BROKEN VOWS

CASSIE MILES

OPERATION PROTECTOR

JUSTINE DAVIS

MILLS & BOON

All rights reserved including the right of reproduction in whole or in part in any form. This edition is published by arrangement with Harlequin Enterprises ULC.

This is a work of fiction. Names, characters, places, locations and incidents are purely fictional and bear no relationship to any real life individuals, living or dead, or to any actual places, business establishments, locations, events or incidents. Any resemblance is entirely coincidental.

Without limiting the exclusive rights of any author, contributor or the publisher of this publication, any unauthorised use of this publication to train generative artificial intelligence (AI) technologies is expressly prohibited. HarperCollins also exercise their rights under Article 4(3) of the Digital Single Market Directive 2019/790 and expressly reserve this publication from the text and data mining exception.

® and ™ are trademarks owned and used by the trademark owner and/or its licensee. Trademarks marked with ® are registered with the United Kingdom Patent Office and/or the Office for Harmonisation in the Internal Market and in other countries.

First Published in Great Britain 2026
by Mills & Boon, an imprint of HarperCollins*Publishers* Ltd
1 London Bridge Street, London, SE1 9GF

www.harpercollins.co.uk

HarperCollins*Publishers*
Macken House, 39/40 Mayor Street Upper,
Dublin 1, D01 C9W8, Ireland

Broken Vows © 2026 Kay Bergstrom
Operation Protector © 2026 Janice Davis Smith

ISBN: 978-0-263-42030-2

0426

Printed and Bound in the UK using 100% Renewable Electricity at
CPI Group (UK) Ltd, Croydon, CR0 4YY

BROKEN VOWS

CASSIE MILES

To the memory of my last trip along the Oregon shore
with Rick Hanson. And all the lighthouses.

Chapter One

Wednesday, three days before the wedding...

"I hate surprises." Nicole Carpenter stomped across the flagstone patio outside Leeward Manor on the Oregon coast. Inside, the wedding guests gathered for cocktails before dinner. Outside, Nicole reached the far end of the patio. A salty breeze from the Pacific stroked her cheeks, and the endless pounding of the surf played background to the DJ in the Manor. She turned toward Alyssa Rossini, the bride-to-be, who had just threatened her with a surprise.

Nicole continued. "Why do you think it's fun to have people jump from hiding places, wave their arms and yell? Don't you remember what happened at my sixteenth birthday party?"

"Not my fault," Alyssa said. "Your dumbass boyfriend planned that fiasco."

"And I broke his nose." *Surprise, surprise.*

"This is different." Lovely little Alyssa twirled a curl of her long black hair between her slender fingers, manicured and painted with Red To Die For nail polish. "You're going to love this surprise."

"Why do we have to be outside? It's chilly."

Alyssa rolled her dark brown eyes. "Just trust me."

Long ago, Nicole had learned that trusting her best friend often resulted in disaster, but when Alyssa made up her mind, there was no point in objecting. The only daughter of Tony Rossini always got what she wanted, including this rushed destination wedding in Oregon. Also, Nicole didn't want to disappoint Papa Rossini, a powerful businessman who, in addition to owning a Las Vegas casino, was CEO of a syndicate with a somewhat shady reputation. Tony's grandfather founded the Safari Casino during the Mafia era. The property had stayed in the family, but the focus had changed. Rossini Enterprises was known for its community service and generosity. Nicole had benefited. Her mother had struggled with a drug addiction and died when Nicole was eleven, and Tony had taken the orphaned honor student into his family. He'd encouraged her studies, paid for her college and med school. When she completed her residency in Portland, Papa Rossini wanted her to return to Nevada. A promise she might not be able to keep.

She loved Oregon. From the patio outside Leeward Manor, Nicole gazed down at a rugged triangle of land, a hundred yards at the widest part and bordered on both sides by coastal forest. The promontory tapered to a rocky point where the Consolation Cove lighthouse stood. Attempts had been made to cultivate a garden and a broad cobblestone path meandered through shrubs and rock formations. The waves crashed against the thirty-foot cliffs at the edge of the headland, and a November wind rushed through leafless trees and moss-covered Douglas fir. She sighed with contentment as she admired the last shreds of sunset above a darkening horizon.

"We're supposed to go to the gazebo," Alyssa said, turning her head to look over her shoulder as if she expected someone or something to appear from the Manor.

"Fine by me. I'd rather hike around out here than sit at a banquet table with people I hardly remember from ten years ago when I graduated high school and left Vegas."

"I missed you so much."

"Same here," Nicole said. Her friend had always played the role of troublesome little sister. Goofy, gorgeous and adorable.

"But I've got to admit, Oregon suits me better. I've always been more earthy and less glitzy. You know that."

Tonight, she'd given in to Alyssa's demands that she dress up by polishing her ankle boots and throwing on a maxi-length, retro, patterned skirt and toasty-brown blazer—the same color as her choppy, unstyled hair. In contrast, the bride-to-be wore a sparkly jacket, skirt and stilettos.

Nicole watched the twilight fog unfurl from the sea, blurring her vision of the gazebo fifty yards away where the officiant would administer wedding vows, much to the chagrin of Alyssa's mom who really would have preferred a priest. For the first time that evening, the lighthouse beacon automatically came on. The light shone for eight seconds. Eight on and eight off was the unique signal assigned to the privately owned lighthouse.

A tall, hooded figure in a long dark gray robe emerged from the forest on their left. As Nicole squinted to see more clearly, his hood fell back and she glimpsed a beard. He quickly covered his head, arranging the hood in a peak. He looked like Death. The Grim Reaper. The fourth horseman of the Apocalypse who rides a pale horse.

Surprise, surprise? "Is this what you wanted to show me?"

"Oh my God, no. If Nonna Rossini saw this creep, she'd have a heart attack." Alyssa waved her sequin-covered arms over her head like a showgirl doing semaphore. As usual, she made a joke to deal with tension. "Hey, Mr. Death, go scare somebody else."

Ignoring her, Death meandered through the sparse autumnal gardens where skeletons of rosebushes mingled with withered thatches of lavender and tattered grasses. When the beam from the lighthouse bathed everything in light, Death raised his arm and pointed at them.

The beacon blinked out.

Though Nicole told herself this specter had to be a sick prank and nothing to worry about, an ominous shudder rippled down her spine. Unlike her friend, she took everything seriously. Always prepared for an emergency, she carried a crossbody purse that held a few medical supplies, an EpiPen and Narcan. A portable first-aid kit. "Who would do a thing like this?"

"I didn't see his face."

"He has a beard," Nicole said. "Who could it be? Have you got any enemies?"

"Oh, puh-leeze. I wouldn't know where to start with an enemies list."

"We should get out of here."

"I'm not letting some creep chase me away. I arranged a surprise for you and nobody is going to mess it up." In her stilettos, Alyssa stumbled gracefully down the hill toward Death.

Sure-footed in her boots, Nicole followed. "He's got something in his hand. Metal. Looks too heavy to be a rapier or a saber. Maybe a machete."

"Gruesome. How do you know about all those blades?"

"I work at a Level I trauma center and emergency room."

"Yeah, yeah." Again, Alyssa rolled her eyes. "You've told me a hundred million times. We're all super proud of you, Doc."

Ignoring the snark, Nicole continued. "In my work, I try to be familiar with all kinds of weapons, how they're used and the type of wounds they cause."

Alyssa came to a halt. "Do you think he's dangerous?"

"Could be. He's armed. Disguised as Death. And lurking around at dusk. I don't think he's here to deliver a singing telegram."

The beam from the lighthouse showed Death coming closer to them. He moved slowly; seemed to be carrying something under his robes.

"Nonna would say Mr. Death is an omen." Alyssa clenched her fists and growled. An odd sound coming from this petite, feminine woman. "All of a sudden, I feel like I'm making a big mistake. I never should have chosen Consolation Cove for my wedding destination."

So true. Late autumn on the Oregon coast usually offered more rain than sunshine, but Nicole wasn't about to make a snotty comment. Alyssa had enough critics. "Summer might have been better."

"But I can't wait." She patted her barely noticeable baby bulge. "I don't want to waddle down the aisle with my preggo belly hanging out. No way! I'm doing this now. Outdoors. Near the lighthouse. That's where Michael and I shared our first kiss."

"Romantic." Against all odds, Nicole hoped her best friend would tie the knot on Saturday, three days from now, and live happily ever after. "Let's go back inside."

"Not until you see your surprise. Besides, I don't really feel like a party."

"Why not?"

"I can't drink. What's more boring than being the only sober chick in the room?"

The beacon shone brightly across the promontory. She saw a man step out from behind the gazebo. Even at this distance, Nicole recognized Hal Jellinek, also known as Jelly, who had come with the bride's family from Las Vegas. Jelly was a big man, literally. He was six feet, four inches and weighed well over three hundred pounds.

"Is Jelly supposed to be the surprise?"

"You know he's my bodyguard," Alyssa said. "I think he's keeping his distance. You know, trying to be unobtrusive."

As if the big guy could hide. Apparently, Jelly had noticed Death. He reached inside his sports jacket and drew a handgun from the holster on his hip. Nicole wasn't shocked by the weapon. Many of the people attending this ceremony would be armed. Alyssa and her groom, Michael Volkov, were the very definition of star-crossed lovers. While Papa Rossini managed a few illegal activities in Las Vegas, Michael's father ran a more sophisticated, white-collar crime syndicate—the Volkov Group—based in Los Angeles. Occasionally, their interests clashed.

Both clans had agreed to suspend hostilities during the wedding celebration, which was one of the reasons they'd chosen a neutral location for the venue. The Consolation Cove lighthouse should have been a sanctuary.

Death responded to the sight of Jelly's gun with an angry howl. At his side, the machete-like weapon gleamed ominously.

"I'm going to help Jelly," Alyssa announced.

Nicole didn't like where this was headed. She touched her friend's upper arm in a probably futile attempt to control her. "This is his job. Let him do it."

Alyssa shook her off and reached inside her sequined jacket to retrieve her slimline Glock—a dainty but effective weapon. She'd learned how to shoot handguns, rifles, Tasers and bazookas before she was out of junior high. Though she'd never been a great student academically, her marksmanship was A-plus. Lovely little Alyssa could shoot the pasties off a stripper at fifty yards. Not that she'd ever do such a thing. As far as Nicole knew, the bride-to-be was a responsible gun owner who had never opened fire on another human being.

Alyssa took aim and shouted, "I got you covered. Drop the machete. Get on your knees."

The crashing surf and wind should have drowned her words, but Death heard. He made a clumsy pivot and faced the two women. He twirled his weapon like a drum major leading a zombie parade.

Nicole pulled her friend back. "Please let Jelly handle this."

"Don't worry. I won't kill him. Aren't you the one who said Death might be dangerous?"

Several shades of gray marked the difference between dangerous and death. "Call Papa. He'll know what to do."

"I'm a grown woman. I can take care of myself."

"And I'm the maid of honor," Nicole said. "It's my job to make sure you don't get murdered before the ceremony."

Jelly shouted, jumped and flapped his arms, trying to attract the attention of the hooded figure. The lighthouse beam flashed off. In the dark, she couldn't tell if Death was coming closer.

When the beacon came on again, he was only about fifty feet away. Gunfire exploded. One shot. Two. Three.

Nicole wasn't sure where the sounds had come from, but Death jolted as though he'd been hit. He pointed at the glaring beacon. Then crumpled to the ground.

The lighthouse tower was over forty feet tall. Just below the beam was a wrought-iron balcony that encircled the structure. The glow from the beacon showed the silhouette of a sniper on the balcony. Nicole looked toward her friend. "Is that one of Papa's guys?"

"I guess so. You know how overprotective he can get."

The light went out. The faded sunlight at dusk didn't give enough illumination to see clearly. The glow of a full moon hung in the sky, but the light wasn't yet strong enough to dispel the night. Nicole squinted. An incredibly long eight seconds passed.

The beacon reappeared.

Death lurched to his feet. Still carrying his weapon, he started running. Unlike his prior movements, his stride was balanced and fast, almost athletic, as he moved away from Nicole and Alyssa. He also veered away from the gazebo and the gardens.

"He's making a getaway," Alyssa yelled.

"Going where?"

"Don't know." Alyssa fired her Glock into the air.

Death kept sprinting. He headed toward the edge of the cliff beyond the forest. His robe fluttered around him.

"You missed," Nicole said.

"That was a warning shot."

But he didn't take the hint, didn't stop. He charged forward and jumped off the cliff.

The beacon extinguished.

Though unlikely that he'd survive the fall onto the rocky shoreline, Nicole didn't readily accept that conclusion. In her work in the emergency room, she'd treated many people who were near death.

A quick response was half the battle. She ran through the dark toward the cliff. If the man who jumped had any chance of making it, she needed to start treatment immediately.

At the edge of the cliff, she leaned against a waist-high rock and gazed down at the rising tide. A surge of vertigo slapped her in the face. Still, she forced herself to peer at the steep, jagged, mostly vertical drop. The cliff was broken into rocky ledges and patches of earth with hardy rough shrubs clinging to them.

Nascent glimmers of moonlight shone on the dark robe splayed across a prickly juniper halfway down. The man inside had vanished. She stared at the crashing waves. The white spray shot high enough to moisten her cheeks.

"Are you okay?" Alyssa called out as she tottered closer on her heels.

"I'm fine."

Cautiously, she eased her way nearer to the edge for a better view. She felt a steady hand at her waist and heard a familiar voice with a slight Texan drawl. "Take it easy, ladies. Y'all be careful."

She hadn't seen him in over two years, hadn't heard his voice or felt the confident touch of his hand. But she knew him. Her heart remembered Ryder Beckham. "Take your hand off me, cowboy."

Chapter Two

Memories surged through her brain, erasing fear and logic and the dusky, foggy scene at Consolation Cove. With her eyes closed, Nicole flashed on a desert night filled with stars. It was nearly two years ago in August. Naked, she stood on the terrace of a penthouse suite on the thirty-fourth floor, overlooking the neon of the Las Vegas Strip and listening to the echoes of gamblers. Winners and losers. *Which am I?* He had approached her with a flute of champagne, caressed her shoulder, nibbled at her earlobe...

Her eyelids snapped open. He was back in her life. Here in Oregon.

Gasping for breath, Alyssa staggered up beside them. In one hand, she clutched her Glock. With the other, she shoved Nicole closer to Ryder. "Gotcha, didn't I? You never guessed."

Surprise, surprise.

Jelly, breathing hard, joined them at the edge of the cliff. He peered over the edge. "Where the hell is he?" Jelly demanded in a gravelly voice. "I saw his ass go flying."

"Me, too." Nicole turned her head and saw that the sniper had descended from the lighthouse. She glared at him. "Did you shoot that man?"

"Swear to God, I didn't hit the guy. I fired a couple of warning shots into the air."

Jelly leaned so far over the edge that she feared he might

fall. He pointed. "See down there. It's sticking up from those rocks. That's the thing he was carrying."

Nicole recognized the shape. Not a machete. Not a weapon of any sort. When the beacon from the lighthouse spilled over the cliffside, she made out the form of a long metal paddle designed to fit inside an industrial-sized vat. She'd seen something like it churning a cauldron of chocolate fudge at the abbey on the edge of the Cascades where the monks made "heavenly" fudge and truffles for sale to the public.

She'd deal with the chocolate later. Right now, there was only one thing on her mind, and he had his arm wrapped around her waist. He hadn't taken his hand off her. If anything, he'd tightened his grip. She faced Ryder, reached inside his black leather jacket and placed her palms on his chest. He was exactly the right height for her. A few inches over six feet. Tall enough that she had to look up to gaze into his dreamy blue eyes. So much about him was perfect. But she wouldn't make the same mistake twice. *Don't trust him.* It had taken two years of intense work while she'd completed her internship and started her residency to break her attachment to him.

She shoved herself away from him. "What are you doing here?"

"I'm invited to the wedding, and I'm real glad to see y'all."

Nicole found that hard to believe. They'd met when she was home for the summer during a break in her medical training. During her month off, she'd worked as a dealer at Rossini's casino—a part-time gig that helped her afford tuition. The pit boss introduced Ryder as a new floor manager and advised him not to make any moves on Nicole because she was best friends with the owner's daughter and prickly as a cactus.

Ryder had taken that description as a challenge. Within a week, he'd charmed her...and everybody else. Nobody had suspected he was an undercover Secret Service agent, investigating a possible counterfeiting scam at the casino. Though he never found credible evidence to link Rossini to the counterfeiters, Ryder had betrayed them all.

She confronted him. "How are things at the Secret Service, Agent Beckham?"

"Things are okay. My job has changed. I'm heading up a—"

"Don't care." She interrupted before his smooth baritone voice could work its magic on her. His slight Texas twang made her think of open ranges and horses and clear blue skies. "I don't really want to hear about what you're doing."

"Hey, look down there." Jelly pointed. He'd spotted something else on the cliff. He stared toward the rocks nearer the lighthouse. "Looks like a body."

Steeling herself against her fear of heights, Nicole squinted through the fog and settling darkness. Ryder handed her a Mini Maglite, the brand used by police. The flashlight fit neatly in her hand. She made a mental note to get one of these for her first-aid kit.

At the farthest point of the cliff, where a rocky shelf descended into the surf, she played the beam at a formation that resembled a wide punchbowl or bathtub. Though they were too far away to see clearly, the rising tide splashed over what appeared to be a man with long legs in a black suit. "Jelly's right."

"Who is it?" Alyssa asked.

"Can't tell." Nicole shot a glance at Ryder. "I don't suppose you brought binoculars."

"In my other jacket."

The sniper held up his rifle. "Use my scope."

Alyssa took the weapon, peered through the infrared lens and focused on the body. After a moment, she lowered the rifle. "I think it's Alan Caldicott, CFO. One of Papa's accountants."

"Call 9-1-1," Nicole said. "Tell them the situation. We'll need help from the Coast Guard to get that man off the rocks."

"What are you going to do?"

"I'm going to climb down there. If he's still alive, it'll be an emergency rescue. If not, I'll keep the body from washing out to sea." She shucked off her blazer and wriggled out of her long skirt, revealing a pair of leggings.

"I can't believe you're wearing pants," Alyssa said.

"It's cold out here." She adjusted her crossbody purse. Her medical supplies would come in handy. "Make the call, Alyssa."

Ryder threw off his leather jacket. Underneath, he wore a crewneck sweater and jeans. "I'm coming with you."

She considered for only a moment. Rock climbing with a buddy was safer than solo, especially since she wasn't wearing the proper gear. Caring for the injured accountant was more important than her broken heart. "I'll go first."

"Let me," he said. "I can catch you if you fall."

"Then what happens? We crash together into the waves?"

"I pull you to safety." He turned away, and she couldn't read his expression. "And rescue your pretty little behind."

He hadn't changed a bit. Still the flirt. Still the sexy Texas cowboy. Still the alpha male who had to be in control. But she wouldn't waste time bickering. "Here's the deal. You go first. And you take the Maglite."

"Fair enough."

She followed Ryder onto the jagged rock face, moving slowly, making sure her footing was solid on each small ledge. The slip-resistant soles on her boots provided decent traction but weren't meant for climbing. She shivered in the brisk wind that swirled the fog above the ice-cold ocean waves sweeping down from Alaska. If it wasn't for the adrenaline pumping through her, she'd be a Popsicle.

As soon as she'd descended lower than the lip of the cliff, she used her hands for balance, clinging to rocks and scraggly shrubs that poked out of the cliff face. Her palms were scratched. Fingernails broken. So much for the manicure she'd gotten today with Alyssa.

Craning her neck, she tried to see past Ryder's wide shoulders. "How much farther?"

"Maybe twenty feet," he said. "But there's not much to hold on to. We need to climb down to a lower ledge."

"I'm right behind you."

He tripped on a loose rock and scrambled off-balance. His arms flung out, attempting to find something to latch on to as he slipped downward. He lost the flashlight when he fell to his knees on the ledge. Cold water splashed over his jeans.

Nicole heard herself cry out in a desperate involuntary plea to the Universe to keep him safe. Was he all right? Was he hurt? She didn't want to care. But she did. Deeply. She'd missed him, had spent countless hours replaying every second of their time together, wishing fervently that she could forgive him. If he was gone forever, there would never be a chance for them to get back together.

When he glanced over his shoulder and waved to her, relief spread through her system. She sucked down a huge breath. Her heart started beating again. She might have been crying but couldn't separate her salty tears from the spray of the surf against the rocks.

"I'm okay," he yelled.

"You're drenched."

"So nice of y'all to notice." They were in trouble again. Just like old times. *So predictable.* Nicole should have expected something like this to happen.

Inching forward and maneuvering on the rocks, she managed to get a clear look at the injured man. His large frame had wedged into a small tide pool. His left leg floated in the waves, pulled by the tide and giving the impression that he was capable of movement. His ghastly white face stood out against the rocks and dark water.

This wasn't Death, the man in the hooded robe. He seemed older, heavier and had no beard. She'd only met the accountant once or twice. Ryder knew him better. He crouched on the rocks beside him.

"It's Caldicott," Ryder said. "I worked with him when I was here before. Nice guy. He has teenaged twins. Both football players."

"Can you find a pulse?"

Ryder pressed his fingertips at the carotid below Caldicott's chin. "I don't feel anything."

"Looks like he has other injuries." His left arm was twisted at an unnatural angle. The left side of his face showed blunt force trauma. "He might have lost his balance and crashed on the rocks."

Ryder pushed Caldicott's hair back from his forehead. "His fall wasn't accidental."

Though the blood had been washed away, she identified a bullet hole burned into the center of his forehead. The shooter had been close. An execution?

BROTHER JULIAN BOBBED in the rolling sea farther from shore than the breaking surf. He was over a hundred yards away from the lighthouse. The dusk and fog made him nearly invisible in the hooded, black drysuit that he'd worn under his habit. The heavy-duty neoprene kept him warmish in the icy Pacific.

The robes had also served to conceal his holstered Beretta with built-in sound suppressor, his mini respirator and the light-weight swim fins he donned almost as soon as he'd dived into the water and taken off like a greased dolphin. He had planned for everything. His getaway harkened back to his younger days when he had the reputation of being a super assassin. That was his true calling. Not the identity he'd assumed a few years ago when he disappeared into the abbey and learned to make fudge.

In many ways, he appreciated the orderly life of a monk. He didn't mind giving up curse words and limited his trips away from the monastery to tend to his personal business. His tastes were simple. The regular schedule at the abbey—from matins to vespers—gave a pleasing structure to his days. But he'd never truly intended to become a monk.

Brother Julian could never obey the sixth commandment. *Thou shalt not kill.* He reveled in murder. The preparation, the stalking, the act and the escape. His shining talent.

Occasionally, he'd slipped away from the abbey to commit violence, but Consolation Cove was his first real assignment since he'd abandoned his regular lifestyle. An interrogation, an assassination and an abduction while surrounded by other criminals. An awesome challenge.

He squinted through his night-vision swim mask at the lighthouse and turned off the breathing apparatus. The miniature tank only held fifteen minutes of air, and he didn't want to waste it. He'd left a small motorboat moored at a marina a mile down the coast and could swim the rest of the way to the location without the respirator, especially since he wasn't hauling a kidnapped girl in his wake.

Despite the euphoria he felt after murder, he couldn't count this assignment as an unqualified success. Earlier tonight, he had lured Alan Caldicott to the lighthouse. Using his false identity as Brother Julian, he'd told the accountant that he had important info to disclose. His plan had been to get answers. Who? What? Where? Encouraging honesty with blows from his freaking candy paddle, he symbolically ended his identity as a monk. But Caldicott was a heck of a lot stronger than he looked. He wouldn't talk.

Impatient, Julian assassinated the accountant with one perfectly centered gunshot to the forehead and shoved him off the cliff. An unplanned action. A reminder to KISS: Keep It Simple, Stupid. Should have just shot the man and walked away. Instead of tumbling neatly into the water, Caldicott had gotten hung up on the rocks.

Julian hadn't wanted him to be found until he'd kidnapped Alyssa. But he hadn't had time to put that part of his plan into effect. Alyssa Rossini had lived up to her reputation for being unpredictable. She and her bodyguard and her friend had been taking an evening stroll toward the gazebo.

At first, Brother Julian had seen her appearance as good luck. He had wanted to take her from there. People usually didn't come to the lighthouse after dark. Not on a chilly, foggy, November evening. Isolation was why he'd planned to use the foot of the cliff for his escape. If Alyssa had been alone, he would have grabbed her, rendered her unconscious and dragged her away through the surf. But he wouldn't have been able to take on her friend, her bodyguard and the sniper.

It was a damn good thing that he'd had a plan B. Immediate retreat. He'd climb down the cliff and disappear into the waves.

He looked back at the lighthouse where he saw Alyssa's friend and her companion struggling on the rocks, trying to keep the dead man from washing away. Julian had been warned about that woman—the maid of honor—who was smart, cautious and had a talent for getting in the way. Her presence had thwarted him.

He resented her interference, blamed her for his failure to snatch Alyssa Rossini and hold her until Tony Rossini gave him what he wanted. He hadn't been given instructions regarding the accursed shrew. It might be wise to kill her before going after Alyssa.

Chapter Three

Wet and cold, Ryder stood at the edge of the cliff near the lighthouse, huddled inside his leather jacket. Not only did he regret stumbling into the frigid Pacific, but he hated looking clumsy and inept in front of Nicole. During their rescue attempt turned recovery mission, his best move had been wielding the mini flashlight, which he had then dropped into the waves. *Only thirty-two and already losing my touch.* Nicole hadn't changed at all in the nearly two years they'd been apart. Still beautiful. Still athletic. And always smart.

He peered down and watched the recovery team from the Coast Guard. They used a basket with a hook and cable device to move the lifeless body of Alan Caldicott into an inflatable Zodiac for transport to their lifeboat. Night had fallen. By the light of a full moon—a November supermoon—visibility was better now than at dusk. The high tide splashed around the four-person team in wetsuits and scuba gear as they performed their jobs with as little fuss as possible. The Coast Guard had responded within half an hour of being notified of an emergency—professional, competent and cool.

By contrast, the scene developing on the shore around him verged on chaos. Rossini friends and relatives who were staying at Leeward Manor charged through the gardens to the cliffside, wanting to help and not miss the action. He recognized some of the men: a pit boss at the casino, a blackjack dealer and a lounge performer in his signature maroon tux. The four bridesmaids clustered together, listening to Alyssa talk about the tall, scary figure of Death. The youngest, a sixteen-year-old cousin, alternated between tears and wild laughter. Alyssa's mother, Stella Rossini, fluttered around the young bridesmaid, telling her that everything would be okay. Stella was glamorous in a fake fur coat. The coastal wind tore strands from her fancy updo that was held in place with a sparkly clip—probably real emeralds to match her eyes. During his undercover time with the Rossini family, Ryder had seen the matriarch when she was angry and resembled a green-eyed hawk with a predator's talons instead of this flighty hummingbird.

Another group stood slightly apart. Three men, dressed impeccably in expensive suits, observed the scene with a disdainful superior attitude that made Ryder think of royalty in the video games he loved to play. These were the kings and princes, the emperor and his court, the conqueror, the general, the tsar. Maybe they came from the Volkov Group.

Of the group, Ryder only recognized young Michael Volkov, the groom, from surveillance photos. Two of the other men—one ginger and one husky guy who was probably a bodyguard—accompanied him. The leader of this little pack showed military bearing, tall and lean with erect posture. His thick white hair crested over his wide forehead and hawklike nose. Clearly, a person of importance. Ryder made a mental note to find out more about him.

He turned his attention to Papa Tony Rossini, who had assumed his natural role as boss. Though barely as tall as Nicole, he cut a handsome figure in a pinstriped suit, tailored to disguise the bulge from a shoulder holster. He sported a silk necktie, gold Rolex, Italian-leather shoes, a diamond pinky ring and a golfer's tan as befitted Las Vegas royalty. After he snarled at Jelly and sent the sniper back to his surveillance perch on the lighthouse balcony, he gathered his people and laid down the law. Everybody cooperate. Don't tell lies. We want to find the murderer, but the wedding will go on. This is an occasion for celebration.

The rest of the crowd on the cliff included the local police, deputies and staties who'd responded to the first 9-1-1. Given the criminal profiles for some of the wedding guests, other law enforcement agencies probably had surveillance nearby.

Tony nodded to Ryder but said nothing and didn't offer a change of clothes. Nicole, on the other hand, was swaddled in a rescue blanket from the Lincoln County deputy sheriff. The manager of Leeward Manor zipped up to her and Alyssa in a golf cart and offered a ride back to the Manor. Nicole looked over her shoulder at Ryder and frowned, probably deciding if she needed to find out more about the murder before leaving the scene. Apparently, she did because she sent the golf cart away with Alyssa, Stella and Jelly on board.

Nicole approached him, somehow managing to look classy while wrapped in a silvery Mylar blanket like a burrito. She stared at his soggy jeans. "You must be cold," she said.

"Is that your professional medical opinion?"

"I don't want you developing hypothermia or going into shock on my watch."

On her watch? "Are you in charge here?"

"Just concerned about your welfare. You're not good at looking after yourself. The last time you were involved with the Rossini family, you were almost killed."

"And y'all treated me." When he spoke to her, his language reverted to the Texas twang of his youth. He turned into a tongue-tied adolescent talking to the prettiest gal in ninth grade. "You probably saved my life."

"It was only a through-and-through shot in the thigh. No broken bones. You would have survived without my help." She confronted him. Her hazel gaze connected directly to his. "The greater harm was not physical."

She's not going to forgive me. That message was clear. Even though he'd cleared the family of involvement in an international counterfeiting scheme and the outcome of his investigation had positive results, Nicole hadn't seen it that way. She'd stubbornly refused to let him off the hook. Couldn't forget that he'd been undercover and lied about his identity. *Liar!* She'd screamed the word at him, and she hadn't been wrong.

He'd never meant to hurt her. Never meant to kiss her or seduce her. He sure as hell had never expected to fall in love with her.

When she'd confided that she wasn't a blackjack dealer but a medical intern, he should have revealed his identity as an undercover agent investigating counterfeiting charges. But he hadn't wanted to blow the case. He'd allowed the lie to continue. Too long. This was the first time he'd seen her since their time together.

"When I was in Las Vegas before," he said, "I spent a lot of time working with Alan Caldicott. He was a big guy into physical fitness, kind of a gym rat. But he was, at heart, an accountant who kept his desktop cleared and his files straight."

"He was compulsive. Liked to have his ducks in a row." She cocked her thumb and forefinger to mimic picking off a row of mechanical ducks in a shooting gallery. "I always appreciated his professionalism. If you want, I'll pass along your condolences to the family."

"Thanks for the offer, but I'll speak for myself. I'm staying for the wedding." Before she could launch into a lengthy list of reasons why he should get out of town, he stepped around her to greet an average-height, sturdily built, dark-haired woman who strode toward him with an unmistakable attitude of authority and a clenched jaw. She reminded him of a cross between his Sunday school teacher and a rugby player. Either way, she was someone who followed the rules and shouldn't be underestimated. Her dark blue windbreaker had FBI stenciled in a warning shade of yellow across the back.

"Special Agent Cheryl Murdock," she introduced herself. "You're Beckham. With HSI."

"Homeland Security Investigations." He shook her hand. *Firm grip.* "Y'all got here fast, Agent Murdock."

She nodded. "We happened to be in the area."

Not a coincidence. The Rossini-Volkov nuptials had attracted more criminals than a festival of *Godfather* movies. Of course, the feds were keeping a watch on all these potential wiseguys. "How can I help?"

"Deputy Yarrow said you found the body."

"He took my statement."

"Mine, too," Nicole said. "I'm an ER doctor based in Portland."

When she gave her name, Agent Murdock turned her head to study Nicole. "I've seen you at the hospital, Dr. Carpenter. You treated three young women who were assaulted last summer and nearly died."

"They pulled through. Physically, they'll recover." She exhaled a tense sigh. "But it will take years of psychotherapy before they're able to cope with what happened to them."

Murdock's gaze narrowed. She turned her scrutiny level to high intensity. "You're Ms. Rossini's maid of honor. You're also a doctor. What is your connection to these Las Vegas people?"

Nicole drew herself up to her full height. With the two-inch soles on her boots, she was almost six feet tall, and she used every centimeter to look down her nose. "My personal life is none of your business, Agent Murdock. And it has nothing to do with the murder of Alan Caldicott. Not unless I'm a person of interest. Do you suspect me?"

The agent didn't back down. "Why were you and Ms. Rossini outside tonight instead of attending the party in the Manor?"

"We were going to the gazebo when we saw a hooded figure prowling around in the garden." She gave a lucid description of the bearded man and his actions before he'd leaped from the cliff. "We went to look over the edge, hoping we could help him. But he'd disappeared. That was when we spotted Caldicott's body on the rocks nearer to the lighthouse."

Murdock turned to Ryder. "Does that fit with what you observed?"

"Yes."

"Why were you out here?" she asked Ryder.

"A surprise arranged by Alyssa. I was supposed to meet Nicole at the gazebo."

"A surprise? Why?"

Though Nicole had avoided mentioning their relationship, he felt no constraint to hold back. "Dr. Carpenter and I developed a friendship a couple of years ago, and Alyssa wanted me to be her date for the wedding."

Nicole scoffed. "Not going to happen."

To avoid going deeper along that path, which was—as Nicole had pointed out—none of the FBI's business, Ryder took control of their conversation. He wanted to hear more about the shooter's motives. And needed to know if Alyssa and Nicole were in danger. "Agent Murdock, have you learned the identity of the hit man?"

"I never said he was a hit man."

"A clandestine meeting and a single bullet to the forehead points to that conclusion."

"Perhaps." Her thin lips tightened.

"Have you talked to the sniper in the lighthouse? Did he see the murder being committed?"

"He did not."

An important point. Apparently, the shooter had killed Caldicott before the sniper had taken his position, which indicated another disturbing aspect: the shooter hadn't left the scene after the murder. Instead, he'd hidden in the forest at the edge of the cliff. Had he been waiting to ambush the two women?

Ryder asked Nicole, "Did anyone else know about Alyssa's matchmaking surprise?"

"Don't know, but I wouldn't be shocked if her plan was common knowledge. Alyssa isn't known for keeping secrets."

Swell. He looked toward Agent Murdock. "When will you have autopsy results?"

"Soon," she said. "But I make no promises about sharing information with you. Perhaps you can tell me about the long, silver object he was carrying?"

"It's a paddle used for churning fudge," he said. "When Nicole and I checked out the body, we saw contusions. The shooter might have used the paddle as a weapon."

"Odd," she said.

Apart from the comment about not sharing, she didn't seem to question his authority. She must have already checked him out and been instructed to cooperate. Ryder didn't know who to thank, but he was glad. During his years in law enforcement, he'd encountered several officers who obsessively followed the rules and were sticklers when it came to jurisdiction. Frequently, they lacked imagination—and imagination is a trait that Agent Murdock might need in order to deal with a killer who dressed up like the Grim Reaper.

"If this murder was a hit," Ryder said, "somebody must have hired the guy. Any suspects?"

"Not yet." Murdock shook her head. "Right now, I want to get a general picture of the scene and the people involved. I'll start with you two."

"Nothing to tell," he said, dismissing her with a wave.

"I'll be the judge of that," Murdock said. "Regarding your supposed relationship with Dr. Carpenter... Who broke up with whom?"

"He's the whom," Nicole said. "I dumped him like yesterday's trash."

His jaw clenched. "I can explain."

"All lies," Nicole growled.

Enough is enough. "I'm leaving now. Give me your phone number."

"I don't think so, Ryder. I don't trust you."

He didn't bother arguing. Just turned away from her, took

a business card from an inner pocket of his jacket and handed it to Agent Murdock. "These are my numbers if you have any more questions about Alan Caldicott. I'll check back later to hear about forensics and fingerprints."

Without acknowledging Nicole, he headed back past the gazebo and approached the manager of Leeward Manor, who had returned with the golf cart. Ryder took the passenger seat. "Can I hitch a ride?"

The ruddy-faced man peeked from under the brim of a captain's hat and stroked his neatly trimmed whiskers. "I'm Daniel DeBarge, otherwise known as Daniel Danger the Salty Dog of Consolation Cove." He thumped his barrel chest. "Pirate king."

"Pleased to meet you, your majesty."

"Staying at the Manor?"

"I was told there are no vacancies."

Daniel glanced toward the edge of the cliff and barked a laugh. "Lest I miss my guess, a room just opened up. Mr. Caldicott won't be staying with us."

"I'll take it," Ryder said. And he introduced himself. His rental car was parked in the lot with his suitcase, laptop and the handgun he hadn't thought he'd need. "So, you're a salty dog."

"Right you are."

"I didn't know there were pirates in these here parts."

"We have a festival in the spring for swashbucklers and friends. There's a ghost from the 1800s who haunts the Manor, clanking his cutlass and growling at the ladies."

Speaking of ladies... Nicole hopped into the back of the four-seater golf cart. "Glad to see you, Daniel. I could use a ride back to the Manor."

If he'd been a gentleman, Ryder would have stepped out and let her have the cart to herself, but he wasn't in the mood to do her any favors. He gave Daniel a nod. "Let's go."

A young man in a suit dashed toward them, waving his arms and signaling for Daniel to stop. Michael Volkov, a law student and next in line to be CEO of the family business, leaped into the back seat beside Nicole. "Alyssa wanted me to check on you."

"I'm fine." Her tone wasn't cold but not friendly, either. Ryder wondered if she disapproved of the husband-to-be.

A manicured but masculine hand thrust into the front seat. "You must be the famous Ryder Beckham. I'm the groom."

When he reached back to shake hands, Ryder looked into Michael's face. Though the moonlight didn't clearly illuminate the young man's features, he saw sculpted cheekbones, a firm jaw and glistening smile like a *GQ* model. "Congratulations, Michael. Alyssa is a lovely woman with a good heart."

"I'm a lucky man."

A well-groomed, redheaded guy with a skimpy mustache and beard hopped onto the edge of the cart. Since there wasn't enough room for him to squeeze into the back seat, he clung to the roof of the cart and hovered while Michael stepped out to introduce him. "This is Dirk Petrovich, my best man."

Unlike Michael, Petrovich didn't offer to shake hands. And Ryder didn't make the first move. When he climbed out of the cart and gave his seat to Michael, he noticed the way Petrovich slid in beside Nicole and possessively tucked his arm around her. A little too friendly for a best man and maid of honor.

Ryder turned away. "I'll walk."

"Thanks," Michael said. "We were getting crowded. Petrovich thinks he needs to accompany me everywhere, like I'm going to run off or something."

Or something. While Ryder watched the cart drive to the Manor, Nicole turned her head and made eye contact with him. In that brief glance, he read a glimmer of affection. Maybe an apology. And a sliver of fear.

Even if she thought he was a scumbag, he wouldn't leave her unprotected.

Chapter Four

Arriving at Leeward Manor, Nicole shook off Petrovich's clingy arm, climbed out of the golf cart and made a quick excuse to Michael about needing to change clothes. Not really a fib because her leggings and boots had gotten drenched. The cuffs and sleeves of her cream-colored blouse had picked up a spattering of bloodstains from when she'd checked Alan Caldicott's vitals. Crouched out there on the rocks jutting into the ocean, working beside Ryder to keep the body from being flushed away in the rising tide, she'd felt saddened by the loss of life but solid. That was where she was supposed to be. Taking an active part. Trying to make a difference. Similar to her response when she treated injured patients in the ER. She always fought her hardest, but sometimes death would not be denied. After that grounded moment on the shore below the lighthouse, she seemed to have come unmoored.

Caldicott—a man she personally knew—had been murdered. His killer and those who hired him were likely also acquaintances. There might be other deaths. Others in the Rossini family might be in danger. And so was she.

Before she could rush inside and make a mad dash to her room, close the door and take a breath, Michael caught hold of her arm. His gray eyes darkened with concern. His voice held a serious note. "Are you okay?" he asked. "Tell me, Nickie, how can I make it right?"

Much as she hated the Nickie nickname, which reminded her of a puppy dog, she didn't snap at him. It seemed that he was trying to be sincere. Not for the first time, she wished that she could bring herself to like this guy. He was a lawyer, and his career trajectory seemed to be on the up and up. But something about him disturbed her. *What is it? Why the negative vibe?* Maybe it was because Michael Volkov reigned as crown prince in a wealthy family with nefarious interests. Nicole had the sense that when he married Alyssa, a business deal would be cemented between Volkov and Rossini.

She forced a smile for him. "I need to get cleaned up. You should go find Alyssa. Or not. Enjoy your last hours of bachelorhood."

"Promise you'll join us. Petrovich really wants to get to know you."

"I'm sure he does."

"You don't like him," Michael said. "You're still hung up on Ryder Beckham."

"Am not," she said with unnecessary vehemence. Childish? Maybe.

In the golf cart, Daniel drove past them and waved his cell phone. "My reservation clerk tells me that your friend Ryder will be staying at the Manor. She found a place for him."

"Terrific," she muttered. Though Ryder might be helpful in figuring out who killed Caldicott, she feared getting close to him. Didn't want to be hurt again.

She shed her silvery Mylar blanket, handed it to Daniel and crept toward the front entrance, trying to be inconspicuous. At the staircase leading to the second floor, a tiny woman with a coxcomb of white hair blocked her way. Born and raised on the Amalfi coast, Nonna Rossini had discarded her peasant clothing as soon as she'd hit Las Vegas. She still wore mostly black with a king's ransom in gold necklaces, bracelets and earrings. A spot of red in her sculpted fingernails appeared when she pointed at Nicole.

"You," Nonna said, "were supposed to protect my grandchild."

Nicole knew better than to put up an argument. Nonna was *always* right. Instead, she tried to switch the topic. "Are you feeling okay? You look a little bit flushed."

"This is makeup, *cara mia*. You could use some."

"How's your blood pressure?"

"I eat the garlic, cinnamon and turmeric. A shot of apple cider vinegar a day." She drew herself up to her full height of sixty inches. "I know how to take care of myself."

Nicole approved of most of Nonna's natural remedies. She was one of those people who would follow her own rules and live to be one hundred and twenty. "And you have a glass of red wine with dinner."

"Sometimes more than one. Oregon makes a nice pinot." She braced her fists on her skinny hips, not allowing herself to be distracted from her main topic. "Caldicott was a family man. Divorced. But still a father. Who would kill him?"

"The FBI is investigating."

"Not good enough." She jabbed a forefinger at Nicole's nose. "You tell your boyfriend, the cowboy, to find the killer and lock him up."

There were so many things wrong with that sentence. "Ryder is not my boyfriend. Not a cowboy, even though he has a drawl and likes to wear jeans. Most decidedly, he's not in charge of this investigation."

Nonna placed a scrap of notebook paper into Nicole's hand. A phone number and address were written on the scrap. "Caldicott's wife is Patrice, and she doesn't live far from here. Suspicious, yes?"

Nicole started to object but changed her mind. Nonna might be right. The murder could be a domestic problem gone wrong. The police always said the first suspect was the spouse. "I'll see what I can find out."

She climbed the stairs two at a time, passing a duo of giggling bridesmaids in skimpy crop tops with matching belly button rings and micro-miniskirts that showed off their year-round Las Vegas tans. Nicole frowned at the younger of the two and said, "Selene, go back upstairs and put on a jacket or something."

"You're not the boss of me."

"It's chilly. You'll catch your death."

"Shouldn't joke about death with poor Mr. Caldicott murdered. One of his sons is here. He's a Duck."

"What?"

"University of Oregon football team. The Ducks."

Nicole nodded. The Caldicott boys going to school here explained their mother's move to Oregon. Nonna must have known. She gave a half-hearted cheer. "Go, Ducks."

The bridesmaids turned their backs and flounced down the stairs, ignoring her advice to put on a jacket. For the ceremony, Nicole would be wearing the same gown as the other four—ruffled, bedazzled and acid-green with thigh-high slits. The designer adhered to the theory that bridesmaids should look as grotesque as possible to highlight the pristine beauty of the bride.

In her room, she closed and locked the door before she peeled off her clothes and jumped into the shower. The piping hot water felt heavenly. She sighed and thought of Ryder, imagined his muscular wrists and forearms, remembered how it felt when his large hands glided down her torso. Her nostrils tickled as she inhaled the steam and remembered his masculine, musky scent. *I'm not over him. Not by a long shot.*

DESPITE DANIEL'S PROMISE, Ryder wasn't able to immediately move into Alan Caldicott's room. The suite—one of six with private bathrooms—had been designated a crime scene. Instead, Daniel escorted his newest guest to a closet-sized space on the third floor next to the dormitory-style room where the bridesmaids were staying.

"No bathroom and no window," Daniel said as he unlocked the door, "but you got the best view in Leeward Manor with those pretty gals flitting in and out. You share the bathroom at the end of the hall with them."

As if to emphasize his proximity to the bevy of bridesmaids, a soprano peal of laughter sliced though the thin wall of his bedroom and pierced his ears. "As soon as Caldicott's room opens up, I want it."

"I should warn you," Daniel said, "that room is haunted by a pirate ghost."

Ryder slipped a fifty into the manager's hand. "I'll pay double the regular rate."

"It's yours."

Daniel stepped aside so Ryder could squeeze past him. The interior of the third-floor room was barely long enough for a double bed. No closet, only a scuffed oak armoire with three drawers below a space where he could hang his wedding suit, two shirts and a heavy sweater. A complimentary bathrobe hung in the wardrobe. In the first drawer, he filed his laptop and briefcase. No matter where he went or what he did, a hailstorm of paperwork accompanied him.

Though desperately craving a shower, Ryder wasn't about to brave the unwanted attentions from a mob of bridesmaids to use the hallway bathroom. He stripped off his cold, wet clothes and dressed in a fresh pair of jeans, a flannel shirt, wool socks and high-top sneakers. He added his gun in a hip holster and a gray thermal vest. Then he hung his leather jacket over the edge of the wardrobe, along with his damp jeans and socks. Should be dry by morning.

He combed his fingers through his dark blond hair and rubbed at the scruff on his chin. Though he could do with a shave, a dusting of stubble made an acceptable fashion statement. And Nicole didn't seem to care what he looked like. In her position as maid of honor, she probably qualified for a room with a private shower. He'd be willing to grovel and apologize—for the ten millionth time—if she'd let him use her bathroom.

After arming himself with a small notebook and pen that fit into an inner pocket of his vest, he climbed across the bed to get to the door and emerged in the narrow hallway. Though not officially an investigator, he might as well gather some information. Avoiding the skinny, claustrophobia-inducing elevator, he descended the central staircase to the second floor. Daniel had given him the number to Alan Caldicott's room—212 on the west wing.

Not surprisingly, the charm of the old Manor building relied on natural wood. As far as he could tell, Oregon was all about trees. The state university teams—less famous than the Ducks at U of O—were the Beavers. The Timbers were the professional soccer team. On the second-floor hallway, there was polished, oaken wainscoting and doors, along with decorative doorframes and crown molding. Must have taken a small forest to create this ambience. On the upper wall were several oil paintings of flourishing live trees.

Two state troopers stood guard outside Room 212 and ribbons of yellow crime scene tape crisscrossed the entrance. Ryder flashed his HSI shield and introduced himself. "I'm looking for Agent Murdock."

A heavy-set trooper raised a skeptical eyebrow. His name tag identified him as C. Chapman. "You're from Homeland Security? I didn't think you guys got involved in plain old murder investigations."

Ryder could have dodged an explanation with the ever-handy excuse of "it's classified" or "counterterrorist investigation." But he preferred to be honest. Nicole's presence acted as a reminder of the trouble he could get into with deception. "I'm here for the wedding."

"Seriously? You know these mooks?"

On behalf of Nicole and all the other law-abiding members of the Rossini family, he was offended. "They were instrumental in solving an international counterfeiting case a couple of years ago. And this ought to be a happy occasion. Y'all should be on your best behavior."

"Except for the murderer," Officer Chapman said dryly as he removed the tape so Ryder could pass into the room. "Murdock is in there."

Ryder found her sitting at a desk, opposite a forensic tech who plucked at keys on a laptop. Murdock set aside the papers she'd been shuffling and gave Ryder a nod. "A lot of info on Alan Caldicott's computer. His briefcase was full of spreadsheets and ledgers."

"He was an accountant," he said. "And so am I."

"I'm surprised," she said. "You don't talk like an accountant. You from Texas?"

"Grew up near Midland." His uncle owned a ranch, and Ryder developed the typical skills—riding, roping, hunting and harvesting. But his dad was an oilman, and Ryder leaned toward office work that required deal-making and accounting. Working at HSI gave him the opportunity to use both sides of his skills.

Murdock arched an eyebrow. "You don't look like a like a pencil pusher, either"

"Appearances can be deceiving."

"Next you'll be telling me you play video games."

"I attend San Diego Comic-Con every year in full cosplay costume." He didn't add that he dressed as Thor. "I'm also on a task force investigating extortion, bribery and racketeering. In HSI, bookkeeping skills are more useful than marksmanship. We learned that from the way y'all at the FBI took down Al Capone for tax evasion."

"All hail Eliot Ness." She gave a grin.

He asked, "Can I take a look at the computer?"

Murdock shook her head. "My crypto guys have first crack."

Not unreasonable. But he had glimpsed Nicole's name at the top of Caldicott's spreadsheet—a general ledger showing assets, liabilities and investments. Ryder only got a vague impression of the amounts, which weren't impressive. Still, he worried. An accountant she did business with had been murdered. That kind of close connection suggested that she might be in danger.

He put some distance between himself and the computer screen so he wouldn't be tempted to spy. His intention was to follow the rules, even though he was talented at coloring outside the lines, ferreting out digital information with quick perusals of computer files and simple hacking techniques. Early in his accounting career, he'd learned to read upside down. When he sat opposite someone at a desk, he could translate the document in front of them.

"Actually," Murdock said, "I have something I can share with you. A news flash."

"Glad to hear it and to help in any way I can."

"I was hoping you'd say that. The HSI database is different from ours."

"Shoot."

"We got fingerprints off the metal paddle thing that the guy in the hood was carrying."

"An identification?"

"There were several smudges and fewer IDs. One set in particular stood out." Her thin lips twisted in a grimace. "His name is John Mitchell, known as Mitch the Bitch. A hit man for hire."

A promising lead. "Anything else?"

"He was famous for pulling off unusual stunts. Some people called him Houdini or the Magician. One of his victims drowned in the middle of a desert. He killed a woman with a poison orchid corsage."

The MO sounded like someone who would dress up in a cowled robe to scare Nicole and Alyssa. The joke was on him. Those two women were not easily terrified. "Doesn't sound like a magician if he left behind prints."

"He wasn't worried about getting apprehended," she said. "Mr. Mitchell was declared dead a couple of years ago."

He swallowed hard. This case was turning interesting. "What's your explanation?"

"Number one, we might have misidentified the prints." She ticked off other possibilities on her fingers. "Two, a glitch in AFIS. Three, he's not dead. His corpse was badly deteriorated, and identification was problematic."

Ryder picked option number three. Not dead. "Can I see his file?"

She took his cell phone number. "I'll transfer the info to you as soon as possible if you promise to give me any details from Homeland Security and Secret Service."

"Done."

His next plan meant talking to Nicole, finding out how she was connected with Alan Caldicott and Mitch the Bitch. Also, he needed to talk to Tony Rossini, and he figured she could facilitate that meeting.

In the wood-framed hallway, he frowned at the row of closed doors broken by the central staircase. Since he didn't know which room was Nicole's, he prepared to call Daniel and ask for the number. Then he saw a clue: Dirk Petrovich. The lean redhead strode across the landing at the top of the stairs, turned right, trotted down the east wing and stopped outside number 206.

When he knocked with two sharp, confident raps, Ryder felt fairly certain that Petrovich had led him to Nicole. He stepped up beside the groom's best man. "Is the party still going downstairs?"

"Oh, yeah. Thought I'd check with Nicole and see if she was ready to have some fun."

"Sure." After chasing Death and finding a dead body, every woman would be up for a drunken bash.

She pulled the door open. With her cozy, teal robe cinched tight at the waist and her choppy caramel hair still damp from a shower, she was in a state of adorable disarray. Ryder wanted to scoop her into his arms and keep her away from Petrovich. She was his woman, even if she didn't know it yet and wouldn't admit that they belonged together.

Calmly, Nicole said, "Petrovich, you should go back to the party."

"Call me Dirk. And you ought to come with me." He pushed the door wider. "I'll come inside and wait for you to get dressed."

Ryder barely suppressed a chuckle. Nicole didn't take orders well. Her calm turned edgy. "Dirk. Go."

"Come on, Nickie. You don't want to send me away."

"Go now," she snapped, then she turned to Ryder. "You, come in here."

He tried to take advantage. "Did you decide to give me your phone number?"

"Not yet," she teased.

"Why do you want to see me?"

"I have a message for you from Nonna Rossini."

Chapter Five

Nicole couldn't believe she'd invited Ryder into her bedroom. Definitely *not* the way to maintain her distance from him. His nearness sucked the air from the room, leaving her lightheaded. His scent tickled her nostrils. They were alone, and he was quick to take advantage. He strode across the patterned wool carpet toward the bathroom, unzipping and peeling off his thermal vest as he went.

"I need a shower," he said.

"Not here." Fists on hips, she glared. "I didn't ask you to come into my bedroom so you could get naked."

"My room doesn't have an attached bathroom."

"I'm sure Daniel has provided some kind of accommodation. A shower down the hall, perhaps."

"That I share with four bridesmaids and probably a couple of others."

Struck by a vision of Ryder locked in the hall bathroom with the perky young bridesmaids clawing at the door and calling to him like sirens from the deep, Nicole couldn't help but grin. "Not my problem."

"What's the message from Nonna?"

"She wants you to investigate. And she gave me a phone number for Caldicott's ex-wife, Patrice, who lives nearby. I also learned that his twin boys are here for the wedding. They play football at the University of Oregon in Eugene."

"Ducks." He pulled his T-shirt off over his head.

She hadn't forgotten how amazing he looked without a shirt. Lean but muscled, with a sprinkle of light brown hair that arrowed down his chest. Though she wanted to yell at him about not taking a shower in her room, her throat went dry.

"I'll be quick," he said. "When I get out, we'll go downstairs to the party and talk to the twins about their father."

Frozen in place, she stared at the closed bathroom door and whispered, "Don't forget to get dressed—completely dressed—before you come out."

She quickly changed into brown yoga pants and a long oatmeal-colored sweater. Grabbing the blow dryer from the top of her dresser, she poked her short caramel-colored hair into shape and then applied lipstick. Her outfit was presentable. Nonna and Alyssa's mom wouldn't be embarrassed by the way she looked.

From overhead, she heard an odd pattern of walking—a thud followed by the more familiar stomp of a boot. *Thud-stomp, thud-stomp, thud-stomp.* She stared up at the ceiling.

Ryder emerged from the bathroom in a billowing cloud of steam. He wore only a towel around his waist. "What's that noise?"

"Put on some clothes."

"I wanted to see if you were in trouble."

Not yet. But she was about to whip off that skimpy towel and... She held back. No matter how much she wanted to lunge at him, no matter how long it had been since she'd scratched that itch, she could control her impulses. "Clothing on. Stat."

Wisely, he retreated into the bathroom. Upstairs on the third floor, the *thud-stomp* got louder. An outburst of wild, ominous laughter rolled through the hallways and echoed. Followed by high-pitched screams. Now, she decided, there might be reason for concern.

Ryder charged from the bathroom wearing jeans, his flannel shirt and his unzipped vest. He carried his handgun. "I better see who's scaring the bridesmaids."

He dashed out the door, and she followed, grabbing her room key and her portable first-aid kit just in case. Nicole paused to lock her door. Weird, unexplainable stuff had been happening tonight, culminating in murder by the lighthouse. She didn't want anybody sneaking into her room and going through her things. The thud-stomper could be related to the cowl-wearing Grim Reaper.

In the third-floor hallway, bridesmaids shrieked and scampered. Ryder took a shooter's stance, lowered his weapon and shouted, "Federal agent. Freeze."

"Don't shoot." The man wore an eighteenth-century tri-cornered hat. His white shirt had flowing sleeves and his leather vest was bulky and old-fashioned. An unsuccessful attempt to look like a pirate of the Caribbean. He raised his arms, waving a curved cutlass. "It's me. Daniel Danger the Salty Dog."

"Drop the weapon," Ryder said.

"It's plastic." But Daniel did as ordered, using his free hand to balance against the wall. He had rigged his full-cut, striped trousers to make it look like he had a peg leg, which must have been the "thud." His other foot was encased in a flamboyant, cuffed, cavalier boot.

Ryder pushed him up against the wall. "What the hell are you doing?"

"I promised these lovely ladies a bedtime story about the legendary local pirates." He wiggled his bottom. "Let me get my leg out of this device."

Ryder stepped to the side so Daniel could maneuver. He sank to the floor, pulled up his trouser leg and unfastened a tube attached to his foot and ankle. Instead of a fake wooden peg, he had two functioning legs. He jumped to his feet, took a backward step and stomped on Ryder's bare foot with the heel of his cuffed boot. Though the move could have been accidental, Ryder didn't treat it that way. He spun Daniel around, shoved his back against the wall and got up in his face.

"No stories tonight," Ryder growled. "Y'all should know better. A man was murdered. It's not a time for fun and games."

"But pirate stories are part of the ambience at Leeward Manor," Daniel said. "It's expected."

"Not tonight. Don't make me say it again." Ryder raised his voice and spoke to the people gathered in the hall. "Y'all go back to your rooms and settle down. If you want a party, there's one downstairs."

"He's right." A willowy bridesmaid—Camilla Botafogo, the daughter of one of Tony's partners, who was a bit older than the others—stepped forward. She was one of those people who automatically commanded respect. "Everyone chill or go back downstairs."

Her words were echoed by Alyssa, who stalked down the hallway toward them like a pint-sized, ebony-haired fury. The crowd dispersed quickly. Without his peg leg, Daniel Danger didn't make a *thud-stomp*. It was more like an offbeat *shuffle-step*.

Approaching the young man standing behind Camilla, Alyssa took his hand in both of hers and gazed into his puffy, bloodshot eyes. "Jimmy, I'm so sorry about your dad."

He mumbled, "He knew something was going to happen. I never should have left him alone tonight."

Nicole exchanged a glance with Ryder. Apparently, Jimmy was one of the Caldicott twins, which made him a potential witness. She placed her hand on Alyssa's shoulder. "We should go somewhere private."

"My suite," Alyssa said. She led their little group down the staircase and they descended to the second floor. As befitted a bride, Alyssa's rooms were twice as large as the others. Not only was the attached bathroom posh, spacious and equipped with a hydrotherapy hot tub, but the king-sized bed had a private room to itself. The main area was a large sitting room with a dining room table and a kitchenette.

After Nicole provided bottled water for Jimmy and a diet soda for Camilla, Alyssa placed a plate of fresh muffins and fruit on the coffee table in front of the brocade love seat where the twosome sat close together.

"Anything else we can get for you?" Alyssa asked.

Jimmy exhaled a heavy sigh and crumpled forward, bracing his forearms on his thighs. His head drooped. Thick, curly brown hair fell over his forehead. In spite of his long, gangly limbs and broad shoulders, he looked like a forlorn little kid.

His voice was shaky. "I want answers, Alyssa. Who killed my dad?"

Camilla patted his back and murmured soothing phrases.

Nicole pulled Ryder forward and introduced him. "Jimmy, this is Special Agent Ryder Beckham of Homeland Security Investigations."

Jimmy bolted to his feet and shook Ryder's hand. "I thought I recognized you, sir. You worked with my father on that counterfeiting scam."

"Alan helped me a lot," Ryder said. "He was a good man. Real proud of you and your twin. Both wide receivers?"

Nicole's heart went out to Jimmy. Tears spilled over his eyelids. With effort, he controlled the tremble in his jaw. "I'm a receiver. My brother plays defense. Sometimes, we line up together to freak out the other team."

"I'd like to ask you some questions," Ryder said.

"Yes, sir."

"In private." He glanced at Alyssa.

"No problem." She ushered the two men to the attached bedroom.

Nicole tore her gaze away from the closed door. She was proud of Ryder for stepping up and helping this kid, even though he wasn't officially investigating. Maybe he wasn't such a jerk, after all.

The bride's private bedroom wasn't a great place for an interrogation, but Ryder had little choice. Though he didn't suspect Jimmy Caldicott was involved in wrongdoing, the kid might have the sort of information that only family would know. Jimmy shuffled across the room and stood in front of a glamorous, long, white, strapless wedding gown fitted onto a dressmaker's mannequin with the veil arranged at the neck.

Jimmy reached out and stroked the skirt. "Soft. What kind of material is it?"

"I'm guessing silk," Ryder said.

Jimmy turned to face him. They stood eye to eye, the same height, but the kid was in better condition than Ryder, whose football days at University of Texas had ended a decade ago. A good-looking young man in spite of his weepy eyes and swollen dripping nose. Worried about the gown, Ryder grabbed a box of tissues from the bedside table and passed it to the kid.

He blew his nose and pitched the tissue in a trash can. "The dress made me think of a photo of my mom and dad on their wedding day. She was really pretty. And he had the happiest grin on his face, like he'd hit the jackpot."

Not the best intro to the topic of Alan and Patrice's former relationship. But Ryder had to start somewhere. He guided Jimmy to two chairs by a window that was covered by floor-to-ceiling drapes. "How long were they married?"

"This June it would have been twenty-three years. They got divorced a year ago. Mom caught him messing around. Stupid move on his part. It's never good to lie."

Amen to that. "I knew it hadn't been long. Alan was still married two years ago when I worked with him. Can you tell me about the woman he dated. Did she have a temper? Or an angry husband who might want revenge?"

"Don't go there," Jimmy said. "Dad wasn't in love with Tiffany, who was single. Like I said, he was just stupid."

"Were there other women?"

"Probably." Jimmy blew his nose again and met Ryder's

gaze. "You're being kind of an ass, talking about the affair. But I'm glad you're investigating. I already talked to that FBI lady, and she gave me the typical attitude about the supposed Rossini crime family. Like we're all gangsters from TV shows who go around whacking people."

"I know all of y'all better than that."

During the time Ryder had spent undercover, he'd met sharp businessmen and professionals like Alan Caldicott who worked for Rossini Enterprises. Normal people with regular jobs. He'd liked most of them and had been relaxed enough in their company to fall in love with Nicole. As a casino owner, Tony Rossini scrupulously obeyed the dictates of the Nevada Gaming Commission. The Rossini organization ran many other local businesses, including two brothels founded by Tony's grandfather. The houses of ill repute were outside city limits, as required by law.

Tony's father had recalibrated Rossini Enterprises. In earlier days, their practices had been more aggressively criminal. Some of the family left over from those times—the hit men and -women, enforcers, bodyguards and thugs—remained active, but ninety percent of the people employed by Rossini were salt-of-the-earth, middle-class folks. Las Vegas had changed. The family's standing in the community was more respected than feared. Nonna supported the church. Tony funded a lot of hospital research. His father died young from pancreatic cancer, and Tony was dedicated to finding a cure.

"I've got to ask," Ryder said, "did your dad have enemies?"

"Hell, yeah. He held the purse strings. People always griped about payments. Everybody always wanting more, more, more." In Jimmy's voice, he heard echoes of his father. "Greedy bums."

"Anybody who might have come after him?"

"I don't think so. And you can take Mom off your list of suspects. Even before she found out about the affair, she was kind of done with being a stay-at-home wife. And she really hated Las Vegas. Moving to Oregon was good for her."

Ryder wondered if there was something magical about this place. Nicole liked it, too. Maybe they were captivated by the fog and rain and mist. The opposite of the Las Vegas desert. "Some people talk about having a friendly divorce, but I don't believe such a thing exists. Did your mom think the terms of their breakup were fair?"

"Totally. Dad was always about the details. He had everything in place. No muss. No fuss. No arguments. They weren't best friends, but he planned to have dinner with her while he was here for the wedding."

Ryder wasn't sure how much of that he could believe. In his experience, parents didn't share gory details with the kids. He'd have to verify things with Patrice. "Earlier you mentioned that something was supposed to happen, and you should never have left your dad alone."

"Something about cyber-crime." Jimmy frowned, and his forehead wrinkled. "And the groom's family is involved."

Ryder's ears pricked up. Because of his background in the Secret Service and HSI, he knew the basics about the LA-based Volkov family. High-class predators dressed in Gucci suits, they specialize in white-collar crime, ranging from fraud to extortion. They live in Beverly Hills and Bel Air. Shop on Rodeo Drive. Their primary business is import-export but—like the Rossini clan—they never deal in drugs or human trafficking.

Handsome, young Michael seemed to perfectly represent his family—shiny on the outside but not-so-pretty when you peered deeper. Ryder wasn't surprised to hear they might be part of a larger criminal scheme. "Tell me about the cyber connection."

"I don't know much." Jimmy shrugged. "Last week, Dad came out to Eugene for a home game. We did good. I caught a touchdown pass and Josh made an interception."

Though Ryder didn't follow college football, he knew the Ducks were undefeated. "What did he tell you about this crime? Any details could be helpful."

"I asked him what he was working on, and he actually talked about it. Dad usually kept a ten-foot brick wall between family and business, but he thought I might be interested because this project was like a video game with order, supply and payment online. Nobody got their hands dirty. He said they were gearing up for another delivery, and it was going to be big."

"What was being delivered?" Ryder asked.

"He didn't know. When I asked, he shut down and said he didn't want to tell me anything specific. He seemed nervous. Shaky. That wasn't like him."

"I remember a guy he used to work with on cyber issues." While he was undercover, Ryder had made a connection with the computer technician. They'd bonded over a discussion of video games.

"Mouse." Jimmy rose from the chair and paced across the room. "He can help you. I'm not sure he's here yet, but he will be."

"Can I get a phone number for your brother?"

"He won't be here until tomorrow. And we're both going to miss the wedding. Saturday is a football day."

Ryder needed to talk with Alyssa's father and get his okay before he started interrogating other employees. He wondered how much Tony Rossini knew about Caldicott's suspicions. Tony might have more pressing reasons than paranoia to assign Alyssa a full-time bodyguard.

"Thanks for talking." He gave Jimmy a card with his phone number and indicated that he should write his number and his brother's on another card. "If you think of anything else, call."

"There is something." He dug his toe into the carpet. "This delivery, whatever it is, will happen on Saturday."

"The day of the wedding," Ryder said.

"Yeah." Jimmy looked toward Alyssa's dress on the mannequin and lowered his voice, almost as if he was speaking to the delicate white gown. "I'm sorry."

Chapter Six

After his successful escape from Consolation Cove, the assassin returned to his home on a rugged hillside overlooking the Pacific coast where he shed his former identity as a brother from the Saint Macarius Monastery. He indulged in a luxurious, cedar-scented shower, dried himself with a thousand-thread-count towel and shaved off his beard. The bone structure of his sculpted jawline pleased him. He looked strong, determined and tough. During the three years off and on that he'd lived as Brother Julian, he'd lost thirty pounds and firmed his physique with regular exercise and a simple diet, which meant denying himself the pleasure of fudge and truffles.

Erasing his beard left a subtle difference in skin tone that he'd correct with self-tanner. Not a problem. He knew all kinds of makeup tricks to disguise his identity, making himself more or less intimidating. Later, when he mingled with the wedding guests, he'd pretend to be a friend of the family. Probably someone from a foreign country so he wouldn't be expected to make small talk. He was fluent in Spanish and knew enough Italian to get by, but probably not enough to fool a native speaker. He'd stick to Spanish.

Stepping back from the bathroom mirror, he viewed his bare chest, six-pack torso and chiseled biceps. With a wink at his reflection, he said, "Look at you, Julian. Not bad for a thirty-five-year-old man."

Starting over in his profession meant honing a new identity. No more dumb nicknames like "Mitch the Bitch." The identity of John Mitchell had expired. He was Julian, named for his great-grandfather with the reputation of being a scoundrel. Julian's heritage. A scoundrel. A respected killer. An assassin.

Still naked, he left the sleek, marble bathroom. His house was small—only three bedrooms—but secluded, tucked into a forest of Douglas fir, hemlock and spruce. The floor-to-ceiling windows in his bedroom and living room framed a distant view of the 235-foot-tall Haystack Rock in Cannon Beach and was only about twelve miles north of Consolation Cove. His walk-in closet held a collection of suits, sweaters and jackets he'd purchased on excursions away from the abbey where he'd pretended to be a monk who'd taken a vow of poverty.

Before he'd staged his own death and gone into hiding, he'd accumulated a seven-figure balance in an offshore bank. The murder of the Rossini accountant had increased his wealth by a hundred thousand. When he abducted Alyssa, he would double that original fee.

Wrapped in a black cashmere robe, he answered the untraceable burner phone on the shelves above his shoe collection. *Why was the idiot calling again?* Julian didn't waste words. "Your payment was received."

"I appreciate the link you provided," said his employer.

He had asked for details regarding a shipment that was supposedly sent by Rossini Enterprises. Specifically, he wanted to know where the delivery would take place and the precise time. After coercive encouragement from Julian, Caldicott had offered up the links and passwords. "You got what you bargained for."

"I have a few more questions." Julian noted the hint of a Russian accent. Not surprising since his employer worked with the Volkov Group and came with a reference from Alexei

Volkov himself. "We know the shipment will arrive on Saturday before the wedding. I want the precise location."

"I asked for clarification." Julian recalled the moans from Caldicott who'd sprawled on the ground below the lighthouse, helpless while Julian administered bone-shattering blows with the metal paddle. He'd crushed the left wrist while warning the man not to cry out. He'd offered a shred of false hope to keep Caldicott talking, telling him that he might let him go if he got all the data he wanted. The desperate man had wanted to tell him everything. "The only location he knew was the Consolation Cove lighthouse."

"That's a tourist site. A risk on the day of a wedding."

Julian had thrust the edge of the metal paddle into Caldicott's rib cage and pressed with all his strength. He'd felt a rib snap. Writhing in agony, the old man had pointed up at the lighthouse and said that was all he knew. "He didn't have all the answers."

"Is it coming by boat or truck?"

"No answer."

"I need more," his employer said. "We already knew the delivery would be somewhere along the Oregon coast. That's one reason I hired you. You know the area. Do you have a place to hold Alyssa after you abduct her?"

Julian stalked into his living room where moonlight shone through the wall of windows onto sleek leather furniture and smoked-glass tables. She'd be safely hidden here. His security measures were top of the line. "I have a place."

"Somewhere quiet and inaccessible. I don't want her blabbing about the location."

"She won't." He had no intention of allowing Alyssa to live after she'd seen his face. Certainly not when she could identify his house.

"Did the accountant tell you what was in the shipment?"

Julian had already given his employer the approximate worth: four and a half million. Caldicott had given up the monetary information but hadn't revealed the nature of the cargo. Since neither Rossini Enterprises nor the Volkov Group dealt in human trafficking or drugs, the consignment was probably weapons. "He refused to say."

"Did he give up names?"

The obvious answer was Tony Rossini, the father of Alyssa, which was why the next move meant using the daughter to get her father to talk. But Caldicott hadn't specifically identified who was giving the orders. No doubt following a misguided sense of loyalty. "No names."

"After you capture Alyssa, call me on my burner. I wish to question her. In person."

It went without saying that if he knew the address, he'd be signing his own death warrant. This was Julian's private lair. "I'll do the asking."

"It's important to me."

Julian didn't care. "No."

"I would settle for face time on the computer."

"This isn't a negotiation."

"You should start by grabbing her friend. Nicole. Start with Nicole."

Julian doubted the friend would have the information they needed. "That will cost you extra. Another hundred thou."

"I'll pay fifty."

"Not interested. Hire somebody else."

After a long pause, his employer barked an angry laugh. "You sure as hell value your privacy."

Which was the primary reason he was still alive. Alone. Always. He disconnected the call without saying goodbye.

NICOLE WATCHED ALYSSA'S glossy black hair bounce with every determined step as she led her and Ryder away from the bridal suite to the party on the first floor of Leeward Manor. Alyssa still wore her sequin jacket and probably had her slimline

Glock within easy reach, but Nicole didn't make the mistake of thinking that her bestie was out of harm's way.

For a very long time, she'd considered herself to be Alyssa's guardian angel. Never applied for the job but couldn't turn away when she recognized a kid who needed help but was too proud to ask. The two of them had come a long way together, starting in elementary school when fifth graders bullied Alyssa and took her lunch money. Later, in middle school, the mean girls whispered and made fun of the Rossini name. Nicole put a stop to that. Not only was she taller and stronger than most of the other kids but she was tough—a defense mechanism that served her well when she became an ER doc. It took a lot to shake her. She'd developed a hide as thick as a rhino to deal with her mom's lifestyle.

After Mom fatally overdosed, Tony and Stella Rossini took her under their wing. She was grateful. She owed them. And she loved Alyssa, even when she was acting like a spoiled brat. Nicole would never let anything bad happen to her girl.

The appearance of the man in the monk's cowl had worried her. For a moment, it seemed he was headed toward them, coming after Alyssa.

Descending the grand staircase, Nicole glanced at Ryder and whispered, "We need to find out who killed Alan Caldicott and get him taken out of the picture before the wedding."

"You and me," he said. "Working together?"

What was that supposed to mean? Ignoring possible innuendos, she focused on the investigation that Nonna had demanded. "Do you have any leads? Did Jimmy say anything that might tell you who killed his father?"

"Something big is supposed to happen on Saturday. The day of the wedding."

"Too vague." She rolled her eyes. Unlike Alyssa, who hadn't outgrown the need to smirk, Nicole tried to avoid cornball adolescent expressions, but Ryder had that effect on her. An ability to provoke immaturity. When she looked directly at him, her attention was shattered by the sheen from his blue eyes, his plump lower lip and the way his dark blond hair, still damp from the shower, curled over his forehead.

"I need to talk to Tony," he said. "If he doesn't know more about what Caldicott was working on, he can point us in the right direction."

That sounded like a plan. "What else?"

"Jimmy mentioned a computer guy his dad worked with. His name is Mouse."

She knew him. "He'll be easy to spot in a crowd. Always wears T-shirts with goofy slogans like 'Programmers Do IT Better' or 'Nothing Artificial About My Intelligence.' Stuff like that."

In the ballroom, Alyssa took the lead. "Stick with me. We'll find Papa."

Big parties and social events weren't Nicole's favorite thing. She carefully dodged Petrovich, who stood beside a tall, distinguished gentleman she didn't recognize. One of the Volkov Group? They proceeded through the throng of people from Rossini Enterprises. Family, employees and friends tried to be respectful about Caldicott's murder while still celebrating the impending nuptials. The result manifested in a layer of nervous chatter overlaid with annoying dance music from the DJ and punctuated by outbursts of rage, tears and semi-hysterical laughter.

As if this emotional soup wasn't enough, some people seemed to recognize Ryder from his time spent undercover at the casino. He didn't know if they'd bear grudges or growl and snarl because he was—after all—a federal agent, i.e., a sworn enemy.

Nicole nudged his elbow. "Maybe you should keep your head down. Not everybody is a member of the Ryder Beckham fan club."

With Alyssa leading the way, they wove a path across the large open space that took up more than half of the first floor.

When special events like weddings weren't scheduled, she'd been told that the ballroom transformed into a restaurant. Near the server's area, she spotted Daniel Danger the Salty Dog wearing his pirate garb minus the peg leg. He waved his plastic cutlass, supervising the caterers and bartenders.

Across the room, arched windows alternated with French doors leading onto the flagstone patio. Polished oak baseboards and crown moldings set off the gold, damask-patterned wallpaper set with brass sconces. A dance floor provided more than ample space for the three couples who still paid attention to the DJ's music. The rest of the space was filled with an array of circular tables draped in the bride's signature purple and acid green—colors that reminded Nicole of a Mardi Gras nightmare.

Though several people signaled to them, Alyssa pressed through the crowd, making a beeline for her father. She broke into his conversation with a deeply tanned golf pro and one of the casino pit bosses. "Excuse me, gentlemen, I need to speak with my father."

"The bride is always right." The pit boss bowed and adjusted his suit coat. Nicole glimpsed his gun in a shoulder holster.

Alyssa pulled her dad outside onto the flagstone patio where the beam from the lighthouse sliced through the fog. In the distance, Nicole saw several officers moving through the mobile LED lights set up by the forensic team to illuminate the crime scene. The distant rumble of the surf reminded her of retrieving the body with Ryder.

Despite her long sweater, Nicole shivered and hugged herself. Tony Rossini frowned at her. Concerned, he asked, "You okay, Nicole?"

She looked into his ebony eyes, which were the same dark shade as Alyssa's but very different. His daughter's eyes flashed and sparkled. Tony Rossini held a ponderous weight of woe, regret and responsibility in his gaze. So many people depended on him, expected him to make things right for them. She considered telling him that everything would be fine and the police were investigating, but Nicole couldn't lie. Not to him.

"I'm worried," she said. "I think the guy who killed Caldicott might come back."

"Finally." He threw his hands in the air. "Somebody else sees that we got a problem."

"I hope I'm wrong."

He nodded to Ryder. "I'm glad you're here. I've seen you in action and think you'll do a better job than the local cops and the feds. Am I right, Nicole?"

Before she could answer, Alyssa piped up. "I knew bringing him here was a good idea."

Tony signaled to his wife. Stella had been standing at the French door watching them, and she rushed outside to her daughter's side. Fluttering and chirping, she pulled Alyssa back into the ballroom to discuss wedding arrangements. Nicole and Ryder were left alone on the patio with Tony Rossini.

Ryder turned to Tony and asked, "What made you suspicious?"

"Ever since Alexei Volkov—that's the groom's dad—suggested this destination for the wedding, I knew something was up. What kind of knucklehead wants his son to get married on a foggy coast when I have a premier location at the Safari Casino? We could have had top-tier entertainment, an eight-layer, custom-designed cake and Michelin-starred chefs. Instead, we've got pigs-in-blankets and a pirate impersonator."

"And a murder," she reminded him.

Ryder dug for more info. "What was Alan Caldicott working on?"

"He discovered a computer hack that could disable law enforcement radios and signals. Something to do with EMP technology."

"Electromagnetic pulse," Ryder translated. "A neat way to

disrupt communications and mask operations in a specific area."

Nicole was familiar with magnetic resonance in MRI scans and radiation used in hospital treatment, but she wasn't an expert. "If an EMP could block communication equipment, it could probably also disable traffic cams and offshore surveillance. Could be used for smuggling."

"Bingo," Tony said. "Caldicott was working with Mouse to get more information. That's where you should start investigating."

Ryder asked, "Do I have your blessing to look into this?"

"As long as you keep my daughter and this one out of danger." Tony shook his hand. "If anybody gives you trouble, refer them to me. What have you got so far?"

Without holding back, Ryder filled him in. Autopsy results on Caldicott weren't available yet. But the long metal paddle carried by the cowled man had probably come from the St. Macarius Monastery north of Salem.

Nicole spoke up. "I've been there. The monks make fudge and truffles to sell to the public."

"I want to check it out," Ryder said.

News to me! "You want to go to the abbey?"

"As good a place to start as any," he said. "First, we should talk to Mouse."

"He's not supposed to be here until tomorrow," Tony said. "Use one of those video call things. Nicole has the family connections on her computer."

Before she and Ryder left the flagstone patio, she gave Papa Rossini a hug and a peck on the cheek. He whispered to her, "I'm glad you're here. My daughter listens to you. More than to her mother or me. Don't let her ruin her life by marrying the Volkov boy."

The handsome young Michael? The father of her unborn baby? Nicole didn't want to break Alyssa's heart. "I'll do what I can."

Ryder placed his hand on her back, a gesture she found both unnecessary and sexy. To Tony, he said, "Thanks for your help, sir."

Turning, she noticed the tall, classy, white-haired gent again and asked Papa, "Who is that man? It seems like I should know him."

"Dmitry Orloff, supposedly a distant relative of the late czar. A friend of the Volkov family and advisor to Alexei. Be nice to him and he might give you a crown jewel."

She and Ryder climbed the staircase together and went to her bedroom suite, which was about half as fancy as Alyssa's with a sitting room and counter, a very nice bathroom and a small, attached room with a queen-sized bed. In here, they'd be alone with her computer. She closed the door and flicked on the lights. When she turned to face him, her intention was to clearly inform him that even though they'd be spending time together, she still didn't forgive him or trust him. Nothing had changed. They were barely friends. Certainly, nothing more.

And then, she kissed him.

Chapter Seven

To tell the truth, she hadn't accidentally fallen into Ryder's embrace. Nicole had purposely planted her lips on his and wrapped her arms around him. While her rational brain screamed negative warnings about getting too close, her body acted with a mind of its own. Call it passion, call it lust, call it stupidity. Instead of telling him to stay away from her, she plunged her tongue into his mouth. Her body molded to his. Her right leg clenched around him.

She closed her eyes and sank backward in time. Almost two years ago in Las Vegas when he was undercover and she worked as a dealer at the Safari Casino, they had merged. Without thinking or planning, they had become part of each other. During those precious weeks, they danced in perfect harmony. His steps matched hers. They shared the beating of their hearts. Echoes of their private rhythms, their favorite songs and their laughter rang in her ears. She could read his thoughts and finish his sentences.

No, I couldn't. Her eyes snapped open. She hadn't known him at all. Everything she had believed about Ryder Beckham was a lie.

In the sitting room of her suite, sanity returned with a dull thud. She tried to step away from him, but he tightened his grasp and whispered in her ear, "Don't leave me, Nicole."

"I didn't mean to kiss you."

"I know."

But while they'd been working together, pursuing their so-called investigation and talking to Tony Rossini, she'd felt... right. Comfortable. Destiny—the same unexplainable force that had dragged her through med school and her internship on the way to becoming a doctor—informed her that she was supposed to be with him.

He imprinted a gentle kiss on her mouth. Her conscious mind objected and told her this was *not* right. *Not at all.* The opposite, in fact. Oh, so wrong.

But she found herself kissing him back. Her left arm coiled around his torso. The right flung around his neck. Her body vibrated and rubbed against his. Nicole was definitely playing the role of the aggressor, taking what she wanted from him. Which might be okay. As long as she was in control, what could go wrong?

Her right hand slid down his chest. His sculpted muscles felt incredible under her fingertips. She reached lower, stroked his torso and paused at his waistband to manipulate the rivet button on his Levi's. He gasped. Then he reacted.

He hoisted her bottom, forcing her to wrap both legs around him as he carried her across the suite to her small separate bedroom. He lowered her onto the flowered duvet and tumbled into bed beside her.

"Unbelievable," she said.

"Wasn't too hard. You're tall but not heavy."

"It was unbelievable that you managed that whole maneuver without breaking the kiss."

"If I let you catch your breath," he said, "I figured you'd tell me to stop."

"Good guess."

"But now we're here." He slid his hand under her long sweater and glided his clever fingers over her rib cage toward her bra. "Might as well—"

"First, we need to talk." If she allowed him to go further,

there would be no stopping until they'd made love. Too sudden, too soon. She shoved his hand away, bounced herself off the bed and turned on the bedside lamp that had an ornate base and a fringed shade. Her suite had an old-fashioned feminine décor that amused her, especially since her behavior was definitely not suitable for a proper lady.

Standing beside the bed, she looked down at the big handsome man who rested on his side with his elbow bent and his head propped on his fist. His compelling gaze followed her every move. In a seemingly innocent voice, he asked, "What do you want to talk about?"

"We ought to figure out what we need to ask Mouse." She glanced at her practical wristwatch with the large readable numbers. Though it seemed like a lifetime had passed since she'd first seen Ryder at dusk, the watch showed the time was only ten thirty. "I can reach him at home. I hope he hasn't gone to sleep."

"Probably not. I'm guessing he's the sort of guy who stays up late playing the latest version of *Wizards, Witches and Warriors*."

"How do you know he's a gamer? Is that some kind of profiler deduction?"

"Have you forgotten?" His lips curved in a self-deprecating grin that activated the dimple on his right cheek. "I have a lot in common with Mouse. I play video games and go to Comic-Con whenever possible."

She hadn't forgotten. Even after they'd broken up, one of her favorite fantasies involved imagining him in his cosplay Thor armor. "I wasn't sure if the sexy nerd routine was part of your undercover disguise or your real personality."

"Sexy nerd? Is that a real thing?"

"As real as Rugged Cowboy or Handsome Prince."

"Whatever," he said. "I don't know how much we should plan our call to Mouse. Logical questions like who, what, when and where. And I think you should do the talking."

"Why?"

"Sexy nerds, like Mouse and me, live to please the ladies. He'll tell you more than he'd tell me."

She found the analytical side to his personality appealing. A little bit sneaky but still… His talents went beyond carrying a gun and knowing how to kick ass. He was smart and dedicated, with eyes on the prize. But was he meant for a long-term relationship? *Oh, hell no.* She stiffened her spine. "Fine. I'll handle Mouse."

He cleared his throat. "Do you want to talk about anything more personal? About us, for example."

"Now that you mention it, you said something when we first met at the lighthouse about how your job has changed. What's different?"

"I no longer accept undercover assignments."

"Why not?"

He stroked a figure-eight pattern on the duvet beside him. An invitation for her to return to the bed. She decided to humor him, let him think he had the power. Primly, she sat on the edge of her queen mattress while he continued. "After what happened in Las Vegas, I don't have the stomach for covert assignments."

"Really?" She teased with a wide-eyed, pseudo-innocent look. "But you're so good at lying."

He rested his hand on her thigh. "I missed you, Nicole. Did you ever think of me?"

All the time. He rubbed her leg. His touch felt warm and soothing. At the same time, arousing. Fighting the urge to collapse onto the bed beside him, she stubbornly stuck out her chin and lied. "Think of you? Not a bit."

"If I expected it'd do any good, I'd apologize again. By now, you've got to know I'm sorry. You can show me that you believe me by giving me your phone number."

"I'll think about it."

She made the mistake of gazing into his blue, blue eyes and

seeing a small flame of sincerity. Like a pilot light. The burner ignited and heat raced from his touch on her thigh down to her toes and back up to her abdomen where it exploded and spread through her entire body like a contagious infection. Her resolve melted. *What could go wrong? This could!* She wasn't over him. Maybe she never would be. Maybe she'd be haunted by unfulfilled passion for the rest of her life.

Determined to stay in control, she bolted from the bedroom. "My computer is out here. Let's make the call."

She rushed into the sitting room and went to the granite counter that had a sink, a microwave and a full array of overpriced snacks ranging from gooey candy to oranges. The undercounter refrigerator held a stocked minibar. She'd added a six-pack of Deschutes beer from Bend. Grabbing a bottle for herself and one for him, she opened the twist tops on both and held one toward him. She didn't trust her shaky hands to pour into glasses without spilling.

He tilted the bottle toward her in a toast. "Here's to our investigation."

Though she tapped her bottle against his, she avoided looking at him. She had to get a grip on her resistance before she dove headfirst into another relationship that ended in hurt. After a swig of smooth pale ale, she took two deep breaths, licked her lips and confronted him. In an almost-steady voice, she asked, "If you aren't going undercover anymore, what's your new job?"

"Supervisory. I'll be spending a lot of time riding a desk—overseeing accounting procedures, monitoring potential fraud and smuggling."

"Your connections could come in handy in our investigation."

He nodded. "Especially since I've applied for a position on the west coast. I'd be based in Portland. Your backyard."

"Congratulations." To her chagrin, her heart twirled in happy cartwheels.

"If I get the job, I'll need to find a place to live. Maybe you can show me the good restaurants and coffee shops. Portland is famous for coffee, right?"

Refusing to be drawn into a friendly chat, she tightened her jaw and stalked across the room to a small table with two chairs. With her laptop centered on the table, she said, "Time to call Mouse. Please summarize what we already know. And what we still need to find out."

He sat opposite her and placed his beer bottle on a coaster with the logo for Leeward Manor and a silhouette of the lighthouse. "Since we won't have an official autopsy for a couple of days, what can you tell me about Caldicott's injuries from what we observed?"

"You want my medical opinion?"

"You're an ER doc. An expert."

She was glad to shift her focus to straightforward medical knowledge. Flashing on a mental picture of Caldicott's face, she recalled his visible injuries. "The likely cause of death was the gunshot wound to the head. Since I didn't have a chance to examine him thoroughly and waves were washing away the blood, I can't say for certain what caliber bullet. I'm guessing a nine-millimeter."

"What else?" Ryder asked.

"He was wearing a suit, so much of his body was covered, but I opened his shirt to determine if we should attempt CPR." Though he'd had no pulse, she wouldn't give up until every hope was lost. "I saw perimortem bruising on his torso. One of his ribs appeared to be broken."

"Could he have gotten those injuries in his fall?"

"Crashing down a jagged rock cliff would produce lots of scrapes and contusions. But the injuries on his chest and gut appeared to be purposeful. As though someone had applied pressure to that area or beaten him. Also, his wrists were circled by bruising. Fingers were broken."

"The fall? Or something else?"

Nicole had seen similar injuries in the emergency room, often in domestic violence cases. "I don't like to draw conclusions from such scant evidence, but I'm guessing the autopsy will reveal that Caldicott had been abused before he was shot. Beaten by the long metal paddle carried by the cowled figure."

"Tortured," Ryder summarized. "The killer was trying to get information from him."

She sipped her beer and stared down at the screensaver on her computer—a sketch of *Vitruvian Man*. Though she hadn't been close to Alan Caldicott, she'd known and respected him. The idea of him suffering at the hands of an assassin disgusted and horrified her. Accidental death was bad enough, but torture wakened terrible images in her mind. All too often at the hospital, she'd dealt with the results of man's inhumanity to other men or women. "Why do people do things like this?"

Ryder reached across the small table and held her hand in his, offering small comfort. His words were even less consoling. "In this case, I suspect the motivation was money. The combination of torture and a bullet to the brain points to a paid assassin."

"Who paid him...and why?"

"Agent Murdock from the FBI identified fingerprints from a man who fit the bill. Apparently, he had a colorful career as a mastermind assassin who arranged unusual murders. Sounds like the sort of guy who'd dress up as the Grim Reaper."

She didn't miss his use of the past tense. "*Had* a career? Had? Is he deceased?"

"Died three years ago. Murdock sent me his file, and I learned that he lived in Las Vegas for a while. Do you remember the name? John Mitchell. People called him Houdini or the Magician or Mitch the Bitch."

"Why does it matter? He's dead."

"Any hint, any microscopic viral blip, can trigger important information." He shrugged. "Call Mouse."

She tapped on the computer keys, logged in to an account

for Rossini Enterprises and entered her password. Her access was limited to midlevel security, mostly used for contacting other employees or family. In a few moments, she had a face-to-face call with the computer engineer who went by Mouse.

Her screen displayed a wide angle of his thin face—a match for his bony shoulders and gaunt frame. His sallow complexion, unusual for Las Vegas, showed how seldom he spent time outdoors. His head was shaved on the sides, leaving a magenta Mohawk and a long thin braid. He wore a short-sleeved T-shirt over full sleeves of tattoos on both arms. The shirt said, "Geeks Rule." His round, rose-colored sunglasses almost disguised evidence that he'd been crying. "Are you okay?" she asked.

"Not really, but thanks for asking, Nicole."

"I didn't know Alan Caldicott well, but I liked him." Nobody deserved the kind of death he'd endured. Her throat tightened, and she paused before continuing. "He seemed kind and efficient."

"He was the father I never knew. I'm going to miss him."

"We're going to catch the people responsible," she said. "I'm investigating."

"No offense, Nicole, but you're a doctor. What do you know about detecting?"

She signaled for Ryder to come around the table and join her on the screen. "Do you remember this guy?"

Mouse smiled, revealing an overbite that suited his nickname. "Ryder, the undercover Secret Service agent and Level Thirty-Six Wizard."

"We're working together on solving this murder," she said. "Jimmy Caldicott, Alan's son, said you probably knew something about a delivery."

"I know everything." Mouse caught the end of his magenta ponytail and twirled it between his fingers. "I first noticed the glitch two months ago. Instead of erasing it, I followed the links and almost reached the source."

"Did the hack involve EMP technology?" Ryder asked.

"Oh, yeah." His eyebrows pulled down and touched the rim of his sunglasses. "Caldicott said you were smarter than you looked. I'm going to miss the old man."

"Send us a copy of your notes," Ryder said.

"My data is totally encrypted. You'll need help interpreting, but I'll send what I've got through this link with Nicole."

"Thanks, Mouse." She reached out as if she could pat him on the back. "Tell us what happened after you found this glitch."

Ryder sat close beside her so he could see the screen. *So close, too close.* She felt waves of warmth radiating from his body. Breathing in his scent, she smelled forest, wind and ocean.

"It's big news, really big," Mouse said. "The delivery is worth four-and-a-half-million dollars."

The number drew her full attention. Her feelings for Ryder would have to wait.

Chapter Eight

Thursday, two days before the wedding...

The next morning, Ryder wakened from a dream about four-and-a-half-million dollars raining down from a lighthouse while the cowled figure of Death did a salsa number with four bridesmaids dressed in acid-green ruffles. He blinked into darkness. His tiny third-floor room had no windows, but he knew dawn was near. His tactical, glow-in-the-dark, G-Shock wristwatch showed the time to be a few minutes before five, which meant he might have a chance at finding the hall bathroom unoccupied.

He got out of bed, threw on the complimentary navy-blue robe—surprisingly plush, considering the threadbare room—and padded down the hall. *All right, all right, all right!* The door was open and no one was inside. He locked himself in. Downstairs on the second floor, Nicole had a well-supplied, private bath with deluxe shower, including an overhead device that made the spray feel like a downpour in a rain forest. She hadn't invited him to join her last night. After their call with Mouse, they'd made plans to visit the monastery where fudge and truffles were made. Then she'd booted him out of her room. A disappointment. Her spontaneous kiss had given him reason to hope. He'd glimpsed a sliver of light at the end of the tunnel before she'd slammed the door and sealed it shut.

He splashed water on his face. Unfortunately, the only towel was a gritty-looking scrap. No problem. He used the robe to dry off and then went back to his room to grab his toothbrush, toothpaste and electric razor. He returned to the hallway in time to see the bathroom door close. Somebody else was already in there. Two fluffy bridesmaids flounced into the hall and formed a line outside the facility. He overheard their banter about the hotness of the best man, Dirk Petrovich, with the ginger hair—an opinion that caused him to demote their intelligence and observational abilities to less than zero. Their high-pitched giggles stabbed into his brain like shards of glass.

Again, he thought of Nicole's deluxe bathroom. Since it was probably too early to call, he texted: Need to use your shower. STAT!

He stared at his screen. Nothing to do but wait. A test of his patience. Saint Macarius Monastery didn't open to the public until eleven o'clock, but they could probably get inside earlier. GPS showed a two-hour-and-twenty-minute drive, which meant their earliest departure from Consolation Cove was 8:40 a.m. According to his watch, it was currently 5:20 a.m. Three hours and twenty minutes before he and Nicole should leave.

Tick-tock. He dropped the phone onto his bed and closed the door to his room. Juggling numbers represented a coping strategy for him. No problem was too big or too small that it couldn't be broken down into numerical pieces and reassembled like a puzzle. He reviewed the tasks to be accomplished this morning and estimated the time necessary. He allotted several minutes—between seven and twenty-one—to contact his HSI supervisor at national headquarters in Washington, DC, which was three hours ahead of West Coast time. Maybe call there first. A possible smuggling operation worth four-and-a-half-million dollars must have generated interest at Homeland Security. Very likely, an investigation was already underway.

He'd make another call to update his soon-to-be supervisor in LA. Also, he'd check in with Agent Murdock to follow the FBI's forensic investigation into Alan Caldicott's murder. Both of those tasks could be done while driving and, as such, really didn't figure into his timing. The same grab-and-go logic applied to breakfast and coffee. He might have to actually stop his rental car to fill up with gas.

While Ryder shuffled numbers in his head, he repacked and prepped to leave. After last night's showdown with Danny Danger, the manager of Leeward Manor, he didn't expect to be offered a better room. No way was he staying another night on the third-floor dormitory.

His belongings rapidly and efficiently filled the suitcase. Years of planning and frequent repetition made him an expert when it came to life on the road. When he'd heard Alyssa's plan—*surprise, surprise*—to bring him and Nicole back together, he'd hoped his nomadic lifestyle might change. Ryder was ready for a permanent home with a lawn and a driveway and maybe a golden retriever puppy.

He checked his phone. She still hadn't responded. Easily he imagined her snuggled under the duvet, cozy and warm, breathing gently. Using his index finger, he stabbed out another text. STAT!

Dressed in a long-sleeved shirt, crewneck sweater, jeans and his leather jacket, Ryder focused on new priorities, starting with getting the hell out of Leeward Manor. The groom's family—otherwise known as the Volkov Group—would arrive today. Maybe he'd take a room at their hotel. Dragging his roller suitcase while carrying his garment bag and briefcase, he descended the grand staircase to the parking lot.

Outside, darkness clung to the sky. The stars and moon had begun to fade into the mist, but it was still a long time until sunrise at about seven o'clock. Standing in the double-door entry to Leeward Manor, he sensed that he wasn't alone. The banging of pans and clatter of mixers from the rear of the Manor indicated that the kitchen crew had arrived. Was there someone else? The muscles across his back twitched. Was he being watched? He slipped his hand inside his jacket and touched his holstered sidearm for reassurance.

The flashes from the lighthouse came with preset, pretimed regularity but were blocked by the tall trees in the forest and provided little illumination. Fortunately, the parking lot was lit well enough that Ryder didn't have to stumble through total darkness. He made his way to his rental SUV, where he stored his suitcase and garment bag in the rear, slid into the driver's seat and shut the door. Though sealed inside, he didn't feel protected. Too many windows. Too much rustling from the wind. The eerie cries from a lonesome gull. The nose of his vehicle pointed into the rugged coastal forest where the cowled assassin had hidden. He squinted and saw nothing moving. Glanced over his shoulder. No one appeared to be close.

In an overabundance of caution, he freed his Beretta from the holster and set it on the passenger seat beside his briefcase. He inhaled a deep breath and slowly exhaled. Maybe he was overreacting to a vague feeling, but nobody ever died from paranoia. He checked his phone. Still no reply text from Nicole. Sending another text seemed too desperate. If the lady wanted to be in charge, fine. He'd follow his own plan.

At 6:07 a.m. in Oregon, the time in DC was after nine o'clock. Not too early to call his supervisor. From a special pocket in his briefcase, he pulled out the satellite phone used for official business and contacted HSI headquarters. Marianne Trevino, Special Agent in Charge, answered her private line on the fourth ring. "Ryder Beckham, how's my favorite cowpoke?"

She never let him forget his Texas roots, and he played along. "Happy as a pig in slop."

"I wasn't expecting to hear from you."

"Why is that?"

"Aren't you supposed to be on vacation this week?"

He noticed the way SAC Trevino avoided giving him any information. Usually he enjoyed a dance with her, but he didn't have time for games. Ryder had only allotted no more than twenty-one minutes for this call. "What can you tell me about a special shipment worth four-and-a-half million that's supposed to be delivered on the Oregon coast on Saturday?"

"A lot of money," she said. "Not a very specific location."

"Tell me something I don't know."

He and Trevino had worked together frequently, including on the investigation into Rossini Enterprises when he'd met Nicole. He knew that she trusted his observations and would share info. Still, she wasn't about to spill the tea without an explanation. She asked, "What's your connection to this supposed shipment?"

"I found the victim's body. Alan Caldicott. He was Rossini's CFO, an accountant."

"You're there for the Rossini wedding." She spoke as though his location was a big surprise to her, though he knew it wasn't. "I suspect that you plan to see Nicole Carpenter, the ER doc who would be a perfect match for you."

"That's why I'm here." No point in denying.

"I hope you have your priorities straight, Ryder. Getting involved with the Rossini family might not be smart."

"They were exonerated from all accusations." He pointed out the obvious. "They helped prepare our case against the real counterfeiters."

"Which doesn't give them a free pass. This time, they might not be clean. Lightning doesn't strike twice in the same place."

Her suspicions were clear. "Is this a smuggling operation?"

"Could be."

Amid the general sounds from the forest and the Manor, he heard the shuffle of a footstep on the parking lot tarmac. He sensed the approaching presence. The watcher was moving closer. He picked up his Beretta. "I want to know what's going on, Trevino. To find out if there's any kind of danger."

"Really?" Her voice sizzled with disbelief. "The danger is obvious. There's been one murder already. From the report, it sounds like Caldicott was killed in weird circumstances. Beaten with a fudge spoon before taking a bullet to the head. And we've picked up quite a bit of data on computer hacks designed to thwart law enforcement communication systems."

"I'm aware."

"A piece of advice, cowboy. Throw Nicole over the back of your saddle and ride out of Oregon as fast as you can."

"As if she'd go," he muttered. "Nicole is the maid of honor. And Alyssa Rossini is determined to get married on Saturday."

A few ticks of silence spread between them before SAC Trevino spoke again. "Here's a proposition for you. Since you're already on site, I want you to investigate. Something is getting smuggled, and I want to know what it is. And the computer hacks need to be disarmed."

"I don't do undercover anymore."

She gave a low, husky chuckle. "You couldn't be undercover if you wanted to. Everybody knows you're a special agent with HSI Secret Service."

His G-Shock watch showed nineteen minutes had passed. *Perfect timing.* "Send me the contacts and details."

"There's not much, but I'll pass it along. Oh, and Ryder…"

"What?"

"Yippy-ki-yay."

He ended the call, dropped the phone and went into attack mode. Someone was out there. In the forest. Lurking behind other cars in the parking lot. At the Manor. Someone was coming closer. Ryder had no intention of being taken by surprise.

He released the thumb safety on his Beretta 92. The other hand hooked into the door handle. In one smooth move, he whipped open the driver's-side door and dove outside onto the tarmac where he somersaulted and rose in a kneeling position with his gun in hand, ready to fire at the shadowy figure who stepped away from his rear bumper.

She made a high-pitched screech.

"Nicole." He lowered the gun. "What the hell?"

The parking lot lights shone on the pale circle of her face. Her hazel eyes popped wide open, showing white around the rim. She'd reacted to his unintentional assault by raising her hands above her head.

"I was looking for you." She lowered her arms. "After I checked your text, I took my shower and got dressed. Then I came looking."

"You could have texted."

"Well, you know how flight attendants always say you should put on your own oxygen mask before helping your children. That's what I was doing."

He wasn't sure if he was supposed to be her child in that weird analogy. Or something else. "You were stalking me."

"Come back to the Manor with me. You can use my shower now."

His tension hadn't yet abated. In this parking lot, they were as obvious as rodeo clowns waving red flags at a bull. The fact that SAC Trevino had given him an assignment reinforced his sense of danger. Maybe Nicole wasn't the only watcher. The killer was still out there, and Ryder needed to shift gears and treat their situation like a real investigation with potentially fatal consequences. His best option might be to take Trevino's advice: throw Nicole over the back of his saddle and ride off into the approaching dawn.

"You're coming with me," he drawled.

"Mind if I ask where we're going?"

He went around to the passenger's-side door, moved his briefcase to the rear and held her hand as she boarded the SUV. Since his minute-by-minute schedule no longer made sense, he improvised. "We'll get breakfast, review our conversation with Mouse and then go to the abbey."

He took his cowboy hat from the back seat where it had been resting upside down to keep the good luck from spilling out. Too late for that now.

Chapter Nine

Nicole fastened her seat belt and stared through the windshield as Ryder adjusted the GPS map display on the dashboard, threw the engine into gear and drove out of the parking lot. Something about him had changed, and it wasn't just the battered cowboy hat that almost scraped the ceiling above the driver's seat. His voice had lowered to a serious tone. The first time she'd noticed this sort of vocal shift was in bed after they'd made love and his inhibitions were gone. The memory brought her a smile.

She turned away from the windshield and studied his profile. His posture had gone from casual to ramrod-straight. His taut grip on the steering wheel flexed the tendons in his hands and wrists. Yesterday, he'd been trying to figure out what had happened to Caldicott in a detached manner, asking questions because it seemed rational. Today, his investigation felt personal and laser-focused. Braced for an attack, his attitude reminded her of a cocked gun ready to fire.

For once, they were on the same page. This morning when she'd gotten his text, she'd been lying in her bed, wide awake. She had sensed approaching danger and wondered if she could convince Alyssa to postpone the wedding. Hadn't they already discovered that the delivery of the mysterious shipment would take place on the wedding day? Not a good omen.

She hadn't realized how much she relied on Ryder's opinion

until she'd dressed, left her room and spotted him clomping down the staircase at the Manor. After all her grumbling and telling him to get away from her, she'd changed her mind and executed a sharp one-eighty pivot. She wanted him to stay. To make sense of their catastrophic breakup. To know—for sure—there was nothing left between them. No words unspoken. No emotions unexpressed. More importantly, she wanted him to solve the murder and make sense of the cyber threat before something else terrible happened.

Returning to her room, she'd grabbed a jacket, strapped on her cross-body pack and zipped her cell phone into it. Outside the Manor, she'd followed him across the parking lot. When he made his phone call, she hadn't interrupted. Before she'd had a chance to approach, he'd leaped from the car and drawn his gun on her, totally freaking her out.

"Who were you talking to?" she asked.

"My supervisor, Marianne Trevino, at Homeland Security Investigations in DC." He glanced toward her. "You met her during the counterfeiting investigation."

Nicole remembered a slender woman with cropped gray hair, dark eyes and fierce eyebrows. Though short, her intensity made her stand out from the crowd. Most of the other law enforcement people she'd encountered during those fraught months had faded into shadow, eclipsed by the presence of Ryder. "I remember her. Now she's your boss."

"Supervisory SAC. Special Agent in Charge." He tapped the brim of his hat in a cowboy salute to Marianne. "She says *hi*."

"*Hi*, back."

"She assigned me to be part of the HSI investigation into what's happening here at Consolation Cove. There are other agents assigned. Good news for us. We'll have easy access to a whole lot of information and expertise."

"Why does she want you involved?"

"Because I have history with the Rossini family. Y'all aren't exactly known for being open and friendly."

The opposite, in fact. A lifetime spent with Alyssa's family had taught her not to trust new contacts who might have hidden agendas. The Rossini reputation came with unfortunate expectations. Many people thought they were a gang of blood-thirsty mobsters toting machine guns and twirling wire garrotes. "That's not fair. How can SAC Trevino suspect us of wrongdoing? She worked the counterfeiting case. She ought to know that we can be helpful."

"And she appreciates your integrity."

"So?"

"Your help on the prior investigation doesn't mean y'all have a free pass. There could be rotten apples. Just because you helped us once doesn't mean you'll do it again."

"But we're the victims here." The HSI attitude irritated her. "Alan Caldicott was the CFO of Rossini Enterprises. Why would we hire an assassin to kill him?"

"You wouldn't."

"Somebody is trying to make it look like we're enabling a device to knock out communication on the West Coast. That's what Mouse said."

"Agreed. Don't jump down my throat." He shot her a glance. "Just so you know, I'm not undercover on this assignment."

Fair enough. Also, she reminded herself, the accusation from his supervisor wasn't his fault. She took a breath and centered herself. Through the windshield, she saw sunrise break over the horizon to the east, turning the skies into streaks of orange and magenta behind the silhouettes of Sitka spruce, pine, cottonwood and fir. Beyond the forest, pockets of fog rose from gorges, canyons and riverbeds, adding a layer of mystery.

"You're officially on the case," she said. "Is that why you're wearing the hat?"

"You used to like my cowboy look."

"I've grown up since then." Not completely true. The rancher in him appealed to her almost as much as the sexy nerd he was at heart. "Are we still working together?"

"That depends." He guided the SUV through the forested coastal range where moss-covered tree branches rose above them while shrubs and ferns crowded the edge of the road. "I won't do anything that puts you or Alyssa in danger."

She hadn't expected that response. Though she waited for a punch line, there wasn't a glimmer of a smile. He was dead serious. Regrettably, it was her turn to agree. "Did Marianne mention danger?"

"She didn't have to. I'm worried enough on my own. Just now, when you were following me, did you notice anybody else in the vicinity?"

"Like the cowled figure of the Grim Reaper?"

"That's no joke," he drawled. "The assassin already used that disguise, so I doubt he'll repeat. Think about it, Nicole. Did you see anyone near the Manor or in the parking lot?"

Her observational skills were top-notch. Closing her eyes, she recalled the moment when she exited the Manor and looked out at the flagstone patio. "There was a guy jogging toward the lighthouse. Didn't see his face. He wore a green Oregon Ducks track suit with the hood up."

"Probably a local."

"If he came from Las Vegas, he'd more likely be dressed in a Raiders pirate hoodie."

He drove the SUV into a wide open swath of the Willamette Valley. Sunlight sparkled like diamonds in the dew. Hilly fields had been cleared during the November harvest, leaving neat rows of grapes to start the next season. He asked, "Do you ever miss the desert?"

"Sometimes," she admitted. "The rainy Oregon winters aren't my favorite thing, but the moisture is great for the complexion. And I appreciate the green-on-green in the fertile fields. I've been trying to get a feel for wine tastings, but I don't have much of a palate."

"Willamette Valley is famous for pinot noir."

When he launched into a commentary on the aroma, clarity and structure of red wine and port, she wasn't surprised. Ryder had developed a wide range of knowledge in his years of undercover work. She wondered if he'd ever posed as a sommelier.

As they cruised through the valley, she pointed out sights and talked about the area. If he took the job in Portland, she'd enjoy showing him the lush landscape and introducing him to an incredible array of seafood. When they drove through Corvallis, she directed him to a busy little café on the northern edge of town. As soon as the waitress appeared, Nicole ordered bacon, eggs over easy and pancakes. He did the same.

When their coffee was served, he reached across the faux wood tabletop in their booth, grasped her hand and gave a squeeze. "I've been considering everything Mouse told us. Do you think he was exaggerating when he referred to a mastermind?"

"Was he lying? The answer is no. I believe he sincerely liked Caldicott and wants to see his killer caught. *Mastermind* is part of Mouse's vocabulary. He spends a lot of time playing computer games with superheroes and demons." She squeezed back and released his hand. "You know more about those fantasy worlds than I do."

He sipped his coffee and licked his lips. "Here's what I got from Mouse's story. A few weeks ago, he noticed a glitch in the computer programming system for Rossini Enterprises."

"But he didn't just call it a glitch. He used computer language that neither you nor I understand." She tasted her own coffee, which wasn't bad for diner brew. "The glitch was related to supply orders for the Safari Hotel."

He nodded. "I keep forgetting how complex the Rossini operation is. A casino, an arena with world-class entertainment, a hotel, import/export business, property development and construction."

"Not to mention financing a new wing for the hospital, a

pancreatic research facility, an orphanage and retirement villages."

"Tony Rossini has a hand in a heap of different businesses."

The aroma of bacon on the griddle tickled her senses and she realized she'd skipped dinner last night. Another sip of coffee wasn't enough to silence the hunger growling in her stomach. She continued their narrative. "When Mouse told Caldicott about the glitch, the CFO advised him to follow up. He took a deep dive, including a visit to the dark web, and discovered hacking on communication sites along the Oregon coast. The supposed mastermind had created a web, using electromagnetic pulse technology, that could interrupt police signals. Mouse was able to observe when the interruption happened."

"Ten days ago," Ryder said. "A twenty-minute break in simultaneous communication for police, the sheriff's departments and state cops. Also, the Coast Guard, FBI and HSI, which is why Homeland is investigating. That interruption made for one hell of a malware assault."

He'd laid it out neatly, except for one thing. "According to Mouse, the hack created false trails leading to Rossini Enterprises."

"Which makes no sense," Ryder said, "unless Rossini has business on the West Coast."

"I've never heard of anything. Not that I'm involved in the inner circle. But I'll ask Alyssa. If there's a West Coast connection, she'll know." Unwittingly, Nicole had validated SAC Trevino's opinion that Ryder's special connection with the family might provide valuable information. "Also, Mouse assured us that Rossini Enterprises doesn't have interests in the West Coast. Let me remind you, he thought this scheme was meant to blame Rossini."

"You're saying it was a frame."

A frame? Yes, it was. She remembered how Mouse chewed his lower lip as if biting back an accusation that couldn't be proved. "Mouse doesn't know who is behind it, but this destination wedding at the lighthouse was suggested by Alexei Volkov, Michael's father. Isn't that what Tony said?"

The waitress returned with their order. Good-sized portions of bacon and eggs with toast and a short stack on the side. Nicole slathered butter on the pancakes and poured maple syrup over the top. The first bite was heavenly. When she shoveled in the next, she looked up and saw Ryder watching her and grinning.

"What?" she asked.

"I like the way you eat. No counting calories for you."

"I wish." She chugged another swallow of coffee to wash down the food. "When I was in med school, I didn't get enough sleep, drank too much vodka and ate too much junk food. To survive, I had to switch to a healthy diet…with occasional lapses into syrup and butter because if I quit cold turkey, I'd be miserable. God, I love butter. I've been known to make special trips to Tillamook for ice cream, butter and cheese."

His grin widened, and she realized how normal their conversation had become. She was happy to let down her guard and invite this interesting combination of special agent, cowboy and nerd into her life.

"The Volkov family," he said. "If they're involved with the hack and the mystery shipment, why would they try to pin it on Rossini?"

She shrugged. "I don't know much about them, other than Alyssa adores Michael. And his best man, Dirk Petrovich, is practically stalking me."

"I overheard the bridesmaids talking. They think he's a hot ginger," he said with a wink. "Don't you know the tradition? Best man and maid of honor are supposed to hook up."

"Not this time," she said with a shudder. "How can we find out more about the Volkov family? Maybe we should talk to the other HSI agents."

"Good idea. The Volkov Group does a lot of import/export business."

"Like Rossini Enterprises, they aren't known for handling drugs or human trafficking."

"Not yet," he said, displaying a streak of cynicism.

Again, she agreed.

Over the years, she'd learned that the Rossini family might not be running a massive criminal endeavor, but she'd be a fool to trust all of them. Papa and Caldicott and men like Mouse worked legitimate channels. They also consulted with legal counsel before undertaking large operations. "How do we get to the truth?"

"First, we lay out the questions. We need to know three things. What is being shipped? When and where exactly will it be delivered? And who is calling the shots?"

"Symptoms," she said, translating to a medical jargon. "We know there's an illness, so we study the symptoms and ultimately discover the cause."

He snapped a bite of bacon between his teeth. "Our first clue is the monastery. The assassin used the disguise of a fudge-maker to get close to Caldicott. We need to figure out his real identity. If he's there, will you be able to recognize him?"

"I'm not sure." She swabbed her toast in egg yolk. "I only saw him for a second on a very foggy night. All I remember is his heavy beard."

"Which could be a disguise," he pointed out.

"Even if he's not there, one of the other monks might remember him. I did a bit of online research about this order based on Saint Macarius, patron of candymakers. He was kind of a hermit, a description that also fits parts of St. Benedict's life. Anyway, the monks believe in silent contemplation."

"Not good for our interviews."

"They also follow Benedictine Rules, which means calls to prayer six times a day. As well as mass on Sunday and on other important dates, like Macarius' feast day." Though she wasn't an expert, she'd visited the monastery and tasted their products. "Whatever they're doing, it works. Their truffles are yum. And the dark chocolate fudge is incredible."

"The monastery isn't open to the public before eleven o'clock." He checked his wristwatch. "We've got some time to kill before then. Let's get coffee-to-go and head out. If you drive, I'll make a call to St. Macarius and set an appointment with the head monk."

"He's an abbot," she said. "You can call him Father."

His blue eyes flashed with a memory. "You used to go to Mass."

"And you used to come with me. But you were never really Catholic, were you?"

"Methodist," he said. "I'm kind of surprised that Alyssa's mom is okay with a wedding service on the beach outside a lighthouse."

"She's not." Nicole felt a bit guilty for not maintaining focus on the wedding events, but investigating the murder took precedence, especially now that Ryder was officially on the case. "We have to be back tonight by late afternoon. There's a wine tasting set up for the guests. Shouldn't be as raucous as the party last night."

"And a good opportunity to meet the Volkov Group."

She wasn't thrilled about the prospect. At least, Ryder's presence ought to discourage Dirk the Jerk from hitting on her.

Chapter Ten

While Nicole drove, Ryder made a series of phone calls from the passenger seat. After eight in the morning, he figured it wasn't too early to contact Agent Murdock and inform her that he was officially investigating on scene for HSI. Now that he'd been assigned to the investigation, she had no hesitation about sharing.

She informed him that the autopsy hadn't been done yet. Her only new info came from her interview with Mouse, which repeated facts Ryder already knew. She readily agreed to send him photos of the metal candy paddle and the habit the killer had been wearing, both of which would come in handy when he talked to the abbot. Also, she'd send him the only known photo of John Mitchell, the supposedly deceased hit man. Though he'd been arrested once, his mug shot had vanished. A Houdini trick? Somehow, his file had uncovered a snapshot.

Next, he touched base with the Secret Service agent in charge of Homeland Security Investigations in the Pacific Northwest to inform him that he'd be joining the team and was on his way to the abbey. The local SAC seemed like a nice guy but overworked. The Consolation Cove investigation didn't rank as a top priority for him. Ryder had a free hand, which was just the way he liked it.

When he got through to the administrative offices of the St. Macarius Monastery, he learned that the abbot was in Portland for the week. His prior, Father Bruno Schmidt, would see them when they arrived and would be happy to cooperate with HSI.

Ryder ended the call, leaned back in his seat and tried to enjoy the ride in spite of the questions hammering in his brain. On the mostly deserted country roads, Nicole kept the speed within 5 mph of the limit as she swooped through forests and hills in the Willamette Valley. The patchwork landscape ranged from harvested wheat fields to hazelnut orchards to wineries to fallow farmland. The SUV zipped past a herd of dairy cows that were so much tamer than Texas longhorns.

"Only a couple more miles," she said.

One of his questions popped into the forefront of his brain. "I keep thinking of John Mitchell. Mitch the Bitch."

"The deceased hit man?" She bobbed her head. "He's a puzzle, all right."

On his phone, he pulled up the snapshot of Mitchell that Agent Murdock had sent. An unposed, casual picture of a round-shouldered man in his late twenties with an innocent-looking round face like Charlie Brown. His curly blond hair flopped over his forehead and his lips pursed in a natural pout. Ryder held the phone so she could see. "This is him."

"Wow." She glanced while keeping an eye on the road. "He's a cutie-pie. Huggable."

"That might be a disguise. Remember his rep. He's a magician. A chameleon." His investigative instincts—which counted for zero in a courtroom—told him that Mitchell was the assassin. If they could find him, everything else would fall into place. "In this picture, he looks like somebody who makes fudge at a monastery."

"As you know, appearances can be deceiving."

"If Mitchell didn't kill Caldicott, how did his fingerprints show up on the weapon? He's supposed to be dead."

"I'm sure there's an explanation." She cocked an eyebrow as she considered. "Could be a failure in the system. You know, records of prints can be wrong or misfiled. Or the identification of the deceased was shaky. A glitch."

"Another one." The so-called glitch that Mouse discovered had set the whole investigation in motion and resulted in Caldicott's murder. "More likely, Mitchell isn't dead. And he might have used robes from the abbey as his disguise."

She shrugged and then pointed through the windshield to a majestic, snow-covered, volcanic-shaped peak towering over the scene. "Mount Hood."

His suspicions paused for a moment while he took in the unreal, distant beauty of the mountain. Other summits were visible, but none was framed so perfectly. Turning toward her, he noticed how her lips had formed an appreciative grin. A healthy glow colored her complexion. Her caramel-colored hair curled wildly in the humidity that had been absent in Las Vegas. Nicole was thriving.

"I'm glad you stalked me this morning," he said. "We make a good team."

"True story. The way I see it, you'll need an interpreter to deal with Father Bruno. Somehow, I don't think the two of you speak the same language."

"We might be more alike than you think. Just because I don't pray six times a day like you said the Benedictines do, it doesn't mean I'm not a spiritual person. Caldicott's murder offends me. The smuggling of unknown goods represents a threat to anybody's sense of morality."

"Agreed."

"The shipment could be human traffic. Or drugs. Or weapons. Whatever it is, I'm standing on the side of right, and I expect Father Bruno feels like I do."

"Different language but the same theme."

Tasteful wooden signage along the two-lane road indicated they were close. She drove through an old-growth forest with thick, towering spruce, Douglas fir, oak and sequoia. At the top of a wide bluff where the approach seemed to even out, they were greeted by a life-sized marble statue of a monk holding a staff in one hand and carrying a book in the other. Ryder asked, "Do you know who that's supposed to be?"

"Could be Benedict himself. He's usually depicted with a book because he was scholarly. His sister, Saint Scholastica, founded an order of nuns. They were a lot alike, both academic and preferring a hermit lifestyle. Some people say they were twins. Also, I think Macarius had a longer beard."

Following more signs, she circled around to the half-filled lot where she parked. They hiked up three flights of steps to a grassy square. A few people in regular civilian clothes strolled on the wide sidewalk. The monks were dressed either in the cowled habit, like the one worn by the assassin, or a cassock. Others wore plain black trousers and shirts with the clerical collar.

Ryder noticed that most people weren't talking or spoke softly. No vehicles were allowed on the bluff. With regular noise buffered by the thick forest, a profound quiet spread throughout the grounds. Around the square, several buildings featured Romanesque-style architecture. All were light gray brick with red-tiled roofs. Since Nicole had visited the abbey before, she took on the role of tour guide. "If I remember correctly, at the far end of the square to your left is a coffee shop and the candy store, where you can also buy souvenirs and books. The three-story, industrial-type structure next to it is the manufacturing, packaging and shipping facility. Every two hours they offer tours."

"Are the employees all from the monastery?"

"Don't know." She whirled, and her plaid rain jacket flapped open, revealing her crossbody first-aid kit. "Right here in front of us is the church and bell tower."

He paused to read the signage that described a seventy-foot-tall tower that housed six bells, the largest of which weighed three tons. They tolled six times a day, calling the monks to prayer. "Have you ever heard the bells?" he asked her.

"Once, in the evening," she said. "Incredibly loud. The pealing from those huge bells rolls down from the bluff and across the valley."

"Is there a bellringer, like Quasimodo?"

"The ringing is activated electronically." She pointed to another informational sign. "This says it's similar to the way the lighthouses send out their beams. The bell tower is a new addition. Installed in 2015." She pointed again. "The long building behind the tower is the cloister where the monks sleep and eat."

"How many live here?"

"I'm not sure. Somewhere between forty and fifty, I think. Are you asking because you're thinking of Mitchell and how he could have hidden here?"

"That's right," he drawled. "Time for us to start digging deeper. Let's see if we can find our way to Father Bruno's office."

They approached a two-story admin building to the right of the church. The structure didn't need a sign labeling its function. The flat, unadorned architecture spoke for itself. The only hint of decoration came in a small frieze of twin cherubs with trumpets over the main door. When they entered, they were met by a receptionist wearing a cassock with a black sash and a black skull cap that reminded Ryder of a yarmulke. He showed them into Father Bruno's office.

The prior appointed by the abbot was a short, muscular man also dressed in a black cassock and skull cap. He hustled around his desk to shake hands. He wore a plain cross and no other jewelry. Nicole had told him that Benedictines took vows of poverty and valued hospitality. The Father sure was a friendly dude. He complimented Ryder's cowboy hat and showed him the rack near the door where he could hang it. Bruno's wide smile almost convinced Ryder that the stocky, gray-haired monk was happy to see them. Not until he'd offered coffee and gotten them seated on a sofa beside his armchair did his beaming cheerfulness slide into something less open.

"May I ask," he said, "why Homeland Security is interested in our monastery? Have we done something wrong?"

Though Nicole immediately reassured him, Ryder held back. He'd learned that when a witness expects to be accused, it's because he or she has done something wrong. If you let them talk, they'll admit the error of their ways. He made direct eye contact with Father Bruno. "We're investigating a murder."

A spark of excitement flickered in the monk's expression. "Are we involved?"

"Could be."

"Like Father Brown or Father Dowling." He bounced in his chair. His strong, capable hands gripped the arms as if to keep him anchored. His secret emerged. "I love a good mystery book. Not the death and violence parts, of course. But figuring it all out."

"This murder took place at Consolation Cove on the coast. We suspect the killer has a connection to the monastery." On his cell phone, Ryder called up the photos Agent Murdock had sent and showed them to Father Bruno. "He wore this habit. And he carried this implement."

The plump, energetic monk nodded vigorously. "The cowl could have come from just about anywhere, even a costume shop. But the metal stirring implement seems to be from our fudge-making operation. It appears to be battered—perhaps we discarded it."

"Can we speak to someone in the fudge department?" Ryder asked.

"You most certainly can." He leaped from his chair and called down the hall. "Brother Louis, come in here."

The receptionist appeared so quickly that Ryder suspected the young man had been standing in the hall eavesdropping. "Yes, Father?"

"Clear my schedule for the rest of the day." He beamed at Ryder. "The game is afoot."

"But you have a meeting and a lunch with the local clergy

and the Sisters of the Blessed Sacrament that can't be missed or postponed."

"The meeting that the abbot keeps ducking," Father Bruno said with a groan. He paced across the large office to the window that looked out on the square. "Business always comes first. Looks like I'll be stuck here until after lunch, but I've got a few free minutes right now. What else can I do?"

"We'll need to establish alibis," Ryder said. "The murder took place late yesterday afternoon, and the location is on the coast, a couple of hours away from here."

"I can't speak for all the brothers because we don't officially keep tabs on them. Though we recommend an early bedtime because the morning prayers start at five thirty." He glanced toward the receptionist. "Would you make sure the conference room is set for the meeting? Then I want you to find Brother Gabriel and ask him to come here so he can help these detectives."

The young monk scurried off while Father Bruno settled back in his chair. He had more to say. "Though the monastery is largely self-sufficient and the brothers are kept busy, we have several nonclerical people who work here at the candy factory and as salespeople. They would also have access to robes and equipment."

"Good point," Nicole said. "How can we get in touch with them?"

"You'll want to talk with our accounting department on the second floor to get a list of people who have access to the grounds."

"I appreciate that," Ryder said. "I'm an accountant myself. And who is Brother Gabriel?"

"A printer. He puts together our programs, pamphlets, advertising copy and a weekly newsletter with all the gossip. He'll be helpful because he knows everything about everybody."

"I have a snapshot of a suspect." Ryder brought up the photo on his phone and passed it to Father Bruno. "Does he look familiar?"

The Father nodded as he studied the screen. "Well, yes, he looks like someone I might have met before. Blond hair, average features. Our founders came here from Switzerland, and this young fellow looks like he might have roots in a Germanic country. The abbot likes to say we arrived with a prayer and a recipe for the best fudge in the world. Does the lad have a name?"

"John Mitchell."

"Doesn't ring a bell." He handed back the phone. "What else can you tell me about the murder?"

Ryder had a lot of experience dealing with questions from interested parties about crimes, and he explained as much as he could without overstepping any lines. When he mentioned the wedding, Nicole interrupted. "The bride's mother would really like to have a priest perform the ceremony on Saturday. Could we borrow one of the monks?"

"We'll work something out." Father Bruno gave a benevolent smile. "It would be a shame to deny the couple the sacrament of holy matrimony. Both Catholic?"

"Absolutely," Nicole said.

"Why aren't they using the priest at their home parish?"

Her lips twisted in a scowl. "The bride is from Las Vegas and the groom from Los Angeles. This is a destination wedding. It's complicated."

"You can certainly borrow one of our monks. Most are ordained and able to perform weddings, but it doesn't sound like there's time for the prewedding preparations. One of our brothers can bless the bride and groom and wish them a long and happy life together, though that doesn't mean they're married in the eyes of the church."

"That might be enough," she said.

When Brother Gabriel sidled into the office, Ryder had considered him an unlikely monk, not the usual recruit for the monastery. Though dressed in a floor-length habit with a stained, pinstriped apron covering the front, Gabe didn't look like a man of the cloth. His thin shoulders hunched. Stringy black hair hung nearly to his shoulders. His face was lined and rugged with a jagged scar across his jaw and another bisecting his left eyebrow. Full sleeves, rolled up to his elbows, revealed several tattoos, including a web that radiated from his elbow—a design common in prison time as a reference to being caught in a spider's web.

When introduced to Nicole, Gabe's bloodshot eyes narrowed as he sized her up. Unsmiling, he asked, "Are you a cop?"

"I'm a doctor." She gestured toward Ryder. "He's a federal agent."

Gabe pinched his lips and held his hostility in check while Father Bruno took charge of the situation and got them organized. "First, we divide and conquer, seeking information and alibis."

"Alibis?" Gabe questioned.

"There's been a murder," Father Bruno explained, "and we can help solve it. We'll touch base again at lunch. Nicole and Ryder, you'll know it's time to eat because the bells ring at noon."

Ryder didn't like the division of duties. He was assigned to talk to the accountants and check out the living quarters at the monastery. Nicole would visit the place where fudge was made. He didn't have a problem with that. But she'd be accompanied by Brother Gabriel, who would introduce her around and show her how things worked. It all made sense, but Ryder didn't like the idea of her being alone with him. There was something dangerous about this unlikely monk.

Chapter Eleven

Dressed as an elderly tourist carrying binoculars and wearing sunglasses, Julian shuffled forward and joined a group of whale watchers at the edge of the cliff below the Consolation Cove lighthouse. Though not the peak of migration season, a couple of blues and humpbacks had been spotted breaching and sky-hopping in the dark waters offshore. The fog had lifted enough for great views from the small deck with a chest-high fence and built-in benches.

Julian adjusted his fisherman's hat over his shaggy gray wig and hiked up his baggy trousers. He hadn't come here to spy on fish or mammals. This was a recon mission, pure and simple. During the two days before the wedding and the delivery of the shipment, he needed to check out the people staying at Leeward Manor and plan his next step in the abduction of Alyssa.

His planning had started this morning before dawn when he'd gone for an early jog around the grounds and along the shore. Crime scene tape had still been in place on the right side of the cliff where Caldicott's body had gotten hung up on the rocks below the lighthouse. The kitchen staff had already arrived at the Manor. And he'd seen Nicole crossing the parking lot and heading toward the rental car for Ryder Beckham who, Julian had learned, was a federal agent working for HSI.

Not that Julian was worried about his identity being discovered. Three years ago, he faked his own death, disappearing before he assumed his identity as a Benedictine monk. To solidify the change, he altered his appearance, going from blond to dark brown. He sculpted his formerly flabby body and had dental surgery to adjust his jawline. He had a fresh look. A new start. Besides, nobody would suspect a dead man.

Standing among the whale watchers, he deepened his current disguise by projecting an attitude of firm but friendly kindness, not unlike Father Bruno. The conversation revolved around the murder, and Julian tsk-tsked along with the others. *What was the world coming to? Who would do such a terrible thing?* Opinion split fifty-fifty. Half blamed the Rossini reputation and called it a mob hit. The others thought he was killed by his ex. Only Julian knew the truth, and that awareness fed his feelings of superiority.

Alternating between peering out to sea and turning his high-power binoculars to the forest and the Manor itself, he decided on two possible approaches if he had to sneak inside the Manor. Creeping through the forest, using the abundant trees and shrubs for cover, or marching directly from the parking lot, relying on a disguise to keep him invisible. Both routes meant disabling surveillance cameras, which shouldn't be a problem. The equipment wasn't high tech.

In casual conversation with the other whale watchers, he learned there would be a wine-tasting later this afternoon with some of the groom's family. His instincts warned him against attending that event. The guy who'd hired him would likely be there. As well as Dmitry Orloff, who had used Julian's services in the past when he was John Mitchell. Neither of them was likely to recognize him, but sharing a glass of wine was a little too close for comfort.

He lowered his binoculars, ready to go home and plan for a time when he could make his move on Alyssa. Before he walked away, he spotted two other people hiking toward the whale watchers. One was a husky woman wearing an FBI windbreaker. Though her companion wore plainclothes, his shoulder holster made an obvious bulge under his sports coat, his shoes were practical and his haircut showed a military influence. Julian pegged him for a local detective and figured it might be useful to eavesdrop.

Swinging his binoculars in a direction nobody else seemed to be looking, he pretended to glimpse a fluke. He pointed, and everyone turned to look. "To the left. Over there."

Julian glanced at the FBI agent and the cop. "That's the first whale tail I've seen all day. You brought me good luck."

"I'm glad somebody is feeling lucky," the cop said. "Seems like we're dragging from one dead end to another."

"You'll catch him." Julian turned away before they saw his satisfied grin. If he'd been keeping score, he just hit a grand slam.

"We're not doing so bad," the FBI woman said. "We have fingerprints."

"From a dead man." The cop stepped up to the railing and stared out to sea. "Let's not talk about it anymore. I wanted to come out here and watch for whales to get a break from investigating."

She stood beside him, rested her forearms on the railing and tilted her chin to catch the sea breeze on her face. The three letters on her jacket danced in Julian's peripheral vision. FBI. They had his fingerprints, John Mitchell's prints.

Foreboding shuddered through him. How could the FBI have obtained that damning evidence? He'd been careful to always wear latex gloves. When he'd decided to use the fudge spoon, he'd enjoyed the irony of something so innocent being put to dangerous use. He'd known there would be a risk that someone might search at the abbey. So what? He wasn't there anymore.

Still, they might connect Brother Julian with John Mitchell. None of the brothers knew his prior identity. Not even Brother Gabe, who'd come closest to establishing a relationship. Buying his cooperation had been easy. Whenever Julian missed a curfew or needed to get away, Gabe had backed him up and provided an alibi in exchange for a neat, crisp, twenty-dollar-bill. The larger payoff went to an old priest who worked with the Volkov Group. For ten thou in cold, hard cash, the priest arranged the proper papers and recommendations for Julian to join Saint Macarius Monastery. Nobody suspected. Julian felt safe. Until now.

Leaving his prints counted as one of the worst mistakes he'd ever made. Not a good way to resurrect his career. He'd slipped up.

An excited cheer went up from the whale watchers. A giant tail fin rose above the sea. Then another fluke. Majestic. Incredible. Julian waved his binoculars above his head and congratulated everyone. Inside, he boiled with rage and fierce determination. This assignment needed to be over.

WORKING WITH DIFFICULT patients in the hospital emergency room taught Nicole how to deal with people in literal life-and-death situations. A simple question to a patient might provoke an outrageous deception. She'd once asked a preteen boy how he'd broken his wrist and heard a litany of stories about being attacked by zombies and fighting off giant squirrels and being chased by an ATV before his mother appeared and firmly, logically, said that he'd fallen while sneaking out of his second-story bedroom. His lies didn't save him from being grounded.

Sometimes, patients dissolved into tears or screamed obscenities. The worst scenario? When they refused to talk to her at all, even though she needed information from them to treat their injuries. Brother Gabe fell into the last category.

She sensed that he had something to hide but disguised his secret behind a scowl as they walked together on the wide sidewalk through the square at Saint Macarius Monastery. Was he privy to all the gossip? Did he know something about the metal paddle used for churning the fudge? In glances, she studied the tats on his forearms for a clue. In addition to the spider web at his elbow, he had a dragon, a demon, a laughing skull and several other scary images. Also, an elaborate and somewhat sexy angel with a harp. Many crosses intertwined with other tats and she wondered if they'd been added later when he'd decided to become a priest.

He answered every comment with a one-word response. His dark brown eyes avoided direct contact. His eyebrows—especially the one bisected by a scar—pulled into a wary frown. His left hand shoved into a pocket in his habit under the pinstriped apron.

Choosing a topic that didn't seem threatening, she asked, "Were you working in the kitchen? You seem to have stains on your apron."

He glanced down as if he'd never seen himself before and brushed at a dark red streak. "This isn't blood. It's beet juice."

"Do you enjoy cooking?" Too simple a question. She peppered him with others. "What's your favorite dish? Do you bake? Is kitchen duty a regular job for you?"

"Favorite dish is poached salmon when we get it fresh caught." He exhaled a sigh, apparently exhausted by the full sentence. Then he continued. "Don't bake. Regular job? Nope. All the brothers take turns on the basic chores in the kitchen, laundry and gardens. I'm in charge of the printing and the weekly newsletter."

She heard a note of pride in his voice. Communication might be possible, after all. She encouraged him to tell her more. "What are the regular features in the newsletter?"

"The usual stuff. Illnesses, accidents and deaths."

He was a morbid little monk. Not so little, really. He was her height with a bony frame under his robes. His active lifestyle filled with chores and obligations kept him in shape. "You must also report on happy occasions?"

"Prizes, graduations and birthdays. Yeah, I write those up. And welcome messages to new brothers at the monastery."

"Does that happen often?" she asked. "Do you have many new brothers?"

"No."

His one-word response warned her off. He hadn't really opened up and wasn't about to get chummy. They walked in silence, passing a long two-story building with a wooden sign in front identifying the McElroy Library with the date of founding. On the opposite side of the square were the classrooms for a small seminary, visitor's center and an auditorium. Opposite the chapel, she saw the coffee shop at the far left. To the right were the no-nonsense buildings where they made fudge and truffles, marked with another sign: Not Open to the Public.

"I visited the Saint Macarius a few years ago," she said, pausing as if lost in a memory. "Took a tour of the candy-making facility and had ginger tea at the coffee shop."

He stopped beside her and said nothing.

She took her phone from her crossbody purse and held it so he could see the screen. "Brother Gabe, please take a look at this photo. Do you recognize him?"

He carefully examined the snapshot of the blond man before shaking his head. "I don't know anyone who looks exactly like that."

An odd statement. The corner of his mouth twitched, and she suspected he was lying. Not exactly a lie. He had phrased his response in ambiguous terms to give himself deniability if she probed deeper.

If Gabe had recognized John Mitchell, it would move their investigation forward and give them a clear focus. No more wasting time speculating about Caldicott's ex-wife or others who might hold a grudge. They'd know a hit man had been hired to kill the CFO. The murder would certainly be tied to the electromagnetic pulse hack and the arrival of the mysterious shipment.

She followed him into the industrial building where a combination of monks, wearing black shirts with clerical collars, and workers from town managed the preparation of several varieties of fudge, including dark chocolate and caramel. Melting, measuring, mixing and stirring with heavy metal paddles. In another section, the fudge was scooped into containers and packaged for sale and shipping. A plump monk with a clipboard, who could have been a twin to Brother Bruno, matched the inventory with the purchase orders to make sure the correct product would be delivered to the right place.

Nicole politely interrupted the shipping clerk. "Mind if I ask you a few questions?"

He hugged his clipboard to his chest, raked his pudgy fingers through his gray hair, and gave her a bright smile. "I'm guessing you want a taste. Am I right? We have free samples in the front office."

She held out her phone. "Do you recognize this man?"

His forehead scrunched. "Give me a hint. Does he work here? Is he from town?"

"Does he look familiar?"

"Can't say that he does." He nodded to Gabe. "You might want to show our guest to the front office. They're better at answering questions."

Gabe did exactly that. He escorted her up a staircase into a large office with picture windows overlooking the floor where the activity was centered. After the supervisor offered her a dizzying array of fudge and truffles, he told her that he didn't know the man in the photo and wasn't aware of any missing pieces of equipment. "Which doesn't mean that nothing has been misplaced or discarded. We're a small operation. Everybody trusts everybody else. Don't need to keep careful watch."

She hated the idea that the hit man might have infiltrated this place of candy and innocence. Looking down at the copper kettles where the final product was stirred to perfection, she asked, "Where do you get your chocolate?"

"Imported from a pristine valley in Switzerland," he said proudly. "We use time-tested recipes from the nearby town.

It's where our Benedictine order originated, and I visit once or twice a year to keep up with new developments."

"Your process seems very efficient," she said. In addition to the inescapable smell of working men and machinery, a sweet scent of sugar, butter and chocolate hung in the air. She licked her lips. If she were employed here, she'd have to triple her exercise regimen to work off the inevitable chocolate poundage.

"We're profitable," he said. "If we decided to expand, we could become a major player in the candy market. Maybe as big as Godiva or Cadbury. But we're not here to become moguls, only to pay our bills, say our prayers and donate to the order."

He directed them downstairs to a glassed-in area where the truffles, large and bite-sized, were hand-made and decorated. These artists, dressed in white jackets, masks and hair coverings, perched on stools beside hygienic tables with conveyor belts. One tray at a time, they piped tiny rosebuds or hand-painted the chocolate. Nicole managed to show the photo on her phone screen to a few more people and got zero hits.

Gabe nudged her shoulder. "We should head back. We're supposed to meet Father Bruno and your partner for lunch."

Her partner? She liked the way that sounded. She and Ryder worked well together as detectives. Last night, she'd awakened a more intimate partnership that also worked exceedingly well. Remembering those moments in her bedroom made her lips tingle and her pulse race. Tonight, she might use the promise of a long, hot shower to entice him to join her between the sheets. Bath, bed and beyond. Probably wouldn't take much convincing, but she wasn't sure it was a wise move.

Outside, where the temperature had dropped and the bluish skies had turned hazy, she fell into step beside Gabe on the long sidewalk. He continued to give her the silent treatment, interrupted by furtive glances. She asked, "Is there something you want to tell me?"

"No." But he peered to the left, then the right, then back

over his shoulder. Acting like he suspected they were being watched or followed.

And she wondered...what if John Mitchell was still here? She might have already encountered him wearing a mask in the truffle room. He wouldn't necessarily be recognizable from the photo because he was a master of disguise. A shudder trickled down her spine, interrupting her pleasant memories. She asked, "Is everything all right?"

Though Gabe didn't have a watch, he looked down at his tattooed wrist as if he expected to see the time. Then he sped up his pace. "It's almost noon. The bells mark the hour."

She looked up as they approached the tower. "I heard them once before, but I was much farther away."

"Six cast bronze bells," he said. "That's over a ton of clanging. They're activated electronically and free-swinging."

"Up close, the sound must be deafening."

"Enough to bust your eardrums," he warned. "Hurry up. Don't want to be late."

But when they reached the tower, he abruptly halted. "Want to take a look inside?"

Entering the tall brick structure appealed to her natural curiosity but seemed like tempting fate. What if they didn't make it out before the bell ringing started? "Seems like a risk."

"I won't let anything happen to you." He clasped her hand and tugged. "Trust me."

She heard the urgency in his voice and sensed that this was more than a sightseeing tour. He had something to tell her and had promised not to hurt her. If she couldn't trust a monk—even a tattooed one with scars on his face—who could she believe?

He rushed her to an entrance on the side of the tower. On a digital access pad, Gabe punched in the code to unlock the sturdy wooden door, grabbed her hand again and pulled her inside. Square brick walls ascended to a bare wooden ceiling below the bells. The ripe smell of bird droppings was dissipated by narrow windows on three sides. The fourth side housed a closet at the ground level and anchored a spiral staircase that passed other rooms.

"This way." Gabe gestured for her to follow. "Climb up here. You can see the bells up close. Not many people get this view."

He must think she was very special or very stupid. "Thanks for showing me this, but I want to get out of here."

"You have to come." His tone became demanding and angry as he pulled her to the foot of the staircase. "You won't regret this."

"Let me go." She dug in her heels and twisted her arm, breaking his hold. A backward stumble threw her off her feet. She scrambled up, dashed for the door and yanked at the handle. Locked!

"Might as well cooperate." He sauntered toward her. "You can't get out. The entry door automatically locked when I closed it, and you don't know the code to open it up. Come with me, and you'll be fine."

Unless I'm deafened by a ton of bronze bells. She unzipped her crossbody purse, raided the first-aid supplies, found a scalpel and unsheathed it. The razor-edged blade looked too tiny to do much damage, but she wasn't giving up without a fight. "Unlock the damn door."

"Be reasonable, Nicole. If those bells start ringing, I'm in as much trouble as you are. Do what I say, and we'll both be fine."

She slashed the air with her scalpel. "Don't come near me."

He pointed to the spiral staircase. "About fifteen feet up is a landing and a door. Do you see it?"

"What's up there?"

"A soundproofed room where the technicians program and maintain the equipment that keeps the bells timed correctly." He turned and walked away from her. "In there, we won't be hurt by the noise."

"Why should I believe you?"

He placed his foot on the first step. "You don't have a choice."

He was right. Above her head, she heard a click—or imagined she heard something—as if the mechanism to start the bells was going into effect. No time to figure out her next move. No chance to escape from this tower.

She dashed up the spiral staircase. Gabe paused on the landing where he plugged in a code to unlock the door. Without explanation, he grabbed her free hand and pulled her into a four-by-six room lined with computers and a small desk. When he closed the door, the silence overwhelmed her.

"We're safe," he said. "This is one of the only places in the abbey that's totally private. No one can see us. No one can hear us."

Which meant she could scream like a banshee, and no one would know. Still holding the scalpel, she asked, "Why did you bring me here?"

"I know the man you're trying to find. He doesn't look like the picture on your phone, and he's a stone-cold killer."

Chapter Twelve

The noon ringing of the bells started with a heavy clang from the largest.

"Three tons," Brother Gabe shouted cheerfully. "Tuned to a musical A."

Though the soundproofing muted much of the noise, Nicole still heard the sonorous throbbing from overhead. Much to Gabe's apparent delight, each of the other five bronze bells added their note to the cacophony. He dropped to his knees, crossed himself and murmured a prayer under his breath while reverberation from the echoes trembled in the air like waves of static. The floor beneath her feet rumbled in imitation of an earthquake. If Gabe hadn't locked them inside this small room, the ear-splitting noise would have deafened her.

Though grateful, she was still outraged and kept the scalpel in her hand, ready to defend herself. Why the hell had he trapped her in the tower? What did he mean about knowing the identity of a stone-cold killer? She waited until the bell ringing had stopped.

Brother Gabe crossed himself again and stood. "I'm sorry for bringing you here against your will."

"If you have some sort of confession to make, you should be talking to my partner."

"The man you want is Brother Julian, but he doesn't look like that photograph. He has other people at the abbey working for him. They report to him. I used to be one of them because I believed he'd been treated unfairly. Then I found out that I was wrong. So wrong. He's evil."

"You said he was a murderer."

"If he knew I was talking to you, he'd kill me." He crossed himself again. "Please, Nicole, forgive me."

His expression softened, and he offered a shy smile. Still reading his attitude, she decided to take a chance and trust him. Reaching into her combination purse and first-aid kit, she found the sheath for her scalpel and covered the blade. Since it was no longer sanitary, she'd never use it, but she didn't want to leave the sharp edge unprotected.

"You called him Brother Julian," she said. "Is he a monk?"

"About three years ago, he transferred to Saint Macarius from an abbey back east. In Maine."

"How does that work? Did he have references or recommendations?"

"A former bishop in the Los Angeles diocese requested the move for him."

A possible connection to Volkov? "Do you know his name?"

"This is where stuff gets complicated." Gabe scowled. His shoulders slumped. "As soon as we met, Julian made me his friend. That happens sometimes. People see my tats and assume I'm some kind of badass. Excuse my language. I know that dragons and skulls and scars don't look sweet and innocent."

Ashamed of herself, she realized she'd drawn the same sort of conclusion. *Never judge a book by the cover.* "Why did you get all the tattoos?"

"My mom was a tattoo artist who also did body piercings. She practiced on me, called me her little pin cushion. Most of the piercings have healed up." He traced his index finger up and down his arm. "And I don't mind the tats. I like how they look. After I joined the priesthood, I got crosses added and had another artist change a witch on a broomstick into an angel."

"How did you get the scars on your face?" she asked.

"A bar fight. Dumb mistake I made when I was a kid."

She drew a reasonable conclusion that, at one time, he might have been a badass.

Now he was embarrassed by it. "Let's get back to Julian. What did he do after he made you his friend?"

"He convinced me that the abbot at his prior monastery had it in for him. And he'd try to get Julian kicked out of Saint Macarius using people from his past. That's where the name of the former bishop comes in. Julian asked me to change it."

"Do you remember what the name was?"

"Not a clue. Anyway, I used the computer in the main office to change that and other things about his records." He crossed himself again. "I deceived the abbot and Father Bruno. Worse, I accepted twenty dollars from Brother Julian for fixing the documents, rewriting his past contacts."

"You believed Julian was your friend."

"I'm so sorry." His fingers twisted in a knot. She could tell how much he was hurting.

"Is Julian still here at the monastery?"

"He left about a week ago, said his mother was ill and needed him to care for her. I know it's a lie." Tears filled his eyes. "I don't know what to do. I don't have the right to ask for your help, but I don't know where to turn. If I talk to Father Bruno or the abbot, I might be putting them in danger."

His story reminded her of traumatic wounds. Gabe might not have a physical injury, but his pain was no less real. PTSD of the soul. Gently, she directed him to a wooden chair in front of the small desk and told him to sit facing her.

She perched on a stool, leaned toward him and offered a smile. "I want you to inhale for four seconds, hold your breath and then exhale for four seconds."

He did as she said for three repetitions, then shook his head. "I can calm down easier if I say a Rosary."

"I understand."

Gabe took his rosary beads from his pocket and started

murmuring to himself. As he smoothly rocked back and forth, she saw him visibly relax. Knowing something of Gabe's history gave her insight into what was troubling him. She couldn't help being sympathetic to a kid whose mom had treated him like a pin cushion.

When he looked up at her again, he had regained his composure.

"This is how I learned that Julian is a killer," he said. "Two weeks ago, he told me that Brother Ezra was trying to get him in trouble. Ezra was a very old man, a great storyteller. He used to help out in the day care center for the people who work in the candy-making process. He wanted Julian to trade rooms with him because he had a better view. There was something else, but Julian wouldn't talk about it."

"What do your rooms look like?" Father Bruno had advised against her going into the living area for the brothers. Though women weren't forbidden, Bruno tried to respect the privacy of the other brothers. "I know they're called cells, but they aren't like prison, are they?"

"Small, simple rooms. A place for reading, prayer and contemplation. Most have bookshelves. Benedictines are into education. Some brothers have artwork or photos. Almost everybody has a cross or crucifix. Nothing to brag about. But comfortable."

"So, Julian's room probably wasn't much different from Ezra's."

"In his room, Julian had created several hidey-holes—loose floorboards or drawers with false bottoms—places where he kept his cash and documents." Gabe shifted uncomfortably on the hard wooden chair. His tension had returned. "Anyway, he wanted me to come with him to confront Brother Ezra. You know, as a witness. But when we got to the old man's room, Julian told me to stay outside."

She had a very bad feeling about what had happened next. "Take your time, Gabe."

"Julian killed him. Suffocated Ezra with a pillow. He didn't admit what he'd done. Just stepped back into the hall, gave me a nasty grin and told me it was settled. The next morning at breakfast, we learned that Brother Ezra had passed away during the night and the funeral would be on Friday."

"Was there an investigation?" she asked.

"Ezra was old and not in the best of health. The doctor called it death by natural causes."

Though she tended to be sympathetic to doctors in difficult situations, Nicole had no respect for laziness on the part of an attending physician. She wanted to believe he or she had taken time to be sure about cause of death. "Are you sure it wasn't natural?"

"Not until I looked into Julian's eyes and remembered what he said. Told me it was all settled. He looked proud and unconcerned. He murdered Brother Ezra and felt no remorse." He rose from the chair. "I have to escape from Julian. I know too many of his secrets. He'll kill me, too."

In the small room, she planted herself in his path. No way was he getting out of here until they reached some kind of plan. "What can I do to help? Do you need a place to stay until Julian is in custody?"

"For what crime?" His voice trembled. "Brother Ezra's death wasn't considered a murder."

She didn't want to mention exhumation and reopening an investigation that might go nowhere. If Brother Julian was, in fact, John Mitchell, he was a hit man with many deaths to his credit. "You could be taken into protective custody."

"No. I've been a coward long enough. Julian is a killer, and he must be stopped." He straightened his shoulders. "I might be the only person who can identify him."

"Surely, there are photos. You're the head of the weekly newspaper. Haven't there been group pictures?"

"Julian always avoided snapshots. The few photos I have of him, he's in shadow or hiding behind his beard. When he first came here, he stayed in his room, took a vow of solitude until his beard grew out. And he concentrated on losing weight and going to the gym. Probably dropped thirty pounds. I knew him before when he was pudgy and clean-shaven. I've got to speak up, to tell your partner."

An idea began to take shape in her mind. This solution allowed them to protect Gabe, identify Julian, aka John Mitchell, and—above all—keep the wedding on track.

IN A SMALL parking lot behind the living quarters at the monastery, Ryder stood beside Nicole, gazing through the gathering mists at a distant but still-spectacular view of Mount Hood. They were waiting for Brother Gabe to gather his things and join them for the ride back to Consolation Cove.

This plan came one hundred percent from Nicole. When she and Gabe met up with Ryder and Father Bruno for lunch, she laid out her idea clearly and emphatically. They would take Brother Gabe to Leeward Manor, and he'd bless the marriage on Saturday. Father Bruno, as acting head of the monastery, agreed with the idea of providing a priest.

Off the top of his head, Ryder could think of a half dozen reasons why they shouldn't saddle themselves with a tattooed priest during an investigation, but he decided to trust Nicole. They hadn't been alone to talk about it until now. Still staring at Mount Hood, he slung his arm around her shoulders. He whispered in her delicate, shell-like ear, "I think you better tell me what's really going on here."

She snuggled a little closer. "I like this. Your arms around me. It's friendly. Like we're partners in crime."

"That's backward. We're the crime fighters." He gave her a squeeze. "Gabe?"

"After we went to the candy-making facility, where nobody recognized Mitchell from his photo, he hustled me back here and locked me in the bell tower."

"Locked you in?"

"Slammed the door, locked it and told me the six bronze bells were loud enough to pop my eardrums."

If Ryder had known this part of the story, he wouldn't have agreed to bring Gabe with them. "Then he unlocked the door."

"Nope, he made me dash up a spiral staircase into a small room where the electronic controls for the bells are kept. The room was soundproofed, but I could still hear the clanging and feel the vibration of the sound."

"Were you scared?"

"Terrified." Her eyes widened, showing white around the irises. "But Gabe was a hundred times more frightened than me. He went through this whole thing to get me alone in the bell tower so we could talk without being overheard."

"Why?"

"He believes that a monk who came here three years ago is a stone-cold killer. That's a direct quote. If this guy thought Gabe ratted him out, he'd take revenge."

"Tell me more about this mobster monk."

"His name is Brother Julian. According to Gabe, he's running a crime ring in the abbey, getting monks to perform tasks for him and paying them off with twenty-dollar bills."

"Cheap labor."

"When you've taken a vow of poverty, any cash is a big deal. A twenty isn't too much, doesn't make you feel guilty." She tilted her head to look up at him. "I believe Gabe. He said Julian avoids having his picture taken. He disguised himself with a heavy beard and lost a lot of weight to change his appearance."

Her theory made sense. "Three years ago was about the time when Mitchell vanished from sight. Hiding out in a monastery isn't a bad idea. Let's pick him up and run his fingerprints."

"We can't pick him up because he's not here. Supposedly, he's taking care of his sick mother. Away from this area." She held his chin in her left hand, turned his face toward her and gave him a light kiss on the lips before she took a step away from him.

Ryder was beginning to appreciate this *partners* thing, but didn't want to end up in the friend zone. She was much more to him than a buddy. "Do we have an address?"

"Not according to Gabe. And you're right about the fingerprints. You should go to his room and collect prints and hairs for DNA before we leave. But we still need Brother Gabe to identify Julian."

"Sounds like you've got everything figured out."

"I do."

"When we get to Consolation Cove, where is Brother Gabe going to stay? Leeward Manor is completely booked."

"You just vacated your room on the third floor."

He liked the direction this was headed. "I could move in with you. Your great big queen-sized bed has plenty of room for two."

"And I also have a sofa in the living room."

"And a shower." Her private bathroom gave him reason enough to move into her room. "I'll get those prints and be right back."

"Okay, partner."

Tonight, he would convince her that he should graduate to the next level. More than partner. More than partner with benefits. He hoped to be her boyfriend. But that sounded like they were in high school. Her lover. He swung open the door to the monastery. He wanted to be her lover.

Chapter Thirteen

On their return drive, Ryder was behind the steering wheel while Nicole, sitting in the passenger seat, talked to Alyssa about the complications arising from her star-crossed wedding. Brother Gabe perched in the back seat, looking through the window with a cheerful expression that made Ryder wonder how often the little monk left the cloisters of St. Macarius. Clearly, the dude needed to get out more.

Gabe had asked if they could drive back along Van Duzer Corridor, a stretch of Route 18 that connected central Oregon and the coast through a forested area. The two-lane road appeared to be surrounded by old-growth trees, which was actually an illusion. In many stretches along the route, the wood had been harvested. A half mile away from the road, the land was clear-cut, leaving a corridor of thick shrubs and moss-covered trees.

Ryder glanced in the rearview mirror and made eye contact with Gabe. "Why do you like the Van Duzer?"

"It gets us to the ocean faster, and we'll have a nice, long drive going south on Highway 101. The monastery has wonderful views of fields and mountains, but I love the beach. Sand between my toes. The sounds of rolling waves. The cries of gulls are calls to prayer." He crossed himself and lowered his voice. "Heavenly Father, I thank You for the vast and mysterious sea."

"Amen to that," Ryder said. "Did you grow up near the ocean?"

"Saint Louis," he replied. "No ocean, but the Mississippi is amazing. And I'm guessing you're from Texas."

"Good guess. And I'm not even wearing my hat."

"You can take the Stetson off the Texan, but you can't take the Texas out of the cowboy." Brother Gabe gazed through the window. "Thank you for this adventure."

Ryder hoped for a happy ending. They'd apprehend Brother Julian, solve the hack, stop the shipment and save the wedding. Best-case scenario, Nicole would be back in his arms for good.

She ended her phone conversation with a loud groan.

"I need to be there for Alyssa," she said. "As her maid-of-honor, I should be handling all these petty little problems so she can float around being serene and beautiful."

"In my limited experience," he said, "that's not how weddings work. When my baby sis got married, that pretty little filly turned into a fire-breathing dragon."

"Bridezilla," she said. "Alyssa isn't like that. Don't get me wrong, she can be plenty demanding, and she carries a slimline Glock in the back pocket of her skinny jeans. But I've never known her to actually shoot somebody who got in her way."

He pointed out, "She drew really fast when she thought you were being threatened by Brother Julian."

"But fired into the air." She half turned to speak to Brother Gabe in the rear. "Nonna Rossini is absolutely thrilled that you'll be there to bless the bride and groom."

"I've only been involved in three weddings," he admitted. "I'm ordained and everything, but people don't like to put me at the altar because of my tats."

"That's not right," she said, "but I understand. It's the judging-a-book-by-the-cover thing. Most of the people you're going to meet are good-hearted, generous and kind, but the Rossini family still carries the taint of former involvement in mob crimes."

Ryder changed the topic. Not that he opposed conversations about things not being what they first appeared to be, but they had a schedule to plan. He didn't want to go down a rabbit hole with Nicole on her new favorite issue that hinted at his former undercover identity. "Before we go to the tasting at the winery, I want to check in with the FBI. Agent Murdock should meet Brother Gabe and can provide additional protection."

His voice rose from the back seat. "Am I going to need protecting?"

"I sure as hell hope not," Ryder said. "But what do you think will happen if you come face-to-face with Julian?"

"You're right," he said. "I should meet the FBI and local police and anybody else you think is on our side."

Nicole said, "Father Bruno was very cooperative about sending you with us."

"He's kind of a crime buff," Brother Gabe said. "I wouldn't be surprised if he showed up for the wedding with a magnifying glass to look for clues."

Like Father Brown and the many other crime-solving priests and nuns. "What's Bruno's last name?"

"Schmidt. Father Bruno Schmidt."

"Sounds like a crime fighter to me." Ryder liked the old padre and wouldn't mind having a discussion with him about amateur sleuths and private eyes.

"Yeah," Gabe said. "He's really good at knowing when you're lying."

Yet, Father Bruno had missed the changed data on Brother Julian's records and couldn't fill in the blanks. Knowing the name of the bishop who recommended Julian would have given them a thread that could lead to his identity. Bruno claimed he'd forgotten. True or false?

THEY CAUGHT UP with Agent Murdock at Leeward Manor in the suite formerly occupied by Alan Caldicott. The manager, Daniel DeBarge, cleared away a room service cart while making a point of avoiding eye contact. Ryder hadn't forgotten the fifty-dollar bribe that was supposed to guarantee him this very room. He approached the wannabe pirate and blocked his way into the hall. "When's my room going to be ready?"

"I don't know." Danny Danger sounded peevish. "The feds have taken over, and they don't tell me their plans."

Nicole nudged Ryder's shoulder. "It's okay. You can stay with me."

"Exactly what I was thinking," he said. Agent Murdock joined them and shook hands with Brother Gabe. Since he'd dressed in black trousers and a black, long-sleeved shirt with clerical collar, his tattoos didn't show. Murdock's wide smile gleamed with approval. "You're the witness," she said. "It's always good to have a member of the clergy testify. If we ever get this guy arrested and charged, you'll be effective in the courtroom."

"Thank you, ma'am. I hope I can help."

"Let's get right down to it." Though the door to the suite was closed, the noise of loud conversations echoed from the hallway. People were getting ready to leave for the tasting at the nearby winery. "We found fingerprints for John Mitchell, a suspected hit man who is supposedly deceased. From what Agent Beckham told me, you believe Mitchell is using an alias. He's Brother Julian, correct?"

"That's right." Gabe pushed his straight brown hair off his forehead. "When Nicole mentioned a killer who dressed like a monk from Saint Macarius and carried a fudge paddle, I thought of Julian. He's a dangerous person. A liar and a cheat. I'm almost certain he smothered Brother Ezra with a pillow."

"Was that death investigated?"

"No, ma'am."

"We'll talk more about it later." Murdock looked toward him. "Agent Beckham, do you have any other, hopefully more tangible, evidence on Brother Julian?"

He went to the desk by the window, opened his briefcase

and took out several plastic evidence bags. "I searched Julian's room at the monastery and came up with a couple of useful things. A hand mirror and a notebook that might have fingerprints you can compare with Mitchell. A comb with strands of hair for DNA. In a hidey-hole under a floorboard, I found a little over two thousand dollars, all in twenties."

"Should I turn this evidence over to my forensic people for processing?" she asked. "Does the FBI have jurisdiction? I don't want to step on toes at HSI."

"I'd be glad to sign these items over to y'all," he said. "From what I can tell, you've already established a task force and are a whole lot more familiar with the area than I am."

"When Julian is arrested," she clarified, "I get credit for the collar."

"And you're welcome to it." He hadn't enlisted in the Secret Service for the glory and never enjoyed talking to the press. "If y'all grab Julian before he kills somebody else, I'll throw you a parade."

She grinned. "I'm SAC on this case, and I want it to go well."

Ryder took her arm and pulled her aside, giving the impression of privacy without leaving the room. He lowered his voice to a confidential tone. "I have a job I'd like to drop in your lap."

"Tell me what you need."

"Brother Gabe couldn't identify Julian from the snapshot you gave me. Apparently, Julian has sprouted a beard and lost a lot of weight. It'd be useful if you had a sketch artist to do a composite drawing for identification."

"I'll get that organized."

"And we need a security detail to protect our witness. This afternoon, he'll come with me to the wine-tasting. Lots of people from both sides of the family will be there. If we're lucky, Brother Gabe will identify Julian right away."

Murdock took immediate action, assigning a uniformed deputy sheriff to make Gabe comfortable until Ryder came back to pick him up. "When you return from the wine-tasting, check in with me. I'll arrange for Brother Gabe's room tonight."

With the immediate situation under control, Ryder went with Nicole to get ready for the afternoon event. They took a quick walk down the second-floor hall to her suite and slipped inside. Though sunshine through the west-facing windows gave enough light to see what they were doing, she turned on the overhead in the kitchenette, took a bottled water from the under-the-counter fridge and perched on a love seat behind a coffee table where a bowl of fresh fruit had materialized. Her head tilted back, she took a long pull on the water bottle before collapsing backward into total, boneless relaxation.

"Tired?" he asked. A needless question. She looked exhausted. Her toasty brown hair curled around her face in a wild, untamed style that he found adorable. When they'd taken off this morning, there hadn't been time for her to pull herself together or put on makeup. The shadows under her eyes emphasized their depth in a darker shade of hazel gray. "Maybe take a little nap before we go to the wine-tasting."

"No time." She swallowed another glug. "We need to leave in forty-five minutes."

"I need to be there," he said. "It's a good event for Gabe to look for Brother Julian. But you could play hooky."

"You don't get it. I'm the maid of honor."

"Don't care if you're the Queen of England. Everybody needs a break sometimes."

"Hah!" She took another hydrating sip and levered her body to her feet—a process that allowed him to appreciate her long legs and supple torso.

He made one more try at convincing her to relax. "Alyssa will understand."

"My best friend is inches away from morphing into a fire-breathing monster. I need to find her and see what fresh wedding disasters have struck. On the phone, she complained about seating charts for the reception, a change in the menu and the flowers being the wrong color of purple. Too mauve when they should be violet."

"Disasters," he said. "For damn sure."

"Clearly, you don't understand what it's like to be a bride. Or a groom, for that matter." Her gaze suddenly sharpened. "You've never been married, have you?"

The chasm of deception that characterized the end of their former affair reopened and spread wide. There was so much they didn't know about each other. "Never even been engaged. Never met the right woman."

"Picky, picky," she teased.

"Maybe so." He shrugged. "I'm the kind of man who knows exactly what he wants. Exactly. When I see it, I'll go after it with everything I've got."

She finished her water and headed to the door. "I need to check in with Alyssa. Be back in a few minutes."

"I'll be in the shower."

"Don't take too long. I need a shower, too."

"You could always join me," he drawled.

"In your dreams, cowboy."

She was so right about that. Whenever he closed his eyes and pushed the investigation out of his head, all his imagination zoomed in on her face, her voice and the way she'd felt in his arms last night. She was the woman he wanted. Exactly.

Chapter Fourteen

At half-past four, the sun had already begun to set, thanks to daylight saving time when the clocks got turned back. Ryder drove Nicole and Brother Gabe from the oceanside Leeward Manor across the coastal range and Willamette Valley to Villa Vitalia—a full-scale winery offering several varieties in a restaurant where tonight's tasting menu would be sampled. Much of their route followed a river through the rolling hills touched with the colors of autumn. They passed farms, fields, orchards and vineyards planted with long rows of grapes, mostly harvested. On a high bluff, she saw a magnificent mansion in the style of a French chateau gleaming in the golden sunset. The landscaping—big-leaf maple, oak, fir, spruce and cypress surrounded the villa. To Nicole, it seemed like the perfect blend of nature, elegance and functionality. Sitting beside Ryder, she almost forgot about the investigation and chaotic, star-crossed wedding.

Instead of parking at the front, he drove around to the rear and found a space in the employee's lot. Normally, she wouldn't complain, but Nicole was wearing high-heeled pumps to complement her burgundy dress. *Should have stuck with boots.* "You know, Ryder, we can valet park at the main entrance."

"If your job is to protect a VIP or witness, you never let a valet hide your vehicle. Always be ready to make a speedy escape. Plus, I want to detour through the kitchen, so Gabe has a chance to check out the servers, cooks and sommeliers. Julian might pose as one of them."

She heard a snort from the back seat. Gabe commented, "He'd make a terrible waiter."

"Why?" she asked.

"Too arrogant."

Ryder added, "He might pass as a sommelier. Some wine stewards are snooty. They make my taste buds cringe like they aren't worthy."

She knew Ryder was keeping it light, downplaying the dangers of their situation, and she smiled at the mental image of cringing taste buds. But she wasn't distracted. She couldn't dismiss the memory of Alan Caldicott's battered body. Poor man. He never had a chance.

Before their little group had departed from the Manor, Agent Murdock had given them autopsy results that reinforced her observations. The metal paddle was used to beat and torture the victim perimortem. A nine-millimeter bullet was recovered from Caldicott's brain, which Nicole had predicted. The FBI ballistics experts would have more information on the weapon and if it had been used in the commission of another crime. The medical examiner listed the other injuries. The killer had snapped a rib, inflicted several head wounds, dislocated the left shoulder and crushed both wrists. A sadistic monster. Exactly the way Brother Gabe had described Julian.

When they exited the car, Ryder quietly repeated his instructions for the evening. "I'll take care of Gabe. Your job is to enjoy the wine, make sure Alyssa is okay and keep your ears open for clues."

She gave him a mock salute. "Yes, sir."

Before she realized what she was doing, Nicole went up on tiptoe and planted a little goodbye kiss on his cheek. *Too friendly? Too aggressive?* She escaped before she started to question herself.

She dashed through the kitchen and came out on the second floor, where the event was already underway. From the looks of things, Nicole guessed that about half of the invited guests had arrived, maybe twenty-five people. Several were seated at a long table with three-glass flights of wine before them and a plump sommelier lecturing about the varieties and the history of Villa Vitalia vineyard.

The guest list for this civilized wine tasting concentrated on important Rossini Enterprises business associates, many of whom were not staying at the Manor with the more raucous, younger crowd. Tomorrow's rehearsal dinner would focus on friends and family of the bride and groom. Scanning the crowd and wondering how she could overhear meaningful clues, Nicole realized that Alyssa, her mother and father hadn't yet arrived.

A polished cherrywood bar stretched along one wall. Behind the three bartenders were sparkling rows of wines, mostly reds, with several choices of pinot noir. Other options included port, sherry and gin infused with juniper berries. One of Nicole's primary duties tonight would be to keep Alyssa supplied with a full glass of some nonalcoholic beverage so she could avoid drinking the wine without calling attention to her abstinence. Her pregnancy wasn't common knowledge.

At the bar, Nicole ordered a merlot from a handsome young bartender in a crisp white shirt and black vest. Though she wasn't a connoisseur, he gave her the wine-tasting spiel about how this merlot placed fourth in an international competition and was known for being a dry wine with black cherry flavor, tannins—whatever those were—and an undertone of earthy roots and vanilla. "Would you like a tasting sample?"

"I'll take a full glass. Thank you."

"Good choice."

She sipped the clear red liquid. Her untrained palate couldn't detect all the subtleties, but she liked the taste and gave the bartender a thumbs-up. Then she scoped out the long room with a huge river-rock fireplace sending out the pleasant aroma of maple. The western wall was all windows, looking out on sunset over the vineyard and the mountains in the distance.

No sign of Ryder and Gabe, but she spotted Nonna Rossini talking to the tall, distinguished, white-haired gentleman she'd noticed before. Papa Rossini had said he was a trusted advisor to the groom's father, which meant he might be a good person to pump for information. Nonna stood barely as tall as his shoulder but appeared to have his full attention. Nonna wore an elegant, floor-length black chiffon dress with a dramatic turquoise-and-sapphire necklace that probably weighed half as much as she did.

Nicole approached them, got kisses on both cheeks from Nonna, who introduced Dmitry Orloff. He kissed Nicole's hand. Very old-school and classy. They talked for a moment about wine and she tried to sound more knowledgeable than she actually was.

Nonna pinned her with a glare. "What's this I hear about you bringing a priest to the wedding?"

"I thought you'd be pleased."

"You know my opinion about a wedding on the beach. The Sacrament of Holy Matrimony is supposed to be in a church. There are ancient protocols to be followed." She nodded to Orloff. "Am I right?"

"Of course, Sophia. You are always right, but I make it a rule to avoid family disagreements. I prefer harmony." He gestured toward the young man seated at a baby grand in the corner, playing a combination of light classical and Billy Joel. "I bid you ladies adieu."

Nonna waved goodbye and turned her attention back to Nicole. "I don't like your priest-come-lately. The only clergy who should be involved is at our home parish in Las Vegas."

"You can always do another more intimate ceremony later," Nicole suggested.

"Where did you find this so-called priest?"

"St. Macarius Monastery. He's one of the brothers. Father

Bruno assured me that Brother Gabe is fully ordained and has performed weddings before."

Nonna's eyebrows raised. "You spoke to Father Bruno?"

Nicole wasn't surprised that Nonna knew the prior of St. Macarius. Nonna Rossini was incredibly active in Catholic charities and had contacts throughout the western states. Nicole verified their meeting. "He's a very nice man who likes mystery stories. I was impressed by the abbey, especially the bell tower."

"Years ago, I contributed to that project." Her long, thin fingers toyed with the turquoise on her necklace. "While I'm in Oregon, I should visit."

"Anyway," Nicole said, "I doubt Alyssa will change her plans to accommodate an official Catholic wedding. Might as well have Brother Gabe bless the young couple and wish them a long and happy life together."

"Still not married in the eyes of the church," she muttered. "I don't know why we had to race out here to get my granddaughter hitched in a matter of weeks. Suspicious. No?"

"Not suspicious. Not at all. Alyssa is just deeply in love and wants to start—"

"She's pregnant." Nonna interrupted with a flash of sudden comprehension. In a softer voice, she repeated, "Pregnant. Needs to get married before she starts showing."

Nicole took the older woman's arm and pointed her toward the bar. "Let's get another glass of wine. The merlot is tasty. All those tannins. Yum."

With a surprising display of strength, Nonna broke Nicole's grasp and faced her. A direct confrontation. "Am I right?"

"I can neither confirm nor deny."

"Hah!" Nonna kept her voice low. "I know I'm right, and I'm glad. It's about time for me to become a great-grandmother. Don't worry, dear. I'll tell no one."

"Not even her mom and dad?"

"Especially not them. My son and his wife are too—" She

rubbed her thumb and fingers together as if to grasp the right word. "Too provincial. Too worried about what people think."

"Aren't you?"

"Hah! I'm Italian from the Amalfi Coast. My people understand how life works."

"Can you be glad about the blessing from Brother Gabe?"

She pinched Nicole's cheek. "You're a good friend to Alyssa."

Silently, she gave her own blessing. *Nonna Rossini, you'll be a great great-grandmother.*

A commotion at the front door drew Nicole's attention to the front entrance where Tony, Stella and Alyssa made their entrance while the pianist played the opening to "The Wedding March" by Wagner and segued into "Just the Way You Are."

Alyssa's parents were charming and attractive in casual chic. A blue suit with an open-collar shirt for him and a figure-hugging, brocade cocktail dress for her. Alyssa in a low-cut, silver lamé gown with an attached cape was spectacular. Her glossy black hair tucked behind her ears showed off diamond chandelier earrings. She caught Nicole's eye and motioned for her to join them.

She bid Nonna goodbye and marched resolutely into the embrace of the Rossini family—the eye of the social hurricane. While she gave Alyssa a hug and cheek kiss, Nicole whispered, "Maid of honor reporting for duty."

A thread of desperation wove through Alyssa's words. "Find Graham, the sommelier. He put aside a couple bottles of grape juice that look like pinot noir."

"Your wish. My command."

"And I've got to pee."

"Come with me." Nicole recognized the problem. Frequent urination was one of the early signs of pregnancy. "I saw a bathroom on my way in."

She spotted Dirk Petrovich coming toward them and swerved to avoid him. Her goal tonight was uncovering leads for Ryder. Not dodging the pushy best man.

Outside the ladies' room, Jelly stepped in front of them to block the door. "I can't let you go in there until I make sure it's safe."

Alyssa rolled her eyes so emphatically that only the whites were showing. "If you don't get out of my way, I'm going to squat right here."

"Just doing my job."

Nicole mediated, as she had so many times before. "You're a good bodyguard, Jelly, and I appreciate your devotion to duty, but give us a little privacy. I'll enter first and make sure the coast is clear."

His double chin pulled into a scowl, but he stepped aside and motioned for Nicole to do her thing. She zipped inside. The four-stall bathroom with three sinks—nothing fancy—was vacant. She quickly escorted her friend inside

Locked in a stall, Alyssa groaned, "Can you believe Jelly? I mean, I'm glad he's watching out for me, but Papa is too paranoid. I'm fine, other than worrying about the wedding. Why would a hit man come after me?"

"Good question." Nicole rolled the possibilities around in her head. "Maybe you know something you aren't even aware of knowing. Speaking of which, Nonna figured out that you're pregnant."

Another groan. Louder this time. "Is she angry?"

"The opposite." Nonna was a wily, old bird. "She's thrilled to be a great-grandma, and she's not going to tell your parents."

Alyssa flung open the door to the stall and went to the sink. "Will you adjust my cape and make sure my Glock isn't showing?"

Nicole fluffed the shimmering fabric to cover the weapon in the slimline holster. "Another reason somebody might come after you is to get revenge on your family. You're aware of that. You've lived with it for your whole life."

"Yeah." She dug into a hidden pocket in the cape and produced a lipstick.

"Can you think of anybody with a grudge against Papa Rossini? Somebody who might come after you to hurt him?"

"Let me think about this."

Nicole glanced toward the bathroom door, imaging Jelly holding back other women who needed to relieve themselves, but she didn't pressure her friend to think faster. Other people might be quick to dismiss Alyssa. Too pretty to be smart. But Nicole knew better. "Think out loud, so I can follow your reasoning."

Alyssa freshened her dark red lipstick and inspected her reflection in the bathroom mirror. Her makeup and hair were perfect, as far as Nicole could tell. "There are the usual suspects," she said. "Guys who have hated my family for decades, since the days when my grandfather was in charge and Las Vegas was corrupt. Like the Wild West."

"Things are different," Nicole agreed. Families came to Las Vegas for vacations. Nobody expected to run into a notorious hit man.

"The biggest takedown in the past couple of years was after Ryder did his undercover investigating and broke up a counterfeiting ring. Caldicott worked closely with your honey."

"Not my honey," Nicole corrected. "We're friends."

"Whatever," Alyssa said. "Anyway, there were threats. Some people blamed Rossini Enterprises and Papa."

And Ryder. He had been at the center of that investigation. Was the counterfeiting operation starting up again?

Chapter Fifteen

Ryder found a quiet space near the bar where he and Brother Gabriel could hover beside a tall, round cocktail table between the bar and the piano player. His rendition of "Killing Me Softly" covered their real conversation about a possible Julian sighting. As they tasted their wine and watched, Ryder did his best to avoid being noticed, slouching to hide his six-foot-four-inch height. The subtle lighting in the restaurant minimized the scars on Gabe's face. Also, he wore a black shirt and collar under a plain black suit that covered his tattoos. Ryder told himself that they were unremarkable. Like flies on the wall.

Earlier, when they'd entered through the kitchen, they hadn't been so circumspect. Ryder had badged a couple of the supervisors, who'd pointed out new employees for special scrutiny. The bosses promised not to say anything, and he doubted they would. They were too slammed, way too busy with the crackers, canapes and wine…bottles and bottles of wine.

Gabe had concentrated hard, not joking around. Finding Julian was deeply important to him. Brother Gabriel had strayed from his calling, betrayed his vows because of Julian's clever deceptions. He wanted to see that guy in jail.

Ryder had given him hints for identifying his nemesis, ways of looking past a possible disguise. Gabe needed to see beyond facial features and hair color, needed to pay attention to gait, posture and gestures. And to listen for Julian's tone of voice. Despite these tips, Brother Gabriel had recognized no one among the kitchen staff and servers.

After they found their spot at the wine-tasting, where the piano man was now playing a medley from *West Side Story*, Gabe squinted at the growing crowd. Over half of them were women. The men—in various shapes and sizes—were dressed in suits and sweaters, casual but not sloppy. After a swallow of pinot noir, Gabe spoke just loud enough for Ryder to hear. "Most of these guys are too old to be Julian."

"Remember what I told you," Ryder said. "Look for similarities to the dude you knew as Julian. Did he tilt his head? Lick his lips? Pick his nose?"

"I'm trying."

"Maybe he dyed his hair or is wearing a wig. He could have trimmed his beard or shaved the whole thing off. Y'all got to think outside the box. He could even be dressed as a woman."

Gabe choked a laugh. "Not Julian. He thinks he's Mr. Macho. He swaggers."

Ryder compared his memory of the FBI snapshot of the blond, huggable hit man with the composite sketch Gabe had created with the FBI computer artist. The current version had sharp cheekbones, thin lips and cold, flat, brown eyes without laugh lines. Overall, he had very few wrinkles. Evil must be good for the skin.

While Gabe continued to check out the guests, Ryder found his gaze drawn to Nicole in her formfitting burgundy dress. She'd taken off the trench coat she'd worn on the drive over here, showing off her tanned, well-toned arms. Patterned black tights outlined her long legs. Instead of her usual sensible shoes, she wore black heels with ankle-straps—not stilettos but still sexy and tall, very tall. In his eyes, she seemed to be bathed in a spotlight while the rest of the wine tasters faded into a dull background. Her strong, confident vibe challenged men and made women want to be her friend. Dr. Nicole Carpenter was something else, something special. Ryder wanted to scoop her up and carry her away to somewhere private where he could tell her how damn pretty she was.

"I see your girlfriend," Gabe said.

"Me, too."

He should have corrected the monk's label of "girlfriend," which Nicole would certainly object to, but Ryder liked to imagine there was a link between them. They were partners, yes. But also friends. Also lovers.

She turned her head. An incandescent beam of light from her mysterious hazel eyes shot across the restaurant and merged with his gaze. Their laser connection passed from her to him to her. His pulse thundered at a hundred miles per minute. Oxygen flooded his bloodstream. He felt lightheaded.

And she calmly looked away.

Brother Gabriel tugged at the sleeve of his sweater and pointed. "Who's that guy?"

Ryder blinked, not wanting to return his attention to his investigation of smuggling and the murder of Alan Caldicott. But he was a federal agent, and this was his job. He looked where Gabe was pointing. At the front entrance, a tall, slender man wearing a bespoke black suit and silk shirt glided into Villa Vitalia as if he owned the place. Ryder knew him from photos but had never met the man in person. He guessed this experience might be like coming face-to-face with an oligarch or a czar. "That's Alexei Volkov."

Following three paces behind him came his supermodel wife, who was not Michael's mother. She stalked, as if on a fashion runway wearing a scrap of shiny material, low-cut on top and real short on the bottom. Her blond hair fluttered around her face. Marrying into that family would intimidate most young women, but Ryder guessed Alyssa could handle the challenge. The Rossini girl was pretty damned intimidating herself.

Like everybody else in the room, he and Gabe watched Alexei make his approach to the Rossini family. His son, Michael, walked over and facilitated a handshake between the two patriarchs. Then Michael hugged Tony, Stella and Nicole, and took his place beside his bride-to-be after giving her a kiss on the cheek.

The piano player had segued into "Tonight," the song from *West Side Story* before the two gangs have a rumble in the street. An appropriate nod to everyone's fears, but Ryder hoped the song wasn't accurate. He didn't want to believe the Volkov Group was involved in the computer hack, the murder, or the smuggling of goods worth over four million dollars. He had a lot to consider. Later tonight, he needed to check in with SAC Marianne Trevino for an update.

Nicole swept across the restaurant to his side and grasped his hand. "Come with me. Michael is going to serenade Alyssa."

Ryder didn't particularly want to watch Michael Volkov make a suave, romantic gesture to his fiancée. Not that he was jealous of the handsome young man who was about to graduate law school and take over a company worth millions. Not at all. Reluctantly, he allowed himself to be dragged to a position behind the keyboard. Others followed, and Ryder made sure Gabe was right beside him.

Nicole leaned so close to his ear that he felt her warm breath on his cheek. "I've got a clue for you," she whispered. "Alyssa said her father had gotten threats from the counterfeiting group you exposed."

He doubted the plausibility of that threat, but he didn't refute her. Having her pressed against his body felt too good to interrupt. He cinched an arm around her waist. "Tell me more."

"Now is neither the time nor the place for intimacy," she said as she moved away. "I just wanted to let you know."

Even though he hadn't been responsible for the arrests from two years ago, he had testified in his role as an undercover agent and had kept up with the cases. He knew that the major players had all been taken into custody, but there were always others with grudges or family members who didn't like seeing their loved ones in federal prison. He needed an update. Another question for SAC Trevino.

Michael approached the piano player and asked if he could fill in for a moment. Seated on the bench behind the baby grand, he flexed his long fingers and played a quick warm-up before he launched into a version of the classic "Greensleeves." Then he directed Alyssa to sit beside him. Gazing in her eyes, he sang in tenor, "Can't Help Falling in Love."

Not jealous. Hell, no. Not a bit. Every female in the room—and some of the males—exhaled sighs of pure longing. So what? No doubt, their hearts throbbed in unison. Who cares? When Michael ended his song, held Alyssa's face in his hands and kissed her mouth, the wine-drinking crowd let out a cheer and applauded.

Nicole tilted her head up toward him and stared into his eyes. "Tonight," she said, "you'll stay in my room. In my bed."

Ryder realized that he was the true beneficiary of Michael's serenade. Forget jealousy. He ought to send the guy a thank-you note. "Wish I could sing."

"You have other talents," she said.

And he knew better than to overplay his abilities. The proof was Dirk Petrovich, who conferred with the piano player as soon as he returned to his bench. After a moment, Petrovich stood up straight, smoothed back his wavy ginger hair and announced, "This song is for our maid of honor. For you, Nicole."

After the piano played an intro, Petrovich warbled "You Are So Beautiful."

It wasn't pretty.

Nicole cleared her throat. "Thanks so much, Dirk. That's enough."

He continued. Louder.

"I mean it," she said. "Enough."

Apparently, the piano player agreed. He segued into a version of "Hit the Road, Jack."

In response to the applause from the crowd, Petrovich

bowed. No matter how pathetic and deluded he seemed, Ryder didn't discount the best man. Idiots could be dangerous.

A guy he recognized from their online meeting popped up beside them. Though he wore a slouchy, gray beanie cap that covered his head and drooped low on his forehead, his magenta braid escaped from the back. Round, gold-frame glasses perched on his nose. Nicole gave him a hug and introduced Mouse to Gabe.

"You two share a couple of things in common," she said.

"Me and a priest?" Mouse shook his head. "Doubtful."

"Incredible tattoos," she said. "When we're done here, you should roll up your sleeves and compare. In the meantime, you can talk about computers. Maybe Mouse can explain the glitch that showed up in the hack."

"Maybe later," Ryder interrupted. "We don't know who could be listening."

"I hear you," Mouse said. "The deeper I get into this, the more I realize that we should be talking to the police."

"Lucky for us," Ryder said. "I am the police."

Using his HSI and FBI contacts, he'd handle this part of the investigation with the cyber-crime experts. Also, he'd review the records from his undercover years in Las Vegas when he'd first fallen in love with Nicole and provided evidence to shut down a massive counterfeiting and money-laundering operation with branches throughout the western United States and into Canada. Later, he'd get a grip on the total operation.

Right now, his focus was finding Julian. So far, their attempt to find him among the wine-tasting guests had been futile. Ryder was anxious to move things along. Unfortunately, Nicole felt obligated to stay with Alyssa and do the maid-of-honor thing.

"I'll ride back to the Manor with Alyssa," she said. "She came in a limo with her parents. Tony and Stella are going to stay here longer, but Alyssa is almost ready to head out. We'll ride with Jelly."

"She's not spending the night with Michael?"

Nicole shook her head. "He's going out with Petrovich and a couple of other guys."

"A bachelor party?"

"Oh, they've already done their wild night on the town. So has Alyssa." She gave a noncommittal shrug. "We're from Las Vegas, you know."

He remembered. "Y'all know how to party."

"The hard part is finding something we haven't done before." She shrugged. "It's awkward when the bachelorette stripper is a guy you saw at Mass on Sunday with his wife and kids."

Brother Gabe gave her a high five. "Amen."

Ryder questioned, "You have a problem with strippers at Mass?"

"It can be awkward."

As it turned out, Mouse had dropped his suitcase off at Leeward Manor but didn't actually have a room reservation. Gabe offered to share the former room of the murder victim, which the FBI had offered to him along with witness protection from an on-site agent. Seemed like a perfect solution.

Ryder, Mouse and Gabe left through the back exit. Mouse and Gabe grabbed handfuls of canapes on their way out, including crostini, Tillamook cheeses, pears and seafood. The shrimp and salmon stunk up the back seat of Ryder's rental SUV. He rolled down his window to catch the breeze and told them to do the same.

He turned in the driver's seat to watch them spread their haul of food on a white towel that he didn't recognize. Probably stolen, but he wasn't about to complain. "Y'all hungry?"

"It's almost nine o'clock," Gabe said. "I missed dinner."

Mouse agreed as he put together cheese on a crostini. "This is good stuff."

"I'm not going to head back to the Manor just yet. I want to make sure that Nicole and Alyssa get out of here safely."

He drove around to the front and parked in sight of the covered entrance. The well-lit area showed wide sidewalks and a drop-off point where valets in red vests retrieved vehicles for guests who were coming and going. Ryder parked and leaned against the fender, watching those who were late to arrive and those who were already headed home.

Big Jelly stood waiting at the valet desk. Nicole, Alyssa and her mother were beside him. Lubricated by the wine-tasting, they chatted and chuckled. All three women looked happy. Ryder hoped that boded well for his night with Nicole. When a sleek, black Lincoln Town Car was driven up to the curb by a valet, Jelly opened the door for the ladies. Alyssa and her mom got in the back. Nicole took the front seat, which bothered Ryder because that was the worst place to sit in case of an accident. Good thing she had her crossbody purse.

Ryder noticed a valet whose red vest had faded to a pinkish tone. He strode away from the entrance to a black midsize Ford Ranger truck parked opposite Ryder's on the driveway. The valet yelled over his shoulder, "I got other things to do tonight. I'm done."

Like a full-sized jack-in-the-box, Brother Gabriel popped out of the rear seat. He stared at the Ranger's tail lights as it pulled away. "That's him."

Ryder stared at him. "What are you saying?"

"That's Brother Julian. Doesn't look like him at all. But I recognize his swagger. And I heard something familiar in the tone of his voice. Follow that car."

Ryder jumped back into his car and slammed it into gear. Julian the hit man was trying to steal Nicole and Alyssa from under his nose. Ryder couldn't let him get away with it.

Chapter Sixteen

Nicole didn't come close to drinking the amount of wine tasted by most of the guests, and she wasn't as excitable as Alyssa and her mom who had their heads together in the back seat, gossiping and giggling. Nicole glanced over at Jelly in the driver's seat, glad to see that he appeared to be calm and sober. She asked, "Did you get to try any of the wine?"

"I'm a beer drinker. Sam Adams with a whiskey chaser if I want to get fancy."

"A boilermaker," she said.

Her mom liked to have a boilermaker with a snort of cocaine. She'd taught her daughter to mix several beverages. Nicole used to joke that her mother's lifestyle left a bad taste in her mouth, but that was the truth. She'd only been falling-down drunk four times in her whole life. The worst episode came after she'd learned that Ryder had deceived her and she'd told him that she never wanted to see him again.

Tonight, in her suite at Leeward Manor, she'd find out if that pronouncement still held true. Had she really forgiven him? Would she ever be able to trust him?

Through the windshield, she looked out on a moonlit valley with wineries, fields for other crops come spring and a grove of hazelnut trees. The farming landscape morphed into the heavily forested coastal range that flattened as it approached the coast. Though it was only half past eight o'clock, few other cars were on the road as they descended to the Pacific shore. Wispy clouds crossed the face of the moon, but the night was relatively clear. She hoped the temperate weather would hold for a day and a half when the wedding would take place.

Jelly glanced in his side mirror and the rearview. "I don't like the way that truck is following. Looks like a midsize, maybe a Ford Ranger."

"Maybe you should pull over and let him pass."

He gave a snort. "I'll speed up and see what he does."

His logic was shaky, but she understood. Some men didn't like to be challenged by somebody who stood taller or bumped shoulders or drove faster. In anything they considered a masculinity test, their testosterone spiked.

She glanced at the speedometer. The needle hovered at seventy on a curving, two-lane road. Not terrible but somewhat concerning. When she turned in her seat to peer through the back window, Alyssa bounced forward, gave her a kiss on the forehead and said, "I love you, Nicole."

"Right back at you, kiddo. You're bubbly. Almost as if you'd been drinking."

"Not a drop. This is hormones."

Nicole scowled. "You're not wearing your seat belt? Why isn't the alarm bell clanging?"

"I buckled it behind my back," Alyssa said. "Didn't want to be restricted."

Her mom said, "I told her to put it on."

"Do it," Nicole said.

"You're a couple of party poopers."

"Don't you mean 'y'all are poopers'?" her mom asked with a high-pitched giggle. "I think Ryder's drawl is so cute."

"Yeah, he's adorable." Through the rear window, Nicole saw the headlights behind them, riding their bumper. She didn't know enough about trucks to guess at the brand. A Ford? A Chevy? Something big, black and scary.

Beside her in the driver's seat, Jelly frowned. He didn't

look scared or particularly nervous, but his grip on the steering wheel tightened and he leaned forward as if urging the car to go faster. The big man was a trained bodyguard. He'd probably done car chases before, but she didn't want to ask and find out he was clueless.

"Do you know how to use a gun?" he asked.

"Yes." She wasn't a super markswoman and hadn't been to a shooting range in over a year, but she'd learned the basics from Papa Rossini.

"In the glove compartment," Jelly said, "I have a loaded Beretta."

"I'll keep that in mind."

When he swerved, her stomach clenched. Her breath quickened. No doubt her fear sparked a flood of adrenaline into her bloodstream. Her foot slammed down on an imaginary brake. In a quiet voice, she said, "If he's tailing us, we should call for backup."

"Get your phone ready," he said, "but don't make the call yet. I'm going to turn up here and see if he follows."

Phone in hand, she prepared to make the call. Papa Rossini was the better choice for sending the cavalry to rescue them, but she preferred Ryder's standing as a federal agent in case things got dicey. Both were on her favorites list.

Without warning, Jelly made a sharp left and fishtailed onto a crossroad that pointed toward the lights of a very small town. His surprise move tossed Alyssa across the back seat, and she shrieked with laughter.

Over his shoulder, Jelly growled, "Put on your damn seat belt."

"You're not the boss of me," she shot back. Hormones or not, she was acting just about as mature as a five-year-old.

Her mother reprimanded, "Pay attention to your bodyguard, Alyssa. That was rude. I'm so sorry, Mr. Jellinek."

"It's okay to call him Jelly, Mom. He likes it."

"He's your elder and deserves respect."

"I'm always polite," Alyssa said, still not hooking up her seat belt.

Their mother-daughter bickering felt familiar. Nicole wanted them to be aware of the possibility of a high-speed chase but didn't want them to freak out. Through the rear window, she saw the headlights appear. *Damn.*

The truck followed at a distance, not too close. "Jelly, should I call?"

"Not yet."

At the center of the small town. which must have been named Oyster Bend because those words were written large over the pharmacy, diner and hardware stores, Jelly whipped a right. Alyssa tumbled, again. Before she got herself resettled, Jelly made another right. Then another. They were back to the road they'd entered town with, and he backtracked to the route they were following before—an action that infuriated the GPS dashboard navigation.

Nicole alternated between checking their speed, reading the GPS and looking out the rear window. After a long ten minutes while Jelly focused on driving through the night, they seemed to be the only vehicle on the road. "Good job, Jelly. You lost the truck."

"Appears so." He eased off the accelerator, and they slowed. "I didn't want anybody on our tail when got to Highway 101."

"Why? That's a main road along the coast. On this stretch of 101, there will be cops, good visibility and two lanes on each side to maneuver."

"Yeah, yeah, and great views of the ocean." He shook his head. "And miles of road with nothing but a skinny guardrail along a cliff."

Though she didn't know much about cars, she knew their Lincoln Town Car ranked as one of the biggest, heaviest and fastest sedans. On the plus side, forcing them off the road wouldn't be easy. The negative, this sedan had the power to plow through a guardrail as if the barrier were made of cardboard. They'd launch into a swan dive over the rocky shore.

The phone she clutched in her hand rang. Caller ID said "Ryder Beckham."

She answered in a flash. "You called me."

"Did you think I couldn't track you down?" he asked. "I work for Homeland Security. I'm a federal agent. Only reason I asked for your number in the first place was to be polite."

"Okay, I get it."

"If I wanted," he drawled, "I could find out the name of your first pet, your favorite color, your third-grade teacher and your date to senior prom. But I wouldn't do that because I respect you, and I respect your privacy."

When she'd first seen the caller ID, she'd been relieved to hear from him. Now, she was ticked off. "Okay, Mr. Agent Man, tell me why you called."

"Where are you?"

"On the way back to Leeward Manor. Jelly is driving."

"Put me on Speaker," he ordered.

She did as he said, and Jelly filled him in on their situation, outlining their route since they'd left the wine tasting. "A little while ago, I thought we were being followed."

"By a black Ford Ranger," Ryder said.

"How did you know?"

"I saw you leave from Villa Vitalia. The Ranger took off after you. I followed him but hung back so he wouldn't notice since I pretty much knew the route you'd take. Then y'all surprised me, vanished into thin air."

"That's when I shook the tail," Jelly explained. "Haven't seen him since."

"Give me your location."

"Getting close to the 101. I just passed a crab shack called Shabby Gabby's with cars parked in front."

"I can alert the state patrol," Ryder offered. "When you

get to the highway, the staties can provide an escort back to the Manor."

"I'm cool," Jelly said.

Unsure that she agreed, Nicole piped up. "We might be safer with police accompanying us. I'm sure Alyssa and Stella feel the same way."

Her reminder about Tony's wife and daughter worked its magic. Jelly's job was to make sure they were safe, no matter how uncool it was for him to accept police protection. "Okay, Ryder, send in the cops. Nicole will call you when we hit the 101."

"I'll do what I can." Ryder ended the call.

Alyssa—still not wearing her seat belt—popped her head into the front. The light from the dashboard reflected off her face. "Were we really being followed? Were we in danger?"

Nicole answered, "Jelly had everything under control."

"Damn right I did," he muttered. "Some jerk was on my bumper, following too close."

She wanted to believe him, but Nicole remembered what Ryder had said about a black Ford Ranger leaving the wine tasting when they did. Couldn't be a coincidence that the vehicle in Jelly's rearview mirror was the same make and model. The person following them could be Julian, formerly Brother Julian, and probable hit man. Her fingers itched to unfasten the latch on the glove compartment and take out the Beretta. First, she'd reassure Alyssa and her mom.

"We're fine now," Nicole said. "Ryder promised to get us a police escort when we reach the highway."

Stella's voice quavered at the edge of panic. "Should I call Tony?"

"We're only about half an hour away from Leeward Manor," Nicole assured her. "We're going to be fine as soon as Alyssa fastens her seat belt."

She eased back in the seat and dramatically clicked the belt. "What can we do to help?"

"Maybe watch out the back window for a black Ford Ranger truck," Nicole suggested as she turned toward the windshield and peered into the moonlit hills and forest on either side of the Town Car. She'd be glad when the state police joined them. Glancing toward Jelly, she asked, "How is this going to work?"

He shrugged. "I don't know. Never had a state police escort before."

When he merged onto the 101, she called Ryder and informed him. "What are we supposed to do when the police show up?"

"You'll figure it out," he said. "I'll make a couple more calls and get back to you."

"Okay." She wanted more reassurance but didn't want to be a whiner.

"I'm not far from the highway myself. It's a real pretty night. Full moon. Not much fog."

"It's beautiful," she agreed, looking out the passenger's-side window. "Call me later."

"Yes, ma'am."

He ended the call and she stared through the windshield. Jelly had been accurate when he'd mentioned the spectacular views from the highway to the rocky beach where the dark waters of the Pacific roiled with frothy, white surf. Offshore, she saw the characteristic sea stacks—tall basalt columns of jagged rock. In the moonlight, they looked like weird creatures rising from the ocean. Some were large enough to provide habitats for gulls and ledges where sea lions could rest.

In the midst of all this natural grandeur, she focused on the guard rail at the edge of the cliff. It looked inadequate, incapable of stopping their Town Car from a death plunge. Nicole was relieved when she heard the police siren behind them.

From the back seat, Alyssa shouted, "The police are here. I see the flashing lights."

Nicole twisted around and peered through the back window.

The blue-and-red flashers from the bar atop the state trooper's car were clearly visible. "I think he wants us to stop."

"Why?" Jelly wasn't happy with that idea. "What does he want to say?"

"Don't know. Ryder didn't call me back yet."

With lights still flashing and siren blaring, the police sedan pulled even with the Town Car and signaled them to pull over. Nicole looked past Jelly and peered in the window of the patrol car. In the ER, she often worked with cops, and this guy looked like he meant business. Bushy black eyebrows pulled into an angry scowl. His jaw stuck out at a sharp angle. He wore the flat-brimmed hat that was part of the state patrol uniform. Something about him didn't feel right to her.

The nose of the patrol car edged closer to the Town Car as if he intended to force them to pull over. From the back seat, Stella and Alyssa shouted incomprehensible directions ranging from "You've got to stop" to "Ram that car."

Jelly tapped the brake, slowing down.

Nicole opened the glove compartment and took out the Beretta. She released the safety and checked to be sure there was a round in the chamber.

Jelly pulled over and parked on a wide shoulder with the patrol car behind him. Before the cop could approach, Jelly removed his gun from the holster and handed it to Nicole. Smart move. If the cop saw the weapon, he might mistake their intentions and shoot first. Jelly climbed out from behind the driver's seat, leaving the engine on and the car in Park.

"What's your problem?" Jelly called out.

The trooper exited his vehicle. Nicole took off her seat belt and climbed over the console into the driver's seat so she could see what was going on.

"Put your gun down," Jelly said as he raised his open palms. "I'm unarmed."

The trooper cracked a grin. "Your error, big man."

He shot Jelly in the chest. Before he could fire again, Nicole stuck her arm out of the car and blasted three shots with the Beretta. The trooper ducked out of sight.

Nicole was in the driver's seat with the engine running, but she couldn't drive off and leave Jelly there. She yelled to the two women in the rear. "Get down."

"Like hell I will." Alyssa ripped off the offending seat belt and drew her Glock Slimline. Leaning out the lowered window on the passenger side of the car, she fired at the patrol car.

Between the two of them, they had the trooper pinned down. He must have realized that whatever he had planned wasn't going to work. He managed to get into his car, backed up and zoomed away.

Nicole slipped out of the driver's seat and knelt beside Jelly. Blood seeped from his wound, much more than her little first-aid kit could handle. He breathed in labored gasps. He was still alive. But for how long?

Chapter Seventeen

When Ryder spotted the Lincoln Town Car parked on the wide shoulder with Nicole kneeling beside it, he reacted instinctually. *She was in trouble.* He slammed his foot down on the accelerator. Frantic to get there faster. Ready to help, to rescue her. *Not rescue.* She'd never accept the role of damsel in distress.

From the back seat of his rental SUV, he heard Brother Gabriel. "Are you okay?"

Mouse chimed in. "Slow down, man."

Ryder swallowed a couple of deep breaths and brought himself under control, though he continued to drive too fast on Highway 101. *What had gone wrong?* He'd only been off the phone with Nicole for a moment. Getting through to local law enforcement had been more complicated than he'd anticipated. *What the hell happened?* Had Julian caught up with them?

Nearing the Town Car, Ryder hit the brakes. He ordered Brother Gabriel and Mouse to stay in the back seat. He parked. Turned on his emergency flashers. Unholstered his Glock. Leaped from the driver's seat. Ran to Nicole's side.

She knelt beside Jelly, who lay flat on his back beside the car. Barely glancing up to acknowledge his appearance, she concentrated on treating a bleeding wound near Jelly's left shoulder by applying pressure using her trench coat.

Alyssa shouted at Ryder from the open window of the back

seat. "Nicole already called 9-1-1. She figured the three of us dragging Jelly into the Town Car would cause more harm than good. We need an ambulance."

Three of them? With a jolt, he remembered her mom joining the two others. At the same time, he realized they had no cover. Out here, on the shoulder of the highway, they made easy targets. "Alyssa, you and your mother stay in the car."

A few minutes ago, he'd put out an alert to local law enforcement, telling them that they needed immediate backup. Immediate as in now, right now. They'd be here soon. In the meantime, he assumed a protective stance between Nicole and the passing traffic, watching with his gun in hand, ready to open fire at the first sign of threat.

Looking over his shoulder, he observed Nicole. Her black-patterned tights were torn from kneeling on the shoulder. Bloodstains spattered her burgundy dress and her bare arms. Her curly hair fell across her face. When she tilted her head up and met his gaze, he noticed a smear of dirt on her cheek. She was more beautiful now than when she'd been all chic and polished at the wine tasting.

"What can I do?" he asked.

"All we can do right now is stanch the bleeding and slow the blood loss."

"How long has he been unconscious?"

"He woke up for a few seconds, then went out again." Her voice sounded strong and steady. An ER doctor to her core. "He hit his head against the fender when he went down. That worries me. He might have a concussion."

As if in response, Jelly squinted his eyes open and said, "I'm fine. Gotta get on the road. Tony is gonna kick my butt."

"You're not going to get kicked," Nicole said. "You're a hero, Jelly."

"Am I gonna die, Doc?"

"Not for many, many years."

He exhaled heavily and closed his eyes. "Gotta take a nap."

Ryder focused on the highway traffic, wishing they had more distance away from the oncoming cars and trucks. "I can move him to the other side of the car."

"Let's not," she said. "I have no way of knowing how much internal damage the bullet might have caused. It's better not to jostle him around."

"Do you want me to call emergency dispatch and see if I can get the ambulance to hurry?"

"If they don't arrive in the next ten minutes, yes. Make calls. Make noise."

Ryder didn't understand why Jelly had pulled over and how anybody had gotten the drop on the experienced bodyguard. "Tell me what happened."

"A patrol car was following us with sirens and flashers. He pulled right up to Jelly's window and motioned for him to pull over. Weird, am I right?"

"Right."

"I had a clear view of the patrolman. Heavy eyebrows. Lantern jaw. He wore a flat-brimmed hat." She shrugged. "I thought he was self-important and a jerk. I see a lot of that in the ER. Patrolmen who think they know more than I do."

"And then?" he prompted.

"When Jelly got out, he left his gun behind. So the cop wouldn't mistakenly shoot him. But there was no mistake. As soon as he saw Jelly, he opened fire. I stuck my arm out of the car and shot back. In the back seat, Alyssa rolled down the window and did the same."

Ryder almost grinned, imagining the gunman's surprise when the well-dressed ladies started blasting away. "Did you hit him?"

"Doubtful. I wasn't even aiming. Didn't need to. The guy took off running and got back into his car. I considered shooting out his tire but decided to let him go. More than anything, I wanted him gone so I could treat Jelly."

When he looked back at her, the moonlight and reflected headlights shone on her face. "You did the right thing."

"Was it Julian?"

"Afraid so. Brother Gabriel recognized him outside the winery. Not from his facial features but from the way he strutted around. You and Alyssa were lucky to get away unharmed."

"Luck didn't have much to do with it."

He stared back at the road. Where the hell was his backup? "Explain."

"I don't think he intended to harm us. He was close enough to take aim, and it was obvious that we were shooting blind."

Similar to when he'd stalked across the grounds between Leeward Manor and the lighthouse. Julian had had a gun at that time, too. If he'd wanted to kill them, he could have used it. "He meant to kidnap Alyssa and you. Is that what you think?"

"I don't know why," she said, "but yeah."

In the distance, he heard the wail of an ambulance. *Finally.* "Sounds like help is on the way. Is Jelly going to be all right?"

"I hope so."

An SUV with the word "Sheriff" emblazoned on the side pulled up in front of them, providing cover from the passing traffic. As soon as he and Nicole were protected, Ryder slipped off his leather jacket and draped it over her shoulders. He crouched beside her. "You're going to be okay."

"How did Julian find us?"

"My guess," Ryder said, "is that he took off after the Town Car when he saw you and Alyssa leave. Julian followed you until Jelly did his evasive driving and lost him."

"Oyster Bend," she said. "That was the name of the town where he doubled back."

"Okay." He'd noticed that Oregonians had a penchant for odd names and signage. He'd have to ask her about that, but not now. His brain was busy putting together facts and conjecture about what he already knew and what she'd just told him.

Julian had left the winery and followed them. That much Ryder knew.

Using evasive driving maneuvers, Jelly had shaken both Julian and Ryder.

The next point of direct observation came from Nicole. She'd told him that the hit man pulled over the Town Car and attacked them. He must have been expecting Nicole and Alyssa to come along quietly when the bodyguard was out of the way.

Mentally, Ryder filled in the blanks. How did Julian go from pursuit in the Ranger to driving a vehicle that resembled those used by the state patrol? His scheme took advance planning and preparation. He must have had the fake patrol car ready and waiting on the route back to Leeward Manor. Grudgingly, Ryder admired his imagination and foresight. He wondered how much the elite hit man was being paid for this job.

"Here's how I think he did it," he said. "His original plan required him to impersonate a state trooper. When Jelly lost him, he raced ahead and got into position to follow you and pull you over. Did you get a good look at his car?"

"Not really. It was gray and had a light bar."

"Easy to fake. Did you notice a police emblem? Or any indication it was a patrol car?"

"I can't remember."

The ambulance parked on the shoulder in front of the Town Car. Two EMTs jumped out and dashed toward them. Nicole stood to meet them. In a calm voice, she reported the basic information. "Gunshot wound in the upper left chest. I didn't find an exit wound but couldn't turn him over to do a thorough examination. Also, he has a head injury, possible concussion. You'll need a gurney."

"We'll take it from here, miss."

"I'm riding with you in the ambulance," she said. "I'm an ER resident at General Hospital in Portland."

Ryder took her arm and moved her out of the way. "I'm not

sure you should go to the hospital. Julian could come after you."

"I need to stay with Jelly." Her voice was determined, unshakable.

He doubted he could change her mind, but he hated the idea of Nicole on her own in a hospital where half the staff were wearing masks. It was the perfect place for Julian to strike. Ryder wanted to go with her and stand at her side, but he needed to organize things here. Another two police vehicles had joined the crowd at roadside.

"You need protection." He confronted her. Whether she liked it or not, he wouldn't allow her to put herself in danger. "Both you and Jelly."

For a brief moment, her gaze softened. She whispered, "Come with me."

Best invite he'd had in a long time. Oh yeah, he wanted to stay with her. Tonight was supposed to be their time together, sharing a shower and a naked night in bed. "I'm needed here. But I'll join you later."

He released her arm and snagged a young-looking deputy wearing a windbreaker over his tactical vest. The name tag under his six-pointed star badge read "L. Farley, Deputy, Lincoln County." After advising him to check in with his boss at the sheriff's office, Ryder instructed him to follow the ambulance to the hospital in Newport and stay with Nicole. Without betraying too much about the investigation, Ryder told him about the threat from an elite hit man. "He could be anybody at the hospital. You've got to be alert."

"Yes, sir." The young man's blue eyes brightened as he adjusted his brown baseball cap. "If I see this hit man, should I arrest him?"

The enthusiasm was great, but the inexperience worried Ryder. "Don't go jumping the gun, Farley. This guy is a master of disguise. Stay with Nicole. He might come after her."

After introducing her to her new bodyguard, he gazed into

her hazel eyes and promised, "I'll join you at the hospital as fast as I can. Stay safe."

She hugged him tightly, fitting her body against his. Her breasts crushed against his chest. "I'll wait for you," she whispered.

"You better." He kissed her forehead. "I want my jacket back."

He watched Nicole until she climbed into the rear of the ambulance, and they drove away with siren screaming. Deputy Farley's vehicle followed.

Once again, Ryder had opted to do his job rather than follow his heart and join Nicole. A visit to St. Catherine Hospital in Newport wasn't his idea of a good time, but almost anywhere would be better than managing the situation at the edge of Highway 101.

With so many cops from different law enforcement entities, a hassle about jurisdiction took place with a lot of bitching and moaning, huffing and puffing. The state patrol won that skirmish, claiming control over the Town Car that could be considered a crime scene. Alyssa and her mom—both witnesses to the crime—needed someone to drive them to Leeward Manor where the staties would interview them. But before the agreement could take place and the tangle of cars could unravel, a stretch limo swept onto the shoulder. Tony Rossini emerged, followed by three other men in tailored suits and silk neckties. Tony straightened his lapels, cleared his throat and took control.

Without raising his voice, he summarized the situation. "It's my understanding that Hal Jellinek, my employee hired as a bodyguard for my daughter, was shot and hospitalized."

"That's correct," Ryder said. He never knew exactly how Tony managed to get his information, but Papa Rossini always knew what was happening and who was to blame. Ryder continued, "Nicole accompanied Jelly in the ambulance. A deputy sheriff is keeping an eye on them at the hospital to make sure there are no other assaults."

Tony nodded to one of his men. "Follow up. Assign two others to the hospital."

Ryder explained that the Town Car was considered a crime scene and would be taken by the Oregon state patrol. Alyssa and Stella needed to be questioned as witnesses to the shooting.

Tony motioned for another of his men to step forward. "This is my lawyer."

"I know," Ryder said.

While the lawyer passed around his business cards, Tony dictated the next step. "My wife and daughter will ride to Leeward Manor with me. Their questioning will be arranged through my lawyer."

One of the state patrolmen opened the rear door of the Town Car for Alyssa and Stella. The two women stepped through the throng of cops and took their rightful places beside the patriarch of the Rossini family. Alyssa smiled and did a royal wave goodbye before she climbed into the stretch limo.

Though they weren't actually colleagues, Ryder had to admire the way Tony ran his empire. Over the years, he had developed a smooth, confident, powerful manner, and he almost always got what he wanted. Shortly after his limo pulled away, the FBI arrived in two separate cars. Agent Murdock marched directly toward him.

"We need to talk," she said.

"Maybe later." He gestured to the law enforcement gang. "These officers have some jurisdictional issues. And I'd be much obliged if you would take it from here."

"Fine," she said with an ironic grin. "I have a riddle for you."

"Shoot."

"What weighs eighty pounds, fits in two suitcases and is worth four-and-a-half-million dollars?"

Chapter Eighteen

2:12 a.m., the day before the wedding...

With Ryder's leather jacket spread over her like a blanket, Nicole curled up in an uncomfortable, metal-frame chair in the waiting room down the hall from the ICU at St. Catherine Hospital on the coast. After Jelly was checked in, he'd been taken into surgery where doctors removed the bullet and repaired internal damage. His left lung was nicked and two ribs broken. In the Intensive Care Unit, he had recovered consciousness under the watchful eye of the nursing staff who refused to allow visitors and kept Jelly resting comfortably. Nicole graded their caretaking as A-plus—conscientious and effective. Not surprising since St. Catherine of Siena was the patroness of nursing.

Exhaling a sigh, Nicole rubbed her cheek against the collar of Ryder's jacket and inhaled the masculine scent of leather, musk and cedarwood, which wasn't a mouthwatering smell like vanilla but pleased her senses because it reminded her of him. He'd called twice with updates on Mouse and Brother Gabriel, who were rooming together at Leeward Manor and sharing computer data with the crypto investigators who worked with the FBI. According to these experts, Rossini Enterprises wasn't responsible for turning off communication between law enforcement along the coast during a one-hour window. The link to the Las Vegas business was bogus. Unfortunately, all these computer geniuses hadn't yet figured out how to thwart the electromagnetic pulse virus from attacking again.

She yawned, stretched her arms over her head and looked across the waiting room to the chairs where her bodyguards—a cute, young deputy named Farley and two of Tony's crew—had taken up residence. They were almost too diligent in watching her every move—insisting on checking out the ladies' room before she went inside, tromping along in a group when she got coffee from the vending machine.

Annoying but necessary, they were almost as persistent as she'd been when she demanded detailed information from the surgeon about Jelly's condition. Though she'd tried to be polite, the doctors had made it clear they didn't like having her peeking over their shoulders, especially when she was insistent about initiating concussion protocols. Much of her work in the ER involved head injuries, and she'd gotten familiar with the symptoms.

Her eyelids drooped shut. She'd only slept in snatches and hadn't eaten anything since the canapes at the winery. Since it was after midnight, this counted as the last day before the wedding. She expected to encounter frantic activity and all sorts of minor problems as the day went on, in addition to solving the murder and figuring out who was smuggling multimillion-dollar cargo into Consolation Cove.

Later. She'd deal with all that later. Right now, she intended to stay in this chair until Jelly was moved to his own room and settled. A fragmented dream danced across her semiconscious mind. The soundtrack was piano music. "Greensleeves" and "I Can't Help Falling in Love." Ryder popped into her head and stared at her with his incredible blue eyes, bluer than the waters of Crater Lake. He tossed aside his cowboy hat and dragged his fingers through his dark blond hair. For some reason, he was wearing chaps. And then, she felt his lips against hers. She felt the beating of his heart against her breasts, almost as though he were inside her. Oh yes, she wanted that, wanted him inside her. A tremble spread to every part of her body. She gasped. Her eyelids snapped open. And she saw him.

Ryder stood over her, his hands braced on the arms of her chair. Was he really there or was she still lost in fantasy? Her gaze slid down his chest. He wore sensible clothes—a windbreaker over his sweater and jeans. Not cowboy chaps. Nor a cosplay costume like Thor. He continued to gaze at her with the sexiest grin she'd ever seen.

Her hand sneaked out from under his jacket to touch his very solid, very real, arm. "You're really here," she said.

"I promised I'd come back."

She straightened up in the chair. "Did I miss anything while I was half asleep? Did the police find the patrol car that Julian stole?"

"Here's the thing. He stole the Ford Ranger when he was disguised as a valet. When he got close to the coast, he changed cars. He had prepared a navy-blue sedan equipped with a light bar on top and a siren. Then he slapped on a state patrol hat and took off after the Town Car."

"How do you know this?"

"The FBI found the abandoned gray sedan. And the Ranger."

She concluded, "So he must have had a third car to make his getaway. Wow, Julian spares no trouble or expense."

"That's what it takes to be a master of disguise," Ryder said. "I'm guessing his plan was to pull you over, shoot Jelly and grab Alyssa. He didn't count on y'all being armed and dangerous."

"He could have waited us out," she said. "We didn't have all that much ammo."

"Not only is Julian a shapeshifter but he's also a survivor. Probably weighed the risk against the chances of getting away with Alyssa and decided to escape."

"A coward," she said with cool distaste. "Lucky for us."

"That's all I know for now."

"Did the doctors say anything about Jelly?"

"He's still in ICU, not allowed to have visitors." He peeled his jacket off her as he handed over one of her own sweatshirts, a pair of black yoga pants and a pair of sneakers. "Alyssa got into your room at Leeward Manor and told me to bring these."

"I'm shocked that she didn't insist on a sequined cocktail dress."

"Your tastes are different."

"What do you expect?" She slipped the sweatshirt on over her dress. The added warmth felt good but she missed the masculine smell of his jacket. "Alyssa is a dainty little flower, and I'm a giant redwood. We'd look ridiculous wearing matching outfits."

"Don't put yourself down," he said. "You're built like one of those Victoria's Secret models."

"An underwear model?" Her eyebrows raised. "How do you know I look like that?"

"I remember." His grin widened, and dimples curled on both cheeks.

When they were together before, he had seen her in all stages of undress, but Nicole had never worn excessively frilly or lacy or satiny underwear. She'd always been a practical cotton-panties woman. "I don't even own a thong."

"Says the woman with 'Babe' written across the butt of her panties." Another grin. "Now I've got a riddle. Ready? What weighs eighty pounds, fits into two suitcases and is worth four-and-a half-million dollars?"

The mention of "four and a half million" clued her in. "This must have something to do with the shipment being smuggled. I'm going to say drugs. Fentanyl or meth or packages of cocaine."

"None of the above."

"Then it's got to be some kind of illegal weaponry or rocket launchers."

"Nope."

"I give up. Tell me."

"Twenty and fifty-dollar bills. Four and half million worth."

Her eyes widened. Working at the casino in Las Vegas, she'd seen huge bundles of cash in straps but never stopped to figure out how much those bundles were worth. She whispered, "Are you telling me the shipment being smuggled is cash?"

"Counterfeit bills," he said. "And it's likely much bigger because twenties are easier to pass than hundreds, especially with the new security stripe, watermark and raised printing. If the shipment is in twenties, it's more like 2,000 pounds and 80 square feet. If it's a mix of twenties, tens and fives, it'll be several times larger."

From his expression, she could tell he was figuring the dimensions and weight in his head. More than any of his other occupations, Ryder was an accountant. Numbers fascinated him. "Why?" she asked.

"The counterfeits have been printed offshore. The shipment will arrive here and be distributed across the country. Most counterfeiters are caught because they work in a limited area and can be surveyed by local police. If they're spread out all over the country, they're harder to root out and find."

"You're right about the twenties and lower denominations."

"In this digital age, not many people rely on physical cash."

"Not even the casinos," she said. Dragging Rossini Enterprises into this scheme made a bit more sense. If the counterfeiters were the same gang that Ryder had exposed, they had the added motive of revenge. They'd hate Rossini for working with the feds.

One of Tony's men who had been sitting across the room came toward them and sat in the chair beside Nicole. "What are you two whispering about?"

"Riddles," Ryder said. "Are y'all fixing to be here the rest of the night?"

"We're on duty until nine tomorrow morning. I guess that's nine today, huh. Then somebody replaces us."

Deputy Farley joined them. "I've got to go. Is that okay?"

Nicole pulled herself out of the uncomfortable chair. Her joints creaked from being in a cramped position. "Until we get Jelly out of ICU and into a regular room, I'd like y'all to stay." Inwardly, she groaned, realizing that she'd picked up Ryder's drawl.

Taking the yoga pants, sweatshirt and sneakers with her, she went to the nurses' station at the center of the hall. This late at night, only two nurses in scrubs were working.

The older nurse, with her long straight hair in a ponytail and a plastic name tag that said "Graham, R.N." looked up as Nicole approached. She gave a weary smile. "Good timing. We're getting ready to move your friend to his own room. You requested private, didn't you?"

She nodded. "I did."

"Well, you're lucky. We have something on the fourth floor, but if we get crowded tomorrow, we might need to give him a roommate."

"Is he awake?" Nicole asked.

"He's said a couple of words, but doesn't make much sense."

"Can we go with him to the room?"

Graham, R.N. glanced at the three bodyguards plus Ryder, who had moved to stand behind Nicole. "I'm not sure you'll all fit in the elevator. Maybe you and one other to start with."

"Thank you so much, Nurse Graham. I appreciate everything you do."

"You're an ER resident in Portland, aren't you?"

"Yes, ma'am."

"Hang on to that sunny attitude after you become a doctor. Kind words go a long way."

Nicole told the guys that she and Ryder would accompany Jelly to his private room. They could follow on the next elevator. Then she dashed into the ladies' room to change into the yoga pants, sweatshirt and sneakers. Her blood-spattered dress went directly into the trash can along with her half-shredded, patterned tights. Her feet were so happy in the comfy sneakers that she almost danced on the bathroom tiles. A glance in the mirror over the sink ended that celebration.

Her curly, unkempt hair had tangled into a life of its own. She'd already washed off her makeup, which meant that the bluish circles under her eyes were natural and permanent until she got some sleep. Since her crossbody purse held only medical supplies and her cell phone, there wasn't much she could do about her appearance.

She rejoined the men in the hallway outside the ICU, where they waited for the gurney and portable IV pole, manned by two orderlies in aqua scrubs, to emerge carrying Jelly. He gave them a wave as he rolled past and was transported into the elevator.

Nicole stood beside the gurney, took his hand and squeezed. She'd spoken to the surgeon earlier and felt confident in reassuring him. "Everything went well. You're going to be fine."

He gave a slight nod. Every move he made seemed to require serious effort. "Wanna go home now."

"Tony sent two guys to look after you."

His mouth twitched as if trying to smile. "Tony's a good boss."

"And you're a great bodyguard."

The elevator reached the fourth floor, and the orderlies did their job, shifting him from the gurney onto the bed. A team of nurses hooked him up to an oxygen canula, checked his IV catheter, attached nodes for the heart monitor and tended to the white bandage on his upper left chest. Though satisfied that Jelly was receiving excellent care, Nicole hated to see the big man like this. A wave of anger washed through her. She wanted the hit man behind bars.

She looked up at Ryder. "Are you any closer to finding Julian?"

"He's disappeared. The guy is slippery. He went from wearing a beard and a cowl like Death to a clean-shaven valet to a state patrolman. Who knows what his next disguise will be."

"How about convict?"

"I'd vote for that."

SHE STROKED JELLY'S forehead and didn't feel a fever. His eyes closed, probably sleeping. Still, she leaned down and spoke to him. "I'm going to leave you now. You have two armed men guarding, so you ought to be okay. I'll be back tomorrow."

He made no response, but she was content to see the steady rise and fall of his breathing. Still alive in spite of the bullet and the concussion. When she stepped away from his bedside, the exhaustion she'd held at bay descended like a tidal wave, swamping her and threatening to carry her out to sea. With her last bit of energy, she sent texts to Alyssa and Tony. Numbly, she watched Ryder organize the two Rossini men who would guard Jelly. He also dismissed Deputy Farley and thanked him for a job well done.

Glad that he'd taken charge, she allowed herself to sink into silence. No need to think. Her brain emptied of conscious thought, and she clung to Ryder's arm as he guided her through the hospital to the exit and tucked her into the passenger seat of his SUV. The chilly night air woke her up enough to speak.

"This was supposed to be our time," she said. "You and me and a shower. And a bed."

"I'm not giving up." He gave her a light kiss on the cheek. "I'm still taking a shower and sleeping in your bed."

"I want more." She slowly blinked and leaned back in the passenger seat. "Rain check?"

"Whenever you're ready."

She trusted him. He wouldn't let the moment pass them by.

Chapter Nineteen

After Ryder parked outside Leeward Manor, he looked over at the sleeping woman in the passenger seat. The beam from the lighthouse swept through the trees and crossed the grounds—a reminder to be wary and not take chances. Nicole had been out cold since they'd left the hospital. He checked his wristwatch. It showed 4:12 a.m., almost the same time he'd started his day yesterday. Time to get back in the saddle.

"Nicole." He whispered her name, not wanting to startle her awake. "Nicole, we need to get moving."

Still sleeping, she adjusted her position, and her head turned toward him. The lights in the parking lot shone on her face. So delicate but strong. So beautiful. Her full lips parted as she breathed steadily. He reached across the console to touch her shoulder and wake her up, then hesitated. Watching her closely, he noted that her eyes appeared to be moving behind her closed eyelids. A sure signal of REM sleep, the most relaxing phase of slumber when the most dramatic and vivid dreams occurred. On the chance that she was dreaming about him, he decided not to wake her.

Instead, he reached under the seat where he'd stashed his briefcase and took out the SAT phone he used to contact his HSI supervisor in Washington, DC. Even though it was only a little after seven her time, early to be at work, he wasn't surprised when SAC Marianne Trevino picked up. "Howdy, cowboy," she greeted him. "Aren't you the early bird? The guy who gets the worm."

"Not this time. The worm made a clean getaway."

After he briefed her on yesterday's events, he brought up the important point. "The FBI has a statement from an informant saying that the shipment scheduled for tomorrow is four-and-a-half-million dollars in counterfeit bills."

"Counterfeiting is our jurisdiction. We should be in on this." She sounded irritated. "Do you have a name for the confidential informant?"

"Daniel DeBarge, otherwise known as Danny Danger the Salty Dog. He's the manager of Leeward Manor and claims he overheard a conversation. He could only identify one of the speakers who works at the Manor in the kitchen."

"Did the FBI take the kitchen worker into custody?"

"They did," he confirmed, "but didn't arrest Danny Danger. They're hoping he'll be useful with other information."

"I hope you passed this intel along to the guy who will be your supervisor when you transfer to the coast. A huge cargo of funny money deserves more attention on our part."

"I notified him last night." And he'd taken pains to not embarrass the guy for missing the boat on this. "He'll be talking with you later today. He agreed with me that the FBI should handle arrests for the smugglers since they already have agents in the loop. But the final word is up to you."

"Yes," she said decisively. "The delivery is scheduled for tomorrow, early afternoon. Not enough time to get organized. And you'll be there, representing HSI interests."

"Yep."

"I'll want a full report," she said. "Any new leads on your hit man?"

"Not a thing."

"My advice," Agent Trevino said, "is to cancel the wedding."

"Yeah, sure." If Alyssa didn't get married tomorrow, she'd turn into a raging Bridezilla. He'd rather face an army of hit men. "That's not going to happen."

Her voice took on a pseudo-sweet tone. "What about your lady friend, Ryder? Have you patched things up?"

His gaze rested on Nicole. "I hope so."

"You keep dreaming, cowboy."

He ended the call and put away his SAT phone while she continued to sleep. When he reached toward her and touched her shoulder, she slapped his hand away. Her eyebrows twitched into a frown. She mumbled. "No, no, no, no."

"What's wrong?"

"So much wrong." She shifted. "So damned much."

Even in sleep, she worried. A lot could go wrong. There were all the issues with Alyssa and the wedding. Also, Nicole fussed about Jelly's care at the hospital, the shipment of counterfeit bills and the hit man who was a master of disguise. She had way too much on her plate, and he wanted to wipe away her stress.

If she'd been alert, she would have objected to having him be the caretaker. But she was still mostly asleep when he lifted her from the passenger seat and set her feet on the ground while he closed and locked the door. Earlier when he'd been at the Manor, he'd unloaded his suitcase and garment bag from the SUV into Nicole's suite. He had no other burden as he lifted her in his arms and carried her across the parking lot. She wasn't a lightweight, but her body felt so warm and cuddly in his arms that he enjoyed carrying her, especially when her arms wrapped around his neck and she snuggled into the curve of his throat.

At the front entrance, he started to set her feet down so he could use the key, but the door swung open. Daniel DeBarge aka Confidential FBI Informant, stood there, snickering and making a big deal of checking his wristwatch. "Did you two have a late night?"

"We've been at the hospital," Ryder informed him coldly. The nosy little snitch knew exactly where they'd been. "Step aside."

Danny backed up. He cocked his head like a pirate's parrot. "I saw you took your stuff out of the third-floor bedroom. Checking out?"

"I'm staying in Nicole's suite. Feel free to give somebody else that garret."

"Aye, matey. Sure thing."

He stared at the little snitch, trying to recall if they'd met when he was investigating the counterfeiting, but Danny didn't look the least bit familiar from past acquaintance. Still, Ryder didn't for a minute believe that the manager of Leeward Manor had "just happened to overhear" a conversation with the smugglers. Somehow, he'd made a connection with guys who ran a multimillion-dollar scheme. No doubt, Danny thought he'd make a buck. A dangerous game.

Still carrying Nicole, Ryder took the elevator to the second floor and went to her suite, where he unlocked the door and deposited her on the bed. He flopped down beside her. Though dog-tired, he didn't want to sleep yet. All day long, he'd been longing for a shower.

Though she barely had stirred while he was carrying her, she bolted upright on the bed. Her first words echoed his thought. "I need to take a shower," she said.

"Me, too."

"I'm filthy and have dried blood all over."

"You can go first." Ever the gentleman.

Her gaze darted around the suite, then landed on him. "How did I get here?"

"Do you believe in magic?"

"No."

Her answer was point-blank and definite. Frankly, he agreed. Though he liked computer fantasy games and occasional cosplay, he'd seen too much of real life to trust in wizards. "I'm speaking in metaphor here. Magic can happen when two powerful people—like you and me—join forces."

She was awake enough to scoff. She hopped off the bed, went to the dresser, took out fresh clothes, and headed for the bathroom where she stood in the doorway and gazed at him. "Thanks, Ryder, for everything. I'll be out in a minute."

He lay back down but forced his eyes to stay open. No matter how tired he was, he wanted magic to strike tonight. Two powerful people acting as one. He wanted to believe that would happen no matter how doubtful it seemed.

IN THE BATHROOM, Nicole peeled off her yoga pants and sweatshirt. Though she'd tried to wipe away the traces of Jelly's blood, her arms and legs had smudges. While working in the ER, she barely noticed the spatter and goop that accumulated on her scrubs during the day. But as soon as she got home, she needed to clean up. Like resetting a clock or rebooting her laptop, she needed a shower to get back to normal.

Before diving into the spacious, frosted-glass shower, she took a moment to acknowledge to herself that Ryder had come home with her and intended to spend the night. *He was here!* The man of her dreams was here, and she'd left him sitting on the edge of her mattress, un-kissed and un-snuggled, despite two years' worth of fantasies. Well, what could she do? Ignore the fact that she was gritty and blood-spattered? No way, she wanted to do this right.

Using the jasmine-scented soap she'd brought from home, she lathered, scrubbed and rinsed. The steamy, hot water sluiced down her body, soothing her senses and erasing signs of gore. Wouldn't it be great to so easily cleanse her mind? The moment when Jelly was shot and crashed to the ground seemed to be implanted in her brain. Vivid and horrendous, the scene replayed in an endless loop.

Nicole couldn't help feeling like she was somehow to blame. She knew more about Julian than either Alyssa or

Jelly. Dealing with him meant a high degree of caution was necessary. She should have insisted on more bodyguards or convinced Alyssa to stay at the Manor, tucked away from the hit man. She'd failed to protect her friend, and Jelly had paid the price.

It wasn't like her to be so careless. She owed the Rossini family. They'd taken care of her since she was eleven. Tony and Stella had filled the role of parents for her. Alyssa was like her little sister. They were her family, and she loved them.

Tonight, she'd let them down. She never should have allowed the hit man to get so close.

She stuck her head under the shower spray and washed her hair with a floral and citrus shampoo—a fragrance that complemented the jasmine. The shower should have revitalized her, but she felt her strength washing down the drain. The brief nap in Ryder's car hadn't been enough. Maybe this wasn't the right time.

Outside the shower, she toweled dry and slipped into a long-sleeved, midnight-blue, satin, button-up nightshirt that fell to the middle of her thighs. With another towel wrapped around her damp hair, she opened the door. Steam poured out of the bathroom into the bedroom.

Ryder was stretched out on the bed, watching her. After a lazy smile, he said, "You look like a goddess rising from the mists."

"That's a very poetic image."

"Not if you're a gamer."

"Right," she said. "I've seen those babes in the computer games. Real women don't look like that. They don't have totally unblemished skin, cascading hair, boobies like grapefruit and teeny-tiny waists."

"I like the way you look. Better than a cartoon heroine." He rose from the bed. Though still wearing his jeans, he'd changed to a plain black T-shirt. His cowboy hat didn't fit with the gamer identity but looked good on him. He sauntered toward her. "You've got those long, shapely legs. And if I unbutton that silky nightshirt, I'm pretty sure I'll see a fine, firm set of—"

"Stop right there," she said. "You need to take a shower before you come to bed."

"Whoa, granny. That's fussy."

She shrugged. "Please."

"You're probably right. After a day's worth of driving, a car chase, a wine-tasting with crackers and stinky cheese, and a visit to the ICU, I don't guess I smell like a rose garden."

"Leather, cedar and musk," she said, remembering the aroma of his jacket. She lowered herself onto the bed. "I'll be right here, waiting for you."

After he placed his hat upside down on the dresser because it was bad luck to rest the hat on the brim, he looked her over and frowned. "I don't want to leave you out here alone."

"Seriously? Do you think Julian will break in and attack me?"

"I think the minute I close the bathroom door behind me, you're going to fall asleep."

He might be right about that. Her brief catnaps hadn't cured her exhaustion. "If that happens, you have my permission to wake me."

"I wouldn't have the heart. Your day has been rougher than mine." He pulled the T-shirt off over his head. "I've got a better plan."

She blinked hard. Her tired eyes were nearly overwhelmed by the devastatingly gorgeous vision of his bare chest and torso. "I'm listening."

He took his phone from his pocket and set it on the bedside table next to his gun. "I'll get in the shower, and you come into the bathroom and do whatever it is you do after you shampoo."

"Wait a minute." She couldn't believe this idea. "You want me to blow dry my hair while you're naked in the shower?"

He held out his hand toward her. When she took it, he yanked her off the bed and into his arms. Brute force. Not something she usually liked, but in this case…she liked being overwhelmed. Her jasmine fragrance mingled with his masculine aroma. Not so bad, after all. He pressed his mouth to hers, sending shock waves through her body. *Forget the smell. And the shower.* She broke away from him. "Okay, I think we can go to bed now, right now."

"Not a chance." He stepped backward into the bathroom. "I like this game."

She watched as he unzipped his jeans and stripped them off. As he stood before her in his snug black boxers, her memories of him merged with reality. During the two years they'd been apart, he'd gotten even sexier, something she hardly believed possible. As if to emphasize her unspoken opinion, he snapped the waistband on his briefs.

In a slightly husky voice, she said, "I'm ready to stop playing."

"Giving up so soon?" He lowered the waistband a few inches, drawing her attention to the bulge inside. "My dear old Texan granny had a saying. 'When y'all start down a trail, it's best to finish the journey to the end.'"

She remembered. "When you were undercover, you used to talk about your Texas family. Was that a lie?"

"I'd never lie about Granny, and I had to be Texan because I couldn't hide my drawl. I grew up near Midland."

"And your father was a rancher?"

"An oil man," he said. "My uncle owned a ranch, and I worked there."

Though she was keeping up her end of the conversation, her focus remained fixated on his boxer briefs. "When we first met, you told me your name was Ryder. I thought undercover operatives used an alias."

"I used Ryder as my last name. First name was supposed to be Sam." He inched the waistband lower. "I'm glad I fudged on the alias. Sure would hate to hear you call out another man's name while we're having sex."

He tore off his briefs, stepped behind the frosted-glass shower doors and turned on the hot water. His blurred silhouette moved suggestively through the streaming water, and she had to turn away before she tore off her nightshirt, leaped into the shower and wrapped her legs around him.

"Hey, Nicole, is there any soap out there that doesn't smell sweet and girly?"

She found a mini bar of wrapped cedarwood on the counter, opened the shower door with her eyes closed and held it toward him. "Here."

"Much obliged."

His hands were wet as he took the soap from her. Though not looking, she felt the steam and the spray. Her fingers lingered close to his slick, naked body. "You're a tease, Ryder Beckham."

"So it's working."

There was no reason she had to stay in the bathroom, but walking away felt cowardly. She turned away from the frosted-glass shower and confronted her reflection in the mirror over the sink. She'd show him that she hadn't lost control. She unwound the towel on her head. Might as well fix her hair.

The roar of her blow dryer covered the splashing from the shower. Knowing that the steam from the shower would activate her curls, she didn't try for a smooth and sultry look. She was done in a few moments, pushed her waves into shape and leaned close to the mirror to apply a smear of rosy-pink lipstick.

She went to the door. "I'm leaving you now. I'll wait in bed."

"Don't fall asleep."

"I'll try not to." *Not a chance.*

His striptease had wakened every cell in her body. She threw back the covers on the bed and stretched out on the crisp white sheets. Sleep was the furthest thing in her mind. After she tried a few different poses and wondered if she should take off her nightshirt, she settled, lying on her side and facing the bathroom door.

When he emerged, she tried to think of a witty comment, but his appearance stole her voice. He wore only a towel around his waist. She had never been a "lights out" kind of lover, and this moment was no exception. She admired the pattern of his chest hair and his lean torso. His long, muscular arms and legs showed a man who exercised often. He whipped off the towel as he approached, gloriously naked, and lay beside her on the bed.

"Take a whiff," he said. "Do I stink?"

"Not bad." Everything about him was sheer perfection, but she didn't want to pay too many compliments and make him cocky. His ego didn't need pumping up. Nor did any other part of his body. "I've smelled better."

He brushed her hair off her forehead and ran his fingers through her curls. "You have good hair."

"Too curly."

"I like the untamed look," he said. "You don't have to fuss with your hairdo. Just shake your head, and it falls into place."

"Enough of the beauty-shop talk." She leaned toward him. "Kiss me."

"Not yet."

His tone made it very clear that he was in charge. He pushed her shoulder and tilted her onto her back. At the same time, he threw his leg across her body, pinning her to the bed. Then he stared into her face, devouring her with his gaze.

"What are we waiting for?" she asked.

"I've been thinking about making love to you for a very long time. And I don't want to rush. I want to appreciate every inch of you. From your hair to your hazel eyes that change color with your mood. Right now, they're glowing like gold." He slid his hand down the side of her face and stroked her throat all the way down to her collarbone. "And your jaw, your slender neck."

She knew he was doing more than taking visual inventory. His rock-hard erection pressed against her thigh. Clear evidence that he wanted her as much as she wanted him. Rising up from the pillow, she forced the issue, joining her mouth with his.

The pressure of her kiss started light and then deepened. He probed with his tongue, forcing her lips apart. When they separated, she was breathing as hard as if she'd run a mile. Her pulse raced.

He started unfastening her shirt, fumbling with the buttons. She arched toward him. "Rip it off."

Ryder didn't need a second invitation. He grasped each side of her satin shirt and yanked. The sound of cloth tearing aroused her, fed the building frenzy within her. He squeezed her breasts, pinched the nipples. Licking and nipping, he drove her straight out of her mind.

Being so far out of control wasn't like her. She had a deserved reputation for being disciplined, practical and predictable. Not a wild animal. Or maybe she was. Maybe we all were.

Since she wasn't wearing any of her sensible cotton panties, they were both naked. When he lay on top of her, she welcomed his weight pressing down upon her. Their freshly showered bodies rubbed together, and she started to sweat. Another shower might be necessary.

In a husky voice, he said, "I need a condom."

"Drawer in the bedside table."

"I'm surprised." He reared back and looked down at her. "Were y'all planning for this to happen all along?"

"Alyssa left them for me."

"Thoughtful." He fished out the condom and expertly slipped it on. "Where were we?"

"You were on top," she said. "Next time, it's my turn."

"I saw you had a whole string of condoms in there."

"Wishful thinking," she said boldly.

She welcomed him back to his former position. He was on top, bracing himself to enter her slowly. With every inch he went deeper and deeper, she abandoned herself to a trembling riot of sensation. Why had she broken it off with him? Why hadn't she forgiven?

Never again would she turn her back on this man. He was her destiny.

Chapter Twenty

After only a few hours of sleep, Ryder awakened to the buzz of his cell phone on the bedside table. He should have been groggy after yesterday's actions that climaxed, so to speak, in last night, but he was instantly alert, revitalized and highly aware of the sweet, warm female snuggled in his arms. Though he tried to reach for the phone without disturbing her, she sat up and tossed her head.

"Answer it," she said.

He cleared his throat and picked up the phone. Agent Murdock greeted him impatiently. "It's after eight, Ryder. Get your butt in gear and meet me downstairs."

"Give me fifteen minutes."

He figured he could wash up, brush his teeth and get dressed in seven minutes. It would take two more to lock up and jog down to the first floor. That left six minutes to be with Nicole. Not nearly enough time to do what he wanted to do.

She clicked on the bedside lamp and leaned back against a pillow with a sheet covering her breasts. An odd position considering their brazen lovemaking. Last night, she'd been all over him with the lights full on, flaunting her beautiful body.

"Good morning," she purred. "You look surprised that I'm awake. I'm an ER doc, remember? I get emergency calls, just like you. Mostly for multicar crashes or natural disasters. All-hands-on-deck situations."

Like him, she was a first responder. "Agent Murdock needs me right away."

"I don't like having you called away, but I understand."

"I don't like it, either. There are a whole lot of reasons I don't want to leave you alone." Most of them wouldn't make it into the federal agent's handbook. "I'm concerned about Julian and his next attempt. Y'all are in danger, both you and Alyssa. The hit man isn't going to stop coming for her."

"We won't be going anywhere. Today, we'll concentrate on wedding organization and getting ready. Tonight is the rehearsal dinner."

"I'm sure Tony will assign another bodyguard or two. You and Alyssa need to stay close to them. Do what they say."

She reached toward him. Her fingers touched his arm and glided down to his wrist. "Maybe you could volunteer for that job."

"Lady, there's no other body I'd rather guard. But I've got to figure out the smuggling plot and put an end to the Julian threat."

"Maybe later, you could come to the hospital with me to check on Jelly."

"Didn't you just tell me that you weren't going out?"

"I've got to see my patient."

When she tugged his hand, he couldn't resist coming close to her and stealing a gentle kiss. Though he wanted more, the day was already started. Reluctantly, he stepped away from the bed, grabbed his jeans and went into the bathroom. About six minutes later, he emerged. Almost ready to go.

While he was putting on his button-down shirt, sweater and gun, he had another thought. "Since you're going to be here all day, would you please arrange a time when I can talk to Alyssa? I want to find out how and why her wedding ended up in Consolation Cove."

"Because it's where she and Michael first kissed."

"Romantic."

But there had to be more to the story. He was looking for a link between Danny Danger and the men he'd overheard. Also, Nicole had mentioned that Alexei Volkov had suggested Leeward Manor as the location for the wedding. The Volkov Group might be involved in the smuggling. He slipped on his leather jacket.

Too many loose ends. He needed to tie it all together in a big red bow. Resolute, he marched to the door.

"Ryder, wait. Aren't you forgetting something?"

When he looked over his shoulder toward her, he saw her sly little smile. "What?"

"Your cowboy hat."

"Thank you, ma'am. Much obliged."

He locked the door when he left, and headed for the staircase. In the dining area, a typical continental breakfast had been laid out on a long table. Several guests helped themselves to donuts, baked goods, fruit and veggies. There was also an omelet station for a hot breakfast with sausage and bacon.

Agent Murdock rose from the small round table where she'd been sitting. In her hand was a large disposable coffee cup. Before he joined her, Ryder grabbed a cup of his own. Together, they went through one of the French doors onto the patio. The heavy, morning fog gave the feeling that they were alone and secluded, but he knew that wasn't so. They walked away from the Manor, aware that eavesdroppers, like Danny, could be nearby. Agent Murdock slapped on a soft, gray bucket hat.

At the edge of the patio, she paused and gazed across the dew-drenched, semicultivated grounds to the gazebo and the lighthouse beyond. "Nice view," she said. "Mysterious and evocative, like the Gothic novels I used to read."

This was the first time she'd volunteered personal information, but he wasn't surprised that her plain, solid exterior masked a sensitive soul. "Did you pass on your love of Gothics to your kids?"

"How did you know I have kids?"

"You've got a mom vibe."

"Two sons, teenagers. They don't think they like Gothics, but they constantly play fantasy computer games with ghosts, wizards and witches."

"My kind of people," Ryder said.

She stepped off the patio and walked onto the path through overgrown garden weeds. "Last night, while you were sleeping, the FBI did some serious investigative work on the navy-blue sedan used by the hit man you call Julian. His fingerprints—the prints belonging to the supposedly deceased John Mitchell—were all over the car, which was rented in Portland to another false identity who paid in cash."

"Did you check the cash? There's counterfeiting involved."

"Give me some credit, Ryder. We verified. Your hit man didn't use funny money."

Considering that they hadn't located the car until after ten o'clock last night, he was impressed by how much they'd accomplished. "Y'all did good."

"There's more," she continued. "He left behind receipts for the purchase of equipment he needed to put together the light bar and siren. Went to stores in Portland. Paid cash."

"Was there CC surveillance in the stores?"

"We got several different images, almost like he was posing. In one store, he wore a slouchy hat pulled down on his forehead and a fuzzy beard obscuring his jawline. In another, it was a ginger wig, prosthetic nose and jaw. Comparing those photos with the artist's sketch from Brother Gabriel, it's hard to believe they're the same man."

Ryder put the information together. "Like he's two different people. In one version, he's a ruthless professional, capable of meticulous planning and thinking ahead. In the other, he makes sloppy mistakes like leaving fingerprints and receipts."

"John Mitchell entered Saint Macarius Monastery three years ago, apparently on the run," she said. "It's possible his time there changed him."

"I hope you're not suggesting he found the Lord and got saved. Even in the abbey, Julian continued his evil ways. Brother Gabe suspects him of the cold-blooded murder of Brother Ezra, suffocating the old man with a pillow."

"A crime that was neither reported nor investigated," the FBI agent pointed out.

Ryder had done his own follow-up. "I contacted Father Bruno, the prior at Saint Macarius, to get more intel. He couldn't tell me who recommended Brother Julian or anything about his life prior to coming to the abbey. His file had been tampered with, which Brother Gabe already confessed to doing."

"And this Father Bruno doesn't know anything more about him?"

"He says no. He thinks the abbot will have more about Julian's past. I should be able to talk to him this afternoon."

Agent Murdock stopped at the edge of the grassy area leading to the gazebo where the seating for the ceremony tomorrow would be arranged. "Weird place for a wedding."

"Kind of romantic." At least, Alyssa thought so.

"Would you want to get married here?"

Ryder hadn't dared to think about marriage until last night with Nicole. Not only was she kind, smart and beautiful, but she was sexier than he remembered. "You know, Murdock, I'd get married anywhere she wanted. No questions asked."

Chapter Twenty-One

In her role as maid of honor, Nicole took her responsibilities seriously. All morning, she'd been glued to Alyssa and her mom, checking the order with the official photographer, verifying the delivery with a local florist and getting a mani-pedi with Alyssa, even though nobody was going to see her tootsies through the dyed-to-match pumps that went with her acid-green, floor-length gown.

After a salad for lunch, she took off for a trip to visit Jelly in the hospital. The reprieve from bridesmaid duties felt like a vacation. Leaving Alyssa with her new bodyguard team—two physically fit young men—she got into the SUV with Ryder, her own private guard. She nodded to Brother Gabe in the back seat.

Ryder settled behind the steering wheel. "Gabe did such a fine job identifying Julian last night that I asked him to come to the hospital with us. He's our early alert system, watching out for anybody suspicious."

"Wish I could do more," he said. Nicole heard a note of shame in his voice. Though he'd nearly deafened her in the bell tower, she liked the little monk.

"If I wasn't for you," Ryder said, "we might not have caught up with Julian in time to stop him last night."

"Me and Mouse are getting close to figuring out who developed the electromagnetic pulse and the hack. We're nearly as good as the FBI crypto team."

When he reached up and adjusted his clerical collar, Nicole wondered if the fit was too tight. Working with Mouse had given Gabe an outlet for his computer interests. She seriously doubted he was keeping up with his daily prayers. Might be time for him to switch his mission in life. "Have you ever thought of getting a job as a teacher in one of the parish schools?" she asked. "Maybe teaching computer science."

"I've been thinking about it," he said. "I'd have to get more education and certification. Maybe at Gonzaga in Washington. They're Jesuit, but I can work something out."

"Gonzaga has a great basketball program," Ryder said.

"Yeah, well, I wouldn't be going there for the sports. I'd be studying. That's how I can contribute to the community and make the best use of my talents. Besides, I'm too short."

"How about those Ducks?"

Ryder launched into a conversation about the U of O team based in Eugene, and Brother Gabriel joined in. Since Oregon didn't have a pro football or baseball team, college level sports took on huge importance. Plus, Ryder had special insight based on talking to one of the football-playing Caldicott twins last night.

Obviously, neither of these guys wanted to hear her commentary about the minutiae of wedding planning. Happily, she could forget the flower arrangements and whether the four-tier cake would arrive on time. With her eyes closed, she leaned back in the seat. Being with Ryder relaxed her. He made her feel safe. Not that she needed a man to protect her, but it was nice to open her eyes and see him behind the wheel, driving them into a future together. Making love last night had cemented the relationship they started two years ago.

At St. Catherine hospital, Ryder cruised into the emergency parking area, probably expecting to take advantage of his HSI status to snag a prime spot. Before he could flash his badge, Brother Gabriel made the sign of the cross and spoke to the security officer who was watching over the parking lot. The guard bowed his head and stepped back.

Nicole grinned. Nice to know there were still places where a monk outranked a federal agent. Inside St. Catherine's, Nicole expertly navigated the labyrinth of corridors to the fourth floor where Jelly's private room was about halfway down the hall. Gabe paused at the nurses' station to greet a nun in a white wimple and traditional habit. Nicole wasn't surprised to find that a monk from St. Macarius Monastery knew the sisters at the hospital.

He gestured for her and Ryder to go forward. "I'll catch up," he said.

Ryder ducked his head and spoke quietly so only she could hear. "I don't think our pal Gabe is going to stay cloistered much longer."

"He doesn't seem destined for a life of quiet contemplation," she agreed as they entered Jelly's room. "Gonzaga, beware."

In addition to the bodyguard Papa Rossini had assigned to watch over Jelly, other guests were in the room. Nonna Rossini and Dmitry Orloff stood at his bedside. Nonna chattered like an angry chipmunk while the tall, austere Orloff looked over her shoulder. When Nonna spotted Nicole and Ryder, she kissed Jelly's forehead and squeezed his hand before she stalked across the room toward them.

Though she kept her voice hushed as befitted a hospital visit, her words rang with intensity. "Nicole, how did this happen? Jelly is a good man. Why would anyone do him harm?"

Really? Nonna was a Rossini. She knew better. Nicole reminded her, "His job was keeping Alyssa safe. It's a hazardous occupation."

Nonna turned her attention to Ryder. "Take off that stupid cowboy hat. Where were you when Jelly was shot?"

Without removing his hat or answering her rhetorical question, he combatted her raging hostility with politeness. "It's good to see you, ma'am."

"Good manners," Nonna said.

"Just trying to keep you happy."

While Nicole approached Jelly, she noted the various tubes and wires monitoring his vitals. Earlier, she'd called his doctor and surgeon for an update on his condition and learned he was doing as well as could be expected. They wanted him to stay hospitalized one more day, but he'd probably be released in time to get to the wedding.

"Looking good," she said as she stepped up to the side of his bed. He seemed alert. His color had improved. "The doctor said you're fine, but he mentioned something about high blood pressure."

"Yeah, my doc in Las Vegas gave me pills. I don't like the side effects."

"There's an alternative," she said. "It's called diet and exercise."

Nonna waved goodbye, and Orloff escorted her from the room. For a moment, Nicole chatted with Jelly about who was assigned to guard Alyssa and how the wedding was proceeding. Then Gabe bustled into the room and Ryder signaled for her to join them.

Nicole stood between her tall, handsome cowboy and the excited little monk. "What?"

"The man with Nonna Rossini," Gabe said. "I recognized him."

"Mr. Orloff?" She cocked her head to one side. "We know who he is. A friend of the groom's family."

"His first name is Dmitry," Brother Gabriel said with extreme clarity. "Father Dmitry. There was a photo of him in Brother Julian's file."

"The file you destroyed?"

He nodded. "Dmitry is the church official who recommended Julian to the abbot."

A link between the Volkov Group and Brother Julian. She didn't like to hear about this possible connection.

Chapter Twenty-Two

At 2:43 p.m., Ryder exited the hospital parking lot. In the passenger seat, Nicole yawned and stretched her arms over her head, scraping her knuckles across the SUV ceiling. "Just think," she said, "in a little more than twenty-four hours, this will all be over. Alyssa and Michael will be married and celebrating at the reception before they take off on their honeymoon."

"What's on the sched for today?" he asked.

"The four o'clock run-through at the gazebo with the whole wedding party. A possible fiasco with a minimum of twenty people. The officiant, five bridesmaids including me and five groomsmen led by Dirk Petrovich. A flower girl and ringbearer, accompanied by parents. The immediate families: Tony, Nonna and Stella on the Rossini side. Plus Alexei and his young wife for the Volkov Group."

"And assorted bodyguards," he said. "How long do you think it'll take?"

"There's a 30/5 rule that applies to weddings. Whatever takes five minutes in real life will eat up thirty minutes in wedding-planner time. My best guess is that we'll be rehearsing until after five, when we go into the Manor for a festive dinner."

He detected a note of dread in her voice. "Expecting trouble?"

"With the leaders of two powerful families facing off, a

gaggle of giggling bridesmaids and the impending arrival of illegal cargo? Hah! What could go wrong?"

"And there's no way to call it off? Or to postpone?"

"If we even try, I promise you that sweet little Alyssa will whip out her Glock and start blasting. This morning, she nearly shot the cell phone when the photographer said he'd be late this afternoon."

Before they started their return journey, Ryder had tried again to reach the abbot at Saint Macarius Monastery, hoping to verify Brother Gabriel's recollection about Dmitry Orloff being the Father Dmitry who'd vouched for Julian and helped him get accepted at the monastery. Still, the abbot was out of touch. Father Bruno promised he'd have the head man call the moment he returned to the abbey.

As soon as Ryder had that confirmation, he needed to interrogate Orloff to find out if he'd known Julian aka John Mitchell was a hit man. Had this supposed priest willingly created a hideout for Julian? Or had he been duped?

In the meantime, he'd take Nicole and Brother Gabe back to Leeward Manor where there were several people to watch over their safety. Driving the same route that Jelly had taken last night, he glanced over at Nicole in the passenger seat. She'd experienced a traumatic event last night, and he wondered if she was affected. Not everybody was accustomed to a high-speed chase with a hit man in pursuit. Not to mention the shoot-out. "Do you recognize these roads?"

"Not specifically this route," she said. "But I've been living in Oregon, off and on, for three years. I'm accustomed to the shady coolness of the forests. The light is different, colored by the endless green of the trees, even in autumn. Then we come out at the beautiful, rugged coast. Why do you ask?"

"I worried that you might be suffering from post-traumatic stress."

"Not my thing." She flashed a confident smile. "I'm the person who cleans up trauma for everybody else. Sure, I'm going to remember what happened to Jelly. But it won't poison my mind. I'm well aware of the PTS symptoms."

Her courage and her intelligence amazed him. "Has anybody ever told you how incredible you are?"

"All the time." She snorted a laugh. "I'm surprised you haven't been trampled by the throngs of my admirers."

"Throngs?"

"Maybe one throng. Jelly likes me."

Gabe piped up from the back seat. "If the abbot arranged a hideout for Julian, will he get arrested? It's illegal, right? Aiding and abetting a criminal?"

Ryder shuddered to think of HSI or any other law enforcement authority taking on the Catholic church. "I don't know, Gabe. I'm not a lawyer."

When the SUV emerged from the forest onto Highway 101 with the spectacular views of offshore rock formations and waves with whitecaps, Ryder understood Nicole's fascination with this part of the world. After living most of her life in the arid Nevada deserts, the ocean was alive and boundless. Today, the skies were slightly overcast. He asked her, "Does the fog bother you?"

"Sometimes," she admitted. "But I don't miss all the moisturizer I used to have to put on to keep my skin from getting parched in Las Vegas."

She could make anything sound good. He couldn't wait to live here. With her.

When they approached the Manor, he saw Nonna Rossini standing on the patio. A small, rigid figure in black, she gazed toward the lighthouse. He parked and sent Gabe inside with instructions to check in with the bodyguards and not to tell anybody else about their suspicions of Dmitry.

He and Nicole circled the front of the Manor and approached the tiny woman with her coxcomb of white hair brushed back by the breeze. The weather was cool but not cold, and Nonna had wrapped an exquisite embroidered shawl over her long black dress. She acknowledged them with a sharp nod, almost as though she expected trouble.

"Excuse me," Ryder said, knowing how Nonna valued politeness. "May I ask you a few questions?"

"Ask all you want." She stuck out her pointed little chin. "Whether or not I answer is my choice."

Hostile. Swell. "How well do you know Dmitry Orloff?"

"He's an old friend, a charming man." She turned her head toward the sea. "I was looking forward to spending time with him during the wedding, but he just informed me that he'd been called away."

"I'm sorry," Nicole murmured.

"Don't be. He wasn't special to me. I enjoyed the compliments and the air kisses, but I'll be fine. I always am."

Ryder kept focus on the main issue. He asked Nonna, "Where is he going?"

"I'm not his keeper."

Her expression changed from slightly hostile to heavy-duty suspiciousness. He saw protective walls going up around her. From this point forward, she'd be careful what she said. "Another question, Ms. Rossini. Did you know he was once a priest, known as Father Dmitry?"

"Of course," she said. "That's how we met. He retired only a few years ago."

"Were you aware of his connection to St. Macarius Monastery?"

She frowned and shook her head. "Doesn't surprise me. He was a bishop when he left the priesthood, so he knew everybody on the West Coast and inland as far as Las Vegas. But he never mentioned St. Macarius."

He escorted her and Nicole back into the Manor and alerted one of Tony's armed guards to keep an eye on them. Though he wouldn't interrogate Dmitry until he had final confirmation from the abbot, he contacted Agent Murdock and asked if her men could keep tabs on the former priest. Nonna's mention of his unexpected departure gave Ryder cause for worry. Dmitry could be fleeing the scene of the future crime. Maybe he didn't want to be here when the shipment of funny money arrived.

As soon as he knew Nicole was safe, he went back outside to make other phone calls, talking to his future supervisor in Portland about new intel on the counterfeiters from two years ago. Nobody—not them and not any of the FBI—had uncovered more about Danny Danger.

Finally, he spoke to the abbot, who remembered his contact with Father Dmitry very well and had believed his endorsement of Brother Julian. The abbot mentioned being disappointed in the new member of their abbey who'd seemed less than committed to the prayer-filled, Benedictine way of life.

Understatement of the year. The serial hit man didn't fit the requirements for being monk of the year. Ryder counted them lucky that Julian hadn't cracked his disguise and gone postal on the fudge-making abbey. Only one possible murder in three years? A miracle!

Before he went back into the Manor, Ryder received a call from Agent Murdock. She gave him a quick rundown of how the FBI had searched for Dmitry, who had checked out of his hotel in Consolation Cove. His phone went straight to voice mail. FBI agents in southern Cal visited his home in Newport Beach. The housekeeper hadn't heard from him. Nobody knew where he'd gone. Dmitry Orloff had effectively disappeared.

Ryder's jaw clenched. He should have detained the former priest sooner. No more slipups. With less than twenty-four hours before the wedding, he needed to wrap this investigation.

On the second floor in Leeward Manor, he joined Nicole and Alyssa in the lavish bridal suite. His conversation with Alyssa required privacy, so he took her into the adjoining bedroom where the wedding dress and veil were still hanging, waiting to make their appearance.

Alyssa closed the door. In spite of the prewedding jitters,

she presented a calm, composed appearance as she met his gaze. "What can I do for you, Ryder?"

"First, I want to thank you for getting me and Nicole back together by inviting me to the wedding. We both needed a shove in the right direction."

A satisfied grin creased her lips. "I'm not as silly as I look. And I knew Nicole was still pining away over you. She deserves some happiness."

"You're not silly, not at all. The opposite. You're smart and clever. I trust your intuition."

He watched as she approached the dress and possessively glided her hand over the satin and tulle. In a quiet voice, almost as though she was talking to herself, she said, "I've been thinking about my wedding for years. I didn't sign up for a complicated mess with counterfeiters and computer hacks, the murder of Alan Caldicott, and Jelly being in the hospital. Papa says Rossini Enterprises isn't involved, and I believe him."

"So do I," Ryder echoed.

"But I'm not so sure about the Volkov Group." Her voice trembled. When she looked up at him, her eyes filled with tears. "If Michael is part of a smuggling scheme, I don't think I can go through with this."

He didn't want to break her heart, but she was right. If her fiancé was a crook, it was better to find out now. "I won't lie, Alyssa. I have concerns. Did Nicole tell you about Dmitry?"

"We don't keep secrets from each other. Never have. Never will." Alyssa dashed away her tears. "Tell me what you're concerned about."

Placing his trust in a civilian wasn't always a smart thing to do, but Ryder had no time for investigative poking and prodding. He needed answers, and he needed them fast. "Tell me about the first time you visited Consolation Cove. Why here?"

"Is this about Danny Danger?"

"I can't answer that," he said.

"Are you telling me this information is classified?"

"Kind of."

She rolled her eyes. "You feds are all alike."

"I can't go into details," he said, "but I need your insight. What sold you on this location for your wedding venue?"

"I wanted to come to Oregon anyway and visit Nicole. Michael's father, Alexei, suggested Leeward Manor. He'd come up here with Dirk Petrovich looking for real estate and met Danny DeBarge."

"Petrovich set up the trip." Ryder hadn't liked the best man from the first moment he'd laid eyes on the tall, muscular, ginger-haired creep. "Petrovich is the guy who has a crush on Nicole."

"One of many," Alyssa said.

Throngs. Ryder hadn't paid much attention to the best man. Had written him off as a loser. No threat. "It was Petrovich and Danny who convinced Alexei."

"Danny gave us a free suite and room service." The smile returned to her face. "Michael and I had a magical weekend."

Though he didn't want to add her husband-to-be to the short list of suspects, Michael seemed to be an integral part of bringing the wedding to Consolation Cove. Evidence to the contrary, he hoped her fiancé was innocent.

"Abracadabra," she said. "It was a done deal."

Ryder had never believed in magic.

Chapter Twenty-Three

"Listen to me, Mr. Younger." Nicole spoke loudly into her cell phone. For what seemed like the ten thousandth time, she explained to the wedding photographer, "The ceremony takes place tomorrow at three o'clock, and you need to be here an hour earlier."

"Yeah, yeah, yeah." He tended to repeat as if he understood, which he clearly did not. "Now what's the deal with today?"

"A wedding rehearsal at four o'clock. By the gazebo near the lighthouse." All of this had been clearly spelled out in the photographer's contract. Despite his name, Mr. Younger was actually quite old—somewhere between sixty and two hundred. It was difficult to make a more exact guess from the photo on his website, which featured little round glasses, a bald head and fluffy white muttonchops. Nicole had reviewed samples of his work and thought he had a talent for catching the hopeful mood of a wedding. Also, he'd been recommended by a friend of Alyssa's mom. "We want some casual snapshots of the wedding party. Since the weather isn't too foggy today, sunset pictures would be great."

"Great, great, great. And all of this takes place at Leeward Manor. Am I right?"

"Yes." Finally, they were getting somewhere. "When you arrive, find me."

"How will I recognize you, Nicole?"

"I'm the tall woman with the short temper."

"Just one more thing," he chirped. "Please, please, please. Can you send me directions?"

She'd already done so. Three times. "Use the GPS navigation in your car."

"I don't trust that modern stuff. It'll send me off the end of a cliff. Know what I mean?"

With a sigh, she flopped onto the bed in her suite. Drawing on the last shred of her patience, she repeated the directions from Tillamook to Consolation Cove. "Is that clear enough for you?"

"Thank you, thank you, thank you. I'm leaving right now."

She ended the call and stared up at the ceiling above her bed. Dealing with Mr. Younger was a clear illustration of the 30/5 rule, which wouldn't be so awful if everything turned out okay in the end. When she heard the door to her suite opening, she bounced off the bed and into Ryder's waiting arms. Cradled in his strong embrace, she felt protected from the frustrations of the day. Her cheek rubbed against his cashmere sweater, and she inhaled his distinct scent of cedar and musk.

"I wish we could stay here forever," she said. "Forget about the wedding and the investigation and just be together. You and me."

He nudged her hair out of the way and ducked his head to nibble at her earlobe. Shivers of excitement went through her as he repeated her words. "Just you and me."

"But we have to get ready for the rehearsal." She had to get changed for the rehearsal and report to Alyssa for maid-of-honor duty. "Seems like every time we're alone in my suite, we're taking a shower and getting dressed."

"Let's try something different."

"I'm game." She tilted back in his arms and looked up at his handsome face. His blue eyes sparkled. "What do you have in mind?"

"The ecologically responsible move would be to shower together," he said.

"And I'm all in favor of saving the planet."

In the bathroom, they helped each other out of their clothes. Not as sexy as his striptease last night, but getting naked rapidly brought them to the same elevated level of arousal. She pressed her body against his and let nature take its course.

IN LESS TIME than she would have imagined possible, they were both clean and satisfied. Ryder insisted on towel-drying her, and she reveled in his touch, especially when he followed each stroke of the towel with a kiss. "Don't get me started again," she warned. "We can't be late for the rehearsal."

While she selected a practical outfit of sienna-brown slacks and a striped shirt under a waterproof jacket, he changed his undershirt and wore the same luxurious cashmere sweater and jeans. In the sitting area of her suite, he went to the minifridge and took out a bottled water. "I talked to Alyssa," he said. "She's smarter than most people give her credit for."

"That's her superpower," she said. "Alyssa bats her eyelashes and hypnotizes people—mostly men—into thinking she's harmless. Then she pounces and gets what she wants."

"She told me that Alexei and Petrovich suggested Consolation Cove for their visit. The best man convinced Michael that this was the place for their wedding."

She couldn't believe he was involved in anything as subtle as counterfeiting and hacking. "Are you telling me that Dirk the Jerk Petrovich is a criminal mastermind?"

"Not likely," Ryder said. "But he might have played a role in the overall conspiracy. The doofus actually does have a law degree."

"Which doesn't give him the credentials to be an evil genius." This crime was more than juggling paperwork. Alan Caldicott had been brutally tortured and murdered.

"I referred Petrovich's name to Agent Murdock," he said.

"And to my future SAC in Homeland Security. Neither of them found an obvious link to the counterfeiting crew, but they're still looking."

She hated the idea that Michael's best man might have betrayed him. If so, he'd put them in danger and was responsible for the hit man. "I'll do some digging of my own tonight."

While she fixed her hair and applied makeup, he gave her the parameters for how their investigation would fit into the rehearsal and the dinner that followed. Since Alexei Volkov and his wife were paying for the meal, Nicole didn't feel responsible for making sure the evening went well.

Ryder told her to cozy up to Petrovich and encourage him to brag. She should find out how close he was to Dmitry Orloff. "And don't go anywhere alone with him."

"Not a chance." Petrovich wasn't her type.

Ryder stepped in front of her and rested his hand on her shoulder. In his other hand, he held a small, clear disc. "I want you to wear this in your boot. It's a GPS tracking device."

She held the disc between her thumb and forefinger. "Why? Do you think Petrovich would try to kidnap me?"

"Him or Brother Julian or any of the others in your throng of admirers." He kissed her lightly on the tip of her nose. "This way, I'll know where you are at all times."

"Have you used this device before?"

"Something similar. I got this from Murdock." He shrugged. "I didn't really come to the wedding to be an investigator."

She nodded. "Alyssa should have one of these."

He produced a second disc from his pocket. "Slip this into her pocket."

They left her suite, hand in hand, and descended the staircase to the first floor. As soon as she stepped outside, she recognized Mr. Younger from his website photo. Others had already gathered and headed toward the gazebo.

She gave Ryder's hand a squeeze. "Happy hunting, cowboy."

Nicole dove into the gathering crowd of family and friends, FBI agents and armed bodyguards.

Just a typical wedding.

AS PER NICOLE'S INSTRUCTIONS, the grounds near the gazebo had been roped off to keep other visitors to the Consolation Cove lighthouse from interrupting the wedding guests. Two rows of white folding chairs had been arranged near the front of the gazebo. Tomorrow, there would be seating for a hundred and fifty. The smallish guest list resulted from the destination. If they'd been in Las Vegas, Nicole would have guessed there'd be four or five hundred, maybe more, in attendance.

As expected, the group for the rehearsal was only about twenty. Standing on the stairs of the gazebo, she made announcements and introduced Wanda. "Our nondenominational officiant for the ceremony. She'll run through what is expected for the ceremony tomorrow, then we'll gather at Leeward Manor for dinner."

Danny DeBarge, dressed in full pirate regalia, skipped up the stairs ahead of Wanda and announced in his pirate voice, "Ar, mateys. We be serving roasted jerk chicken, meatball/cannonball stew, mango salad and vegetarian options. Ar, it be a fine dinner. Yo-ho-ho and a bottle of rum."

Wanda brushed him aside. Though she was not part of any organized church or religion, she offered a prayer of thanks to the setting sun, the trees and other natural wonders like sea lions, gulls and whales. Flipping her waist-length braid over her shoulder, she started giving orders. Moving people around like chess pieces, she started with the flower girl and the ring bearer.

Though Nicole had done nothing to summon him, Petrovich sidled up to her. "I've hardly seen you at all this weekend," he said. "Have we got a problem, babe? Are you avoiding me?"

This would have been the perfect opportunity to tell him to get lost, but she wanted to get him talking, giving her information. She smiled and made an excuse about being so busy with her maid-of-honor duties.

"Tell me about yourself," she said. "I know you work for Volkov Group, but what exactly do you do?"

"In the legal department, I work on contracts, but mostly I'm an expediter."

"I don't know much about the import-export business. You'll have to tell me more."

In an insulting mansplaining tone, he outlined his duties, which seemed to be making sure the import and export orders were properly filled, designated and billed. He was a glorified shipping clerk, which seemed like a good position for someone to initiate a smuggling scheme.

They were paired throughout the rehearsal ceremony, which gave him another chance to call her "babe" and convince her that he was incredibly important to the overall operation of the Volkov Group. He also told her all about his long-term friendship with Michael, how they knew everything about each other. "I always have his back. He always has mine."

With very little encouragement from her, Petrovich droned on and on. He had opinions on everything, and she disagreed with most of them. She almost looked forward to the frequent interruptions from vendors and others who were working on the wedding.

At dinner, she and Petrovich were seated at the same table with Alyssa and Michael. Their position should have been an honor, but the atmosphere at the table was chilly. In low, intense voices, the bride and groom argued. Nicole heard the phrase "cold feet" mentioned and strained to hear more. She desperately hoped that Michael hadn't teamed up with his best man/best friend to run a counterfeiting scam.

The dinner ended with a speech by the very handsome Alexei Volkov, who made a grand display of shaking hands with Tony Rossini. They were going to be in-laws. Best of buddies. Mutual partners.

When his speech ended to great applause from the crowd, Alyssa fled from the dining room, leaving Michael scowling. As quickly as she could extricate herself from Petrovich's grasp, Nicole followed. She dashed up the staircase to the second floor and tapped on the door to Alyssa's suite. When there was no answer, she walked to the windows at the end of the hall and peered out into the darkness.

The beam from the lighthouse swept across the landscape and illuminated the poorly lit employee parking lot behind the kitchen. At the edge of that light, she spotted Danny Danger, still dressed in his ridiculous pirate garb. In his arms, he carried a bundle. Nicole caught a glimpse of the cascading black hair. He was carrying the limp form of Alyssa. What had he done to her? Where was he taking her?

With no time to consider the consequences, Nicole dove into the enclosed emergency exit stairs and clattered down to the ground floor. She had to reach them before they disappeared from sight. She burst from the staircase and ran toward the spot where she'd last seen them.

A faint glow illuminated the edge of the forest. Thick, moss-covered trees made an almost impenetrable wall. Where were they? What the hell was he doing with her?

The pirate appeared from the shadows. Light reflected from his puffy sleeves and glistened on his long-haired wig. Alyssa was nowhere in sight. Barely hesitating, Nicole charged at him. Adrenaline fueled her rage. She could take him.

A few feet from him, she pulled up short. This wasn't Danny.

"Finally, we meet." He showed her the six-inch hunting knife in his right hand. "I'm Julian."

Chapter Twenty-Four

His left hand clenched her arm, his grip as tight and unyielding as a vise. He twisted Nicole around so she was standing in front of him. The point of his knife poked into her back. "Don't make a sound," he said in a dark whisper.

Like hell I won't. She struggled wildly. Years ago, she'd taken a self-defense class but couldn't remember any of the moves. The first thing they'd taught involved calling for help, but she could barely draw breath.

"If you cooperate," he whispered, "there's a chance that you and Alyssa will survive. If not, she's dead."

Julian didn't waste time on idle threats. She'd seen no hesitation when he'd shot Jelly. She gasped. "Where is she?"

"Stop wriggling," he ordered.

Still, she fought back. The tip of his blade pierced the skin near her waist. She felt the penetration through her flesh but experienced no pain. Her body had already gone into the first phase of shock.

She had to think, to reason with him. Forcing herself to stop struggling, she said, "I can get you what you want. Tony Rossini will pay any price to have his daughter back. Her groom will also pay."

"We can talk," he said. "But not here."

He yanked her backward into the shield of trees, and she realized the cleverness of his latest disguise. If any of the kitchen staff saw them, Julian would pretend to be Danny playing a prank on one of the guests.

The forest closed around them.

Nicole tried to calculate the time between when she'd seen him carrying Alyssa and when she'd come face-to-face with Julian. Couldn't have been more than five minutes. Not enough time for him to go very far.

He came to a sudden halt and whipped her around like a rag doll. She lost her balance and fell to one knee. Instinctively, her hand went to her side where he'd poked her. She felt the blood, and the thought occurred to her that he might kill her. In her work at the hospital, she had faced death many, many times. But never her own demise. Not fair. She'd just reunited with Ryder. They deserved future happiness together. Never before had she been so determined to live a long, fruitful life.

"Snap out of it," Julian commanded.

Her eyes blinked open and she saw the full-size sedan parked on a two-track dirt road beside them. "I'm not going anywhere with you until you tell me what you did with Alyssa."

"You're a difficult woman." He peeled off the wig and revealed his short brown hair. "Your friend was easy to handle. I zapped her with a stun gun and shot her up with a knockout drug. When she was unconscious, I carried her to the car. She's tiny. It was easy."

She stared at the knife. If she could disarm him…

"You." He pointed accusingly. "You're too heavy to carry."

With a pang of sad regret, she remembered. "Ryder didn't have a problem hauling me from the parking lot to the Manor."

"If you want to keep your boyfriend and Alyssa safe, you'll do what I say." Julian popped the trunk on the car. "Get in."

Inside the trunk, Nicole saw Alyssa curled in a ball and motionless.

THE LAST TIME Ryder had seen Nicole, she was running up the staircase to the second floor of the Manor. When he followed, he hadn't been able to find her. He opened the door to her suite and checked inside. Not there. He went to Alyssa's suite and knocked. Nobody answered.

Panic twisted his gut. He couldn't lose Nicole. Not when they had finally found each other again. Ryder drew back and prepared to kick in the door.

Michael Volkov joined him in the hallway. "Wait. I've got a key."

Ryder caught his breath. "Open it."

Both men charged inside. Ryder had drawn his weapon, and he noticed that Michael was also armed. They quickly searched and found no sign of either Alyssa or Nicole.

In the hallway, they encountered Danny DeBarge, dressed only in a T-shirt and boxers. He braced himself against the wall in the hallway. His head was dripping blood, and he looked faint. Ryder didn't waste time. "Nicole and Alyssa. Y'all have two seconds to tell me where the hell they are."

"I need an ambulance," Danny whined.

"Talk first."

"I'm injured. And somebody stole my clothes."

Ryder put two and two together. The somebody who'd stolen Danny's costume was probably Julian. Disguised as Danny Danger, he was roaming the grounds. Both Alyssa and Nicole were missing. Ryder didn't like their odds of finding the two women unharmed. He called Agent Murdock and told her to search for somebody wearing the pirate costume.

"Ambulance," Danny repeated.

Ryder got up in his face. "You're dreaming if you think I'll give you a helping hand. You're working for the counterfeiters."

His eyes widened, feigning surprise. "Not me."

"You've been acting as the FBI's confidential informant, and I want to know how you're getting your intel."

Danny pleaded with Michael. "Help me."

He got no sympathy from the groom-to-be. "Answer the man."

"Maybe I did a few favors," Danny admitted.

"Who are you working for?" Michael asked.

"You really don't know." Danny laughed, and his face contorted. "I'm getting payoffs from your best man. Dirk Petrovich."

"You two deserve each other." Disgusted, Michael shook his head and looked at Ryder. "I think Dirk's still downstairs. Let's go."

Ryder had seen Petrovich with Nicole until she'd broken away from him and run up the staircase. He couldn't have abducted her. It had to be Julian. Taking the responder for the tracking device from his pocket, he activated the GPS. A tiny green dot blinked, indicating where Nicole was headed. Ryder strode toward the stairs. "I'll pick him up later."

Michael followed. "I'm coming with you."

Ryder paused on the staircase and looked into Michael Volkov's eyes. He remembered the young man's love-besotted expression when he sang to Alyssa. Now, he read terror and desperation in Michael's face. Ryder made a judgment call to trust this young man, mainly because he needed someone to read the GPS while he drove and there wasn't time to shop around. "Try to keep up."

Chapter Twenty-Five

By the time Julian's car stopped, Nicole had treated her wound using a gray sweatshirt she'd found in the trunk, applying pressure and tying the arms around her waist. She'd nearly revived Alyssa, who was still dizzy but mostly okay. Crammed together in the trunk, there wasn't room for CPR or anything more complex. Nicole's wake-up method consisted of gently tapping her friend on both cheeks, whispering encouragement and saying her name as much as possible, calling her back to consciousness.

She heard the car door slam. "He's coming for us, Alyssa. Remember what I said. Pretend you're still asleep. Alyssa?"

"I am. Not. Awake."

"Close your eyes."

Nicole tried to get her legs under her so she could leap. If Julian gave her an opening, she intended to attack and tear the knife away from him. Her wound wasn't deep enough to be lethal, but she felt the loss of blood, her life slowly draining away.

The trunk opened. She blinked in the overhead light from a garage or carport.

Julian stood waiting. While driving, he'd shed the pirate costume and dressed in a crew neck sweater and cargo pants—an appropriate outfit for the casual kidnapper. In his right hand, he held a semiautomatic gun. At this point-blank range, he couldn't miss.

"Both of you, out of the car and into the house. Now."

"Alyssa is still unconscious," Nicole said, trying one last delaying ploy. In her boot, she had the GPS tracking device Ryder had given her. He'd come for her. If she could hold Julian off, Ryder would rescue her. "Alyssa can't move."

"Then you'll have to carry her." He leveled the gun so she was staring down the bore. "You're in no position to bargain. Alyssa is my target. Whatever happens to you is nothing more than collateral damage. Get her into the house. Now."

There was no choice but to obey and desperately hope that Ryder's GPS tracker would lead him to her before she was shot. Struggling, Nicole managed to get her friend out of the trunk and onto her feet in a carport beside a modern, one-story house up the hill from the Oregon shore. Weaving back and forth, Alyssa was only halfway faking her semiconscious state. Whatever drug Julian had given her had a lasting effect.

Inside the house, he directed them down one step to a lower level furnished in glass and leather. The sectional sofa faced a wall of windows overlooking a spectacular night view of the Pacific waves burnished by the light of a full moon. She would have been impressed if she hadn't known that Julian paid for this panorama with his profits from murder.

She sat beside Alyssa on the sofa. "She's dehydrated. Needs something to drink."

He gestured toward the kitchen in the upper area directly across from the entrance. "Bring her water from the fridge. She needs to be alert enough to talk."

"Is that why you abducted her? To get information?"

"And to put pressure on Tony." He glanced at his wristwatch. "There's a clock on this conversation. I need to call my contact within the hour. If that doesn't happen, I have no need for Alyssa. Or for you."

Taking two bottles of water from the fridge, Nicole eyed the knife block on the counter. She grabbed a paring knife with a pointed tip and slipped it into the waistband of her slacks near the location of her wound where the tied sweatshirt hid the knife hilt.

When she approached the sofa, Julian snatched the water bottle from her hand, screwed off the lid and splashed the ice-cold water in Alyssa's face. When she sputtered awake, he drew back his left arm and slapped her hard.

"Stop it." Nicole rushed toward him.

He raised his weapon. "Sit down. This doesn't concern you."

Outrage coursed through her body, but she did what he said. Beside her on the sofa, Alyssa wept softly. Nicole opened the other bottle and held it to Alyssa's lips. "Drink this."

"Here's the deal." Julian strutted back and forth in front of the window. "You're going to tell me everything you know about the smuggled counterfeit and the hack that made it possible. Do you hear me, Alyssa? If you refuse or claim you know nothing or tell me a lie, I'll take it out on Nicole. *Capisce?*"

"I understand," Alyssa said.

Julian gave them an evil grin. "Mess with me, and I'll start by shooting off Nicole's left pinkie toe."

"Ask me anything," Alyssa said.

"Who is the smuggler inside the Volkov Group?"

"Dirk Petrovich," she said without blinking an eye.

If Alyssa was lying, she was doing a good job of it. Her voice was strong. Her poise, unshaken. Nicole believed her.

"Was the computer hack designed to make Rossini look guilty?" Julian asked.

"Yes," Alyssa said. "For revenge. Rossini Enterprises played a part in the arrests of the counterfeiters."

Before she could say another word, the front door crashed open. Dmitry Orloff stood framed in the doorway, with an elegant, pearl-handled Colt Python revolver aimed at Julian. In his sonorous voice, he announced, "I'll take it from here."

For a moment, Julian's façade slipped. Orloff's appearance confused him. "Why are you here?"

"Don't disappoint me by being stupid," he said. "I'm the man who hired you for this job. Surely, you aren't surprised."

"I had suspicions." Julian was clearly bluffing. "But I thought you were with the church."

"I'm a devout man, but I'm not a fool," Orloff said. "When you got yourself into trouble three years ago, I arranged for you to live at St. Macarius Monastery until I needed you."

"If you call that living," Julian muttered.

"You've done all right for yourself." Orloff's voice was silky but ominous. He closed the door and crossed the room with wide strides, stopping at the end of the sofa. In Nicole's mind, he was too close for comfort. She averted her gaze, not wanting to draw his attention to her and Alyssa. At the same time, she worked the paring knife free from her waistband and gripped the handle.

"I've done what you asked," Julian said, "and I'm ready to be paid."

"You're a greedy bastard. I've kept my eye on you. I watched you sneak away from the abbey and set up offshore accounts. You bought cars, created new identities and even purchased this property."

"I established a new life."

"The brothers are a trusting lot. You took advantage of them."

Julian backed away, perhaps realizing that he made a distinct target silhouetted in front of the windows. "What's your problem?"

"Before you went into the abbey, you were an acknowledged expert in the art of murder," Orloff said. "But you've gotten out of practice. Made mistakes like leaving behind fingerprints and cash receipts. You showed your hand to the authorities instead of taking advantage of being presumed dead."

"Don't know why you're complaining. You got what you wanted." Julian's voice was a harsh mixture of anger and fear. "Caldicott out of the way. And these two lovelies abducted."

"You alerted several law enforcement officers, Brother Julian. I simply cannot afford to be associated with you." He made the sign of the cross and said, "May God have mercy on your soul."

Orloff raised the Colt Python, took aim and fired a single shot. A direct hit to the center of Julian's forehead. The hit man collapsed to the floor like a marionette whose strings had been severed.

Orloff turned to them and executed a stiff bow from the waist. "My apologies, ladies. I wish I could have spared you this unpleasantness."

Thinking fast, Nicole tried to disarm him by putting a fresh spin on what she and Alyssa had witnessed. "You have our deepest gratitude, sir. You saved our lives."

A smile teased the corners of his lips. "Clever girl."

"If there's anything we or our families can do to show our appreciation, we'll be happy to comply."

When he tilted the Colt Python toward them, she knew her ploy hadn't changed his mind. He intended to kill them. Ryder hadn't come to her rescue.

In desperation, Nicole rose to her feet. She held the paring knife stiffly at her side where he couldn't see it. "Tomorrow is Alyssa's wedding day. Please don't deny her that moment."

"You must be familiar with the concept of loose threads. Leaving you alive threatens the very fabric of my existence."

"Nonna Rossini will help us." She took two rapid steps toward him. "She'll find a way for us to disappear."

"I wouldn't ask her to compromise herself."

"Please."

Nicole made her move. She lunged, dove through the air and crashed into him. The force of her attack staggered him. Orloff lost his balance. He went down. She was on top of him, wielding her knife, slashing toward his throat.

He was faster. Using his heavy gun, he slapped the knife from her hand. Rising from the floor, he threw her aside.

A gunshot rang out. Nicole squeezed her eyes shut and winced, expecting to feel the lethal bullet penetrating her body. She heard Ryder's voice.

"Drop the weapon, Orloff. Lace your fingers behind your neck."

"There has been a mistake," Orloff said. "I have come to the rescue of these ladies."

"Tell it to the judge. You are under arrest."

After Michael got Orloff handcuffed, he gathered Alyssa into his arms. Whatever they'd been arguing about before was forgotten in statements of love and caring.

Ryder ordered Orloff to kneel on the floor. When he came to Nicole, his smile vanished. "You're bleeding."

"Not anymore," she said. "It wasn't Orloff. Brother Julian stabbed me."

"I already called for backup. They'll be here any minute." Gently he guided her to the sofa and helped her lie down. "We need to get you feeling better right away. You and Alyssa. You ladies have a wedding to attend tomorrow."

Saturday, the day of the wedding...

RYDER THOUGHT ALYSSA was beautiful, but he couldn't take his gaze off Nicole in her bedazzled, acid-green, ruffled gown with the thigh-high slit.

He couldn't wait to ask her to be his bride.

Chapter Twenty-Six

Six months later, Consolation Cove, the day of another wedding...

Just before sunset, the white folding chairs were arranged in rows in front of the gazebo at the Consolation Cove lighthouse. Nicole gazed up at the landmark tower and remembered the first night, when she and Alyssa had seen Brother Julian disguised as the cowled figure of Death. The warning beacon from the lighthouse marked their days and gave them hope.

Ryder's transfer to Homeland Security Investigations in Portland had been expedited based on the part he'd played in solving the hack into law enforcement communications and the smuggling of four-and-a-half million in counterfeit cash. Dirk Petrovich—a small fish in a much bigger pond—had been all too willing to point fingers in exchange for a slot in witness protection. Needless to say, he wasn't anybody's "best man," and certainly not a friend of Michael Volkov's. After the funny money had been seized, everybody agreed that the twenty-dollar bills were among the best they'd ever seen.

Alyssa, who was massively pregnant and ready to pop, joined her for a stroll around the lighthouse. Though Nicole's dress was a cool shade of pearly white, it didn't bear much resemblance to a wedding gown. Linen instead of silk. Pleated instead of ruffled. Practical instead of fancy, which pretty much described her.

She and Alyssa paused on the oceanside of the lighthouse and congratulated themselves on how well everything had turned out. Michael proved to be an adoring husband who would certainly be a doting father. Ryder was everything Nicole imagined him to be. They'd bought a house together in Portland, and she was assured of a position in the ER when she wrapped up her residency.

"Everything is going so well," Alyssa said.

"Dmitry Orloff doesn't think so."

"He's in prison, still awaiting trial and still claiming some kind of immunity based on his former occupation as a bishop."

"Apparently, his 'get out of jail free' card doesn't work," Nicole said. "I've heard that Nonna visits him every couple of weeks and brings cookies."

Alyssa rolled her eyes. "She says prison is the best way to make sure a man is faithful."

"Tony and Alexei turned out to be best buddies."

"Never would have predicted that," Alyssa said. "But I'm glad. Papa needed a friend."

The new manager of Leeward Manor, replacing Danny Danger who had been fired, popped around the end of the lighthouse and waved to them. "Hey, ladies. There's somebody here looking for you."

Without waiting for an invitation. Ryder came around the lighthouse and swept Nicole into his arms. "You look beautiful."

"You're not supposed to see the dress before the wedding."

"Rules are made to be broken," he said. "Brother Gabe wants us to get started. Since we've done all the preparation and jumped through the hoops to have a blessed ceremony, it'd be a shame if we didn't get started on time."

"Fine with me." She wrapped her arms around his neck

and kissed him hard. "I can hardly wait to get started on the honeymoon."

She'd waited a long time to take on the label of "wife" and was willing to forgive him almost anything as long as she agreed with him. There would be no betrayals, no lies and no broken vows. Only love would come between them as long as they both would live.

* * * * *

OPERATION PROTECTOR

JUSTINE DAVIS

Chapter One

"What's he carrying?"

At his wife's words Quinn Foxworth looked up from the report he'd been studying. Hayley was leaning to look out the window beside the front door of Foxworth Northwest headquarters on the east side of Puget Sound. She was in the entryway, close enough for him to see, but he had no idea what to expect. He only knew it had to be Cutter, because only their dog could bring on that half-puzzled, half-"what now?" tone in his wife's voice.

Geez, dog, it's not even seven in the morning yet.

He was smiling as he thought it.

And then Hayley gasped, dropped the jacket she'd been about to hang on the rack near the entrance, and dashed toward the door. Instantly, knowing Hayley never overreacted, he followed at a run.

When he got through the door, Hayley was kneeling next to their sometimes too brilliant dog. Who was carrying a small, black-and-white puppy with his mouth, so very gently you would have thought it was his own.

At first Quinn thought the tiny creature was just wet. But the moment he got down beside Cutter and the dog even more gently set the puppy down, Quinn could see that it was indeed wet. But not with water, though it was raining hard enough to make even the thick-coated Cutter look soaked. Because the water running off the pup onto the sidewalk beneath him was...

pink. And when Quinn touched him, then pulled his hand back and looked at his fingers, he was sure what the wetness was.

Blood.

"He's hurt," Hayley said urgently.

In that moment the little thing looked up at him, and he couldn't miss the fear and confusion in the big brown puppy eyes. Something snapped in Quinn.

"I don't see an obvious wound, but let's get him to Dr. Moore," he said.

As if they'd planned it out, they each started to move. Hayley ran inside and grabbed a small stack of towels, while he went and collected their jackets and the keys to their SUV parked in the gravel lot outside the building. Cutter stood guard until Hayley got there and began to ease the puppy with the jagged pattern of black-and-white patches of fur onto one of the towels. Then they both headed for the car, Cutter at their heels letting out an anxious whine.

"We've got him, boy," Quinn assured the dog. "But you might as well come along so Dr. Moore can say hello." He knew the reliable veterinarian would want to. He'd often told them that Cutter was his most remarkable patient in his thirty years as a vet.

Hayley made a phone call as they started down the long driveway. They knew the experienced Dr. Moore always left time in his busy day for emergencies, so their wait at the homey-looking white building was short. The presence of the blood—and the Foxworth name, for they'd become a little more than famous in this area—made it a priority.

The young vet tech who made the initial exam agreed with Quinn that there was no apparent wound, but they took the pup back for a more thorough check.

"Poor little guy," Hayley said as she paced the small room. "He was so scared."

"Leave it to Cutter," Quinn said, standing in front of the poster diagramming a dog's circulatory system, trying to focus on it instead of the trembling little creature they'd brought here. The dog he was referring to let out a soft woof. He was well-known here in the small veterinary hospital, and as a certified therapy dog, was the only animal other than the office cat who was allowed the run of the place.

"He's so polite!"

"He's so sweet!"

"He makes me feel so much better when I pet him!"

They heard at least a couple of those every time they brought their too-clever dog in, which was actually reassuring for both Foxworths, because it reminded them he was a pet, and not just the canine who had become such an integral part of the Foxworth team, be it at home or on one of their cases.

It had happened so fast that Quinn sometimes forgot about the time before. But coming to the vet reminded him, because of the deeply etched images in his mind, of when this dog had burst out of the trees and changed his life forever by bringing Hayley to him. And had risked his life to help them during that operation.

The dog had become the very heart of Foxworth, so often recognizing a case before they did, and knowing how to tell them in ways that were undeniable. He tried to imagine his life now if it had never happened. He could not. It made his throat tight just to try. Because without Hayley he would have no life, not one worth living anyway.

Something nudged at his knee. He looked down and saw Cutter, looking up at him steadily with those amber-flecked dark eyes. He knew the dog had sensed his emotions. Automatically he reached to stroke the soft fur, no longer surprised at the soothing feel of it.

He looked over at Hayley, who was sitting in one of the wooden chairs by the door. She wore her worried expression. And that tightened his throat again, because it was so like her to be worried about this little puppy who had appeared out of nowhere, even if they knew absolutely nothing about him.

When the door from the back of the hospital, where they did all the routine procedures, opened and they saw Dr. Moore himself, Quinn knew Hayley had felt the same little jump as he had. They'd expected the tech to come back with the results. But they relaxed a little when he set the page he was carrying down on the exam table and bent to welcome Cutter, who had instantly gone to greet the kindly man who saw to his health.

"And how's my most clever patient ever today?" the man asked, and Cutter answered with a nudge of his nose and a happy tail wag.

After a moment he straightened and looked at the humans in the room. Quinn had learned a lot about reading people from the woman he so loved, and he had the feeling the good doctor was a stride or two beyond curious.

"Well, leave it to you folks to make my day interesting," he began.

"Is he all right?" Hayley asked, sounding a little anxious. "We couldn't see any injury that would have bled, but—"

"He's fine. No injuries internal or external. He's a good weight, clean and healthy."

"So, not a stray," Quinn said.

"No," Dr. Moore agreed. "He's well cared for. We're getting him all cleaned up now, and he should be out in a couple of minutes."

Quinn and Hayley looked at each other, and Quinn knew they were both thinking the same thing. "The blood that was on him," he began.

Dr. Moore's brow furrowed. "That's where it gets very interesting. As I told you, it wasn't his."

"Maybe his mom?" Hayley asked.

"No," Dr. Moore said. "So, knowing what I do about the Foxworth Foundation, I went a little further."

"Hit us with it, Doc," Quinn suggested.

Then, flatly and with a grimace, the vet said, "The blood wasn't canine. It was human."

Chapter Two

Ali Moran had only come home to get some dry clothes. The predicted rainstorm had arrived several hours early, and she'd ended up both soaked and more worried than when she'd started out on her search a couple of hours ago. That it was her own fault that her beloved new puppy, Zigzag, already shortened to Ziggy, had somehow slipped past the newly installed fence she'd had put in just for him, only made things worse.

She should have been outside when he'd started barking, right after she'd heard an unusual sound. But her phone had rung as she'd let him out, and it had been a client who would determine just how well they'd be living the rest of the winter, so she'd gone back to answer it despite the early hour. She'd cut the call short, but by the time she'd stepped back outside on her back deck, Ziggy was nowhere in sight.

She'd been outside ever since, searching. Every corner, behind every shrub in the yard, even crawling under the deck to be sure the little guy wasn't hiding. She'd only brought him home a couple of weeks ago, and while he'd seemed to adjust rapidly—probably more rapidly than she had since she herself had only been in this house for a week longer—maybe he hadn't been as happy as he'd seemed with his new home.

Or you.

It was true she'd never had a dog before, because her mother was beyond fastidious to the point of persnickety, but she'd read and studied and even taken an online course about new puppy life, and thought she'd had it down.

And then reality bites... Again.

She shook her head sharply as she traded her wet sneakers and socks for warm, dry rain boots. She straightened up, then slid her phone into her pocket, thankful she'd gone on a picture-taking binge when she'd first gotten Ziggy, so she had plenty of shots to show the neighbors and ask if they'd seen him.

But that would be the easy part. She was more worried about the woods behind the houses here on the dead end of the street. The long-untouched forest was why she'd chosen her cottage, the last in the small row, and the smallest on the street, especially dwarfed next to the big, remodeled-to-excess place next door.

She gave a mental apology to the residents, seven-year-old Grace more than her mother, Liz, a brusque, rather imperious woman Ali had quickly realized had been the one who simply had to have a bigger, grander, more impressive home than anyone else, to show off.

In a strange way, people like her were responsible for Ali doing what she loved. Because her interiors service—she refused to call it decorating, since that was exactly what she didn't do—catered to those who wanted attractive, functional homes, not showplaces that made you afraid to set down a glass or put your feet up after a long day. Which was why her website header was: It Doesn't Matter How Pretty It Is If It Doesn't Work for You.

She needed to check those woods first, she decided. Ziggy was just a little puppy, and no matter how big he might get later, right now he was easy prey for whatever predator might be living back there, from coyotes to bobcats to owls. At least the gorgeous bald eagles pretty much stuck to the abundant fish in Puget Sound, just a few blocks away.

She had to find him. She couldn't take another death. It had taken her a very long time to become even functional after she'd lost Josh. Even now her eyes teared up at the thought. They'd been supposed to have a long, happy life together, not merely a few years, ending in a flash of agony.

She shook off the too-familiar memories, pulled on her hooded slicker and braced herself for the wind and rain. She had the back door open when a knock came at the front. Her heart leaped. Maybe one of the neighbors had found Ziggy. Maybe it was Grace, who adored the pup and had come over several times to play with him.

She practically ran to the front door and yanked it open. There was a dog there, all right, but certainly not Ziggy. It was a big, partly reddish brown creature with shiny black fur over its head and shoulders. The eyes that looked up at her were dark, flecked with tiny bits of amber, and looked infinitely wiser than the eyes of any dog she'd ever seen.

Or most people.

He'd apparently brought his humans with him, because the man held the leash snapped to his collar. She'd just spotted the metal tag in the shape of a boat that hung from that collar when the woman spoke.

"Does this little guy look familiar?"

Only then did Ali realize the woman had been cradling a small bundle inside her rain jacket. A head poked out, and the moment he spotted her, the pup gave an excited little bark.

"Ziggy!" Ali yelped in relief.

The woman laughed. "I can feel his tail wagging madly. I guess that answers that."

"Thank you so much," Ali exclaimed as her visitor disentangled Ziggy from her jacket.

"Don't thank us," the man holding the leash of the much larger dog said. "Thank him."

He indicated the dog who was sitting calmly between them. Once she had her precious pup safely cuddled in her arms again and she could breathe normally, she gave the man a questioning look.

"He found your boy and brought him to us," he said.

"Our office is just down the road that way," the woman said, gesturing toward the sound.

Scrambling to regain her equilibrium, Ali belatedly realized they were standing out in the cold.

"Please, won't you come in? It's a little messy, I just moved in three weeks ago, so things are still in flux, but I have hot coffee on."

"Hot anything sounds wonderful," the woman said, with a smile that had Ali instinctively trusting her.

They stepped inside, Ali shut the door and ushered them into the living room, which was thankfully in good shape. All the clutter and unpacked boxes were elsewhere.

"I'm Ali Moran," she said. "And this little rascal is Zigzag, for obvious reasons." She'd named him the moment she'd seen the pattern of black fur running the length of his back from head to tail in a zigzag shape.

"And I'm Hayley Foxworth, this is my husband, Quinn, and this clever boy—" she reached out to pet the bigger dog, who was sitting politely at their feet "—is Cutter."

She'd heard the name Foxworth before—it was hard to live here and not be aware—but she had no idea if these folks were connected to those Foxworths she'd seen in the news. They seemed too…normal to be that famous, though.

"Well, I must thank you officially," she said, leaning over toward the other dog. "Is it all right?" she asked, pausing when she realized she was about to pet a strange dog she'd never seen before. And a dog who looked like a fluffier version of a lot of police and military dogs she'd seen on screen.

"Yes," Quinn said.

"And it'll be more all right when you do," Hayley added. Ali smiled at that, understanding because she now knew the happiness and pure stress relief she got from petting Ziggy.

But then, as her fingers stroked the dark head of the bigger dog, she realized suddenly she hadn't understood anything. Because the feeling of calm and ease she got, as if it were coursing upward from her fingers on that thick fur, was unlike anything she'd ever felt before.

Her gaze shot back to the woman, who was smiling. "See what I mean?"

"I...wow. What is he, some kind of therapy dog?"

"Among countless other things," her husband said, dryly but still lovingly. "We try to keep up, but he's always a few steps ahead of us."

There was something about the way Quinn Foxworth was looking at her that made her remember how this had all started.

"I honestly don't know how he got out," she said. "I've looked at the new fence and it's intact. I know it's short, but—"

"So is he," Hayley said.

"Yes," Ali said, glad she understood. She didn't want to get a reputation in her new neighborhood for being a negligent pet owner.

She explained how she'd come back in for her phone, had heard a string of barks from Ziggy, but then quiet so she'd assumed—which she would never do again, she swore—the pup had simply been barking at some passing squirrel or rabbit, since they were common here.

"He's not used to the wildlife yet, and everything seems to fascinate him," she said.

They chatted some more, and she couldn't help thinking she wished these were her next-door neighbors. Except for Grace, whom she'd miss. And so would Ziggy. And finally she felt comfortable to ask the question that had been hovering.

"Are you by chance connected to the Foxworth Foundation?"

Hayley smiled. "That would be us."

Ali's eyes widened. "Wow. You guys are amazing. I've read about you, and how you help the little guy. It does my heart good to know that you're out there, looking out for people who have been treated so unfairly."

"Whether they were treated that way by other people, or by life, we try to help," Hayley agreed.

"As long as they're in the right, the Foxworth Foundation is there," Quinn added.

Ali sighed audibly. "Wonderful. Thank you for…being."

They'd finished their coffee, and Ali noticed it was Quinn who stood and gathered all the mugs and took them into the kitchen, all without comment.

"At the risk of being clichéd, I love what you've done with the place. Welcoming, comfortable and functional."

Ali laughed. "That's practically my business motto."

"Business?"

"I do residential and business interiors, for people who want function over form, but still want to like what they're looking at."

Hayley looked around again, and slowly began to nod. "I can see you're good at it, just from this. Clean lines, but not cold."

"Thank you," Ali exclaimed gratefully. "That's exactly my goal."

"Ali?"

Quinn spoke from where he'd walked after dropping off the coffee mugs, over by a side window that looked out toward the house next door. Grace's house, as she preferred to think of it, since her mother seemed to have no desire to be on a first-name basis.

"What?" she asked.

"When you heard Ziggy barking, did you hear anything else?"

Her brow furrowed. "I heard something right before, but it was far away. So I thought he was just barking at the noise, or I've got a family of rabbits living out there he always yips at, so I thought he'd seen one… Why?"

It was Hayley who answered her. "Forgive us for not telling you right away, but we wanted to check you out before we got into this. When Cutter brought Ziggy to us, he had blood on him. Quite a bit."

Ali gasped. "What?" She immediately looked back at the puppy in her lap, running her hands over him urgently.

"He's fine," Hayley assured her. "We took him to our vet to be sure. It wasn't his blood."

For a moment Ali felt as if she could breathe again, but then the implications of what Hayley had said sank in. "Then what…?"

"The blood," Quinn said from his spot over by the window, "was human."

She blinked. Human? How on earth? "But… I'm the only one here, and I'm not— I haven't—" She broke off, at a total loss.

"I believe you," Quinn said. "Because I think I know how it happened." He turned then to look at them. "I think that sound you heard came from next door."

"What?" She felt like she'd missed something in a complicated story she was reading. She got up, started toward him, wondering what he'd seen. When she got there, he pointed toward the back of the house across the side yard, where a window was clearly broken.

"You want my best guess," Quinn said, "Ziggy heard the breaking glass, barked at the person who broke it—and apparently cut himself up in the process—and who obviously didn't want to be discovered, so he ran over and grabbed your pup to shut him up."

Ali sucked in a harsh breath. And cuddled Ziggy even closer.

"But he didn't hurt him," Hayley, who had joined them now, assured her. "Our vet checked him thoroughly."

Ali looked at the broken window at the back of the house next door. It did make sense, but if it was true… A memory hit her then of that time little Grace had climbed through a window to come over to play with Ziggy.

"Oh no," she said, staring, feeling more than a little stunned. "That's Grace's room."

Chapter Three

Ali hastily explained about her charming, dog-loving little neighbor, but then hesitated. Hayley, who had come up beside them, urged her on.

"Something's bothering you," she said. "Is it about Grace?"

Ali took a deep breath. She didn't want to spread rumors that were based only on her admittedly limited observation and assessment of her neighbors. She was the newcomer to the neighborhood and had no right to pass judgment on people she barely knew. But Grace…

She was thankful Hayley didn't push but instead gave her time to think. She remembered all she'd read and heard about the Foxworth Foundation, all the good they'd done, on a huge scale. Even taking down the crooked governor of the state. Surely they wouldn't get involved here, when she truly had no idea there was really anything wrong?

But she'd also read about them standing for the little guy in the right against the big guys in the wrong. Helping people who had no fame, no position, no influence to barter. She'd even read they had begun by recovering and returning a stolen locket to a little girl, the child's only memento of her dead mother.

In the end, looking at that shattered window, she decided. Because what if that blood had been Grace's, what if she'd broken that window to get out?

"Grace is sweet, loving, and adores Ziggy. I saw her climbing out a back window—that window—of the big house to get here once, but I accepted her explanation that the house was being cleaned and she had to stay out of the way. So it took me a while to realize that she was sneaking over here to play with him without her mother's knowledge. When I asked her about it, she said her mother would kill her if she found out she was coming over here. I assumed she was exaggerating, like kids do. I've met her mother, and while not the warmest person I've ever met, she seems okay."

"But?" Hayley prompted.

In for a penny... Ali went on, still doubting her own decision, but something about this woman made her trust. "But... Grace was shivering. Panicky. As if she were genuinely terrified. And all of a sudden I wasn't so sure—"

The other dog, Cutter, suddenly let out a rolling, almost demanding sort of bark. Both Foxworths spun around. The clearly revved-up animal was at her rear door, looking back over his shoulder at his humans. The bark came again.

"I guess he needs out?" Ali suggested. Before she even finished, Quinn had quickly gone over to the dog.

"That's his 'You need to see something' bark," Hayley said.

Things started to happen so fast Ali was a little boggled. The Foxworths were out the back door with their dog so fast it occurred to her perhaps that person who'd broken the window and grabbed Ziggy might still be around, and the dog had heard him or scented him somehow. Hastily she put the puppy in the playpen she'd set up for him, and followed their visitors outside.

She got through the back door just in time to see Cutter clear her four-foot fence as if it were no taller than Ziggy. Quinn was next, clearing it as easily with one hand on a fence post, as did Hayley. She had less faith in herself, and headed for the gate.

They were into the trees and out of sight by the time she got out of the yard. She paused to listen but heard nothing, not even the dog who had trumpeted the announcement that had made his humans leap into action. They knew him, she thought as she ran, they must be sure this meant something.

Maybe I was right before, thinking he looked a little like those well-trained enforcement dogs.

She went carefully, slowly, not knowing what might be ahead. She at last caught up to them in a small space between some towering evergreens. They were standing facing one of the largest trees, Quinn and Hayley behind their dog, who was a yard or so in front of them.

Their dog, who was staring at the man sitting at the base of the tree, cradling a bloody arm against his chest.

The window. He *was* still here. And Quinn had been right—this was the source of the blood that had ended up on Ziggy.

"Guess your burglary didn't go too well," Quinn was saying.

"I'm not a burglar." The man said it flatly, wearily.

Feeling it was safe now—somehow she knew that either the dog or Quinn Foxworth would stop the man if he tried anything—Ali picked up her pace. She supposed she should be grateful the guy hadn't actually hurt Ziggy, but—

Just as she got close enough to take in the entire scene, the strangest thing happened. The Foxworth dog's demeanor shifted entirely. He went from bristling and on guard to something altogether different. His head came up, he stretched his neck out, his nose aimed at the bleeding man. He tilted his head, as if curious. The man was looking at the dog in turn, warily.

Cutter walked toward him. The injured man shifted, starting to get to his feet, as if he expected the dog to attack.

"Don't think about running," Quinn advised, but made no move to call back the dog.

And then Cutter reached the man, sniffed at him closely, gave a little whuff that sounded oddly like the animal had made a decision. The man was still edgy with the dog right there, but the dog himself seemed different. Calmer, yet no less…determined? She sighed inwardly. She had a lot to learn yet about dogs, if she was imparting human thoughts and emotions to this one.

And then Cutter turned around, facing his people, and sat at the bleeding man's feet. He stared up at the Foxworths steadily, unwaveringly.

"Oh?" said Hayley, as if the dog had somehow spoken.

Quinn grimaced. "Really, dog?"

Whatever Cutter had been trying to communicate, clearly the couple understood it. Ali had the feeling this was far from the first time this had happened. Maybe she hadn't been so wrong after all.

"Apparently so," Hayley said.

Quinn let out an audible breath. "Well, we had December off at least."

"And a lovely December it was." Hayley was smiling now, and Ali was a little boggled by how relaxed they both suddenly were, when the man who had tried to break in next door was sitting right there. Not to mention they'd just had an entire conversation that made no sense to anyone else.

She stifled the pang she felt, thinking of when she, too, had had a relationship like that, and shifted her gaze to that man on the ground now. He looked as puzzled as she felt.

He also looked familiar. He was a big guy, she could tell that even as he remained crouched there. Long legs, muscular arms—the left one blood-soaked even wrapped in what looked like a strip torn from his plaid shirt—slightly shaggy dark brown hair, and bright blue eyes.

Her pulse jumped. She'd seen those eyes before.

Grace's eyes.

The image captured in the photo Grace had once shown her, a clearly precious thing to the child, flashed through her mind. She remembered the girl pulling it out of her pocket, whispering that she had to hide it or her mother would take it away and burn it.

It showed a couple-of-years-younger Grace, a delighted grin on her face, getting a ride in a wheelbarrow pushed by her equally grinning father.

By this man.

"You're Grace's dad," she said, staring at him.

The man stiffened. "You know my girl?"

She nodded. "I moved in next door three weeks ago."

His expression cleared immediately. "You're Ali?"

Surprised, she nodded again. But she was even more surprised by the utterly and unmistakably grateful expression that came over his face then. And when he spoke it was with a sincere tone that matched that look. And surprised her even more.

"Thank you."

Chapter Four

Colby Kendrick had known he was in trouble the moment that puppy had started yapping. He'd had no choice at the time except to grab it and try to quiet it. His ex-wife slept like a log—usually a drugged one—but he couldn't risk it. So he'd picked up the dog, who had wiggled so much it hurt his bleeding arm to hang on to him, and then he'd put him down on the ground back here in the trees so he could try to stop the bleeding. And as he'd hoped, the territory outside his fenced yard fascinated him enough he'd just started sniffing and exploring.

But now Colby was obviously in more trouble than he ever had been in his life.

That was what he got for sitting here in the rain for what, a couple of hours? But Liz had been so furious about the window he had been worried about his little girl. He heard the whole fight from here in the trees. His brave, courageous little girl who had immediately told her mother she had broken the window accidentally.

He didn't think Liz would physically abuse her, but at this point he wasn't certain of anything. And he wasn't about to leave Grace alone, even if he was bleeding.

And that was when everything had changed. When that other dog had arrived. He'd looked like a police dog or something when he'd first come racing out of the trees at him, and Colby had wondered if he was about to get bitten on top of everything. But it all changed again, and he was acting like a well-behaved pet. Well-behaved and...friendly.

"We need to have a discussion," the tall, powerful-looking man who had come up beside the dog said.

That was when a sudden thought struck him. "Did she call you? You work for them?"

"Them?" The woman who had come with the man spoke now. He assumed they were a couple, presumably the owners of the dog. There was something about the way they were together...

He nearly laughed aloud at himself, for thinking he had a clue. After all, he'd thought Liz loved him, too.

"Who?" the man asked, and there was an edge in his voice that said he wasn't a guy to mess with. And that instinct Colby trusted. So he answered.

"The Hollens."

He saw recognition of the name cross both of their faces. But unless he was completely wrong—entirely possible—he also saw a tinge of distaste.

"Hollen? Grace told me that was her mother's last name."

Colby's gaze snapped to Ali. And it happened again, just as it had the first moment he'd looked at her, before she'd explained and he realized she was that new friend Grace had told him about. That hair, the color of the reddest leaves in autumn. And her eyes, green like the other woman's but different, lighter, like the first growth of spring. And that voice, low and deep and rich, sending an oddly shivery sensation down his spine. He hadn't had a reaction like this to a woman in...forever.

Never let it be said your timing doesn't suck, Kendrick.

"Yeah. She never changed it when we got married. She was on the outs with the family then, but the name was...socially significant, she used to say."

"They are kind of...famous around here," the other woman explained to the new arrival. The man beside her snorted audibly, and he knew he'd been right about the distaste. "We're not a densely populated county, but if there's a family that is known by most residents, one way or another, it's them."

"You mean they're…a big deal?" the redhead asked, an undeniable emphasis on the last two words, as if she were quoting them.

"So they think," the man said. "Big real estate moguls, who like to buy up beautiful parcels of rural property and turn them into concrete canyons. Never mind the trees or the wildlife. Or that the roads and local facilities can't handle it." His tone matched that snort, and Colby felt a spark of hope. If that was how they felt about the Hollens…

"That's what Grace said about her mom. That she thinks she's a 'big deal.'"

"And I'm not," Colby said wearily. "And don't want to be. Never did. Which is why the divorce." He grimaced. "She thought I'd want to take advantage of the connection and move up—way up—in their world."

The woman called Ali hesitated, those lovely eyes looking troubled. "Her mother wants to change her last name to Hollen, but Grace doesn't want to. They fight over it, apparently."

Colby bit his lip but couldn't stop the moisture from welling up in his eyes. They'd fought over her first name, too. Grace had been his choice. She'd won that one, and the name on the birth certificate was Brianna, after her father, Brian. Well, she'd sort of won. Until Grace got old enough to choose for herself, and refused to respond to anything but Grace.

The redhead moved suddenly, crouching down as if she wanted to be on his level, eye to eye. The big dog nudged her, gently, and she looked at the animal. And Colby would swear, if it wasn't crazy, that the dog nodded.

Then she looked back at him and said, very quietly, "She told me she loves you, very much, and she wants to keep your name."

He lost the battle this time, and had to swipe at the tear

that was starting down his right cheek. He didn't dare try to speak. Was sure nothing could get past the knot in his throat her words had caused. He felt a touch on his left hand, and his gaze shot back to her face.

And then, somewhere out of left field, she asked in a normal voice, "Did you and Grace really build that birdhouse? Or should I say, bird apartment complex?"

He knew he was gaping at her, but he couldn't seem to help it. But his throat loosened up enough that he thought he could get some words out.

"Yes. Yes, we did. Last summer, at my place." Then his brow furrowed. "She still has it?"

"No. I do."

He blinked. "What?"

"It's in my garage for now, out of sight," she said, nodding toward the cottage-style home he'd always liked better than the overdone thing Liz had insisted on. "Grace said that's what you do. Build things."

"Yes. I'm a carpenter," he said, a little defiantly. "A good one. It's what I love to do. I never wanted to build skyscrapers or industrial parks. Just things for…people."

"And birds?" Ali asked gently. He nodded. "She asked me to hide it for her. To keep it safe."

His eyes closed. He had to suck in a deep breath. And couldn't keep the note of bitterness out of his voice when he said, "Yeah. Her mother wanted to burn it."

"And she tried to. It's a little scorched on one side, but no real damage that couldn't be fixed, I think."

He jolted upright. "Tried to? Who stopped her?"

"Grace pulled it out of the firepit in the backyard."

He swore, harshly, not even trying to keep it under his breath. "She could have been hurt."

She was looking at him now as if what he'd said had decided her somehow. She looked up at the couple, who had been oddly silent through this exchange. And then the dog moved, reaching out to gently nuzzle his hand. The uninjured arm, he noticed, although the dog couldn't possibly understand that. His instinctive response was to pet the dark head, but he did so warily, given how the animal had first approached him.

The moment his fingers stroked over the dark fur, he felt an impossible wave of calm go through him, a reassuring kind of feeling. That he could feel that now, in the midst of near-panic about his baby girl, the pain in his arm and the specter of the Hollens hanging over him, was a little unsettling. As was the fact that it was coming from this dog he'd just moments ago feared was going to rip his throat out.

"Question," said the man towering over him. Colby looked up, waiting. "You broke the window?"

He hesitated, decided trying to lie wasn't going to do him any good, since he sucked at it, as Liz had often told him. And there was something about this guy, some air of authority or something, that told him it wouldn't be smart to lie to him anyway.

"Yes. It was locked, and Grace was in there, curled up on her bed crying really hard. Screaming, in fact. I was afraid maybe…it had become physical."

"Has it been before?" the woman asked, her tone sharp. The man's wife, judging by the ring on her finger, sounded oddly concerned for someone who didn't know him, or Grace, although they apparently at least knew of Liz's family.

"Not that I've seen any sign of, and believe me, I've checked."

"What happened then?" Quinn asked.

"Grace got up and came running to the window when I broke it, but then Liz stormed in. I ducked just in time, when I heard her stomping down the hall."

He shrugged, wincing as it tugged on the cut on his forearm. He also felt a splat on his nose, as rain began.

"So she didn't see you?"

"No." He closed his eyes, and gave a slow, aching shake of

his head. "Grace...she screamed at her that she broke it, trying to get away from her."

"Quick thinking," the man said.

His eyes snapped open and he looked up at the man again. "My Grace is a very, very smart kid."

"Her mother could have called the police. You could have been caught. You're hurt and bleeding. Yet you're still here. Why?"

"I couldn't leave Grace here alone with her when she was that angry." He nodded toward the big house, which was visible through the trees. "Here at least I can still hear what's going on, and see if she leaves with her." He lowered his gaze again. "She's always threatening to vanish with her, to keep her away from me."

"Is there a custody agreement?" the woman asked.

He laughed bitterly. "Sure. But when your name's Hollen you don't have to worry about those little details."

"May I suggest," Ali said, "that we take this inside before the rain really gets going again? I have some first aid supplies, we can take a look at your arm, too."

"Good idea," the other woman said.

"Very," said the man, as the skies opened up again.

Colby didn't move. Looked toward the big house. "It's okay," Ali said gently. "You'll still be able to see the house from inside."

"And there will be four of us to watch," the other man said briskly.

Colby got to his feet slowly, warily. He looked from Ali to the other man, then back to her. For some reason she was the one he trusted, if only because Grace trusted her, and as he'd said, his girl was a very, very smart kid.

He nodded toward the couple. "They're friends of yours?"

Ali smiled, and it was breath-stealing. "I think they will be, although we just met. They brought my puppy home, after he—" she nodded at the big dog "—brought him to them."

Colby winced. "I'm really sorry about that, I had to quiet him or Liz would have seen me. Then while I was trying to stop the bleeding, I lost track of him."

"He's home safe now, thanks to Cutter, here." She seemed to be watching him rather carefully when she added, "And these are Cutter's people, Quinn and Hayley Foxworth."

He blinked. "Foxworth?"

"Nice to meet you," the man said blandly. "Now can we get inside before we're all drenched?"

Colby followed the trio toward the cottage. The dog, however, stuck to his side as if he were his owner, not the couple ahead of them. Maybe he was a herding dog or something, making sure the straggler stayed in line.

Foxworth?

It couldn't be, could it? But it would certainly explain why Ali had been watching him so intently when she introduced them. Because Foxworth was a name well known in these parts. He knew it, not just because of the headlines when they'd toppled their twisted governor, but because of a job he'd done last year. Was this just coincidence, them showing up here? He'd known they were based in the area, but had no idea they were this close. He—

His racing, tumbling thoughts broke off as the dog at his side nudged his hand. He automatically reached to pat the dark head, and felt it again, that soothing, somehow reassuring rush of sensation he couldn't even begin to explain.

He gave his head a sharp shake, trying to clear it. He was all tangled up with the emotions he'd felt when he'd heard Grace wailing, when he'd seen her tearstained face. Plus, he hadn't slept last night, nor had he eaten, so he knew he couldn't think straight just now.

Maybe that was why he just numbly followed these people he'd never even met before.

Or maybe it was that reassuring dog.

Chapter Five

My dad's the best. He loves me more than anything. My mother keeps trying to scare him away, but he promised he'd never give up.

Ali remembered Grace's firm statement, spoken with utter conviction. She remembered hoping the child was right, that it wasn't some idealized image of her father she clung to.

Now she was certain.

She'd gotten her first aid kit from the cupboard she stored it in, and at Hayley's suggestion gave it to Quinn.

"He's had to deal with worse," she'd said.

"Military?" Ali guessed. At Hayley's nod and questioning look she explained, "I did a job for a retired commander in the Navy. They have that air…"

Hayley smiled widely. "Yes, they do."

Now they were standing by the window with the best view of the house next door, while Quinn had Colby's arm stretched out on her kitchen counter, already cleaned up with the antiseptic she kept on hand. She remembered the feel of his hand when she'd touched him. Not soft, office-bound hands, but tough, roughened hands. A working man's hands.

"Could go either way," Quinn said. "Stitches might help, but not sure they're really necessary. It's long, but not too deep."

"I can't leave until I know Grace is okay."

"I figured as much," Quinn said, clearly unsurprised.

"There are some butterfly bandages in here that could hold things. You'll likely have a righteous scar, though."

"Won't be the first," Colby muttered.

Ali watched him as Quinn worked, saw him wince once, but otherwise remain expressionless.

It wasn't until his arm was cleaned and bandaged and Colby had flexed it slightly that he looked up at the man who had been efficiently doing the work. He seemed to hesitate, then asked, "You're not…those Foxworths, are you? *The* Foxworths, I mean?"

One corner of Quinn's mouth quirked upward. "Depends on what you mean by that."

"Ogilvie. Flood."

So he did know, Ali thought as he named the disgraced politicians Foxworth had helped bring down. Their disgustingly crooked former governor, and the even more disgusting senator turned powerbroker—or at least that had been his plan before Foxworth had uncovered that his wife's death, which he had milked for all it was worth, had been a murder contracted by him.

Ali glanced at Hayley, who was smiling. "Read the news, do you?" she asked in a cheery tone.

"When I think I can stomach it," Colby said sourly.

Quinn laughed. "I'm with you there."

"But I only paid attention to that because I'd already heard of you. From a guy I've done some work with."

Fascinated, Ali watched the exchange, getting the feeling there was more to this than just recognizing a well-known name.

"And that would be…?"

"Local building contractor. Guy named Drew Kiley."

Ali blinked. She knew that name, had seen signs for Kiley Construction at sites in the area. He'd built a couple of buildings in town that had become gathering places, because they were beautiful, well designed and constructed. She'd even read that he'd been offered some very big projects but had turned them down, because that wasn't what he wanted to do.

She also knew she hadn't mistaken the sudden change in demeanor in both Quinn and Hayley at the mention of that name.

Nor, apparently, had Colby.

"So you are that Foxworth," he said. "The ones who helped him."

"He was our third case, after Hayley and I met," Quinn said.

"He told me his life was a mess, and then it got worse, but you guys stepped in and saved it all. Him, his wife and their little boy."

"Drew," Hayley said, "understated his part in saving it all. As usual."

Colby smiled slightly, and nodded. "Sounds like him. He's a good guy. And great to work with. We kind of see eye to eye on things."

Quinn nodded, then tilted his head slightly. "So, if we call him and ask about you, he'll have good things to say?"

Colby blinked, pulled back a little. "Yeah. I think so. I hope so. But why—" He stopped abruptly when Quinn pulled out his phone, clearly intending to make that call right now. "Say hello for me," he added, sounding a little bemused.

Ali was a little surprised at how quickly Quinn had the head of the company, Drew Kiley himself, on the line. After a quick moment of greetings exchanged, Quinn asked to put him on speaker for the rest.

"We're here with someone who says he's done work for you. Colby Kendrick."

"Colby?" came a deep, male voice from the phone. "He's there?"

Quinn nodded at Colby, who answered. "I'm here, Drew."

"You okay? Grace okay?"

"For now, I think."

"But there's a problem?"

"We're still assessing," Quinn said. "I just wanted your take."

"My take is that Colby Kendrick is a great guy. And one of the best carpenters I've ever worked with. That Village Center project you guys like so much? He's the one who saved that undertaking."

Ali kept watching, fascinated by all of this. "It was just an idea that worked," Colby said, sounding almost embarrassed by the praise.

"A genius idea," Drew corrected. "Turning that narrow breezeway into a full, covered patio with a play area not only made it a better community center, it solved the problem of how and where to run the power and plumbing lines to the new building."

"It worked," Colby repeated.

"That it did. You made us look really good. And I'd hire you full-time in an instant, you know that, right?"

Ali saw Colby swallow as if his throat was tight. "Thanks, man."

"Quinn, anything I can do?" the man on the other end asked.

"We'll let you know, Drew. Thanks."

"Any time, you know that," the man said. Then he added, rather vehemently, "He really is one of the good guys, I promise."

"Thanks for confirming it." Quinn ended the call.

Confirming it, Ali thought. So Quinn had already thought so? She wasn't surprised. You didn't run an organization like the Foxworth Foundation without being a pretty good judge of people.

Only then did she notice their dog was staring at Quinn, and when Quinn looked back, he gave a short, sharp little yip.

"Yeah, yeah," Quinn said with a wry smile. "I know, you told us so."

"Told you…what?" Ali asked, fascinated by this dynamic. And the more time she spent around the Foxworths and Cutter, the more she wondered if she had the knack at all to deal with a dog.

Hayley was smiling when she answered her. "That look he gave us when we first found Colby here? That's his 'fix it' look."

"Fix it?"

"As in there's something wrong that we can fix," Quinn said.

"And," Hayley added, "that he's decided this person deserves our help."

Colby tilted his head, a thoughtful look coming over his face. "Drew's kid, Luke... I remember him saying you had a magic dog."

Both of the Foxworths laughed.

"Seems that way sometimes," Quinn said. Ali found that fascinating, since she never would have guessed the tough-looking guy had a fanciful streak.

"Is he ever wrong?" Colby asked, looking at the dog a little warily.

"Hasn't been yet," Quinn said. "Besides, how could I ever doubt the dog who brought Hayley to me?"

Colby looked bemused again, so much that Ali wondered if he'd quite absorbed what had just happened here. She felt the sudden need to make it clear.

"So...you'll help him, and Grace?" she asked.

"Looks that way," Quinn said.

She looked at Colby, saw it register. He drew back slightly, looking from the dog to Quinn to Hayley. "You mean...?"

"You've got the Foxworth Foundation behind you now," Hayley said gently. "And we'll get this sorted out, whatever it takes."

Colby swallowed, staring as if in disbelief. Ali had the thought that his ex had belittled him so much that he couldn't quite believe an organization on the level of Foxworth would actually help him. She'd convinced him he wasn't worth that kind of help. Ali felt a little nauseous. She knew people like Liz Hollen existed, but so far she'd managed to keep them out of her life.

And she was seized with the urge to help Colby get this one out of his.

"Yes, we mean it," Quinn assured him when Colby didn't—or couldn't—speak. "So you need to mean it, too. We'll have to probe, ask questions you might not be comfortable answering."

"Just remember," Hayley put in, "that we're not them, and we won't hold anything against you short of maybe murder."

"Not yet," Colby said dryly.

"We'll need to know it all. And you need to answer any questions honestly, even if you can't see the reason we need to know."

"I...all right."

"We'll need to keep a close eye on Grace. Do you live nearby?" Hayley asked.

He shook his head. "I'm a few miles away." He lowered his gaze. "It's just a little place but I like it."

Ali didn't doubt that "little" was in comparison to the place next door.

"Okay," Quinn said. "We can set up and work from our headquarters, which is a lot closer."

"Why don't you stay here, to keep an eye on things?" Ali said.

Colby's head came up sharply, but it was Quinn who answered. "We're used to working from anywhere, but it could get a little chaotic. Coming and going and all."

"I don't mind. I already like Grace so much. It would be an honor to help."

Colby sat there at the kitchen counter, staring at them all for a long, silent moment. Then he slid off the barstool to his feet. He looked at Ali. "Where's your pup?"

Her brow furrowed. "He's in his playpen. Why?"

"I want to go thank him. If he hadn't started barking and I hadn't grabbed him... I'd still be facing this alone."

And in that moment all Ali could think was what a fool Liz Hollen was.

Chapter Six

"Lay it out for us," Quinn said. "Just be honest, that's all we ask of anyone."

They were sitting around Ali's dining table, a nicely built piece with cushioned chairs that invited longer stays. Colby had a feeling they were going to be very glad of that before this was over.

"Do you want me to leave?" Ali asked.

"No," he answered instantly. "Unless you want to. You've already helped Grace…"

"And I'd like to help more. So I'll stay, if it's all right with you."

He was a little surprised at how all right it was. How much he wanted her to do just that. Because from the moment he'd set foot in this place, it had felt…welcoming. And he hadn't missed that while there were some unpacked boxes in the far corner of the living room, the bookshelves along the wall opposite the big windows were already stocked. And stocked with every kind of book he could imagine, heavy, hardbound tomes, paperbacks, large books of photographs of all sorts of places and things.

It felt like home.

It was a moment before he could shift his attention back to the Foxworths.

"Where do you want me to start? The beginning, the end...?"

"How about the beginning of the end," Hayley suggested.

His mouth quirked at that. He was still having a little trouble believing this was really happening, that he had this operation, with the incredible reputation for helping people trying to fight the bigger behemoths around today, on his side.

On Grace's side.

"Liz and I got married young," he began. "That was the first but not the biggest mistake. The biggest was that neither of us had any idea of who the other really was. I knew her family was—" he glanced at Ali "—a big deal, but she insisted she had nothing to do with them, so it didn't matter."

"A bit of youthful rebellion?" Quinn suggested.

"Yeah. But after Grace was born they patched it up. Which I thought was a good thing."

"But it wasn't?" Hayley asked, as if she already knew the answer.

"Not for me. Because it came with a lot of mistaken assumptions."

He started to lift his hand to shove back that stubborn lock of hair that always fell over his forehead, but the cut on his arm twinged and he stopped the movement. He took a deep breath. He could only hope they'd understand. Drew's story encouraged him to go on.

"She assumed that I would immediately grab at the chance her family offered, to become part of their...empire. Become an executive, leave the dirty business of doing actual, physical work with my hands behind."

He hadn't meant to sound so bitter, but apparently he didn't quite have that leashed yet.

"Because of course who wouldn't rather be trapped in a high-rise office rather than being out here in nature, among the peons, creating things," Ali said, her tone nearly as sharp as his had been.

Colby's gaze snapped to the woman sitting at one end of the table. He'd been a little surprised at himself when he'd realized that for some reason he didn't mind that she was going to hear just how stupid he'd been. But now she was jumping in to defend him. To defend him more than his then wife ever had, when Ali didn't even know him beyond what Grace might have said.

"And what was your mistaken assumption?" Hayley asked.

His mouth twisted wryly. "That she knew me. That she understood this was who I was, and I was doing what I wanted to do. And… I assumed she understood me. Enough to know I wouldn't be happy doing anything else."

"And loved you enough to let you do it?" Ali asked, her voice soft now.

"Yeah," he said, his jaw tightening. "My biggest mistaken assumption. When the truth was, I embarrassed the hell out of her. I made decent money, it wasn't like she had to do without, but she was embarrassed when she had to introduce her husband, *the carpenter*, to their ritzy friends."

He'd tried to put the same tone of distaste in his voice that Liz had used, and thought by Ali's look of utter disgust that he'd succeeded. He glanced at Quinn, who he thought wore an expression that seemed just as disgusted. Which was proved right when the Foxworth man muttered a description of women like Liz that made the tension inside Colby ease a bit. It even made the two women here and now smile, although he could see them try to suppress it.

They saw it. They really did. They weren't at all impressed by the Hollen name, or their status and standing in the county. But then, after what the Foxworth Foundation had accomplished in the last few years, they had no reason to be. They were, in fact, a much bigger name than the Hollens themselves.

And there was nothing guaranteed to make ol' Brian Hollen, Liz's father, madder than that.

"So what happened after she reconciled with her family?" Hayley asked.

He shrugged. "She got madder and madder at me for not following her plan. Then one day I came home to an empty house. She'd packed up herself and Grace and gone. I wasn't home more than five minutes when a guy knocked on the door and I was served with divorce papers."

He'd never forget that horrible day. Staring at his little girl's room, stripped of everything that made it Grace's. Except, he'd noticed through numbing shock, the things he'd gotten for her. Those were left behind in garbage bags.

He tried to describe the next steps in the grim journey, but he wasn't sure he'd gotten it all through the gray, light-dimming curtain that descended in his mind every time he thought about Grace, his poor little Gracie, caught in the middle of a battle she couldn't understand.

"Then I made yet another mistake," he said grimly. "I assumed—that damned word again—that Liz just wanted to be rid of me, that she still loved Grace and wanted her to be happy."

"And instead she used her as a weapon," Hayley said gently. At his startled look she gave a sad shake of her head. "We've seen it before. Too often, sadly."

He sucked in a deep breath, so relieved at this immediate understanding of—and belief in—his situation that for a moment he couldn't go on.

"When I hired a lawyer, I didn't realize I'd need the most bloodthirsty shark around. So it was the full cadre of Hollen attorneys and all the Hollen money against me. I ended up with the right to three hours a week and one weekend day a month with Grace."

"Ouch," Quinn said.

"Bad enough if Liz would have abided by it. But she didn't. She was always finding things to take up the whole weekend, things that were for Grace's benefit, so she said. And the last time I confronted her about it she told me to back off or I'd never see my girl again."

This time he did shove that hair back, deciding he needed that little jab of pain to keep him on track, and not spiral into the morass of regret and sadness that tried to swamp him every time he tried to deal with losing his little girl. And it did help him focus, enough to go on.

"The local sheriff's office doesn't have the staffing to come out and stand by every time I go to pick Grace up, but I know damned well that if I even accidentally lay a hand on Liz trying to get Grace away from her I'll be in jail faster than I can blink. And then I really might never see her again."

"What's your worst fear about all this?" Hayley asked gently.

He didn't have to think about his answer. "That she'll make good on her threat to disappear with Grace, to go somewhere her family has access to but that I'd never be able to set foot, lowly being that I am."

He thought he heard Ali say something, but it was too low for him to make out the words. The tone, however, was perfectly clear, and it steadied him.

Quinn and Hayley exchanged glances. "I'll call Gavin," Quinn said, in the same moment that Hayley said, "I'll call Carly."

Colby blinked. He thought about the accounts he'd read of the big scandal a few months ago, wondered if he was remembering right. "Gavin…?" he began.

"De Marco," Quinn confirmed.

Colby went still. Very still. Having a good lawyer was one thing. Having world-famous Gavin de Marco on your side was an entirely different atmosphere. He did okay financially—at least he thought so, as long as he wasn't compared to the Hollens—but a guy who could probably charge a thousand dollars for a three-minute phone call was beyond heady, it was downright absurd for a common carpenter.

"I...could never afford him," he said, feeling oddly as if he was watching a ship leaving the dock, a ship he'd hoped—however briefly—to be on.

"That's not your problem," said Quinn briskly. "Gavin works for Foxworth now. And we foot the bill. Because when we take on a client, it's not for money. It's for what's right. And the only thing we ask of you is to help us help someone else down the line."

"What a wonderful rule to live by."

Ali's voice was soft, but still full of awe when she said it. And Colby certainly couldn't disagree. Still...

"I did break that window," he said. "Grace was..." He had no words for how seeing his little girl nearly hysterical had affected him. "I had to get to her somehow, and I knew if I just knocked on the door Liz would do her worst."

"You didn't try calling the sheriff?" Quinn asked.

"I..." He grimaced again. It was becoming a habit. "I don't have a working phone at the moment. I just this morning discovered Liz was tracking mine, and monitoring my calls and messages, so I bricked it. I don't know how she got the spyware on there, but she did. Probably one of the Hollen tech people did it for her, she's not that tech savvy."

Hayley's brows rose as she spoke. "And location tracking?"

Damn. He hadn't thought of that. "Probably," he said wearily. "That's why she came raging back to Grace's room so quickly. In fact, that's probably why Grace was crying in the first place, now that I think of it. Her mother must have known I was in the area, and gloated that she was going to get me thrown in jail. That's her usual approach when Grace gets stubborn."

"Where's your car?" asked Quinn.

"Around the corner, so Liz wouldn't see it." He groaned inwardly. "You think she's tracking that, too?"

"Possibly." Quinn glanced at Hayley.

"I'll call Ty as well," she said.

Quinn looked back at him. "Let's get this started," he said briskly.

And for the first time Colby felt a jab of a feeling he'd thought lost long ago.

Hope.

Chapter Seven

"Okay, we've got the basics set," Quinn was saying as Ali brought the fresh pot of coffee she'd brewed out to the table. They'd made those phone calls they'd mentioned, and results were already happening.

Ali was feeling much more cheerful now. Foxworth, *the* Foxworth, was going to help. In fact, their clever dog already was; he'd been playing with Ziggy and keeping him out of the way while they organized things.

Quinn was looking at a rather sizable laptop he now had open on the table. A young man with a trace of a Texas sort of accent had dropped it and some other things off ten minutes ago, pausing only for a brief introduction as the local Foxworth tech guy, Liam Burnett. He was also apparently helping orient a new hire—from what Ali heard, a man who had helped them on that big-headline case with the senator last year.

"How's Cort doing?" Hayley had asked.

"About as well as he could be. But he says he'd rather be working and learning than sitting at home grieving. Rafe's taking him on for the next stage as soon as we wrap this case."

Ali gathered the man had been widowed shortly after that headline case had wrapped, and she had felt an all too familiar jab of empathy for someone she'd never even met. Then Liam had headed back out to deal with the other case they were handling.

"You do a lot of multitasking?" Ali asked now.

"We've often got more than one case going," Hayley said. "Liam's in the final stages of his, so he'll be available later if we need him."

"And by the way," Quinn said, looking over at Colby, "he noticed a crew installing security cameras next door."

Colby sighed audibly. "I'm sure I triggered the rush, but she has been telling Grace she would. Saying it was for her sake."

His expression made it clear he didn't believe that. And frankly, at this point neither did Ali.

"Liam said just be aware, that the models they're installing have an extremely wide angle of view."

Colby went still. "Meaning they'll cover down to Grace's room?"

"Probably. And probably recording 24/7."

"I guess I should be thankful she doesn't have a video of me breaking that window. I shouldn't have, but Grace…she was screaming, I thought maybe she was hurt—"

Quinn held up a hand. "We'll deal with that, if we have to."

"You mean if she has me arrested for trespassing or something," he said sourly.

"Gavin's up to speed," Quinn said. "He'll be standing by."

Ali saw the look of awed wonder cross Colby's face. She didn't blame him, she'd feel the same way if she was looking at potential trouble and had Gavin de Marco on her side.

"And," Hayley said, almost cheerfully, "we've got a counter ploy. Liam also dropped off a couple of similar cameras for us to set up, so we don't get caught staring out the window at them all the time." She glanced at Ali. "That is, if you don't mind us putting them up outside."

"No, of course not," she said.

"Good. We can stream the feed from here to our headquarters as well. You can watch from there, Colby. I presume her employee over there would recognize you?" Colby nodded, but said nothing. "Then at this point we don't want you being seen anywhere near the house. We don't want her making any connection between you and Ali that might make her pull Grace back."

Colby nodded again as Quinn picked up the devices Liam had left and headed outside.

"And," Hayley said, picking up something else Liam had left behind, a box with two cell phones that looked rather heavy-duty, "you each take one of these. They're our own phones, with links to each of us and headquarters. The red button here is the emergency call out to anyone close by, if you need it, or if you need a fast answer to something."

Ali nodded as she and Colby both took one. Then he turned his head to look at Ali. She saw him swallow as if his throat were tight. And there was a warmth in those blue, blue eyes of his that told her he meant what he said next, deeply. "I... thank you. Again. For worrying about Gracie. For helping out now. For...everything."

"I'm pretty fond of that little girl of yours," she said with a smile. "And," she added pointedly, "I trust her judgment."

And I trust those eyes.

She couldn't help thinking of the last time she had gone with her instincts on that particular thing. When she'd looked into a man's eyes, trusted. And with that man she'd found love and an all too short three years of happiness before fate and illness had stolen it all from her.

And now in Colby Kendrick's eyes she saw all she needed to see, the love and worry for his daughter, the desperation, the gratitude he was feeling. It was all genuine, there was no wall around it, and it was no facade put up to fool others. This man was for real, and even if all this was only visible because of his near panic about Grace, it was still real.

His heart was real.

Some part of her mind tried to point out that she'd met the man all of a couple of hours ago, and she didn't disavow it entirely. Just mostly. Because it was outweighed by the memory of the pure adoration in little Grace Kendrick's face as she spoke of him.

Judging by how quickly he was back, Ali guessed this wasn't Quinn Foxworth's first time installing security cameras. He went back to the laptop and worked on it for a moment, then nodded.

"All right," he said. "We've got the entire back side of the other house on one, and the front and driveway on the other." He looked out to her great room, then back up at Ali. "And if you don't mind, we can cast this to the TV so we don't have to always be in front of the little screen here."

She nodded immediately. "Any movement would be more obvious, too, on the big screen, wouldn't it?"

Quinn smiled at her. "Exactly."

Moments later they were settled in the great room, on the couch in front of the fireplace and TV. The previous owner of the house had included the rather complex setup in the sale, thankfully, since that was not at all her forte. And actually, the evergreen framed view of the big house wasn't unpleasant. In fact, it could almost be an acceptable screen saver, if you were into that kind of thing. She herself preferred mountains and wilderness, and this time of year, snow. But then, that was why she lived here in the first place.

"When's your next scheduled time with Grace?" Hayley, who had been reading things on her phone for a while, finally looked up and asked.

"Friday, after she gets out of school."

"Do you pick her up there at the school?"

He laughed, and there was that bitter undertone again. "She won't allow it. Wants me to come to the house to get her, so she can be there."

"To remind you she's in charge?" asked Ali with a grimace, starting to truly dislike the neighbor she'd barely met.

His gaze snapped to her when she spoke, and he looked both surprised and…grateful? What, that someone saw his side?

Or was it perhaps simply that someone was listening to him? And actually wanted to help? Obviously it was taking him a while to get used to that, to having help.

"That's our first step," Quinn said. "We make sure someone is always with you when you pick her up. As a witness. We've got Liam, and Teague if he gets back from Oregon when scheduled."

"I could help with that," Ali suggested.

Hayley smiled at her. "I don't think so. If Colby shows up with a woman, I'm guessing it'll really set her off. And you being a neighbor might make her suspicious."

Ali looked at him. He shrugged. "Yeah. No one could possibly replace her. Besides, she doesn't want me, so of course nobody else would either."

"So she lies to herself, too?" Ali asked, making her tone as saccharinely sweet as she could.

Colby blinked. He averted his gaze in an almost shy way. But slowly, a smile curved his mouth.

Sure, nobody would want to kiss that gorgeous mouth, Ms. Superior-to-us-all.

"I'm thinking maybe I should make solo contact," Hayley said to Quinn. "We can come up with some pretext, so I can get close enough to feel out the situation. Get her to trust me with whatever plans she might have."

"Pretext like what?" Ali asked.

Hayley shrugged. "We'll have to think of something."

"Or not," Ali said. "Let me do it. I already have the perfect in, the new neighbor thing. I can make a downright nuisance of myself, when motivated."

She was smiling now, liking the idea. Not just of helping Grace, but helping her father. She glanced at him. He was shaking his head, as if in wonder.

"Why would you do that? Why are you doing any of this? You don't even know me."

"Yes, I do. From everything Grace has told me about you.

From that picture she showed me, of you pushing her in a wheelbarrow."

"She has that? And showed you?"

"She's saved it from her mother's purge. And yes, she showed me. And she's told me stories."

He let out a compressed breath. "I'm sure she has. My girl's a storyteller. She writes them all down. I think she'll be a writer someday. She—" He stopped abruptly, paling a little.

"What?" she asked, aware that both Quinn and Hayley were listening to them.

"I…that's how I first knew how bad it was. The last time I was in that house, when I got there before Liz, Grace let me in before the housekeeper could stop her. I saw a story she'd written back before the divorce. About a little girl who lived with a monster and had to hide all day until her daddy came home and she was safe."

Ali gasped aloud. Hayley reacted visibly, and Quinn's gaze narrowed into a stare Ali thought would intimidate anyone.

It took Colby a moment to go on. "That story showed me I'd never had the happy family I thought I did. And it made me worry about Grace. About her safety. Enough to fight for custody even though I knew I'd lose." He let out a long, weary sigh. "Enough to risk breaking that window today to get to her."

"What were you going to do?" Hayley asked, sounding merely curious.

"I'm not sure." Colby gave her a wry, almost embarrassed look. "I wasn't exactly thinking straight just then."

"Who would be?" Ali said quickly.

"Then we'd better get rolling," Quinn said.

And from across the room Cutter gave a short bark that sounded oddly like "About time."

Chapter Eight

"Colby Kendrick, meet Juvenile Detective Carly Devon."

Colby shook hands with the tall, obviously fit woman with the cropped, tousled blond hair. Despite the chill, she was wearing a short jacket that he belatedly realized was so she could easily get to the weapon on her hip.

He'd been a little nervous about them calling in law enforcement, and a bit more afraid that a female juvenile officer would lean toward Liz's side. But Quinn had insisted she was a straight arrow, and it didn't matter who she had to stand against, she'd proven she'd stand for the right.

And if he went by the way the dog, Cutter, greeted her, he'd have to believe it.

He cast a glance toward the kitchen, where Ali and Hayley were planning out her approach to Liz. He had the feeling he was going to be thankful Ali couldn't hear them, given the questions he was likely about to be asked.

"I heard you built the new veterans' meeting hall out at Douglas Rockford's place," she said after petting the dog.

That unexpected observation startled him as much as that steady, assessing, bright blue gaze unsettled him. Together they made him feel as if he were being tested somehow.

"Where'd you hear that?"

"My husband. Parker Ward."

Colby blinked. He remembered the man on Drew Kiley's

team, and the stories of how he'd nearly destroyed his life by turning whistleblower on his evilly corrupt boss. "You're Parker's wife?"

"Yes." She smiled. "I kept the old name because it was too big a pain to change all the legal and badge-related stuff, and Parker didn't care."

"He's had…bigger things to worry about," Colby said.

It was coming back to him in a rush now, how Foxworth had helped Parker, too, in the end hooking him up with Drew's company. Had this woman helped in that?

"Indeed he has," she agreed, and pride echoed in her voice. The kind of pride he'd never heard in Liz's voice, talking about him. "But he told me how much all of Drew's crew liked working with you. And that you'd volunteered for the veterans' hall project."

"I…yeah." It was starting to hit him, all the people he knew or had worked with who had Foxworth to thank for the better lives they had today. He knew they'd also helped a guy who had ended up at Sarge's encampment for veterans. Plus, they'd helped Sarge himself when setting up the refuge for vets who needed a place to get their feet under them again had run afoul of some bureaucrat.

"He also said that you did it for materials cost only."

He shrugged. "Sarge is doing a great thing there. I wanted to help."

He saw the woman nod as if she'd heard what she'd expected to hear. Then she looked at Quinn and said, "So, that…theoretical situation you wanted to discuss?"

Colby's jaw tightened nervously at the "theoretical." Quinn had promised him they'd stay in what-if territory, that they would not reveal anything that would make the detective feel as if she had to step in. At least, not yet. He had to trust them, these people he'd only met hours ago. And when it came to Grace's welfare, it was hard to trust anyone. But the Foxworth name was as unassailable as any name could be, at least around here.

"Seven-year-old child. Divorced parents. Father, working guy, clean record and clearly loves the girl. Mother, wealthy family, with influence she uses like a sledgehammer. Also uses the girl as a weapon against the father. No physical abuse that we're aware of."

The detective shifted her gaze to Colby. "Let me guess, she's also making the father seeing his daughter as difficult as possible?"

"Yes," Quinn answered for him.

The woman's gaze never left Colby. Clearly she knew he was the father in question. "And how far has the father had to push, to see his child?"

"So far just the broken window I mentioned," Quinn answered, "to check on the girl who was locked in her room, nearly hysterical."

Detective Devon nodded, still looking at Colby. And then she shifted her focus to Cutter, who had walked over and sat at—in fact on—his feet, but turned to face her. The dog looked up at her steadily. And as if that had been the deciding factor, she looked back up at Colby and said, very quietly, "I won't step in officially unless I absolutely have to. Unless I'm ordered to. Does she have that kind of influence?"

He let out a weary breath. "Afraid so."

"Mostly local, though," Quinn put in. "Not so much on the other side, or down in Olympia."

"All right," the detective said. "That tells me who not to ask for information, if I need it." That caught Colby off guard and his eyes widened. And then Carly Devon smiled, widely, and shifted her gaze to Quinn "Guess I'll stick to Brett."

"Always a good plan," Quinn said with a grin.

Under the circumstances it took him a moment to put it together, that they were referring to the other local detective who had been instrumental in that takedown of the crooked governor, Brett Dunbar. And once more he felt that wave of wonder, that he had people like this on his side.

"I checked as you asked, Quinn, and as of half an hour ago, no reports on a broken window from that address," she went on, snapping him out of his reverie.

"Figured," Quinn said. "So she's not playing by the common rules."

"She doesn't think she has to," Colby said before he could stop himself. He had to remind himself to word the rest carefully. "Plus...she's the type who might keep that as a secret weapon. Her family's big on that."

"Tell her about the story you found," Quinn said,

It was difficult, sharing how wrong he'd been about the life he'd foolishly thought he had. But that story Grace had written, those two and a half pages of her surprisingly well-formed printing, had been the thing that changed everything, the thing that had opened his eyes.

"You know," the blonde said when he'd finished, her tone carefully neutral, "a lot of people would have shined that on as just a kid's vivid imagination, maybe after watching some movie with a monster in it."

He shook his head. "Not Grace. When I talked to her about it, she said it was real, that she only made it a monster in case Liz found it. So she could pretend just that."

The detective's brows rose. "Smart indeed."

"Yes. And she doesn't lie." Surprising himself, he smiled. At the detective's questioning look he explained. "Once when we were in a hearing, the family court officer asked her if she liked her home. She said yes, but it would have been better if I'd built it. Then they asked her if she had her own room, and had enough clothes and things. And she said yes, after her mother got her own stuff. So they asked her if she had everything she needed, and she said no."

His throat tightened, and he couldn't go on. But it appeared he didn't have to, because Ali had come up behind him and said quietly, "And I'll bet she said it was because she didn't have you."

He nodded, not even surprised at her accurate guess. He was remembering that hearing so vividly now his eyes began to sting all over again. He looked up at Ali, marveling anew at how she had stepped up on his side when they'd met less than—he glanced at the time stamp in the corner of the camera feed on the flat-screen—five hours ago.

He didn't realize he was shaking his head until the detective asked quietly, "Problem?"

"No, I just… This morning I was dealing with this alone, with my gut telling me I was going to lose and be lucky if I didn't end up in jail. And now…" He gestured toward Ali first, then Quinn and Hayley as they came out to join them.

"They do have a way," Detective Devon said after being introduced to Ali. Then, smiling widely, she said, "I owe them—and their boy Cutter—for my current state of delirious happiness. And I'm just one in a long line."

"You met Parker on one of their cases?"

She nodded, confirming his earlier guess. "And the team matchmaker," she said, nodding toward the dog, "decided then and there Parker and I needed to be together."

Ali laughed at that. "The team matchmaker?"

"You laugh now, but just you wait."

Colby wasn't sure what that was supposed to mean, but he was too transfixed by the delighted look on Ali's face to speak.

The detective got to her feet, looking at Quinn and Hayley now. "All right, I'll do a bit of research, find what you asked about. If anything changes, you need more, or need me to step in, you've got the number."

"Thanks, Carly. Say hello to Parker for us."

"Oh, I'll do more than hello," she promised with a wink.

"That," Hayley said with a grin after she'd gone, "is a happy woman."

"And Parker's a happy—and lucky—guy," Colby said.

"What was that about Cutter being a matchmaker?" Ali asked.

"He just knows when two people should be together, like she said," Hayley answered.

Colby was sure he looked as doubtful as Ali. Enough that Quinn grinned at them. "He started with me and Hayley, and he hasn't let up since."

If there was anyone Colby would have thought wouldn't buy into that kind of fanciful idea, it was Quinn Foxworth. And as if he'd read the thought, the man laughed.

"Yeah, I know. And I was a very, very tough sell. I mean seriously, a dog? But if you still don't believe after nearly twenty times without a miss, you're not hard to convince, you're blind."

He shifted his gaze to his wife, who had walked over with Ali. The wife he so clearly loved and apparently would not have were it not for that dog who was now sitting watching them intently.

"You get a plan worked out?" Quinn asked.

"We did," Hayley confirmed.

"All right." He shifted his gaze to Colby. "Big question I have to ask. Do you know if there are any weapons in the house? Does she own any?"

Colby blinked. "Uh… I don't think so." His mouth twisted. "She considers herself above such things, but I know the Hollens have armed security when they need it."

"Typical," Quinn said, then shifted back to his wife. "So what's the plan?"

Hayley looked at Colby. "First of all, to ease your mind, Cutter is now acting as Ali's for the duration. He'll keep her safe, and Grace."

He couldn't deny he was relieved. But also puzzled. "But he hasn't even met Grace."

"But he'll have her scent," Ali said, "and Hayley says that's enough."

"How…?"

"I have a sweater she forgot last time she snuck over here."

"We'll give Cutter a good sniff," Hayley said, "and that with the command 'protect,' he'll know what to do." She smiled. "Not that he wouldn't even without that. The 'protect the children gene' is built in, from what we've seen."

"So I'll go over with him, pretend he's mine. She doesn't hate dogs, does she?"

"No. As long as they don't track dirt into her house, she doesn't react much to them."

Ali wrinkled her nose. Colby almost smiled. "I'll still try to make nice with her," she said. "Grace told me she likes fancy wine?"

Colby smothered a snort. "Yeah. Top-of-the-line stuff. French, mostly."

Ali smiled. "Hayley says they can handle that."

Colby looked at the other woman questioningly. Hayley nodded. "We have a couple of bottles that were a gift from a client. Very high-end. Not to our taste, so now it can be put to good use."

"Anyway," Ali went on, "I'll take her the wine, and if I can get her to drink some and relax a little so we can…talk. And since I know nothing about conducting an inquiry or investigating—" she held up what looked like a pair of pearl earrings "—I'll have Foxworth in my ear, guiding me."

He should have guessed, given what Foxworth had accomplished around here, but somehow it was only now registering just how sophisticated and well-equipped they were. But was it enough, when his little girl was involved?

"But if she finds out Grace has been sneaking over here—"

"We're going to send Grace a message to stay quiet about that. Cutter will deliver it."

He blinked. "What? How?"

"He'll manage. He always does," Quinn said.

"Will she recognize your writing? In a note?" Hayley asked. "We need her to be sure it's you."

"I always put a star after I sign it. Because…she's the star of my life. So she'd know if it wasn't there, that it wasn't really from me."

"Brilliant," Ali said approvingly.

He smiled at her, but it was a bit wry. "Not feeling it, at the moment."

"Then we'll fix that, too," she said, with a certainty he wished he could feel.

And he'd like a lot more of that look she gave him, too. After years of Liz's haughty looking down her nose, he definitely liked Ali's smile and, even more, her obvious approval.

Whether he deserved either, he wasn't sure.

Chapter Nine

Ali clipped on the second earring, glad that they were a subtle style. They looked so normal she was almost startled when she heard Hayley's voice in her ear.

"Copy?"

"You're loud and clear," she told her as she came out of the bedroom and into the great room. The time was getting close. Her new neighbor had returned home from work or wherever she'd gone for the afternoon—did women on her level really work?—and Grace was ensconced back in her bedroom, according to the new camera aimed that way. Everything was in place. While Quinn would also be listening, they'd decided Hayley would take the lead in the communications.

"She's the best at picking up the subtle stuff," Quinn had said. "And she understands women better—" he'd thrown his wife a loving glance "—much better than I do."

"Your biggest problem," Hayley said now, "and I speak from experience, will be not automatically answering verbally when I say something. I'll try to keep it to a minimum, so you don't get too distracted. I'll feed you background info we've gathered, if it seems appropriate, and might help."

"And I'll feed her ego," Ali said, remembering their earlier discussion.

"Yes. And play up to her, like you've heard of her family

and you're impressed." Hayley shifted her gaze to Colby, "Any goals or causes she'd be particularly receptive to?"

He let out a short, sharp laugh. "Anything that makes her feel more important. Her family supports a few charitable causes, but it's all for the PR. She doesn't really believe in any of them. In fact, it annoys her to have to pretend she does. Even her grief organization to help widows and orphans is about making her feel she's better, stronger than they are."

That jabbed Ali deeper than she wanted to let on. Colby had no way of knowing, of course, so she kept her gut-level reaction hidden.

"Interesting," Quinn put in. "We have a contact who dealt with that organization say much the same thing, that Ms. Hollen seems to be in it for the photo ops, that when it comes down to actually dealing with or even talking to the people she's supposedly trying to help, she's mostly absent."

"What about close women friends?" Ali asked.

Colby turned his head to look at her. "She doesn't trust anyone, male or female, who might be…tougher than she is. Doesn't want them around her."

"Because they might show her up?" She was guessing, but from what she'd heard so far it seemed to fit. And Colby nodded.

"And then she'll go to any length to take them down."

Ali thought for a moment, then looked at Hayley. "I'm thinking maybe Cutter's my therapy dog? Emotional support dog? He's certainly got the knack."

"That he does," Hayley agreed. "And that's a good idea, especially since he's actually certified as a therapy dog, with clearance to visit hospitals and rehab facilities."

Colby moved suddenly, leaning forward to put his elbows on his knees and his head in his hands. He'd been looking decidedly edgy about this from the beginning, but now he was slowly shaking his head.

"Colby?" Ali asked gently.

He looked up, and the concern in those eyes of his touched her to the core. "Just be careful," he said in a pleading tone. "If you got hurt somehow trying to help us, I…"

He let out a long breath that sounded exhausted. She sat down beside him. He clearly cared, so much, and was worried. And she knew now that it wasn't solely for Grace, but for all of them. He truly was not used to this kind of help, or maybe any help that could or would stand against the Hollens, and that alone made her even more determined.

She wanted to hug him. To hold him, to reassure him. And it had nothing to do with the fact that, to her eyes, he was gorgeous. Yes, physically, tall, built, obviously strong with that thick dark hair and those brilliant blue eyes, but for her it was the caring that did it. The risk he'd taken for his little girl. Now the worry for her, for all of them. That was what appealed to her on the deepest level.

Cutter walked over to him and nudged his right hand. Seemingly automatically he reached down and stroked the dog's dark head. Then he went still, staring into the dog's dark eyes.

"I think," Ali said very quietly, "the therapy dog thing will be an easy sell."

He looked up at her. "It's…amazing."

"Between him and a bottle of this ridiculously spendy wine, how can we go wrong?" she asked lightly.

She saw him let out a long breath, and he closed his eyes for a moment, with his hand still on Cutter's head. Then he looked up at her.

"Can you drop he's also a guard dog, please?"

"I can do that," she promised, and gave in to the urge to put her arm around those broad shoulders. Shoulders that had carried this unpleasant load alone for too long.

But he wasn't alone anymore, and she was going to see to it that he knew that.

And in the end, Liz Hollen would know it, too.

It went much more easily than she'd expected. From her

purposely hesitant introduction at the door—"I hope you don't think I'm imposing, I know someone like you probably doesn't have much time, but when I heard your name I couldn't help but want to meet you."—she seemed to hit the right notes.

And when she introduced Cutter as her emotional support and guard dog, she saw something flash in the woman's dark eyes that told her Colby had been exactly right. Liz Hollen liked women who were, in her eyes, weaker than her. And Ali knew from the way she took charge of the meeting at that point that she'd found the right way in.

Her mind was racing to assess, with too many brain cells searching for how and why Colby had ended up with this woman in the first place. But when Liz went over to her well-stocked wet bar and was focused on opening the bottle she'd brought, she remembered to slip the note Colby had written to Cutter. Amazingly, the animal took it carefully in his teeth and kept his wet tongue away from it—how on earth did you teach a dog to do that?—as she bent and whispered "Find."

Cutter's nose had been twitching since they'd walked in, and Ali guessed he knew his goal, Grace, was here. She had also noticed him watching Liz like the guard dog she'd said he was, as if he knew without being told that this was someone to be wary of. The enemy, even.

The instant she whispered the command, the dog quietly headed down the hallway. A moment later she thought she heard a slight sound that could have been a door opening. Then an exclamation that she tried to cover as her own with an exaggerated "Oh!" as she walked over toward the wet bar, acting as if she were fascinated with the framed print that hung on the wall above it.

"Is that a Hector?" she said.

"Well done," Hayley said in her ear.

Liz, who had looked up at her words, set the now open bottle aside as she got two glasses out of the cabinet.

"Yes," she said, "it is. An original. I met him at an exhibition in LA, and he practically gave it to me."

It took all she had to say with what she hoped was the right level of admiration, "I'm sure. It would be great publicity for him to be able to say someone like you had one of his pieces."

Ali had to physically stop the eye roll she wanted to make. She was familiar with the current fad of cartoonish drawings turned into what the man called art, and privately thought he likely had to give them away, because who'd want to buy them? But she knew she was thinking too logically, and that with a fad like this, the desire was to be in the crowd that treasured trappings more than reality.

Then she heard the slight sound of Cutter returning, and the dog came back to her side. Mouth empty, she thought, just as he gave her what she would have sworn was a nod, indicating mission accomplished.

And apparently Grace both understood and accepted her assignment. She could just imagine the child reading that note.

Gracie,
Your friend Ali is helping us. Her puppy brought us some friends, including this dog, Cutter. Ali is pretending Cutter is hers, and you need to pretend you don't know her until you meet her now, okay? Just wait a few minutes after you get this, then come out.

We're going to make it better, sweetie. I promise.
Love, Daddy ⋆

"What was he doing?" Liz asked, a little sharply.

"Cutter? Oh, I hope you don't mind. He likes to look around, but he's done now," she said, hoping Hayley got the message.

"Message delivered," Hayley said on the other end, confirming her hope.

Liz shrugged. "I don't mind dogs. People tend to trust people with pets."

Well that's an interesting and ice-cold assessment of the benefits of dogs...

Ali went on, gushing a bit but trying not to go over the top. She was already a little amazed at how the woman seemed to eat it up, or rather, take it as her due. "I can't blame him. Your home is so beautiful."

"Thank you," Liz said. Then, in what Ali guessed was, for her, a polite tone, she said, "Your place is rather cute, in a diminutive way."

Zap!

This was where she normally would write someone off. *No, be honest*, Ali told herself, *you would have written her off the moment you walked in this overdone mass of fakery.*

"It's nothing compared to this," she said, again trying to judge just how saccharine to get. She had a feeling the woman's ego required a lot of feeding.

Now that a few minutes had passed, Liz poured a bit of the wine into her glass and tried it. She nodded in approval, and looked at Ali with what she thought was a bit of surprise.

Because of course us peons know nothing about good wine.

Then the woman picked up the bottle and looked at the label. "I didn't realize they'd come this far," she said. "I'll have to let my father know. He might want to invest."

"Subtly letting you know how bucks up they are," Hayley said in her ear, her tone so dry it was all Ali could do not to laugh.

Liz topped off her glass, and filled one for Ali. She gestured out toward the grand salon—*she really, actually called it that!*—and they went to the big, luxurious couch and sat. Frankly, she thought her own was much more comfortable than this overstuffed, polished leather thing you slid all over every time you moved.

Cutter came and sat politely at her feet.

"He seems very well-behaved," Liz said, sounding as if she were still reserving final judgment.

"He is. And very tidy."

"You mentioned he's also a guard dog?"

"Yes, he is. A good thing for a woman living alone, I think?"

She went with the uptick at the end, as she had been doing, since it made it sound like everything was a question, which in turn made her sound more uncertain and less of a threat.

"You may be right," Liz said, studying Cutter more intently now.

"And I just love him," Ali gushed. "He's so good with my new puppy. And you should see him around children, he's a great playmate. And he makes sure nobody bothers them."

Liz's head came up. "So he's protective of kids?"

"Very."

"Would he warn you if…someone he didn't know was around?"

"Absolutely. He wouldn't even let them get close. Sometimes I—"

She broke off at the sound of footsteps in the hallway Cutter had vanished down earlier.

Grace had not missed her cue.

Chapter Ten

Quinn had given Colby an earpiece to wear so he could listen, although the transmit function was disabled. The Foxworth man had started to explain why, but Colby shook his head.

"I get it. I'm liable to explode if I have to listen to her for long."

Quinn nodded in approval. Colby settled the tiny device in his ear just in time to hear Grace's voice.

"Who are you?" Bless his girl, she was playing it perfectly.

"I'm your new neighbor," Ali said brightly. "I just moved in next door a couple of weeks ago. And this is my dog, Cutter. I thought you should meet, so he knows you're friends. I have a puppy at home too, but he hasn't quite learned how to behave yet."

He thought he heard the sound of movement, as if the dog were walking across the hard floor. Toward Grace, if he had to guess.

"He's pretty," Grace said, and he could tell from her voice she meant that sincerely.

"And he's very sweet. Go ahead and pet him," Ali said, then added with the same sort of obsequiousness he'd heard so many use with Liz, "Assuming it's all right with your mom."

"Mother?"

Colby saw Quinn's glance. "She always calls her 'mother.'

She told me that one of her friends said 'mommy' was for a mother you loved."

Hayley's head snapped around. She covered the small mic that came around in front of her mouth. "She put that together on her own?"

He nodded. "I never said anything about it. I try never to say anything bad about Liz in front of her." His mouth twisted. "Probably for my own sake as much as Grace's."

"Wise decision," Quinn said. "Cuts down on the 'He told Grace this or that' claims, if and when it comes to that."

"Exactly."

"That," Hayley said as she uncovered the mic again, "is one smart girl."

Colby only nodded.

"Could I come over and play with him sometimes?" Grace asked. "If it's all right with my mother?"

"Of course you could," Ali said. "What a lovely idea."

"Why on earth," Liz asked, "would you want to have her over there bothering you?"

There was a second-long pause during which Colby guessed Ali had shifted to look at Liz. It also gave him that time to rein in the surge of anger at his ex's dismissive words about the child he so loved. *Her* child, who she clearly did not love. Not like she should, anyway.

"You have raised a wonderful daughter, Ms. Hollen," Ali said, somehow managing to give Liz the credit, which Colby knew would go over well. "I'd be delighted for her to come over any time to play with the dogs, since I work from home anyway."

"What's your work?" Liz asked.

"I'm an interior designer," Ali said.

They'd talked about that, and how even though she hated the title, it was more likely to impress Liz. And it would also make her reaction to that ridiculous painting more believable, he thought now.

"And I know Cutter would love it," Ali added. "She'd be totally safe, with him around."

"He would…protect her?"

"He would protect her against any threat," Ali said.

Colby saw Hayley nod approvingly, and gathered they must have discussed that exact response. Judging by her satisfied expression, that they'd chosen it to include Liz herself, although Liz would never interpret it that way. The only threat she ever saw was him.

"So I can go?" Grace asked.

She sounded as if she were holding her breath, waiting for an answer that would determine…everything. She was handling this so well, as if she understood exactly what was going on. How on earth had ordinary him managed to father the most brilliant seven-year-old in the world?

"I think that would be all right. As long as you don't make a nuisance of yourself. And tell Irene where you are." A pause, then an explanation. "Irene is my housekeeper and child minder."

Colby heard a tiny sound he was certain was Grace suppressing a squeal of delight.

"She knows not to act too happy," he said at Quinn's look. The Foxworth man gave a short shake of his head, and Colby saw that his jaw was tight.

"I'll make sure she knows when Grace comes to visit, Ms. Hollen," Ali said.

"I think," Liz Hollen said slowly, "you should call me Liz."

Colby sat up straight.

"Damn," he said under his breath. Hayley turned her head to look at him. "She's got her," he explained. "She doesn't give first-name rights to anyone she hasn't decided she can trust."

He got to his feet then, because he had to. He could feel it swirling inside him again, that feeling of hope. He was pacing when Liz started what he'd figured would be coming.

"It's only fair to warn you, Ali," Liz said, "Grace's father is a good-for-nothing slacker who thinks he still has rights, and he may come looking for her."

There was a soft whuff it took him a second to recognize as coming from Cutter. To his surprise Grace said nothing, so there was a brief silence before Ali said, "Oh, dear."

"If he does while she's there, just call me and I'll handle it."

"What if you're not home?"

"I'll still see to it. I have people."

"Well, that's a relief, that you have it handled."

"Ask if she has a photo of him," Hayley said quickly into the mic, and Ali did so. Colby wasn't sure what that was for, but he was sure there was a reason.

"Here," Liz said. "Be on the lookout."

"His driver's license?" Ali asked. Liz had a copy of his DL? How had she managed that?

"I snuck a photo of it one time when he was here to visit Grace. I thought I might need it one day."

Always planning ahead, that was Liz.

"Does he still look like that?"

Colby blinked at that, wondering why she'd asked when she knew perfectly well he didn't. Well, not much.

Liz let out a rather unladylike snort. "Hardly. He's much... scruffier now. I held him to a certain standard, and he was quite handsome then, but he quickly reverted to type once we separated."

Colby rubbed a hand over his stubbled chin, but resisted shoving his hair back again. She just never stopped, never passed up a chance to slam him, even to, in essence, a total stranger.

A stranger who's helping you for no reason other than kindness and liking Grace.

A stranger who had gotten past Liz's considerable walls in less than an hour. Speaking of brilliant females...

He heard a sigh that he knew had to be Ali because Liz would never betray that much emotion. "I hate it when men do that. Appear to be one thing, or pretend, but turn out to be something else altogether."

Instinctively Colby winced, even knowing those words weren't an accusation of him, but part of the plan.

"Exactly," Liz said, with a firm sort of approval. And then she turned to Grace—he could tell by the change in her tone to an irritated sharpness—and began to instruct her.

"You may visit, if and when Ali says it's all right. You may pet the dog, but I don't want you coming home dirty or muddy or covered in dog hair, do you understand?"

Grace's tone was sour. "How about if I don't—"

He heard that small whuff of sound again, and his girl stopped abruptly. That had to have been Cutter. There was a sound of movement before Liz repeated her demand.

"Do you understand?"

"Yes, Mother."

Quinn looked at Colby. "What do you think she was about to say?"

"Probably 'how about if I don't ever come back,'" Colby said. "Which would have made Liz beyond angry."

"Then that's what Cutter sensed. And stopped." Colby looked at him curiously. "Just like before, he could tell whatever Grace was about to say would likely set Liz off. Don't ask me how, he just knows when things are about to go sideways."

He was still looking doubtfully at the obviously tough, experienced man who was saying something that seemed ridiculous about a dog, when Hayley spoke into the mic.

"Go ahead with our plan, Ali. Just make sure you bow down first."

Then he heard Ali speak again. "I have an idea, Grace. You know that big window on the side of my house?" There was a pause, and he guessed Grace must have nodded because Ali went on. "How about if I put a big blue piece of paper in the corner, maybe with your name on it, whenever it's okay for you to come over."

"That would work."

He could hear the excited undertone Grace was trying to suppress. He doubted Liz would; she never paid that much attention.

"You must always, always check with your mother or Irene first," Ali cautioned, and he gathered that was the bowing part. He was a little amazed at how thoroughly Hayley in particular had grasped exactly what kind of woman Liz was, and what she would require in the way of sucking up. But then, Foxworth had dealt with several people of an even higher echelon than the Hollens.

Ali went on, and there was a lighter, almost teasing note in her voice now. "And if I put a red paper in that spot, please come over as soon as you can, because Cutter really needs someone to play with."

Grace couldn't smother her gleeful squeak at that, but to his relief Liz didn't react or call a halt to the whole thing.

"I'll have a friend from school visiting for a while," Ali added, "and poor Cutter may feel neglected. So if he really, really needs to play, he may come looking for you."

Colby went still. Had they worked that out, too? He looked at Quinn. "Is that a way to get her out of there if necessary? You send the dog over?"

Quinn nodded. "And if we do, he won't leave without her."

This dog of theirs was starting to sound like some Special Ops guy or something. Maybe he was, maybe he'd been a military or police dog or something. He was still boggling over that idea when he realized that Ali was saying goodbye.

"See you soon, Grace."

"Okay." His little girl was making a valiant effort to hide her excitement. It was something he knew all too well.

"That sounded pretty uninterested," Hayley said with a glance over at him as she straightened up from her intent, monitoring position.

"She has to hide anything she really likes or wants. If her mother finds out she'll use it against her."

"Well, we were convinced before, but doubly so now," Quinn practically growled.

Colby looked back at Hayley. "I'm guessing you're the 'friend from school' she mentioned?"

"Yes. So Ms. Hollen won't be surprised to see another person here."

Ali came in through the back door, Cutter at her side. Automatically Colby got to his feet. The redhead bent to stroke Cutter's head.

"You are *such* a good dog," she crooned. "And so smart!"

She straightened up to look at the Foxworths, who were smiling at their clever pet. Or fellow operative. Probably both.

Then she walked into the room, shifting her gaze to Colby.

"And I don't ever use this word, but your ex," she said with a sour twist of her mouth and an eye roll, "is a bitch."

He couldn't help it—he let out a snort of laughter.

"I know, you warned me," Ali said, "but holy cow, she's…"

She waved her hand as if there were no way to describe the woman she'd just left. Colby couldn't argue with that, so he merely nodded.

"And you," Hayley said, coming over to take the earrings Ali removed, reminding him to pull out the earpiece they'd given him, "handled that perfectly. You got more than we'd hoped. So now that we have the groundwork laid, we have to plan what's next."

She sounded so confident it filled Colby with hope all over again. And he couldn't stop himself from taking that half step between them and giving Ali a heartfelt hug.

"Thank you," he said, his voice more than a little hoarse.

"Grace is a treasure. Thank you for trusting me to be a part of this."

He no longer had any doubt that slicing up his arm on that window was the best thing that could have happened.

Chapter Eleven

"I have only one question," Ali said as she took a seat next to Colby on the sofa, her last—truly it was—slice of pizza in her hand.

He was wiping his fingers with the napkins that had come with the delivery—albeit it had been another Foxworth man called Teague, not the guy from the actual pizza place—and now stopped to look at her. She had the feeling he hadn't been eating well lately, or maybe at all, judging by how much and how fast he'd bolted that down.

"Only one?" he asked, with a half laugh that was clearly self-directed. Lord, that woman had done a number on him.

She glanced from where they were seated at the counter back toward the table, where Quinn and Hayley were working out whatever planning they had left to do, although she couldn't imagine what they could possibly have overlooked. But once certain they wouldn't be overheard, and because she genuinely wanted to know, she asked her question.

"How did you end up with her?"

He took in a deep breath and let it out slowly, audibly. "I claim ignorance. I met her my freshman year in college. I had no idea who her family was. All I knew was she was a couple of years ahead of me, she was…well, gorgeous, and she took an interest in me. Much to my surprise."

She tilted her head as she looked at him. "I don't find it surprising at all."

His eyes widened. He stared at her for a moment, opened his mouth, then closed it again, as if he could think of nothing to say. He lowered his gaze to the crumpled napkin in his hand.

How could such a simple thing flummox him so? He had to know he was a good-looking guy, who would catch any woman's eye. Even Liz, bi—she caught herself, she'd meant what she'd said about not liking to use that word—witch that she was, had seen the appeal.

"So she was gorgeous, practiced, a little older, more experienced in manipulation... No wonder you fell for her."

"If that's your way of saying I was a gullible, naive idiot, then yeah." He grimaced. "I was stupidly happy that she wanted to get married. But it was...miserable. I knew it wasn't working. But then she got pregnant with Grace. After telling me she was on the pill."

She knew she hadn't mistaken the bitter tone that had come into his voice. She remembered the call Quinn had made, to the contractor whose name she'd seen on such beautiful work.

My take is that Colby Kendrick is a great guy.

Then, even stronger, what Colby himself had said hit her...
She was embarrassed when she had to introduce her husband, the carpenter, *to their ritzy friends.*

A fierce sort of anger began to bubble up inside her. The impression she'd gotten in person added fuel to it. It was quite clear Liz Hollen was the kind of woman she had to try very hard not to hate.

"She really did a number on you, didn't she?"

He let out a long sigh. "I was supposed to join the family firm. Rise to the top and all that. But I had no interest in that. Which is why she divorced me."

She thought again of what Drew Kiley had said, about his idea that saved one of her favorite places. "Why would someone who can do what you do want to become a paper pusher?"

He blinked. And again his mouth opened as if he were going to speak, then closed again as if there were no words to be found. She wished he'd stop doing that. Not just because she didn't like the idea of him being too wary to talk to her, but because darn it, it made her keep looking at his mouth. And that was something she was not used to even thinking about.

But something in the way he was looking at her, something in those blue eyes, made her add, "Paper pushers who deal with other people's products or property are a dime a dozen. People like you who can build or make those things, now, they're worth something. A lot, because it seems like we have fewer of them all the time."

She saw him swallow as if his throat was tight. He looked away then, but she heard a low, rough-sounding, "Thank you."

A phone across the room rang, and when she looked over, Quinn was pulling his phone out yet again. She wondered what it must be like to run an operation with as many threads and connections as Foxworth obviously had. He listened for a moment, then said, "Thanks. Nice to know."

She felt a little nervous suddenly, because when he'd said that he'd been looking at her. And when he slid the phone back into his pocket he came toward them.

"Seems you two have a connection," he said, looking from her to Colby.

She shot a glance at the man sitting on the stool beside her, just in time to catch him doing the same to her. For a moment the only kind of connection she could think of was the one she'd been pondering before, when she'd caught herself watching his mouth a little too much.

Had she been that obvious? True, she was out of practice, focusing entirely on her work now, and building her business. But—

Quinn looked at her. "The name Doug Rockford ring a bell?"

"Yes," she said.

At that, Colby gave her a startled look. "You know Sarge?" he asked.

She nodded. "I designed the interior of his new building at the veterans' camp."

Colby was smiling when he said, "I built it."

"And both of you did it for nothing," Quinn said.

"I love it," Hayley said, beaming as she came up beside her husband, "when we're proven so thoroughly right about our people."

Quinn grinned at his wife. "You mean when he is," he said, nodding at Cutter, who was lounging near the fireplace.

"That, too," she answered cheerfully. Ali saw Hayley realize both she and Colby were looking from her to the dog and back, and she laughed. "You'll get used to it. We had to. Because he's never been wrong. Confused once, but never wrong."

"Confused?" Ali asked.

"That was the first time he met my brother," Hayley said, still smiling, "whom I was very angry with at the time. So Cutter was a bit torn."

Ali found herself smiling again. And thinking about what the woman had said about "our people." As if, once they'd decided to help you, you were family. She glanced at Colby. He could use that kind of support. And so could adorable little Gracie. And helping them help him was making her feel better than she had in a very long time. Since Josh's death, in fact.

"Now," Hayley said briskly, "we need to work on timing and details. Colby, it's clear your daughter is a very smart young lady, but—and we need the most honest answer you can give—how good is she at keeping a secret?"

He took in a deep breath and let it out slowly. She could almost sense him turning from the lighter topic of Cutter's apparent skills back to the matter at hand. She wondered briefly if the Foxworths had lightened things up for those moments intentionally. She wouldn't be surprised; they were obviously very good at what they did.

"She can do it, as long as she understands why," Colby said, sounding cautious. Then, in a more depressed tone he admitted, "But if she gets mad enough, sometimes she'll blurt something out before she thinks."

"Why, you'd think she was human!" Ali put all she could of mock astonishment into her voice. Colby's gaze flashed to her, and one corner of his mouth twitched.

"Can't picture you getting that mad," he said.

A chill went through her at the words. "Oh, I can," she said, and now her voice was grimly level. "Unfortunately uselessly."

He tilted his head slightly, clearly wondering, but Hayley called them back to the current situation and Ali silently thanked her for it.

"If you think she'd let it out that Ali's helping," she began.

"She just needs to understand," Colby said. "How important it is not to tell her mother…anything. Then she'll keep it secret forever if necessary."

"We need to lay out some boundaries," Quinn said, clearly on his wife's wavelength. "Grace coming here doesn't necessarily mean you'll see a lot more of her."

Ali frowned. "But he could be here." She glanced at him again. "You could come any time. Or stay."

And again he looked a little stunned, and she wondered what it must be like to feel so beaten down, so abandoned, that the concept of someone willingly helping was utterly foreign. Even in the worst days after Josh's death she'd never felt that.

Hayley's tone was understanding but firm as she explained. "It would be nice if you could see more of her while we're working this out, but if she might let it out at an inopportune moment, it could blow everything."

"But she already knows I'm involved," Colby said. "That note…"

"Yes, but keeping a note quiet versus seeing her beloved daddy in person are two very different things," Hayley said.

"Plus, we don't want Ms. Hollen or her helpers to see him here."

Hayley was still watching Colby, and Ali knew she was sensing the same current of tension in him.

"We'll get there, I promise," Hayley said to him, "but we have to start slow. We have a lot of work to do, and some of it will be dead ends, until we find the right path. Are you okay with that?"

He grimaced. "You mean can I keep it reined in?" He looked from Hayley to Quinn and then to Ali. She thought she saw something flash in his eyes then, something she could only label as hope.

Then he looked back to Hayley. "I think I can. Now."

Chapter Twelve

Colby took the mug of hot chocolate Ali handed him. It smelled luscious, and he'd noticed while she was making it that it was more than just heating up some milk and a mix. His first sip woke up every taste bud and seemed to warm him to his toes. She smiled, and he guessed his was the usual reaction to the chocolaty, cinnamony with-a-touch-of-marshmallow concoction.

He'd also noticed, as she'd handed him the mug, something he'd missed before. The lighting hadn't been right, or his mind had been so totally otherwise occupied. But now he'd seen it, that slight indentation or line on her left ring finger. Like from a ring long worn but only recently removed. He wondered if perhaps that was why she was so understanding. Maybe she'd just been through a divorce of her own.

Hayley and Quinn were back on their phones again, arranging who knows what. He was still stunned at the evidence of the size and scope of Foxworth, and their apparent resources.

And it had all started with Ali and her pup, who was currently playing a futile came of tug-of-war with Cutter, who held the rope toy so carefully it was like he knew his playmate was younger and more fragile. As he obviously did, from their description of how he'd brought Ziggy to them.

Who would have ever thought bleeding all over that little mutt would have led to…this?

She came around the counter and sat on the stool to his right. Without really thinking about it, he looked down at that finger again. He'd been right, he could see the faint indentation and tan line. He doubted she got very tan, with her complexion that fit with the red tones in her hair, but it was still there, just barely.

He wanted to ask, even though he told himself it was none of his business, really. He could make up some reason, like asking if they needed to worry about her ex showing up, but he didn't want to do that. But he couldn't seem to quash his need to know.

"There was a ring there for a long time," he finally said, making sure it wasn't a question so she could ignore it if she wanted.

She turned her head to look at him. "Yes. Nearly ten years."

"You did a lot better than I did," he said wryly.

"If you call being a widow better."

His eyes widened, and he felt his gut tighten as if she'd punched him. "I… I didn't… I'm sorry. And I'm just going to shut up now, before I say something worse."

"It's all right. You had no way of knowing."

He stared into her vivid green eyes, and even he couldn't miss the pain there. But she didn't seem on the verge of tears or anything, so he risked asking, "When…?"

"He was killed in a car accident four years ago. But I only took the ring off when I moved in here."

"Is that…why you moved?"

She nodded. "I spent those years in the home we made together, unable to let go. But I finally realized I had to, or I was going to stay mired in misery forever."

He tried to imagine what that would be like, to have a woman love you so much she couldn't get past losing you. He couldn't. He'd never even been close to that.

He tried to choose his words carefully, not wanting to step in it again with her. "While he was here, he was a lucky man.

To have you, I mean." He shook his head, that still sounded bad. "That was stupid, too. Shutting up now," he muttered.

"To the contrary, Mr. Kendrick. That was a lovely compliment."

Before he had to come up with some stumbling response to that, Quinn rescued him.

"All right, let me run this by you both. Hayley will stay here a few days to get a feel for things, under the cover of being your friend from school, Ali. She'll be open about it, and if at some point it feels right, you can introduce her to your charming neighbor."

Quinn's tone was beyond sarcastic on those last two words, and it made Colby almost smile.

"We'll use my maiden name, Cole, in case she might recognize Foxworth," Hayley said.

Quinn went on. "Also, in shifts, another of our team will be here—not necessarily inside, Ali, so don't think you have to have houseguests the whole time."

"It would be fine if I did," she said. "And by the way, there's a door into the garage—" she gestured toward the side opposite Liz's place "—and then into the house, so you can come and go as needed out of sight. I'll get you my extra key and door opener."

Colby stared at her again, boggled anew at her willingness to trust what were basically strangers to her.

"We don't want to interfere with your work any more than necessary," Hayley said.

"I'll be fine," she insisted. "I can close the door to my office, and put my headphones on. That way I'll never even know you're here unless you pound on the door. And I'm a little light right now anyway, my next big project doesn't start for a couple of weeks."

He wondered whose life she was going to make comfortable, organized and functional. Lucky people, whoever they were. A while ago he'd gone back to look at the place he'd helped build for Sarge, and had been amazed at how whoever had done it had managed to make it a welcoming dining hall, meeting room, office space and functional kitchen all in one.

Now that he'd met her, he wasn't surprised at all.

"All right. Colby, one of our crew will be going with you when you go to pick up Grace for your scheduled visitation." The man glanced at his wife, and Colby got the feeling they'd discussed this at length. "It would be me, except Hayley thinks I'm a bit…overkill."

Colby couldn't help chuckling at that. "You do have the air."

Quinn shrugged, and it was Hayley who, grinning, went on. "We'll start with Liam. He's more the lean, wiry type, not quite as imposing. And that drawl of his distracts people from seeing just how strong he is."

"Perfect," Colby said, remembering the man's accent and his lazy grin. "Because Liz will take that twang as meaning he's stupid. To her, anybody from certain places she would never set foot must be."

"Her mistake," Quinn said flatly.

"I'll bet," Colby said. "He didn't strike me as the least bit stupid."

"He's at the top of the tech tier at Foxworth Northwest," Hayley said. "And smart as the proverbial whip." She grinned again. "Smart enough to use people's misperceptions to get what we need."

"He'll be wired into us so you don't have to wear an earpiece," Quinn went on. "Unless you make a habit of it?"

"Actually, I do. Loud power tools and all. I don't think she'd wonder about it."

"All right," Quinn said. "Then you can be live with us too. We'll get you set up with one of ours."

"Does that mean I don't get to wear the pearl earrings?" He put all the innocence he could muster into his voice. Ali, who had been taking a sip of hot chocolate, nearly spit it back out again, laughing. Hayley laughed as well, and even Quinn chuckled. And it all made Colby able to genuinely smile.

Hope, he thought, was a powerful antidote to despair.

"Careful," Ali said after she swallowed. "She might like that enough to take you back."

"More likely she'd slit my throat and steal them," he said dryly.

"Did I mention we have a prize-winning ex-military sniper on our team?" Quinn said, just as dryly.

Colby blinked. "Uh…no, you didn't."

"But he's about to get married," Hayley put in, "so we'd rather not call him in if we don't have to."

Colby wasn't sure how to take the cheerful yet apparently serious tone. He had the feeling that, even with what he knew of them from people they'd helped, he'd vastly underestimated the Foxworth Foundation.

Chapter Thirteen

Ali couldn't imagine what it was like, having the woman who supposedly loved you enough to marry you and have your child use that child to manipulate you from the day she was born.

She stood looking out the front window at the garden, which had been one of the big selling points to her. The garden where Grace loved to play because of all the little places to hide. She gave a sad shake of her head at the thought.

Hayley came up beside her, having spent the night as planned. Cutter had stayed with them, which delighted Ziggy and made Ali feel wonderfully safe. It was quite a knack that dog had.

"You don't look happy," Hayley said.

"I just feel like I should have realized," she said. "When Grace came over here, I didn't realize she'd had to sneak out. But she loved to be—" she gestured to the window "—out there, because of all the little places to hide among the bushes and behind where the tree branches brush the ground. I thought it was because she and Ziggy made up a game, she'd hide and he'd find her. But now I wonder..."

"If she's just learned to hide whenever possible?"

Ali nodded sadly. "There were other hints. I see them now looking back."

"But you'd only just moved in, only just met Grace, so you couldn't know for sure, at least not yet."

Ali looked at the other woman. "Are you always so tactful?"

Hayley smiled. "Not always. But I do try."

"You make me wish you really were my friend from college," Ali said.

"And that is the nicest compliment you could give me. So let's say I am, we just got a late start."

Ali smiled back at that.

"Quinn just texted me," Hayley said, nodding at the phone in her hand. "He and Colby are on their way. And Liam finalized his case, so we're set for him to be with Colby tomorrow when he goes to pick Grace up."

Ali couldn't deny the spark of…something that ignited at the thought of Colby being here again soon.

"And for what it's worth, if you had any doubts, our top tech guy in St. Louis did some digging. To the upper crust of the county, Colby's known only as Liz's ex she's well rid of. But to just about everyone else he's an honest, hardworking guy who gives back. Did you know the local fire department gave him a civilian medal?"

Ali drew back a little in surprise. "No."

"He was working up on Cedar Hill Drive when a residential fire broke out a couple of doors away. Propane leak. There was an explosion, and a fireman was trapped, and seriously injured. The others were all on the other side of the building, so Colby went in and brought him out."

"Wow," Ali said, meaning it. "I didn't really have any doubts, but still…"

Hayley smiled and kept going. "And then the fire department turned up info that he'd been a hero twice before. Once he was doing some late-night emergency repair work at a house in a neighborhood out on the peninsula. He spotted something at the house next door. Turned out there'd been something miswired there, and a fire had started. He called it in and got over there and got it put out before the truck even arrived. There was a family of six in that house, and they could have all died. Third time it was a medical call, where he did CPR on a neighbor until the medics arrived. They said the man would have been dead if not for him."

Ali was smiling herself now. Widely. "So what you're saying is, to Liz and her ilk, he's a nobody, but to the people who matter, he's a hero."

"Exactly." Hayley grinned at her then. "I knew I liked you."

"Ditto," she said back to her.

Cutter, who had been delicately wrestling with Ziggy on the floor, suddenly scrambled to his feet. Ears up, he trotted toward the door into the garage, even though as far as she knew the dog had no idea where it led.

"Ah," Hayley said. "The guys are here."

Ali hadn't heard a thing, but she was already learning not to doubt either the dog or this woman. And when, a minute or two later she heard the sound of a voice coming from the garage, it verified her instincts.

Quinn greeted his wife as if he hadn't seen her in a week rather than just overnight. Ali found herself studying Colby, who watched them for a moment with a look of almost sadness before he turned away as if he couldn't watch the two who so obviously adored each other any longer. She and Josh had been like that once. Teased by their friends for the constant displays of affection.

But Colby Kendrick clearly had never known that feeling at all, which left her wondering which was worse, having it and losing it, or never having had it at all. She had thought Tennyson had it right, and seeing Colby's expression in that moment confirmed it for her.

"Irene took Grace to school at the usual time," Hayley said, in the tone of someone making a report. "And we are going to have to be careful. Grace was looking over here the whole time. I would guess she was wondering if you were here, Colby."

He nodded, and when he spoke he sounded resigned. "And if Liz figured it out, she'd unleash holy hell."

"About that," Quinn said, "Liam did a little digging last night." A brief grin flashed across the man's face, and changed him from the very imposing former military Special Ops guy Hayley had told her about last night into a handsome charmer. "He's very good at it, enough to compete with Ty in St. Louis. But he also knows a lot of local lore, so that helps sometimes. Anyway, after Colby mentioned there had been a change of venue in the middle of their custody case, from here locally to over on the other side in the city, Liam got out his virtual shovel. Turns out the Hollens have…let's say a lot of influence over the judge it was transferred to. Which explains why it went so hard against him."

Ali stiffened. She looked at Colby. "So they bribed somebody, or coerced somebody, into making that change happen?"

"Our judicial system, fair and balanced," he said, and she couldn't blame him for the bitterness in his tone.

"This," she said, not caring that the *s* came out like a hiss, "is seriously making me angry."

"Can I interpret that as you're still willing to help?" Quinn asked, looking mildly amused.

"You can interpret it as meaning that as long as Grace isn't hurt in the process, whatever it takes to bring Liz and her family down a notch, I'm in."

As if she'd felt his gaze on her, she looked back at Colby. He still seemed astonished at the simple fact that she wanted to help. After a moment he said quietly, "I like the order you put that in."

"Grace is the most important thing, obviously."

He sucked in a breath and let it out slowly. "To me. To her, not so much. Winning is the most important."

"And she's used to winning against you?" Quinn asked.

He nodded. "She knows I'll back off because of Grace. That I can't fight her."

"It's more important to outthink your enemy than to outfight him."

Ali saw Colby blink, draw back slightly at Quinn's words. "Quoting Sun Tzu?" he asked.

Quinn smiled. "Former occupational hazard. You're familiar, I gather?"

"Yeah. My dad became a big fan when he was in the service."

Ali thought she saw something change in Quinn's expression, as if finding out Colby was the son of a veteran had confirmed something for him.

"What branch?" Quinn asked.

"Army," Colby said. Then, sadly, "He died five years ago. But at least he never had to deal with…this."

"So we will," Quinn said, his voice showing the sympathy he didn't mention in words. Men indeed had their own ways, Ali thought. "With the aid of our ancient strategist."

Colby smiled, gave a short nod as if shaking off the grief that had to still linger. "But if you're going to talk about waiting to take the enemy unprepared, I've got to tell you, she never is."

Quinn smiled back. "I was thinking more along the lines of 'The whole secret lies in confusing the enemy so that he cannot fathom our real intent.'"

Colby looked thoughtful. "All warfare is based on deception?"

"Exactly."

"You have something in mind?"

"A few things. And so does Liam, and so will Teague. Plus we have a lot of former clients who dealt with custody situations we can call on."

Ali sat watching the two men, taking an enjoyment she didn't quite understand in the conversation. And judging by the slight smile on Hayley's face, she was, too. "It's a good thing you two are in charge, getting all philosophical about it," Hayley said, obviously teasingly.

"A very good thing," Ali said. "I'd be planning to grab Grace and run. Which obviously, with her family's pull, would not go well."

"Don't think I haven't thought about it," Colby said, looking at her rather curiously. "But I wouldn't have expected you to feel that way."

Ali shrugged. "Neither of my parents were prizes, but given the choice, if my father had been half the man you are, I'd have gone with him gladly."

He stared at her, looking almost stunned. And that made her ache inside all over again.

And she had the delicious thought that someday, eventually, when all this was over and Grace was safe, she'd like to put Liz Hollen on her expensively clad butt.

Chapter Fourteen

"Don't worry, man. I'll put on my stupid hick suit, and she'll barely even see me. I know her type."

Colby looked at Liam Burnett, who was grinning at him. Friday had arrived, and they were prepping to head over to get Grace. "I'll bet you do," he said. "At least you're smart enough not to have married one."

"Me? Nope. My Ria's the best thing that ever happened to me, along with Foxworth." He gave Colby a sideways look. "But hey, we're all blind about some stuff. And it took me a darn long time to understand what really matters. And your little girl really matters."

"Yes," Colby said, his voice suddenly rough. "Yes, she does. For me, she's all that matters." He meant it more than ever. And felt stronger saying it now, with Foxworth on his side.

He looked around the building where he'd met up with Quinn and Liam this afternoon. He'd been a little surprised that there was no signage, no indication that this was the headquarters of one of the most well-known operations in the northwest. Quinn had said they kept a low profile, but not even a sign? Just a long gravel drive winding among trees, ending in a parking area next to a three-story, rectangular building painted nearly the same color as the evergreens that surrounded it except for a large, open meadow to the rear, spreading out to where the trees began again.

There was a large, hangar-style building to the right of the main one, with a concrete pad in between.

"A helipad?" he'd asked.

Quinn had smiled. "For Igor."

It had taken Colby a moment to get there. "As in... Sikorsky?"

"Seemed fitting."

"Don't get him started on Wilbur," Liam warned with a grin, "or we'll be here all day."

"Let me guess...you've got a plane, too?"

"We do. But Liam's right. We need to focus, so I'll shut up about it."

And so they had gone inside, where he was again surprised, this time by the homelike atmosphere. It had looked like an industrial type of building from the outside, but inside was welcoming and warm. There was a fireplace with a large sofa and some chairs gathered in front of it, around a large coffee table. Then a small kitchen in one corner, and in the opposite corner what appeared to be a bedroom and bathroom.

"I don't think we need the meeting room upstairs, at least not yet," Quinn said, "so let's get comfortable."

Once they were seated, the gas fire had been turned on, adding a pleasant visual to the room along with some needed warmth. It was a comforting, inviting place, and he couldn't help smiling.

"This looks like Ali could have designed it," he said.

"I think she and my wife have very similar tastes in that area," Quinn said. "If she'd left it up to me this'd be a lot less...nice."

He said it with smile and a very satisfied expression. The kind Colby had noticed Quinn got every time he saw, spoke to or apparently even thought about his wife.

Liam was in the small kitchen, apparently prepping a large pot of coffee. Which was a good thing for Colby, because he'd had a very disturbed night. He would have thought having all this help all of a sudden would have made for a more restful night, but as usual before his afternoon with Grace he'd been restless.

He was taking his first sip, wondering what kind of preparations Quinn had in mind, when the front door opened.

"I'm spoiled," said the man who came in and paused to shed his rain-dampened coat and hang it on the rack just inside. "I'm used to the butler opening the door for me."

Liam laughed, then explained to Colby, "He means Cutter. He's really who that handicap button is for. He hears you coming and has the door open before you even get out of your car."

"I think I believe that," Colby said, remembering what he'd already seen of the clever animal.

"Don't ever underestimate that critter," Liam said, then excused himself to go upstairs, saying he had some setup work to do.

Colby wasn't sure what setup work was, but the thought was blown out of his mind as the new arrival turned and walked into the main room. And Colby gaped. All the photographs and newsreels he'd seen of the man over the years hadn't done him justice. Hadn't been able to capture the sheer presence of the man. With eyes as dark as his hair, his gaze was intense and penetrating.

Colby remembered seeing a clip of him talking about his first big break, having to step up from assistant counsel to lead when the senior attorney had died of a heart attack mid-case. He'd called himself the understudy who made good, which Colby had thought rather modest, given the worldwide fame he'd achieved after that.

"Colby Kendrick, meet Gavin de Marco," Quinn said.

They shook hands, and even with the forewarning he might be involved, Colby wasn't prepared for the feeling he was under the close scrutiny of a very, very perceptive man. But what he was prepared for even less was the man's first words.

"I gotta say, Colby, at first I thought you had the biggest

pile of bad luck. Yours is the worst parenting plan I've seen in a while, especially with no proof of abuse."

Colby blinked. Then seized on the most important words. "At first?"

"Then I remembered who you were dealing with. I assume you had no idea both your attorney and the judge who heard your custody case were in the Hollens' back pocket."

He stared at the famous face, unable to even respond.

"I didn't think so," de Marco said. He shifted his gaze to Quinn. "No concrete proof of that yet, but it's undersurface knowledge among some circles that they've got a nice mutual support system going."

"I'm curious," Quinn said. "Did they always have that family law judge, or only after Grace was born?"

"After," de Marco confirmed. He glanced back to Colby. "But right after."

Colby's brow furrowed. "She was planning this that early? Back when Grace was a baby?"

De Marco gave him a sympathetic look. "I don't know if your ex herself was involved at the beginning. From what I've learned about her parents, it could well be they decided to cover that base early, just in case."

"That sounds like her mother," Colby said sourly.

"So how did they acquire this influence over both lawyer and judge?"

"Again, only rumor, but strong ones. The attorney has a drug problem—" he again looked at Colby sympathetically as he added "—albeit a well-hidden one."

Colby groaned. Maybe Liz was right, he truly was too stupid to live in her world.

"As for the judge," de Marco went on, "rumor has it he has a penchant for young boys. That that's why he went into family law because it brought him…possibilities."

Colby recoiled in disgust. He stared at de Marco. "And you think the Hollens have proof of that?"

"That's my guess. But," he cautioned, "it is only a guess."

"And a guess from Gavin de Marco is worth five from anybody else," Quinn said.

"I don't know whether to thank you or throw up," Colby said sourly.

De Marco smiled understandingly. Then he looked back at Quinn. "You want me to keep probing on that?"

"Yes, keep digging, while we stay focused on Colby's situation. If we get the chance to take all of them out later, after Grace is safely removed, then we'll do it."

Colby stared at the man who spoke as if something like that was all in a day's work. "All of them?"

Quinn met his gaze steadily. "The lawyer, the judge…and the Hollens." He said it like a man with full confidence it could be done.

But then, he was sitting here with Gavin de Marco, so that alone sort of implied anything could happen.

They talked a little longer, but Colby wasn't sure how much of it he took in. By the time de Marco left, he was still reeling a bit.

"He'll give you his best," Quinn said as the door closed after the famous attorney. "Especially now."

"Now?"

Quinn smiled. "Gavin just got back from his honeymoon, and I have a feeling kids are on the agenda soon."

Colby wondered what it would be like for a kid to have a father famous around the world. A father to be proud of.

My daughter needs to be proud of her father, not ashamed because all he can do is pound nails.

Liz's words, which he had only later realized was her last-ditch effort to get him to change his mind, his life, echoed in his head now. He was glad when Liam came downstairs to rejoin them.

"All righty, I've got my background into the system, in case your ex or her kin get nosy."

Colby never would have thought of that, but realized he should have, because he knew Liz made a habit of investigating anyone and everyone she had even a passing interaction with. She'd told him she was always looking for talent, but now that he knew the truth he had the feeling she was also looking for dirt.

"Let's get this show on the road," Liam said. "You ready?"

Colby nodded.

"Remember who I am?"

"The kid I took on as an apprentice."

"Yep. Just another dumb carpenter."

Colby's mouth twisted. "She's the dumb one, if she buys that."

Liam's tone became suddenly very serious. "If she bought it about you, she's worse than dumb." Then a grin flashed. "Heard you were trading Sun Tzu quotes with the boss."

"I...yeah, sort of."

"I don't know much about the man, but one of the boss's favorites really rang my chimes. About defeatability and undefeatability."

"'Undefeatablility lies with ourselves. Defeatability lies with the enemy.'"

"Yeah, that one," Liam said. "You oughta keep that one in mind. We're in the right, Colby. That's our strength and power. And it makes them defeatable."

Somehow hearing that from this guy—who had no other reason to help than that "we're in the right" belief—made that burgeoning hope grow even larger.

Chapter Fifteen

It was very strange, Ali thought, to be sitting here at the Foxworth headquarters, watching the camera feed on the big flatscreen and hearing the words spoken through an earpiece, while the scene was actually happening live right next door to her house.

It was also fascinating. The Foxworth man, Liam, had dressed the part, at least what was probably the part in Liz Hollen's mind. A worn, rather ragged shirt and a pair of equally worn khaki cargo-style pants. Hung in a loop sewn into the side seam of the right leg he had what Quinn told her was a nail puller. It looked to her like it could be a rather effective weapon if necessary. He also had a utility knife in one pocket, which could serve the same purpose if you didn't mind getting up close and personal. Yet they were logical things a carpenter would have handy.

As for Colby, he looked...nice. Really nice. As he probably normally would try for when he came to pick up Grace for their precious hours together. Clean, new-looking jeans and a lighter blue long-sleeved Henley, with a flannel-lined jacket half-zipped against the chill. Oddly, she found herself fixated on how he moved, how he walked up to his ex's front door in long, graceful strides, although he'd probably be embarrassed by the word graceful.

They had just driven up the Hollen driveway in an older

pickup truck that also fit the image, a vehicle Quinn explained they kept on hand for just such situations. The excuse they were going to use was that Colby's car had broken down and Liam had offered the ride.

And as she sat watching and listening with the Foxworths, she was a little amazed at how accurately they had pegged her neighbor. Colby had told them she always had Irene, the woman she called her child minder and housekeeper, answer the door, so she could keep him waiting on the porch.

"Have you even set foot inside that place?" Ali had asked when they'd been planning.

"One," Colby had answered dryly.

"One-foot distance, or one foot?" she asked, smiling despite herself.

"About both. She threatened to call the cops if I went any farther."

"Lovely."

"I didn't mind. Place is as cold as a winter storm in the Cascades. Not like your place."

She'd been glad Hayley had interrupted them at that point, so she didn't react and speak out of the sillily warm feeling his words had given her.

So now she sat watching, rather nervously, what Quinn had called the first phase of the operation. Cutter padded over and sat beside her. Ziggy was quietly snoozing in the bigger dog's bed, worn out from all the playing the two dogs had done this morning. She automatically reached out to stroke the dark fur on his head, and felt again that odd sense of calm. And remembered how the dog had raced ahead when she, Hayley and Ziggy had arrived, how she had laughed when he'd raised up and batted at the large, square handicap door switch, opening it for them.

"Here we go," she heard Liam say as the front door was pulled open.

Ali watched as Irene looked curiously at Liam, then at

Colby. She said something, so quietly it came through as an unintelligible murmur. Her expression was too neutral for Ali to read. Even as she thought it, Hayley confirmed her feelings.

"She either doesn't care, or she's experienced enough not to show her own feelings while at work."

"Colby said she's always been civil to him at least," Quinn said as the woman closed the door, leaving the two men on the porch.

A couple of minutes ticked by, and Ali was growing more and more irritated on Colby's behalf as he was, clearly intentionally, kept waiting.

"She's quite the manipulator, isn't she?" she muttered.

Hayley nodded. "Frequently used way to remind people you're in charge is to keep them waiting."

"Because of course your time is more important than theirs."

Hayley gave her a sideways look. "You have some strong feelings about this."

She let out a sigh. "I hate people who play power games all the time. It's one of the reasons I left the city and came here."

"Well, there's a lot fewer of them here, I promise," Hayley said.

As distraction Ali looked around the room again. It had the air of a comfortable great room in a well-designed house, which had been a surprise to her because of the commercial look of the outside. If someone had hired her to take the utilitarian building and make it feel like a home, it might well have ended up something like this. Which made her like these people even more than she already did. And now it was personal, not just by reputation.

"And who is…this?"

Liz's voice, with more than a little undertone of distaste in it, came clearly through the earpiece, and Ali's gaze shot back to the screen. As predicted, she was looking at Liam as if he were some sort of insect that had found his way too close to her door.

"Liam," Colby said. "New apprentice."

"Really." It wasn't a question, and her undertone was one of disbelief. Probably that anyone would want to learn a trade that was actually useful.

"My car broke down, so he gave me a ride," Colby explained.

"Too bad you can't afford a decent one," Liz said.

"Pleased to meet you, ma'am." Liam had apparently had enough of being ignored. Ali drew back, smiling because she couldn't help it. He had truly poured on that Texas drawl. And it made Liz's nose curl and go up even farther.

And then she spotted the truck. The truck that was so obviously a working man's vehicle, with racks above and a ladder and a tool box in the bed.

"You expect my daughter to ride in…that?"

"I cleaned it out, ma'am, I truly did," Liam said earnestly, still with the exaggerated drawl, as if trying to impress in a job interview.

"We're not leaving town," Colby said.

"You'd better not."

"Yeah, yeah." He was sounding weary now. Or better, bored with dealing with her. She couldn't help smiling at the difference Foxworth had already made in his outlook. His voice had the same tone when he said, "Will you call Grace, please?"

Yes, bored, especially the almost blatant insincerity of the politeness. And she guessed there was nothing that would insult someone like Liz more than being found boring.

There was a moment of silence, and Ali got the definite impression Liz was weighing whether a battle now and over this was worth it. Apparently she decided it wasn't, because she then turned her head and yelled toward the back of the house.

"Grace, now."

So quickly Ali knew she had to have been anxiously awaiting the call. Grace appeared in the doorway, looking up at her father excitedly. She gave Liam a puzzled look, but clearly getting away with her father was more important than any questions she had. She grabbed Colby's hand and started for the porch steps.

"You have until 6:03," Liz said loudly as they headed for the truck. "And don't ruin her dinner."

Grace didn't look back, but now that she was close to her dad Ali heard her mutter, "It's already ruined if she's there."

She had to smother a sharp laugh so they could hear anything else, and she saw Hayley was also chuckling, and Quinn was grinning.

"I like this kid," he said.

They heard the vehicle doors slam shut, and then Colby making sure Grace was belted in. The motor fired up, and they started to back out the long driveway.

"That woman's like crossing a mule with an alligator," they heard Liam mutter, in his real voice now. "Not a critter I'd want to ride."

They heard a giggle, clearly from Grace. And Ali wondered yet again how Colby kept himself from just grabbing the smart, adorable child and running to somewhere, anywhere, his ex couldn't find them.

Judging by the change in background noise, they were on the street. The cameras showed only the empty porch now, front door closed, so she focused entirely on the vague sounds of a vehicle driving coming through her earpiece.

Then came Grace's voice, with a worried note.

"Are you okay, Daddy? The man who came to fix the window said it was bloody."

"I'm fine, sweetheart." Ali felt her throat tighten at the pure love that rang in the man's voice. "It was just a cut, and... I think it turned out to be worth it."

"You're funny. How could a cut be worth it?"

"You'll see in just a minute," Colby promised.

Ali knew it was true, because she'd just driven that same route about an hour ago. She remembered them saying their headquarters was just down the road, but she hadn't expected it to be this close. She'd noticed the entrance when she'd gone by before, but had thought it was to a house nicely hidden back in the trees.

An idea struck her, but she only made a mental note of it when Cutter got to his feet and trotted to the door. Once more he hit the door switch with a well-directed paw, and it began to swing open. The dog squirmed through the moment it was open far enough.

"They're here," Hayley said.

Ali hadn't heard a thing, but obviously Cutter had. She got to her feet. She felt a little anxious, but at the same time glad the Foxworths had included her in this. They all needed to be on the same page, Quinn had said.

"What is this place?" Grace asked with lively curiosity evident in her voice.

"This is where I hang out," Liam answered her, sounding like he was grinning.

Then, almost simultaneously, Ali heard the sound of tires on gravel, and Grace's exclamation. "There's Cutter! Is Ali here? Is that why we're here?"

She felt a burst of inner warmth at the hopefulness in the child's voice. It was a new feeling for her, and she couldn't deny she liked it.

When the door swung open again, Cutter was the first through, with Grace beside him, stroking his back. Then the child looked up and spotted the humans in the room.

"Ali! You are here!" The girl ran to her and threw her arms around her in an energetic hug. Ali hugged her back, beyond moved at the child's open trust. Especially having heard the difference in her while speaking of her mother.

"I am," she said, smiling widely.

A small yip drew Grace's attention. "Ziggy is here, too!"

"I didn't want him to feel abandoned. He and Cutter played until he needed a nap."

Ziggy ran excitedly toward his friend, tail wagging madly. Grace dropped down to her knees to hug the puppy to her.

"Shall we all sit, and we'll work out our plan of action?" Hayley suggested.

Grace's head came up at that. She looked as if she wasn't quite sure what it meant. She looked at her father, who smiled warmly back at her. He took a seat on the big couch and beckoned her over. She hesitated, then decided, and scooped up Ziggy before she ran over and climbed up beside him, the puppy on her lap. Ali noticed that Colby immediately reached out to pet the dog as well, as if it was the natural thing to do.

Funny what small things tell you.

She took a seat on Grace's other side, delighting in how the clearly deliriously happy Ziggy couldn't stop squirming, trying to collect pets from all three of them. Her gaze met Colby's, and for a moment seemed to lock in place. For an instant she was surprised she hadn't heard a click, because it felt as if two parts had connected somehow.

She wasn't sure what that meant. Or didn't mean. All she knew for certain was that she wanted to help these two, and that she was happy Foxworth was going to let her.

Chapter Sixteen

"Do you remember that movie we saw last summer, about the kids who fought off the bad guys?" Colby asked his daughter.

Grace nodded immediately. "I remember. They won!"

"Yes, they did, in the end. But it took a long time, remember?"

She nodded again. Then she looked around at the adults in the room, as if she were trying to figure out what that movie had to do with any of them being here, or with anything else.

"Remember why they nearly lost?"

"Because that little snitch Mitch couldn't keep his mouth shut," she said, sounding disgusted.

"You told me you never would have spilled the beans no matter what."

"I wouldn't have," Grace exclaimed.

"You ready to prove that, Gracie?" he asked softly.

Her brow furrowed as she stared up at him. She was very good at reading him, and he knew she'd realized he was dead—and maybe deadly—serious. "What? What's happening, Daddy?"

Colby took a deep breath. "We're going to fight, baby."

"Fight?" She looked puzzled. "Fight what—" She broke off and her blue eyes, so like his own, widened. "Mother?"

He nodded. "And her whole family, if we have to. Just like those bad guys in the movie."

He saw eagerness bubbling up in the child's expression. He also saw the moment when she tried to tamp it down. She glanced over at the Foxworths. "But...who are they?"

"They're friends," he said. "They're Cutter's people."

"Oh."

Grace relaxed a little, as if that was all she'd needed to hear. As if in her book, anybody who owned a dog like Cutter had to be all right. He wasn't sure she was wrong.

Then she shifted her gaze to the woman sitting close beside her. "You, too, Ali? Like Daddy said in his note, you're helping us? Really?"

"As much as I can," she said.

"I knew you were good. Cutter said so." Grace looked thoughtful. "That's why you're letting me come to your house?"

"I'd want to do that anyway," Ali assured her. "But yes. If you ever need a place to go in a hurry, you can come to me. And if I'm not there, we'll figure out a way you can get inside."

"I can do that," Liam said, almost lazily. "We'll rig up a handprint lock. I'll show you how it works."

Grace studied the young Texan for a long moment. "You're with them, aren't you?" she said, pointing at Quinn and Hayley. "You don't really work with my daddy."

Liam looked surprised, but he was smiling. "Well, now, aren't you as bright as a new penny," he drawled.

"You're talking funny again," Grace pronounced, and Liam laughed.

"And you're bein' smart again," he retorted.

Grace giggled.

At that sound Colby felt such a rush of feeling, of gratitude, of thanks, and so many other tangled emotions that he couldn't get a word out past the knot in his throat.

"You really can keep this secret?" Ali asked, leaning down to look Grace in the eye. "Because that's very, very important."

As if she sensed the truth of this, Grace sat up straight. She gently put Ziggy on the floor, then looked directly into Ali's eyes. "I can," she said firmly.

"Your mother's pretty sneaky," Colby warned. "She'll get you talking about something else and try to make you slip up."

"I know. She does that all the time. I've heard her. It's how she gets secrets out of people."

Ali gave a wondering shake of her head. "Are you sure you're only seven?"

Grace grinned suddenly. "I'm a smart seven."

"That you are," Colby said fervently.

The first day after their meeting at Foxworth, Ali put up a blue piece of the construction paper she sometimes used for mock-ups in the window. Within ten minutes Grace was racing across the yard. She and Hayley met her at the back door, where Cutter was already waiting.

Since it was a Saturday and they hadn't seen Liz leave, she was careful to ask the child, "You talked to your mother?"

Grace made a sour face. "Yes. She said I could come."

"Okay, Grace," Hayley said. "Now we need to call your mother."

That startled the child. "Why?"

"Not because we don't believe you, we do. We know you wouldn't lie to us. But you know how your mother wants everyone to obey her?"

"Daddy calls it bowing down to her."

Ali couldn't help smiling. "And I'd agree. But she needs that. I think…" She hesitated, but telling herself the child had more than proven herself smart enough to understand, she went on. "I think she likes it when people are a little afraid of her."

Grace simply nodded. "I know. I see her sometimes when she's yelling at somebody on the phone. She sounds really mad, but…she's smiling."

Ali felt a jab of repulsion at the twisted mentality that would take. But it vanished in the wave of admiration that followed, for just how smart Colby's little girl was. The emotion was touched with a bit of sadness, however. No child this bright and precious should have to deal with a mother like she had. Her own had been no mother-of-the-year nominee, but she hadn't been vicious.

Ali had to steady herself before she made that call.

"It's Ali next door," she said with all the bright cheer she could muster. "I wanted to double-check that Grace cleared her visit over here with you, like she promised."

"She did," Liz said. "But good for you for checking. Wise decision."

Gee, thanks, Your Highness.

"Just wanted to be sure," she said.

"If she gets to be a nuisance, send her home."

"Cutter's tolerance level is pretty high," Ali said, managing a fairly credible laugh. "But I'll make sure she's home in a couple of hours."

For a moment after the call she stared at her phone. A nuisance. Nice.

"It's supposed to start raining in about an hour," Hayley was saying to Grace. "Until then you and Cutter and Ziggy better play out here in the backyard, where you'll be visible. Then when it does start to rain you can come inside and she shouldn't think a thing of it."

Ali reached into the basket that sat beside the back door. "Here," she said, handing the girl a rubber bone.

The girl looked at the slightly gnawed-on toy. Hayley laughed and explained, "I think Cutter is trying to teach Ziggy to fetch, but he needs somebody to throw it so he can show him what to do."

"I can do that!"

Grace looked deliriously happy. Ali wondered how much of that was simply because she didn't have to hide it over here.

She and Hayley sat on the back porch. And after about ten

minutes, she was looking at Hayley in amazement. "He really is trying to teach Ziggy how to fetch."

"That dog," Hayley said, "could teach just about anybody to do just about anything."

"You've obviously trained him well."

Hayley looked back at the girl and the two dogs. "Wish I could take the credit, but he came that way. At a time when I desperately needed him." Then she looked back at Ali. "He showed up on my doorstep shortly after my mother died."

Something in the way the other woman was looking at her told Ali what she wasn't saying. "You know. About...my husband, I mean."

Hayley nodded. "Foxworth does our research."

Ali thought about that for a moment. About the idea of being "researched" by an organization the size and scope of the Foxworth Foundation. It was intimidating, and a bit scary. But that was outweighed by something else.

"You checked me out because you wanted to be sure I truly wanted to help Grace."

"Yes," Hayley said simply.

Ali let out a long breath. "All right."

"You're okay with it?"

She nodded. "Grace deserves that kind of care."

"Yes."

Ali gave the woman she was starting to wish really was a longtime friend a sideways look. "I assume you did the same with Colby?"

Hayley smiled. "We did. You'll have to trust us as he did about you, he's all he appears to be. A good guy to the bone."

She blinked... *as he did about you?*

As if she'd guessed what had rattled Ali, Hayley said, "Understandably, he's not completely confident of his own judgment about women. The reason is right over there, and by the way, she's looked out the window toward us at least twice since we sat down here."

Ali let out a long breath. "I'm really glad you're here. This... undercover stuff is so not my milieu."

"Yet you're doing it so well," Hayley teased, making her both smile and relax a little.

The first drops of rain hit the roof over the porch in almost the same moment that Ziggy finally seemed to grasp the concept of fetch. At least, he brought the rubber bone back to Grace, with a proud Cutter trotting behind.

"A good note to end on," Ali called out to them as they neared. "It's going to open up so get inside before you get soaked. I think some hot chocolate is in order."

Grace gave a happy little whoop, and the trio trekked inside.

She had only known the child for a short time, but the change in her demeanor seemed both blatant and wonderful.

Almost as wonderful as being a part of this.

Chapter Seventeen

Colby told himself he liked meeting with Ali because she told him things about Grace, things he sorely missed, things he didn't know because he wasn't allowed enough time with her. He liked meeting with her simply because she was spending afternoons with Grace and freely shared every aspect of that. She told him everything his girl had done and said in those five days so far, and he could convince himself it somehow made up, in part at least, for the huge hole in his life.

Especially when she told him how Grace talked about him, and he knew the child understood that even when he wasn't physically there with her, she was always first in his thoughts.

This was their second meetup here at the Foxworth headquarters, marking exactly a week since he'd made that surprisingly great decision to punch out the window of Grace's room. Ali didn't seem to mind at all spending time talking about her time with Grace, and he seized on that gratefully. That was the big reason he looked so forward to meeting with her.

He even almost believed that was the only reason.

"—Hayley amazed me, pulling that off."

He snapped back to the moment. "What?"

Ali looked at him. "When Liz came over and started quizzing us about our days in college together. I was terrified, we hadn't really talked about it, but she had me believing it." She looked up at Hayley, who had just topped off their mugs of coffee with that delicious blend he kept meaning to ask about. "Made me understand exactly what you meant when you said Foxworth did their research."

"Oh." He wasn't sure what else to say.

"She not only knew I'd gone to Washington State, she knew my major, and tossed off that we were both in about three campus organizations together."

"That you were really in, I gather?" he asked. Ali nodded. He glanced at Hayley, who nodded at him. "And Ty—he's our head tech guy out of St. Louis—had me planted on the rosters within the hour," she said, "so if she checked, or had someone check after she got back home, there I'd be."

"And she would," he said. "She never trusts anybody completely."

"It makes me wonder how she trusted enough to even have a child," Ali said.

Colby let out a disgusted breath. "That was her last shot."

"At what?"

"She thought since nothing else had in nearly five years, that having a child might wake me up."

Ali drew back. "Wake you up?"

He nodded. "Make me realize I needed to give up this silly idea of what to do with my life and take what her family was offering. For the sake of the child."

She seemed to go very still before saying, with a note of near-disbelief, "So she used your sense of responsibility against you."

"From what we've found," Quinn said as he sat down opposite them, "she—and the rest of her family—use any tool at hand against anyone who's not following their plan."

"Pretty much," Colby agreed. "I'm sure that's why she... picked me. She figured I'd jump at the chance to be on their level. I was supposed to leave my stupid, useless life behind and grab the opportunity I didn't deserve but they were going to give me anyway."

"Because of course, anyone would," Ali said, and he felt a kick of warmth at the utter disdain and sarcasm in her voice. And for a brief second he wondered what it would be like to hear that low, husky voice under other circumstances. Intimate circumstances.

He reined it in and went on. Admitted something he rarely did, even to himself. "If I had it to do over again, knowing what I know now, knowing Grace and the kid she would become...maybe I would have done it."

As if the dog had sensed the change in his voice, Cutter came over and sat at his feet, resting his head on Colby's knee. He reached out to stroke the dark head, and oddly, felt a sort of calm, as if it were radiating from the dog through his fingers. He looked up, a little disconcerted, to find Ali staring at him.

When their gazes locked, she said quietly, "I'll bet you would. For the sake of the Grace you know now, you'd have given up your life. Figuratively...or literally. You'd die for her, wouldn't you."

It wasn't really a question, but he answered as if it had been. "I would. To save her I wouldn't hesitate a minute."

"And deep down, even though she might not think of it in those words, she knows it. What a gift to give your child."

Her words warmed him in a way he hadn't felt in a long time. The kind of warmth he'd felt the first time his baby girl's tiny hand had reached up to touch his face as he held her, the first time she'd piped out "Da-da," the first time he'd made her laugh in delight. Something deep, deep down and glowing, some sense of value and worth he'd lost.

Or Liz had trampled out of him.

"But think about this," Ali said quietly. "If you had given in, if you hadn't had the courage to fight and had gone down that Hollen road... Grace very likely would not be the girl she is now. They would have smothered her with their wealth, power and attitude just as they tried to do with you. The child you love so much, and who adores you, probably wouldn't exist."

He had never, ever thought of it that way. He stared at this woman who had, in the space of a week, become an integral part of his existence, part of the operation that gave him, for the first time in so long, hope.

Even the usually brisk, businesslike Quinn seemed to have been moved by her words. "And there you have it, Colby. The wisdom of the world, given to you on a platter."

Colby nodded slowly, unable to speak. Then Liam came down from what he'd gathered was their meeting and computer level upstairs, and Quinn was back to his usual job of solving problems.

"I think we can get away with Liam going with you again tomorrow," he said.

Colby shifted his brain to the issue now at hand. It was an effort. This emotional crap drained him faster than anything else.

"Agreed, given her opinion of my work vehicle, which is only a bit higher than her opinion on the one Liam drove. And only that because it's an SUV, not an actual pickup."

"And her opinion of me," Liam put in cheerfully. "I'm too stupid to be a problem to her. We can nurse that for a while, I think."

And the next day it worked just as Liam had said. This time the Foxworth man stayed in the truck, and as they'd planned, Colby told Liz he was too intimidated by her to get out. He could tell she liked that idea, enough that she didn't seem to question that it had been a full week for him with no vehicle of his own.

After the usual quiz about where they were going and what they were doing—"Local, as always, and for a walk in the nature park"—they were permitted to leave.

What he hadn't mentioned was what was happening before that stroll in the nature park. Which was a stop at Foxworth, where Hayley, Quinn and—he hoped—Ali would be waiting. And when they turned onto the gravel drive to the big Foxworth building and he saw her car, his pulse took a little leap.

As they pulled to a stop the door swung open, apparently triggered once more by that clever dog. Cutter raced along the walkway, and Grace called out his name in delighted greeting. Colby hurried to let her out to greet the dog, who had been followed by the little wiggle-butt, as Ali lovingly called her pup.

"Ali's here!" Grace crowed, and raced toward the door as if she was as eager to see her neighbor as she had been the dogs. She looked back over her shoulder. "Hurry up, Daddy! Ali's here."

Which was reason enough for him. He just didn't know how Grace knew that.

Colby couldn't describe how cheering this was, sitting here with people who saw the real Liz, the liar and manipulator. Not to mention Cutter's rather amazing knack for giving comfort with just a touch on his dark head.

Hayley brought a tray with coffee mugs, and one filled with hot chocolate for Grace. They sat sipping for a moment, and Colby felt himself relaxing now that Grace was safely with him.

"I don't know how I can ever repay you for all this," he said, looking from Hayley to Quinn.

"Oh, we'll think of something," Quinn said.

"Already did," Hayley said, grinning. "That is, if you'd be willing to take on a real apprentice or two, later, when this is all wound up. We have a couple of outreach programs run by former clients, and they can always use willing employers. We foot the bill for it, of course."

"Deal," Colby said instantly, knowing he'd do anything he could for these people who were doing so much for him, and for Grace.

"I've been thinking," Ali began after a moment, sounding a bit hesitant.

"Do you ever not?" Colby asked, not bothering to hide the note of appreciation in his voice. Ali smiled at him, quick, bright and heart-stopping.

"We're open to all ideas," Hayley said encouragingly. "What?"

She looked at Colby. "What's your work schedule these days?"

"My work's on hold at the moment," he said brow furrowing, not sure why that mattered to Ali. "My girl's much more important. Why?"

"Just... I was thinking about some dog walks. And that maybe after a bit longer, when Liz is used to Grace coming to my house, we could convince her to let Grace come with me on those walks."

"That would be nice," Colby said, still a little uncertain where she was going with this.

"And now that I know how close this—" she gestured at the building around them "—really is, Grace and I and the dogs could be here in maybe ten minutes at the most."

It hit him then. A meeting place. She was offering a meeting place. For him and Grace.

"But I..." He glanced at the Foxworths. "The family court order..."

"There is that," Quinn said. "We'll get Gavin's opinion on it, to see how much of the coincidence defense could apply."

"But if I keep meeting her here—"

"We may have to limit the encounters," Quinn said.

"Or," Hayley said thoughtfully, "what if you had to get out of your place for a while. Maybe it needs work done, and you had to temporarily vacate. So your friends offered you a place to stay." She nodded toward the bedroom and bathroom he'd noticed the first time he'd come here. "That little suite is here for just that kind of reason."

He supposed he was gaping at them now, but he couldn't help it.

"We're what, about halfway between Liz's house and yours? So you'd be close, but not so close it would make her suspicious if she spotted you," Quinn said. "It would be a lot easier to pass off as coincidence if you happen to…run into Grace outside your allotted visiting hours."

Grace had been looking from one speaker to the other, her brow furrowed, as if she weren't sure she was getting this right. But it only took her a moment to figure it out. She stared at Ali. "You mean you and I could walk the dogs here and Daddy would be here already?"

"Yes," Ali said quietly.

Grace turned sharply toward him, got up on her knees and threw her arms around his neck.

"Daddy! We could see each other every day!"

"Well, not quite that often. But…more. If, I mean really if, you can keep it secret."

"I won't tell her. I won't even talk to her!"

"Can't do that," he cautioned. "She'll figure out you're hiding something. Maybe just yes or no answers." He grimaced. "Make that yes, Mother, or no, Mother."

"Less said, the better," Quinn agreed.

Grace's brow furrowed. "She'll ask. Pushy. Like she always does. Not like she cares, but like…"

"Like she's the boss and you have to report in," Colby said, having been on the receiving end of that himself.

"Yeah," Grace agreed.

"Maybe," Ali suggested, "just three-words-or-less answers. Like 'I'm reading,' or 'I have homework,' or 'walking the dogs,' or most importantly, 'I don't know.'"

"And always, the last time you saw me was our last official time," Colby said, "when I came to pick you up and she knows it. Can you keep that straight?"

Grace gave him an eye roll. "Of course I can. I'm—" she slid a glance at Liam "—bright as a new penny."

All five adults in the room, including him, burst out laughing. Ziggy let out a string of happy yips. And Cutter looked at them all as if he were saying, "I told you so."

Colby thought maybe he'd underestimated the dog he'd already admitted was very, very smart. Then he realized Grace was staring at him. Then she threw her arms around him again and gave him a fierce hug.

"What, baby?" he asked, hugging her back.

"You laughed. Really laughed."

He lowered his chin to rest on her silken hair. "I love you, Gracie." It came out a little gruffly, his throat was so tight.

"I know, Daddy. I know she's wrong."

"Wrong?"

"When she says you only pretend to love me, to get back at her."

He felt every muscle he had tense. He heard a tiny sound he thought had come from Ali, and at the same time sensed the Foxworths go very still.

"That," he said, "is the biggest lie she could ever tell."

When he finally looked up again, he saw Ali looking at them, her eyes shining even in the indoor light. She was blinking rather rapidly, and he realized the shine was tears. And that made some deeply buried, frozen part of him begin to stir.

"Liz Hollen could tell me grass was green and I wouldn't believe her," Ali said.

Grace laughed at that. He felt it as much as heard it, that sweet, beloved sound, and it let him regain some kind of control over the emotions that were rocketing around inside his brain.

"I don't know how to thank you," he said to Ali.

She gestured toward them. "Seeing this is a pretty good thank-you."

"That it is," Hayley said quietly.

"I was also thinking, before," Ali said after a moment, "that I should make a big deal about asking her permission for Grace to come with me dog walking. Kowtowing, and all that."

"She'll love that," Colby said dryly.

"Good idea," Hayley agreed.

"Keep in mind she might try to follow you," Quinn said, "until she's sure that's all it is. She seems the suspicious type."

"And then some," Colby said. "I think she has before, a couple of times."

"Then you and the dogs should stop out back," Hayley said. "They can play in our meadow out there. It's Cutter's favorite play spot, and he'll keep the pup in line. And you can say that's why you come here, because they can play off leash."

"And for now," Quinn added, "if asked you have no idea who we are, just that we let the dogs play here."

Colby realized Grace was listening intently, her gaze shifting to each person who spoke, as if trying to process everything. "I know it's complicated, sweetheart, but it's all to help us."

His little girl nodded. Then she looked at Ali. "You helped first."

Ali smiled. "And I'm going to keep helping."

Grace smiled back, warmly. Then she scooted over to give Ali a hug as well. "I knew you were nice. That I could trust you."

"And that," Ali said, "is the best start to the New Year I've ever had."

Colby sat there watching the two, thinking she wasn't the only one.

Chapter Eighteen

Colby sat at the small picnic table, watching Grace attack her cinnamon roll in her own distinct way. She loved the concoction from a famous local bakery, with the slightly hollowed out center filled with even more of the luscious frosting. She carefully tore the soft roll into pieces as she went, dipping each one into the center to be sure each had its share of the good stuff, as she called it. And he knew when she was down to the last piece she would wipe it across the plate to catch any escaped drops, and then lick any residue off her fingers before finally admitting it was gone and wiping her hands with the napkin.

His girl did love these cinnamon rolls.

He took another sip of the strong, black coffee he'd ordered. Liam had dropped them off in the picturesque little town and gone about some Foxworth business, and would be back to pick them up for the unhappy trip back to "the mother," as Grace always put it.

He sat fighting down the usual ache he felt on these days, that in far too short a time he would have to take her back to that house and that woman. Which gave him another battle to fight, that of his own stupidity, and wondering how on earth he'd ever fallen for her mother. Especially when—

"I wonder if Ali likes these too," Grace said out of the blue.

Colby blinked. Because the thought she'd interrupted would

have ended with "—when there were women like Ali Moran around."

"I…don't know. She hasn't lived over here that long. Maybe she's never had one."

Grace's eyes widened. "We need to get her one."

"I…"

"Let's buy one and take it to her."

"Honey, I can't."

"Why?"

"Because it has to be a secret that… I know her."

She frowned. Not in an unhappy way, but in that way that told him that agile mind was racing. "Oh. Because then *she'll*—" she didn't explain what she, just made it clear with the emphasis "—make me stop seeing her, if she thinks you and Ali are friends."

Yes, his girl was smart. And she'd had to learn to survive under the current regime. "Exactly," he said.

Grace frowned again, and this time it was the unhappy kind. And it ripped at him. He felt as if he were trapped in some cell made of unbreakable glass, where he could see the outside, could see his daughter and what she was having to live with, but couldn't do a damned thing about it.

He shoved it out of his mind. He only had an hour left with her today, and he didn't want it weighed down with his own frustration and unhappiness. But that became a harder task when, as they walked down to the harbor to look at the boats—and hadn't he sometimes thought about buying a nice big one and taking off for parts unknown with Grace—she spoke again, in as close to a sulky tone as she ever got.

"I don't want to go tomorrow."

He sighed. He knew Liz was taking her to the city for the weekend. And he was very much afraid he knew why.

"I won't get to see Ali or Ziggy or Cutter, for two whole days," Grace said.

"I know."

"I don't like it over there. There's nasty stuff painted on all the walls and signs and they cut down all the trees."

He couldn't argue with that, remembering his last trip over there, thankfully some time ago. He just wasn't a city guy at heart, yet another part of him he'd have had to crush to follow Liz's diktat.

"Maybe, if you ask right, when you get home she'll let you go over and say hello, at least."

Grace made a sour face at that, no doubt imagining what it would take to ask in a way that would get her the answer she wanted. Then she brightened. "Maybe Cutter will come over and get me. Ali said he might if he misses me."

"Now, that's an idea," Colby said.

But he couldn't help wondering how long Liz would put up with the dog interfering. He doubted she'd ever figure out it was planned, because she barely gave other humans credit for that kind of intelligence. Not when compared to herself, anyway.

Still, it might be worth a call to Ali, asking her if she could send the big dog over when she saw they were home. Actually it would be Hayley who would do it of course, he was her dog after all, but…he could still call Ali to ask.

That he wanted to do that so much should be a warning, he told himself. The last thing he needed right now was to get himself all tangled up over a woman, even if she was the first woman he'd reacted to like this in…maybe ever. With Liz he'd been blinded by the flash, the confidence, the demeanor he now knew was very well practiced to conceal the reality.

With Ali it was genuine. She was just as gorgeous, in her own green-eyed way, with that red hair that made him think of nights in front of a warm fire. And on the inside, she was genuine, honest, open and caring, everything Liz was not. Her insides were like that warming fire, not Liz's dark, cold, swirling, muddy evil.

"Daddy?"

"Sorry," he said quickly, snapping out of his reverie. "I was just thinking about calling and asking if they—" he chose the nonspecific word carefully "—could send Cutter over once they see you're home."

Grace lit up. "Would you? I know Ali would if you asked her."

"I will," he promised.

"I wish Mother would let me have a phone. Then I could call myself. And I could call you, too."

"Sweetheart, I have a feeling that's exactly why she won't let you. I'd buy you one myself, except if she found out, it would make things worse. Much worse." At the look on her face his stomach knotted. "But think about it," he said, trying to cheer her up, "how many people get messages delivered by a very clever dog?"

It worked, because she smiled widely at the memory. "Hey, I could send messages with Cutter to Ali, then she could give them to you. Mother doesn't pay much attention to him."

"I'll talk to them about that. I can't go there, I don't want your mother not trusting Ali, but I think our new Foxworth friends will figure something out."

Grace seemed delighted with the idea that she could easily reach him. "I could write you a note every day!"

She was so entranced with the idea of communicating via Cutter that he didn't point out she could do that while at Ali's anyway. "And I would treasure every one," he said instead. "And what a cool way to do it."

Her brow furrowed thoughtfully again. "But if you write me back, she might find it. Where could I hide them?"

"Maybe Ali would keep them safe for you."

She brightened. "She would! I know she would."

When their time was up and he had to get her home, he felt better than he usually did, probably because Grace was happier. Even Liam noticed the difference, and teased Grace about not getting him one of the treats he also loved.

"Next time I will, promise," she said.

She clearly had come to trust the young man with the twang, just as he had. "I like how you play stupid and she believes it," she'd told him when she'd first gotten into his truck today, making Liam grin.

"Don't forget," she said as they arrived at Liz's door, three minutes early because he figured she'd have the sheriff already dialed in ready to call if he was one second late, "I'll be back Sunday afternoon."

"I won't."

Liz's only response to their arrival was to double-check her watch, then order Grace to her room. She didn't say a word to Colby, merely shut the door in his face.

"Chatty, huh?" Liam asked as he got back in the truck.

"I kind of prefer her that way," he admitted wryly.

"I can see why." He started the engine and backed out of the driveway. "That girl of yours is a pistol."

"She is."

"I'm glad Cutter found y'all, so Foxworth can help."

Colby looked at the man driving. "I never would have expected them to get involved in something this...small."

"It's not small, to us. Because what matters is what's right, not how big a case is. We're not in it for the headlines—" he grimaced and rolled his eyes "—even if we have been collecting them in the last couple of years or so."

What's right.

Colby took a long, deep breath, still not quite adjusted to the idea that he had these people on his side. That he just might be able to free Grace, even a little bit, from that chewing machine that was the Hollen family.

Chapter Nineteen

Ali realized with a little jolt she'd been pacing the floor. She never did that. But the house felt so...empty.

She walked over to where Ziggy was wrestling happily with his stuffed owl. He hadn't managed to break the hooter yet, so the quiet sounds still emanated from the little thing, seeming to inspire Ziggy to keep pawing at it. She didn't mind the noise. She'd bought the toy specifically because she figured she'd be hearing a lot of it, and it was the least annoying sound of all the squeaking things she'd heard as she stood there in the pet store.

She leaned down and picked up the pup, who was surprised, but judging by the way he immediately began licking at her face, happy. Which was an improvement on this morning, when he'd spent an hour or so exhausting himself—and her—by searching every corner of the house repeatedly, looking for his missing playmate.

She understood. She missed Cutter, too. She adored her little imp, but she couldn't deny there was something about that dog, something special. When he was here she was petting him so often, just to prove to herself that she hadn't imagined that odd feeling of comfort, that gentle soothing, that he somehow managed to transmit. She'd noticed, when they'd been at the Foxworth headquarters, that Colby did it, too. And he got the same puzzled but smiling expression she probably wore every time she did it.

She missed Hayley, too. She was a little surprised at how wound up she'd gotten in all this, and above all how much she wanted to help Colby Kendrick somehow get out of this awful situation. Sure, the big mistake—marrying that harridan next door—was his, but how long should he have to pay for it?

And Grace, sweet, smart little Grace shouldn't have to pay for it at all. She hadn't chosen her mother.

Ziggy wiggled in her arms, demanding to be let down. She set him gently on the floor, and he scampered off. She didn't bother to follow him this time, because she knew the path. He'd be checking every room in the house just in case Cutter had been hiding, or had snuck in in the last ten minutes.

The house must seem as empty to him as it does to me.

She assured herself it was just going to take time to adjust. And Hayley's visit, in the guise of her college friend, was over anyway. She'd made her assessment of the creature next door, which had been even more severe than Ali's own, given Hayley had more experience dealing with the type. But while Cutter had gone home with his mom for the weekend, he would be back, Hayley had promised.

"Working undercover?" Ali had joked.

"Exactly that," Hayley had said, with a knowing look that said she wasn't joking in the slightest.

As Ziggy trotted busily down the hall toward her office, Ali found herself wondering if Colby had moved into the Foxworth headquarters. Maybe he'd be doing that this weekend, while Grace was gone. And—entirely unrelated, she assured herself—she had the thought that before she even broached the idea to Liz, she should find out exactly how long it took to walk from here to there, especially taking into account Ziggy's curiosity about everyone and everything, and his much shorter strides.

Decided now, she went back to the bedroom to change from her comfy sheepskin boots into some sturdier shoes for walking. The rain appeared to have abated for now, but as she well knew, it could return with a vengeance at any moment, so she grabbed her slicker with the hood from the rack by the front door. She stuffed a small towel in one pocket in case she needed to dry Ziggy off, put her phone and ID and keys in another, and they were off.

By the time they were two blocks down, she was laughing at herself. She had so underestimated how long it would take for Ziggy to walk even this far. When the time came she might have to carry the little one, and let the well-trained to keep pace with a human Cutter set the speed. Then Ziggy could walk all the way home. Colby and Grace wouldn't have quite as much time together as she'd hoped, but she was sure they'd both think it was better than nothing.

And if she ended up in trouble with the Hollens in case they discovered it had been not accidental but planned, then so be it. She'd count it as a matter of pride to have people like them mad at her. Legal trouble would be a little rougher but with— she still grinned inwardly at the thought—Gavin de Marco on their side, even the Hollens would think twice about starting that gear grinding.

In the end it took them just over twenty minutes. If she carried Ziggy and hurried, she thought she could cut at least eight minutes off that. That would give them that much more time together.

And you have to give it to them. No staying and hovering just because it makes you feel good to see them together.

She hadn't counted on Ziggy somewhat hysterically realizing, no doubt by scent, that this was Cutter's place. The little guy pulled on the leash until she was afraid he'd choke himself.

"He's probably not here, Ziggy," she explained. "He's home with Hayley and Quinn, not here."

But what about Colby?

She yanked her mind off that path, and tugged the pup toward the open meadow behind the building. She didn't think the Foxworths would mind, given it was their idea. And Ziggy seemed willing enough, since she wasn't pulling at him to leave. And he could apparently scent Cutter in the lovely open space as well, because he went back to sniffing madly. He was so excited, his tail wagging so fast, that if it had been longer and he lighter she thought he might lift off like the helicopter she assumed that pad on the other side of the building was for.

She laughed as Ziggy took a short tumble off the small rock he'd tried to climb over, rolled and came up on his paws, looking at her as if to say, "I meant to do that!"

"Very graceful," she complimented him.

"Ali?"

She spun around, startled. She hadn't heard a thing, she'd been so focused on Ziggy. Her heart gave another jump. Colby. He was here. Standing there, just a yard or so away, smiling at her. He had the best smile, and she wanted to see it more often.

She realized she was just standing there, gaping at him.

"Sorry," she said, flustered. "I didn't know you'd be here already."

But I hoped...

She raced on before she let that thought slip out. "I wanted to find out exactly how long it would take to walk here. Turns out with Mr. Little Guy, it takes longer than I thought, so I figured on the way here I'd carry him and then he can get his walk on the way back. We don't want *the mother* to get mad at how long Grace and I are gone, or worse, get suspicious about it."

He was staring at her now, and she thought she must have sounded like some wound-up idiot. She tried to think of something to say, something calmer, less jittery, but she couldn't. And she couldn't trust herself to deliver it calmly even if she did think of something, because he made her so darned...edgy.

"You sound just like Grace when you say that. 'The mother,' I mean."

"She does have it down," Ali agreed, able to smile almost normally now. "So, you're moved in here, temporarily at least?"

He nodded. "Didn't take much. Not like my place is too far away, for whatever I forgot." He hesitated, then said rather quickly, "I just put coffee on. Want to come in?"

She couldn't think of anything she wanted more just now, but only nodded because she was afraid of what she might blurt out.

"I still have trouble believing these guys," he said as they stepped inside, waving at the interior as if to indicate the Foxworths in general.

She bent to let Ziggy off the leash. He was fairly well housetrained already, although not perfect, but since he'd just spent a long time outside she figured it was safe enough. Just sniffing out where Cutter had been would keep him busy for a while.

"What really impresses me is how little they blow their own horn," she said as she straightened up. "You go looking and aside from brief mentions in some news reports—many of which the reports say they limit—the only things you can find are posts and comments from the people they've helped."

"I know." He shrugged as he poured coffee into the two mugs he'd gotten from one of the upper cupboards. Obviously they'd showed him around. "I did some looking, too. Mostly out of shock."

They took the coffee and sat in front of the fireplace. Ziggy, interestingly, immediately trotted over to Colby and nudged at his leg. Then he raised up and put his paws on the seat beside him. And Ali couldn't deny that she liked the fact that he immediately and very gently lifted the pup up onto the couch between them.

Ziggy circled a couple of times then plopped down. He let out a long sigh as if utterly exhausted. As perhaps he was, walking that distance on his short little puppy legs.

"Yep, I'll definitely carry him here," she said, reaching out to stroke his soft fur.

A moment of silence spun out, then Colby said, his voice sounding a little tight, "I really don't know how to thank you for this. For offering to do this, to take all that time to get Grace here."

"We don't have the mother's permission yet," she cautioned.

"I know. But that you'd offer to do it at all..." He trailed off, staring down into his coffee mug as if it held the answer to all the world's questions.

She only wished it were that easy, especially for him. He deserved it. Grace deserved it. And she was more certain of that than she had been of anything since Josh had died.

Chapter Twenty

Colby watched as the puppy snuggled up to Ali.

I get it, dog. I'd like that, too.

He yanked his gaze back to his coffee mug.

"Colby?" she asked, and he knew she'd seen his sudden jerk.

"I just…" He struggled for a moment, then blurted out the first coherent question he could think of, nodding at Ziggy. "Does he help?"

She smiled softly and reached to stroked the soft fur. "Yes, he does. He's so…interested. In everything. That was something I lost for a while."

"After your husband died?"

She nodded. "I didn't care about anything, for a long time. Then my neighbor's dog had puppies, and I met this guy. He was the littlest of the litter, and the quietest. His siblings kept knocking him down. It's silly, but I felt like we could…understand each other."

"Not silly at all," he said, his voice a little rough at the images she was putting in his mind.

"I missed my husband so much, I needed something, anything, to fill at least some of the hole he'd left. And once I had Ziggy, I started to remember things besides the awful ending. Like how Josh was the one who pushed me to start my business, who supported me trying. He always had my back, always told me I could fly if I'd just trust my talent enough to lift off."

He wondered what that must have been like, to have someone so on your side, so encouraging…instead of someone telling you the work you loved was useless, pointless and something to be ashamed of.

"What did he do?"

She smiled. "He was a locksmith."

"Well, that's useful."

"It is. Do you remember when the automatic locks at the emergency room at the local hospital went haywire about five years ago, and nobody could get in or out?"

"I do. It was all over the news, nearly caused a riot." He knew where she was going then. "I read they called some guy out in the middle of the night and he had it fixed in like twenty minutes. That was your husband?"

"It was."

He thought he recognized her expression. "You were proud of him," he said softly, wondering what that would feel like.

"Very. And he of me. And that," she went on, "is how it should be. A marriage, I mean."

He looked at her then. "You don't have to remind me. I realize that now."

"I can't imagine purposely making someone I supposedly love feel the way she's made you feel."

"No, you couldn't, could you?" He had no doubts about that. Ziggy squirmed and let out a sleepy little woof. He reached out and petted the little guy. "Sometimes… I felt like a stray dog who got adopted, but then dumped because he wanted to hunt or herd instead of being a lap dog."

"To do what he was bred to do," Ali said, getting it immediately, not to his surprise.

"Exactly. And to me, her world was like trying to herd sharks."

Ali grimaced. "How on earth did you last as long as you did with her?"

He shrugged. It seemed foolish to him now, beyond foolish. But it was the only answer. "Because I promised forever."

"And Grace."

"Yes." He let out a compressed breath. "She deserved better than the hell she's gone through. She deserved parents worthy of her. With a marriage that wasn't built on…"

He really didn't have any words for that, and waved a hand in defeat.

"You mean a marriage like, say, Hayley and Quinn's, for example," she said.

"Yes. They are…remarkable."

"Did you know they met when, thanks to Cutter, he had to kidnap her?"

Colby blinked. "*Had* to?"

She nodded. "In the proverbial black helicopter. Have one of them tell you the story. It's pretty amazing."

He gave a slow shake of his head. "Seems everything about them is."

"Yes. It does my heart good to know there are good people like them still around these days. To help good people like you."

Colby looked at her for a long, silent moment. "What a mom you'd make," he finally said, his throat tight. "The kind Grace should have had."

He only realized what could be read into that after he said it, but Ali didn't jump onto the inference that he would have preferred her as Grace's mom, too.

Because that's not who she is, she doesn't take advantage of every stupid thing you say.

"Thank you," she said quietly. "That is one of the biggest compliments I've ever gotten." She lowered her gaze to the pup. "We wanted kids. In fact, we stopped any prevention a few weeks before he was killed."

He didn't know what to say to that, and for once managed to keep his mouth shut before he said something that would make it worse. So he did the only thing he could think of. He reached over and laid his hand on top of hers where it was stroking the pup.

Her hand went still but she didn't pull away. She stared down at his hand atop hers and then, to his shock, she turned hers over and wrapped her fingers around his.

"Grace may have one of the worst mothers on record, but she's got you, and that makes up for a lot."

He didn't mean for it to happen. It wasn't a decision he made any more than petting Ziggy seemed to be. He meant only to thank her with a kiss on the cheek, to make up for the words he couldn't find. But she turned her head just then, her lips brushing his, and it became something much more.

She was so warm, so soft, so comforting and thrilling at the same time, that he couldn't stop himself. And she didn't seem to want him to, which only kicked him into overdrive. He tasted the lingering zest of the coffee, but only for a moment before all was erased but the singular, fiery taste of Ali herself. Sweet and sharp, luscious and so very alive, all at once. It was nearly overwhelming and when he finally broke the kiss he had a brief moment of trying to remember how to breathe normally.

She was staring at him, looking a bit as if she were in shock. *Of course she is, you had no right!*

"Ali, I'm sor—"

She put a finger to his lips, stopping his apology. "Don't you dare say you're sorry. Not for that."

"But—"

"I understand. It was impulse. Unexpected." He thought he saw a faint rise of pink in her cheeks. "I liked it." His heart seemed to take a little leap. "But right now…we have to focus on Grace, don't we?"

That easily, and so very gently, she brought him back to earth. Back to reality. He couldn't look at her when he nodded.

"So, we put…that on hold. But Colby?" He did look at her then, because he had to. "Just on hold, okay? Don't bury it."

She already knew him so well it seemed impossible. Because that was his gut-level response, kill it, bury it, because he had no right to even think that way let alone do anything about it. He wasn't sure he would even if there wasn't this huge, malevolent cloud hanging over him.

But there was, and Ali was right. Grace ever and always had to come first. And he would see to it that she did.

Chapter Twenty-One

"Ali said I had to ask you."

Grace was wearing the perfect respectful expression. The child was carrying it off as if she'd rehearsed it a dozen times. As, in fact, they had over the last couple of days, since she'd gotten home from the city. Grace had said it was awful, that her mother had made her dress up and say nice things to a bunch of people she didn't even know.

"Consider it a rehearsal for this, then," Ali had suggested, and the child had lit up at that idea.

"She said that, did she?" her mother replied now, shifting her gaze from her daughter to Ali.

"Of course," Ali said, with just the right tone of deference she'd practiced right along with Grace. "I wouldn't dream of assuming it was all right for her to come along on our walks without checking with you first."

Ali thought she saw a flash of something in the other woman's eyes. She was fairly sure it wasn't gratitude. Maybe pleasure? Satisfaction?

More likely acceptance of the obsequious manner and tone as her due.

Taking that as incentive, she went on, still with that practiced smile. "You have my number, so of course if you need us to come back right away just call or text and we'll come back at a run."

"And just where do you plan on taking these walks?"

"I've been staying fairly close, not leaving the general neighborhood," she promised, leaving the interpretation of neighborhood open. "I need to learn my way around a bit, find some open places for the dogs to play. Ziggy needs to learn how to be on a leash, and Cutter needs the exercise. That last won't hurt me, either." She tried to make her smile look ingratiating but not fawning. "And maybe Grace will sleep better if we work off some energy."

That seemed to register, and Ali wondered if the woman was thinking the child might be less recalcitrant if she was more tired. Ali also noticed the woman barely glanced at either of the dogs, and in Cutter's case that seemed a good thing. Especially since the dog was rather casually inserting himself between Grace and her mother. Or maybe she was just imagining that. The dog was so smart, maybe she was giving him too much credit. But somehow she didn't think so. When she'd brought the dog back a couple of hours before Liz's expensive car had arrived, Hayley had explained once more how Foxworth had never gone wrong by trusting the dog's instincts.

Ali and Grace waited for a decision, but apparently there was one more thing the queen had to be sure of.

"And if I said no?" Liz asked, as imperiously as if she truly were that monarch that kept popping into Ali's mind.

"Then that's the way it is," Ali said simply. "You are her mother, and what you say goes."

Again that look flashed in the dark eyes Ali couldn't help thinking of as shadowy, but that was likely her overactive imagination. Or maybe the memory of that story Grace had written. Colby had shown it to her the day she'd first walked with Ziggy to Foxworth—she fought down the memory of that kiss—and she'd read the couple of pages with interest that had gradually turned to dismay. No wonder this had been the turning point for him. It was a simple yet appalling tale, and it made her want to grab Grace and run herself.

But apparently she'd hit the right tone, the right amount of submissiveness, because the woman nodded.

"All right," she said. She looked at Grace. "You may go on these walks, as long as you check every day to make sure I don't have something else planned for you. Is that clear?"

"Yes, Mother."

Liz shifted her gaze to Ali. "You're awfully generous with your time, to spend it with a troublesome child."

Ali had to tamp down her reaction to that statement, made right in front of the child in question. That Grace barely reacted told her this wasn't an unusual occurrence.

"Just trying to be a good neighbor," she managed to say lightly enough.

"Thinking I might return the favor some day?" Liz asked, and Ali could almost feel the thunk as the woman slid her into one of her mental slots, that of someone trying to curry favor with the queen.

"I hope that never happens, of course," Ali said, "but it's nice to have friends close by, isn't it?"

And I'd run all the way to Foxworth before I'd ask you for the time of day.

"Hmm," was all Liz said.

Ali had had more than enough of the woman. She turned to Grace. "You ready to go?"

"Yes," the child responded instantly. Ali could almost feel the child's glee as she started toward the door. She put a hand on the girl's shoulder to warn her not to let it show. She added a little squeeze as a reminder, and Grace looked back.

"Thank you, Mother."

Liz looked almost startled. Her glance flicked to Ali, who gave her the best smile she could manage, wanting the woman to think she was pounding home to Grace the respect due to the woman in charge. It seemed to work, for the smile she got in return seemed more sincere than any she'd gotten from the woman yet. Not that that was saying much.

They were down to the sidewalk in front of Ali's house before Grace couldn't hold it back and giggled. They made it past the stand of tall evergreens, which masked them from the big, fancy house, then Grace turned and threw her arms around Ali in a huge hug.

"Good job, sweetie," she told the child. "Now, let's get going. I'm going to carry Ziggy, so we'll get there quicker. You take Cutter's leash." Grace gave the dog a wary look, given his size, but took the leather lead. "Hayley promised, he knows his job is to protect you, Grace. You have your very own guard dog."

As if he'd understood, Cutter tilted his head and swiped his tongue across the back of Grace's hand. The girl giggled again, and Ali thought she would do a great deal to hear a lot more of that lovely sound. She reached out to pet Cutter's dark head. Her hand stopped mid-stroke, and she looked up at Ali, wide-eyed.

"He makes me feel so much better!"

"I know. It's amazing, isn't it? He gives me that same, warm, everything's-going-to-be-all-right feeling."

"Yes, that's it."

"Now, let's get moving, m'girl, so you can get to the other guy who makes you feel like that."

This time it was a full-on laugh, and such a joyous one that Ali felt like she would do a lot more than merely invite a child on a walk with her to hear it. And tried to ignore the feeling welling up inside that that same guy made her feel the same way.

The walk did go much faster with Ziggy in the sling she'd picked up for that very purpose. And the pup seemed content enough for the moment, with Grace and Cutter to watch, although he squirmed around now and then.

"You can do all the sniffing you want on the way back," she promised him.

They were there in about half the time it had taken her with

Ziggy on foot. Her own pace slowed, and Grace stopped dead, staring at the big, black helicopter that sat on the pad she'd noticed earlier. Quinn was next to it, leaning into the...cockpit? Cabin? She wasn't sure what it was called on a helicopter. Cutter let out a short bark and Quinn spun around. And only then did Ali see the man on the other side, who had apparently been also leaning in, looking at the interior.

Colby.

"Daddy!"

Grace took off at a run. Her father turned to her and did the same. He swept the child up into his arms, taking care, Ali noticed, not to yank on the leash she held. Quinn, smiling widely, came over and took it from her, then unclipped it from Cutter's collar.

"You take some time," he told Colby, "then meet us inside."

Cutter had greeted Quinn quite happily, but stayed close to Grace when he walked over to Ali.

"He really does know she's his job, doesn't he?" Ali asked the head of Foxworth.

"He does. And he'd take down anyone who tried to hurt her."

"I had the funny feeling today, when we were talking to her mother, that he was purposely putting himself between them."

Quinn smiled. "I'm sure he was. He knows who the threat is."

"Wow. That's beyond just smart."

"He's beyond smart. He's...inexplicable."

Quinn said it with a shake of his head and an expression that told her that hadn't been an easy conclusion for him to reach. Or at least, admit to. She'd learned a bit from Hayley about his background in the military, where he'd worked with some very smart dogs, and wondered when he'd realized this particular dog was even more amazing. She remembered how it had been Cutter who had apparently directed the assessment of Colby, how the dog had sniffed, assessed and then sat at his feet looking up at his humans. Given them his "fix it" look, as they called it.

Because Cutter had decided Colby was the good guy in all this. And they believed him.

With that, even though she'd only just met them all a few days ago, she agreed.

Chapter Twenty-Two

Colby wished it could have gone on and on, this time with his precious girl. She was chattering so fast, so excited that this had worked and they were together, it was hard to keep up with her. She'd always been so quick, and seemed quite able to think in multiple directions at once. She'd been putting together four-to five-word sentences at just over two years old, which her doctor had said was a sign of how quick and smart she was.

He'd had a dream about her once, Grace as an adult, standing at some podium, receiving some big award. He'd been there with her, cheering proudly, but Liz had been nowhere in sight. He'd awakened feeling a bit guilty about that, given they'd still been married at the time. Maybe he'd sensed what was coming even then.

Or maybe it was just wishful dreaming.

"—gonna fly somewhere in that?" Grace was pointing at the helicopter.

He smiled. "I don't think so. But it would be fun, wouldn't it?" She nodded, a wide smile on her sweet face. "They have an airplane, too, down south at the airport."

"Wow."

"Yeah. They're a pretty big deal around here, these Foxworth folks."

"And they're helping us."

"Yes. Yes, they are. So I guess we should go in and talk to them, huh?"

"And Ali. She's helping, too."

"I know."

Ali was a woman going about her life, building her own business while recovering from a terrible loss. That was enough to consume most people, but yet she was going out of her way, spending time, effort and emotion to help them. And doing it well, given she'd been able to convince Liz to let Grace accompany her on the dog walks.

He was still pondering that when they rounded the corner of the main building. Cutter trotted ahead, raised up and batted at the automatic door switch with his front paws, and the door swung open. Grace giggled happily.

"He's so smart."

"He is."

"And Ziggy is so sweet and snuggly."

The memory of the dog snuggled between him and Ali on the couch rocketed through his mind, but it was seared away by the heated memory of that kiss. That kiss that had awakened feelings in him he'd never known, sensations he'd never felt before.

That kiss Ali had refused to let him apologize for.

"I really like Ali a lot," Grace said with finality.

"So do I." *Oh, boy, do I.*

As they followed Cutter into the Foxworth headquarters, he had to remind himself yet again that he had also agreed to put all that on hold. He knew it was the right thing to do, for Grace's sake in the main, but so many other reasons as well. But obviously the wall he'd built in his mind to keep those thoughts at bay needed a bit of reinforcement.

And he tried. He was going to head for one of the single chairs by the fireplace, but Cutter got in the way. And then Grace was tugging at him, and they ended up settled on the couch with Ali on the next cushion. Grace was beside him, clinging to him—or maybe it was the other way around—Colby found himself wondering what on earth Foxworth would come up with now. Liam came downstairs, nodded at both him and Ali, and grinned widely at Grace.

"How's my favorite child genius?"

She rolled her eyes at him, but she was grinning back. "You're funnier when you're playing stupid."

Liam laughed as he sat in one of the armchairs at the end of the big couch. He picked up the remote control from the coffee table and aimed it at the flat-screen. "Just some general research," he explained with a glance at Colby. "You know this guy?"

An image appeared on the screen. The man, who looked about sixty, with a beard and what hair he had left both dark in color, seemed vaguely familiar but he couldn't put a name to him.

"That's Mr. Wells. He's a lawyer," Grace piped up cheerfully. Every adult in the room turned to stare at her. Grace shrugged as if it were nothing. "He was at the meeting the mother dragged me to. At her father's office."

Her father. Not "my grandfather." No, Grace had never felt a part of that side of the family, and Colby couldn't deny the fact that it warmed him. She was indeed a smart girl. Maybe even the child genius Liam had called her.

"Your mother," Quinn said carefully, "met this man at the Hollen offices in the city?"

Grace nodded. "That's why she went."

"Why did she want you there?" Colby asked.

"She didn't," Grace answered with a shrug. "She just didn't want me here."

Colby looked at Quinn, whose gaze had narrowed, then back to his daughter. "Couldn't Irene have stayed with you?"

"She would have, but the mother said she didn't want us alone in the house overnight, without her there."

He reached the only conclusion he could think of. He

looked back at Quinn. "She suspects it was me who broke that window."

Quinn nodded. "Looks like."

Grace was looking at them both now, puzzled. "Of course she does. She always says you might try to steal me. When she's pretending she cares about me."

"What else does she say, Grace?" Hayley asked gently.

Grace shrugged again. "Just that I'd better not be stupid and go with him." She shifted her gaze to Colby. "And that if you ever do, you'll be really, really sorry." Her brow furrowed. "But that the…undertaker? Is that a person? She said the undertaker will be happy."

Colby felt a chill ripple over him. "Well, that's a new one," he muttered. As bad as she'd been, Liz had never threatened to kill him before.

"She's escalating," Quinn said, and his voice was grim enough that even Grace picked up on it and looked worried.

"Daddy, what does undertaker mean?"

He didn't really want to tell her. But he didn't want to lie to her, either. She was too smart anyway, and she'd know. But then Hayley spoke, in that quiet, gentle way she had.

"What your mother said means she wishes your father would go away and never bother her again."

"Oh. She always says that." She looked from Hayley back to Colby. "But if you go away, you'll take me with you, won't you?" she asked anxiously.

"I'm not going away without you," he promised her.

"Okay," Grace said, smiling now, as if that were all she'd needed to hear.

"Trust," Ali murmured, just loud enough for him to hear. "A beautiful thing to have earned."

He liked the way she put it, not that it was a gift—which it was, to him—but that he'd earned it. But then, Ali always seemed to see things that way. That he deserved any good thing that happened. Like Foxworth being pulled into his life by her own little pup, via the apparently far too clever Cutter. Who was now acting like a well-trained guardian for his precious little girl.

The Foxworths, Cutter and Ali. He'd never had a run of luck like that in his life before. He supposed that was why he was a little wary of trusting it now.

That word again. Trust.

I trusted you! I trusted you would see the sensible path, that you would realize what you had to do, the only possible thing to do. Not that you would cling to your pitiful former life. I trusted you would see the enormity of the gift my family is offering!

Liz's long-ago tirade was etched into that part of his brain he tried not to visit. But he'd never really had much ammunition to fire back at her accusations. Because she'd been right about the size of the opportunity the Hollens were offering. He could become a mover and shaker, someone of importance, of influence.

What she'd been wrong about was thinking he wanted that.

He supposed that was the moment he'd realized where they were headed. Because it was the moment he'd realized that her shouted words about trust no longer meant much to him. That he didn't care anymore if she trusted him. In fact, he'd even resigned himself to not caring if anyone ever trusted him, not if Liz's kind of life was the price.

But now…

Grace trusted him. The Foxworths trusted him. Ali trusted him. If the value of trust was directly related to the value of the person offering it, then it meant something.

To him, them trusting him meant everything.

And he would do anything not to betray it.

Chapter Twenty-Three

Ali watched as the girl and the two dogs romped in the meadow. Even this time of year there was lots of green, and the expanse out to the towering evergreens—even, she thought, a few redwoods—was dotted here and there with some maple trees she knew would have been brilliantly red just a few months ago in fall, and various shrubs she was willing to bet would explode with colorful flowers come spring.

And she thought the tree they were next to was a magnolia. She'd bet it would smell wonderful when it was in bloom, and knowing what she knew of Hayley, that that was probably the reason it was so close to the patio they were standing on. Colby was beside her, also watching intently, while Hayley was on her other side, enjoying the show along with them.

"What a beautiful space," she said to Hayley as Grace's laughter rang out.

"It is." She smiled. "We love it so much we got married out here. Which seemed to have started a Foxworth trend."

Ali laughed. Hayley had told her about the string of marriages both done and upcoming, all of which she credited to Cutter.

She watched Grace do a cartwheel that was nothing less than…graceful.

"She's well named, in several ways," she said to Colby.

"Grace is her middle name," Colby said. "I wanted it to

be her first, but Liz insisted she be named after her father, Brian. So legally, she's Brianna." He couldn't help smiling then. "But when she got old enough to understand, which for her was about age two, she refused to answer to it. Would only answer to Grace. Even Liz finally gave in, since legally she's still Brianna."

"So you've already beaten her once."

Colby blinked. "I...never thought of it that way, but yeah, I guess so."

"We'll beat her this time, too," Ali said, very conscious of using "we."

And Colby's gaze seemed to heat slightly as she said it, enough that she was glad when Quinn stepped out and came over to them. He'd been inside looking for something, although he hadn't said what.

He stopped beside Colby. "Call in your girl for a minute, will you?"

Ali noticed he didn't even hesitate, but called out to Grace to come over. The girl did, still looking wonderfully happy as she told the two dogs to keep on playing, she'd be right back. Ali saw Hayley notice what her husband was carrying, and give a very slight smile, as if she understood. All Ali could see was that it was a small tubelike thing in silver metal.

Quinn asked Grace to go inside with him. Ali liked the way she looked at her father first, not taking another step until he nodded. Then he moved to follow her. He glanced back at Ali, questioningly, and she in turn looked at Hayley.

"Go ahead," Hayley said. "I'll stay out here for...demonstration purposes."

Now she was really puzzled. But she followed the trio inside, curious.

Quinn ushered them to one side, away from the glass back door. So they couldn't see? Or couldn't be seen?

"Hear how quiet it is inside here?" he asked Grace. "How you can't even hear Ziggy barking?" The child nodded, looking as puzzled as Ali felt. Then Quinn handed her the little silver tube. "Here. Take this end, and blow through it, three times quick and short."

And suddenly Ali knew. She waited as the child did as instructed. And as she now expected, Ali heard nothing. It was as quiet as before in the well-built headquarters building.

"It didn't do anything," Grace said, looking at the thing in her hand. "Did I do it wrong? I did just like you said—"

A sound came from the back door, and Ali felt a rush of cooler air from outside and knew it was open. A split second later Cutter was racing into the room, coming directly to Grace and inspecting her urgently.

"A dog whistle," Colby murmured.

"Yes," Quinn said.

"But Daddy, it didn't whistle," Grace said, looking at him for an explanation while she petted Cutter, who was calmer now that he could see for himself she was all right.

"Not so we could hear it, no. But Cutter could."

"How?"

"Dogs can hear much better than we can. And they can hear sounds we can't hear at all. Like really high-pitched sounds."

"And that," Quinn said, "is what that whistle is designed to do. Put out a sound so high we can't hear it, but dogs can."

Grace was smiling now. "That's cool! Like a secret signal or something."

Ali saw Colby give Quinn a startled glance, as if he'd realized what this was really all about.

Quinn nodded in affirmation. "You hang on to that. Keep it with you, all the time while Cutter's staying with Ali. And if anything bad happens, or you get scared, you blow it. Cutter knows what it means, and he'll do what he just did. Come running."

Grace's eyes widened. "He'll come to help me? And...she won't know I called him, because she can't hear it either?"

"Exactly," Quinn said with a smile. "And nothing will stop

him. Like now, he ran right past Hayley, because he knows keeping you safe is his job."

"But if I'm in the house and can't get out," Grace began.

"He'll raise such a fuss it'll interrupt anything going on. And believe me, unlike that whistle, everybody within a mile will hear that boy bark if he wants them to."

"Which means I'll hear him and call for help," Ali said.

Quinn smiled and nodded. "You use that phone we gave you, and whoever's closest will head that way." He shifted his gaze to Colby. "You're the one who has to be careful. You don't want to give her any excuses, so unless there's physical danger to our girl here, you hang on until one of us gets there."

Ali saw Colby's jaw tighten. Clearly he did not like that idea of staying back when his girl was hurting or scared.

"Trust us." Hayley said it softly as she came up beside them.

"If she's in trouble or danger, we'll come in like a tidal wave, unstoppable," Liam said, the first words he'd spoken in a while.

"And let the chips fall where they may," Quinn said. "We'll deal. But you need to stay free and clear so our girl here will have a place to land."

Grace was starting to look a little concerned. Ali wasn't sure how much of what they were saying she fully understood, but even knowing her less than two weeks she wouldn't underestimate the child's quick mind.

And neither would Hayley, who quickly diverted the discussion. "Here's something else, Grace."

She held out another small metal cylinder, but this one was shorter and bigger around, about the size of a flashlight battery. It had what looked like a screw-on lid, and a clip device on the other end. She opened it, and Ali saw there was a strip of paper rolled up inside it.

"It's blank," Hayley explained, "ready for you or us to write on."

She closed it back up, and clipped it onto Cutter's collar,

next to the blue name tag in the shape of the boat from which Ali guessed his name had come.

"For messages!" Grace yelped.

"Yes." Hayley smiled at her. "Like we talked about before. It's easier for him than trying to hide it in his mouth—and drier." Grace laughed as Hayley went on. "It's a little old-fashioned, but kind of cool, huh?"

Grace nodded. Then she looked up at Ali, who saw the expression she'd come to know meant the girl's mind was racing. "So you can send one to me, but what if I need to... Wait! I can use the whistle, then Cutter will come, and I can put in my message!"

"Come see us in about ten years, Grace," Quinn said with a grin. "We'll hire you."

"Hire?"

"That means you'd get to work with them, doing for others what they're doing for us," Colby said, his voice level now, apparently resigned to his rather removed role in this. Oddly, she found herself liking him even more for hating being sidelined.

"Wow! That would be the best!"

She was so excited now that Ali was glad they would have the walk home for her to calm down a little. Unlike a normal mother, she didn't think Liz would be pleased to see her daughter so happy.

Chapter Twenty-Four

Saying goodbye had been hell. It always was. It just felt so wrong, to watch his little girl leave him.

But at least he now had more opportunity to see Grace than he had had in over a year. He'd rather it be every day, but had to agree with Hayley's warning that if it became too regular, too routine, it also became more likely that Grace would inadvertently say something that would give them away. His girl was brilliant, and she knew how important it was to keep this a secret, but she was also seven years old.

He couldn't deny that he felt better that she was with Ali, for at least a bit longer. And Cutter, too. That little demonstration today had thoroughly convinced him of both the dog's cleverness and his awareness that his main job was to protect Grace.

When Quinn started to go outside to roll the helicopter back in its hangar, Colby leaped up to follow.

"I need to do something. Anything," he said.

"Not used to not working, huh? Careful or you'll end up building my new tool rack," Quinn said as they walked toward the helipad.

Colby's mood shifted almost instantly. "Tool rack? Show me what you need and I'll get on it."

Quinn laughed. "Somehow I thought that might be your reaction."

"Anything that'll keep me from thinking too much about... things I can't do."

"I know it's got to be hard taking a back seat. But for now, while things are still stable, it's for the best."

He waited until they had the aircraft back under cover—a job that was a bit easier than he'd expected—and Quinn had shown him where he wanted the rack and what kind of tools it needed to hold, before he asked what had been eating at him.

"What happens later? If Liz really does blow up?"

"Then we do whatever is necessary to protect Grace."

"I believe you. I just don't know what that might involve."

"Steps," Quinn said. "If it looks like she's escalating, we'll take advantage of Ali's offer and station people at her place, for a quick response." He gave Colby a wry smile. "Sorry it can't be you, because if she spotted you over there..."

"Yeah, I get it. Not happy, but I get it."

"If I were you, I'd much rather be with Ali too," Quinn said, with no trace of joking in his demeanor. Colby looked away quickly, wondering just how much he'd betrayed without realizing. Probably would be hard to miss how he kept... looking at her.

Quinn went on as if he hadn't noticed. "Next option, or maybe simultaneous, would probably be Gavin. He's already digging into all the custody paperwork, and letting her know he's connected should make her take care. Then if necessary, involving Carly."

"And if Liz goes completely off the rails?"

"Then it's all hands on deck, and no holds barred, and a few other metaphors."

"They own a lot of properties in a lot of places," he warned. "And she's always threatening to take Grace to one of them, where I'll never find her."

"But I will," came a voice from behind them. Liam was walking into the hangar. "I've already got quite a list. They're good at hiding things behind fake corporate names, but not that good."

"You're just better at finding than they are at hiding," Quinn said with a grin at his operative.

Colby stared at the two men. "You're already finding the places she might go?"

"Too bad their attempts to buy a piece of that island fell through. That would have been a good place to run to. With that nice private jet they've got hangared over on the other side."

Colby was staring at the guy now, who just grinned back at him. Was their access that good, or was he one of those hacker types who could get…anything online?

Liam went on. "But they've still got some properties that would be possible places to hide out." He shifted his gaze to his boss. "Only two on the list where we don't have someone who owes Foxworth to call on."

"All right," Quinn said. "Give me the locations and I'll see what I can find."

"Owes Foxworth?" Colby asked.

Quinn looked at him. "That's what we meant, before. When we help someone, the only payment we ask is that you help us help someone else down the line." He lifted a brow at Colby. "Which means when all this is done and settled and Grace is safe, we may be calling you some day."

He said it so confidently, as if it were a given, that Colby felt his throat tighten. *Grace is safe*... That was what had to happen, and he would do whatever it took to make it so.

"Anything," he said, meaning it.

"We'll make a note," Quinn said, smiling slightly. Then he turned back to Liam. "Anything else?"

Liam grinned at him. "I'm also finding some interesting financial hiding places. Things I'm guessing they wouldn't want publicly known, which could come in handy."

"Excellent."

Colby couldn't think of a thing to say at this display of reach and efficiency. But something must have shown in his face, because Liam turned to face him.

"Think of it as stockpiling ammo. We don't want to have to use it, but if we need it, for that brilliant kid of yours, we'll have it."

He watched the guy leave, no doubt heading back to collect more of that ammo. When he looked back at Quinn, he was grinning as he watched his tech expert go. Then he met Colby's gaze.

"Your Grace has charmed all of us, it seems."

"She's...a miracle," Colby said, his throat tight yet again. He hadn't felt this much positive emotion in a very long time. Enough to think that maybe, just maybe, they could do this. Not necessarily beat Liz completely, but at least make life better for both him and Grace. And once that was done, maybe, just maybe, he could think about him and Ali.

Just thinking the phrase, just linking the two of them mentally, caused a jump in his pulse rate.

If I were you, I'd much rather be with Ali too.

Quinn's too-observant statement rang in his mind, and he made himself face the truth of it. Yes, he would much rather be with Ali. It would mean he was closer to Grace. But that wasn't the only reason he'd rather be in that cute little cottage that was so much more appealing to him than the grandiose mini-mansion Liz had had built next door. No, the other reason would be its owner. The woman who had disrupted her life completely to help a child and a man she hadn't even known two weeks ago.

The woman who made him feel...different.

Why would someone who can do what you do want to become a paper pusher?

People like you who can build or make those things, now, they're worth something.

He didn't think he would ever forget the words she'd said, or the tone of utter certainty in her voice when she'd said them. He'd always loved what he did, taken a certain pride in it, but had never expected anyone else to. His clients approved, yes, and he got the occasional "Well done," or "Nice work," which he treasured, but that was from strangers. Not from someone whose opinion mattered…personally. And Ali Moran's opinion mattered to him on a level he didn't think he'd ever felt before.

And it had even before he'd kissed her.

Chapter Twenty-Five

"Grace just sent me a message via Cutter," Ali said into the Foxworth phone they'd given her. Both Quinn and Hayley were on one phone, and Colby was on another. They were set up for a video call, which made the three images rather small, but visible. Ziggy was in her lap while Cutter sat at her feet, and she adjusted her phone so his head was visible, thinking he was as big a part of this as any of them. Maybe bigger.

"Is she all right?" Colby leaned in toward his own screen.

Ali hastened to answer. "She's fine. She's upset, but fine. The note says—" she unrolled the curled scrap of paper again to make sure she got it exactly "—'Daddy, she wants to mess up our day together. I heard her talking about going to the city again that day. On purpose.'" Ali set down the little note. "Can she even do that, Colby? Take her away on your visitation day?"

"She's done it before," he answered, and she knew she was right about the bitter note in his voice, because it was matched by his expression. "She always makes sure it's for some 'educational' thing, so it's hard to deny. Threatens to take us back to court if I say no, because there's some kind of override proviso in the agreement."

"What there is," Hayley's said, clearly angry, "is some kind of overreach. I think we might need Gavin to step in sooner than we thought."

"Agreed," Quinn said, sounding flatly irritated as well. "Ali, can you try and find out someplace public the mother—" they'd all taken to Grace's terminology, and it made Ali smile in spite of everything "—will be one day soon?"

"Of course I'll try," she answered instantly. "I'll have to watch for when she's home, but—"

"She'll be home tomorrow," Colby cut in. "She's always there when I pick Grace up, and there when I bring her back. She's probably got an alarm set so she can call the cops if I'm a second late with her, like she always threatens to do."

"So she'll already be edgy," Hayley said. "That could be good. Ali, if you pour on the empathy, how awful this is for her, having to hand her child over like that, she might open up a bit more. Be careful not to pour it on too thick, though."

"But thicker than you'd think you can," Colby put in. "Because she believes that of course everyone feels for her and wants to help her."

"Because she's just so darned special," Ali drawled out in her best imitation of Liam's accent, and had the pleasure of hearing Colby chuckle.

"Exactly," he said.

"To quote our old friend, 'The opportunity of defeating the enemy is provided by the enemy himself,'" Quinn said.

"Sun Tzu again?" Ali asked, grinning.

"There's a reason he's still relevant after over two thousand years," Colby said, and she was glad to see a trace of a smile on his face.

"I'll find what we need," she promised. "And I'll send her a message back with Cutter, saying we're on it."

"Tell her to act like she doesn't really care," Colby said. "To shrug it off."

"Because the more upset she is, the more her mother will know it's a good weapon?" Ali asked.

"And she won't hesitate to use it."

"All right. I'll tell her in the note. And tell her you'll explain more tomorrow, when you have your afternoon with her."

"And tell her she can't let it slip she's been in touch," Colby said.

"I think she knows that. She did a beautiful job the other day when we came back from our walk. She gave me the biggest wink then told her mother that the dogs made her almost forget about your day coming up."

She smiled when she heard Colby chuckle. "Sometimes my girl is downright scary smart."

"And the two of you together are quite a team," Hayley said.

Ali liked the sound of that. And it made her even more determined to get the information they needed out of Liz tomorrow.

And in the end she did, much more easily than she had expected. She waited until Colby and Grace had been gone for nearly an hour. She'd spent half that time pacing the floor, going over and over it in her head until she was afraid she'd be so wound up she'd blow it by being too obvious. Plus she had to quash the rather fierce desire to be with them.

This was their time alone together, and she needed to respect that. It wasn't like she had any right to intrude on that precious interlude. No matter how much Colby kept thanking her.

She decided to take Ziggy and Cutter out to play in the backyard, hoping that would stop her obsessing about the task ahead. And it did, because before long she was laughing at their antics. Ziggy because he was such a sweet, silly puppy, and Cutter because the difference between this playful, gentle creature and the protective guardian he could become in an instant never ceased to amaze her.

Then she steeled herself, put the not quite housebroken Ziggy in his playpen with several toys, gave the pup a treat, then leashed Cutter and headed next door. She figured the more Liz saw of the well-behaved canine the more she'd ignore him when necessary. Plus, to Liz it probably made her seem weaker, unable to even come next door without the support animal at her side. Which was exactly what Ali wanted her to think.

And in the end, it was easier than she'd dared hope. She had her pretext, a flattering question about where she'd gotten that lovely, elegant dining table—which Ali in truth thought overdone to the point of being grandiloquent—and that alone did the trick. Liz gave her the name of the custom shop down in the city that was the county seat, saying that it was across the street from the best restaurant in the county, where it so happened she would be meeting for lunch with a county official a week from Monday, about a new Hollen project.

She just can't resist pointing out how important she and her family are.

That evening, after loading up both Cutter and Ziggy to make up for abandoning the pup this afternoon, she drove to Foxworth to report in. She let herself enjoy for a moment that Ziggy greeted Colby delightedly, batting at him for more when he dared to stop petting him. She started to take a seat on the other end of the couch, but Cutter was in her way and didn't seem inclined to move. In fact, he nudged her with enough energy that she almost had to sit down or fall down. And so she ended up in the same spot she'd been in the other night.

When Colby had kissed her.

She had to yank her thoughts away from those vivid memories to face the Foxworths and lay out how it had gone with Liz.

"That'll do nicely," Quinn said. He looked at Colby. "We'll just arrange for you and Gavin to be at a nearby table."

"What if she doesn't recognize Mr. de Marco on sight?" Ali asked. "She seems self-absorbed enough to not be aware even of someone on his level."

"She'd know the name," Colby said, "but you might be right she wouldn't recognize him in person, especially unexpectedly."

Hayley smiled. "No problem. So happens the manager of that restaurant is one of those people we mentioned. We helped out his son a while back. He'll be happy to play the concerned host, personally making sure everything's all right at the important Ms. Hollen's table, and in the process mention how excited he is to have both her and the world-famous attorney in his restaurant."

Colby simply shook his head in wonder. Ali understood. The expanse and power of Foxworth was amazing, and she loved that it was built on a foundation of helping ordinary people in the right, and how all those people became part of fighting back against self-appointed royalty like Liz and her family.

"Can you bring Grace here tomorrow?" Quinn asked. "She'll need to know to tread carefully the next few days, so we should go over what's coming."

"I'll get her here," Ali promised.

Quinn and Hayley then went over to the office area to make some of those necessary calls, leaving Ali and Colby sitting in front of the cheerfully burning fireplace. She noticed he'd rolled up his shirtsleeves in the warmth from it, and that his arm was healing nicely.

"You won't even have much of a scar, if any," she said, nodding toward the mark that was down to a faint pinkish line now.

"I'll just add it to the list." He shrugged, still staring into the flames. "I've got a few."

"Outside and inside," she said quietly.

He looked at her then. "But now I've got hope," he said. "And that's in large part thanks to you."

She smiled, but shook her head. "All I did was happen to be next door."

"And help my girl. Even before you knew…anything."

"She's so cute and charming, how could I not?" Her nose wrinkled. "So very unlike her mother."

"Thank goodness," Colby muttered.

"I'd say it's more thanks to you than anything. You've kept her sane and real and good amid Liz's nastiness."

She saw something in those blue eyes, something warm and wondering at the same time. She hated that such a simple compliment could mean so much to him, but at the same time was glad that it did.

And let herself hope that part of it was that the compliment had come from her.

Chapter Twenty-Six

Colby sat looking at the fire again, twirling the half glass of wine he held, wondering what it would be like if this were… real. If this was home, if the dogs sprawled in front of the fire were his.

If Ali was his.

The longing that boiled up in him was searing, in more ways than one. She was, by just being herself, showing him how utterly bankrupt his marriage had been. Even in the early days, when he'd been caught up in the fantasy, marveling at his luck that the gorgeous, rebellious Liz had wanted him, it hadn't been like this. And looking back now, he realized the clues had been there all along, he'd just been too blinded to see them. It should never have been a surprise that she would be drawn back into the Hollen web, and eventually insist he walk away from the work he loved and join the family cabal.

He wondered how much of her initial attraction to him had been part of that rebellion. A lot, he suspected, because nothing could offend their sensibilities more than having a lowly carpenter as part of the family. They'd been a united front from the moment Liz had, as they'd put it, come to her senses and come home. And it was a front he was not welcome in.

That he'd never wanted to be part of that world removed some of the sting, but not all. And most of what was left was directed inward, at himself for not realizing the obvious much sooner. But then Grace had come, and he'd had no choice but to stick it out as long as he could.

He took a sip of wine, hoping to pull himself out of the useless pondering. Ali had stayed after the Foxworths had left, of her own volition, saving him from making a fool of himself asking her to.

"Funny, isn't it? Cutter, I mean?" Ali said now, gesturing at the dogs.

He snapped himself out of the last of the painful reflections of the mistake his marriage had been.

"What?"

"I mean how he stayed here, even though his people left. The way he came over and sat by you and just looked at them, like he was saying his job was here."

"From what they've told me, that's pretty much how it works," he said, looking at the bigger dog who was lying with one paw thrown protectively over the puppy.

"He certainly is the politest of houseguests," she said. "And he's a great puppy sitter, too. I think Ziggy is going to be heartbroken when this is over and he leaves."

She shifted in her seat to look at him. He wasn't sure he dared look back at her, not when they were here alone, in front of a warm fire, sipping wine, dogs snoozing at their feet. It was too sweet. Too homey. Too much something he wanted so desperately he couldn't even put it into words.

"And it will be over, eventually," she said quietly. "I've been doing some more reading, and Foxworth definitely gets things done."

He steadied himself, staring at the wine left in the glass. "I'm realizing that. They seem to have every aspect covered."

"So...do you think you could stop worrying quite so much?"

He did look at her then. "I doubt it," he said wryly.

"Because you'll always worry about your girl."

"Always."

It was a moment before, with a soft smile that did that crazy thing to his gut again, she said, "You remind me of Josh."

He went very still. He wasn't at all sure how he felt about the comparison to her late husband. "Is that…a good thing, or a sad thing?"

"A very good thing. If he gave his word, it was golden."

"I… You must miss him."

"Every day. But I also know I have to get on with my life. It's what he would have wanted. And," she added, "why I moved here."

His mouth quirked. "And look what that got you into."

"What it did was give me a chance to help the most nearly perfect child I've ever met." She smiled, widely. "And Grace is going to be so excited, that something's actually going to happen. I get the feeling she's wanted to fight back for a long time, but was afraid to. Afraid of what her mother would do."

Colby sighed. "Rightfully so. If she argued with her, or worse, tried to get away, Liz would probably lock her in her room every minute she wasn't actually in school."

"I meant," Ali said softly, "afraid of what her mother would do to you. You're who she's protecting."

He stared at her. "Grace…protecting me?"

"Did you not realize that the love between you flows both ways? She would do anything for you."

He didn't know what to say. The thought of his precious girl protecting him, worrying that much about him instead of herself, was nearly overwhelming.

He realized his hand had tightened so much on the stem of the wineglass it was surprising he hadn't broken it. Not wanting another bloody mess to deal with, he carefully set the glass down on the end table. Oddly, Cutter's head came up, and he stared at Colby as if he'd sensed something.

"I'm okay, dog," he said, not even caring if it sounded silly.

"He's an observant one, isn't he?" Ali said. "And Colby, I

think you're a lot more than okay. And it's going to get nothing but better from here on."

He gave a slow shake of his head. "I don't know which surprises me more, you or that dog."

He winced inwardly, wondering if she'd be offended by the comparison. But she wasn't. No, Ali laughed.

"I'm honored to be put in his company. He's amazing."

He should have known. True, he'd only known her a couple of weeks, but he'd never been more certain about anyone. And certain in a deep, rock-solid way he'd never felt with Liz, or anyone else. Josh Moran had indeed been a very lucky man.

He's dead, you idiot. How does that make him lucky?

That thought sent him meandering off into other territory, specifically a poet and his famous line about it being better to have loved and lost than never loved at all. He wondered if Ali felt that way.

And if her husband had known how lucky he'd been.

"Colby? Are you all right?"

He snapped out of it. "Just...thinking," he muttered.

"About what?"

"Love," he said before he thought. "And loss. And if it really is better."

She looked oddly startled. "Been reading Tennyson?"

"Not lately." She was staring at him, and he frowned. "What, you're shocked a carpenter can even read, let alone poetry?"

She pulled back sharply, then jumped to her feet. She started to walk away, but just as quickly Cutter was there, blocking her path. Her escape?

"Ali, don't," he said, getting up nearly as quickly as she had. "That was...reflex."

"You mean all those lovely hardcover books in the library in Liz's house weren't yours?" she asked, a little too sweetly.

He couldn't help it, he snorted at that. "For her, books are wall decor. She used to get really irritated if I actually took one off a shelf and opened it."

The tension in her expression seemed to fade away. "No wonder she didn't like my house, the one time she came inside. To inspect, I'm guessing."

He remembered the cozy little house, and how much he'd liked it, not just the floor plan and the quality of the build, but the atmosphere it already held, even after the short time she'd lived there.

And he remembered the books. One of the first things he'd noticed when he'd stepped inside that day that seemed like both yesterday and a lifetime ago. All looking both read and cared for.

"She finds reading a waste of time," he said. "But she knows many of the people she deals with value it, so she pretends with all those volumes she's never touched, let alone opened."

"So we add total hypocrisy to the list," Ali said.

He grimaced. "It's a long list." He drew in a deep breath, and said what he knew he had to. "I didn't mean what I said. It really was just a reflex. Something I would have said…to her. I should never have said it to you. And I'm really sorry I did."

Ali looked at him for a long moment, then nodded. "Apology accepted. I think sometimes when a sore spot gets poked often enough, it gets to where it doesn't matter who does the poking, or even if it's really a poke at all. We just…react. And I reacted the way I did because I'd been thinking about that same poetic line just a while ago."

He couldn't stop himself, he crossed the short distance between them and pulled her to him. Hugged her, and tightened it when he felt her head come down to rest on his shoulder. He could feel the slight tug from that not-quite-healed spot on his arm, but he ignored it.

Because nothing was worth letting go of her.

And for a moment, just a moment, he let himself think of a life after this, and Ali being a part of it. He quashed the thought. There was too much to get through first, and he had to stay focused.

But for now, until she had to leave, he held her.

Chapter Twenty-Seven

"I really like that they need to go for walks on the weekend, too," Grace said as they started their walk. "But tomorrow I can't come with you."

"Oh?" Ali asked.

"I have to go with her somewhere, all dressed up and silly-looking."

"You, my dear, could never, ever look silly."

Grace smiled, but it didn't last. "I hate when she's around all day and I have to hide in my room."

Ali considered what to say as the dogs led them down to the sidewalk in front of the big house. Cutter, as always, was polite on leash, and better yet, he was teaching Ziggy to behave as well. Stops to sniff were allowed, but pulling so hard Grace had to fight him was not.

Of course, as soon as they were out of sight—they had to be more circumspect when Liz was home—she would pick up Ziggy and hand Cutter's leash to Grace and they'd double their speed.

"I'm sorry you feel like you need to hide," she finally said.

Grace made a face. "I'm afraid she'll get mad and take away all my time with Daddy. I don't trust her."

"Then it's good that you can completely trust him."

The frown became a smile. "I do. And I think I trust the

Foxy people." That made Ali smile. The child had started using the term when she decided the Foxworth Foundation was too long to say all the time. "And I really trust you," Grace added matter-of-factly, as if it were a given.

Ali stopped in her tracks. Grace stopped beside her and looked up, puzzled. She couldn't stop herself, she leaned down and gave the girl a rather fierce hug. "Thank you. That's one of the best birthday presents I've ever gotten."

Grace's eyes widened as Ali released her. "It's your birthday?"

"Well, tomorrow is."

"I didn't know. I should have got you a present."

"You just gave me a huge one."

"But there should be something else," the child protested, sounding almost upset.

"Tell you what," Ali said as they started walking again, "write me a story."

Grace looked intrigued. "About what?"

"Whatever you want. Maybe—" she gestured toward Cutter and Ziggy "—about two dogs who become friends."

Grace's face lit up. "Okay. But we're past the trees, so now you can pick up Ziggy so we can hurry."

Ali nodded and Grace reeled in the puppy. She settled him in the sling and he seemed happy enough, looking around with just as much interest as when he'd been on the ground sniffing everything within reach.

When they got to Foxworth, Grace let Cutter off the leash as they neared the front door to the big green building. He started toward the door; Ali was even looking forward to seeing him hit that auto switch and open the door himself again. But then he unexpectedly changed course and headed not for the main office, but for the building on the other side of the landing pad, where Colby had said they hangared the helicopter and stored other vehicles.

The dog looked back, as if to be sure they had registered the change in destination.

"I guess we follow him, huh?" she said.

"Of course," Grace replied.

The big doors were shut, but the human-sized one was open. And when they got a little closer she could hear the sound of hammering.

"Daddy!" Grace exclaimed, and started to run.

By the time Ali got there, Grace was up in her father's arms, both of them all smiles. She hesitated in the doorway, thinking that now she knew the child was safely with him she should leave them be. But then Colby turned to look, and the smile on his handsome face left her seemingly unable to move.

She'd never seen him like this, in work mode. It was warmer in the hangar than she would have expected, so he was down to just jeans and a T-shirt. A T-shirt tucked in, showing her just how built he really was. Not an ounce on him that didn't look fit and muscled.

"Come on in," he said.

"I... You two need alone time."

"Come in, Ali," Grace insisted. "Look at what Daddy's building."

She was curious, so with a silent promise she wouldn't stay, she walked over to them.

"Quinn said he needed shelves and a rack for the tools, for all the equipment they store in here. He doesn't like the metal ones. Too noisy, he said."

She looked around at the tools stacked up along the far wall. "Wow. That's a lot of stuff."

Colby nodded, still smiling widely. As if having his little girl with him and work to do was all he needed to be happy.

"With the helicopter, a couple of generators, an ATV and three extra vehicles for various purposes, they need a lot of different tools."

Ali gave a slow shake of her head as she looked around at

everything he'd mentioned. Colby set Grace back down, and the girl proceeded to dart off to explore those same things.

"Sometimes," Ali said, "I have to remind myself what a big deal they are, they seem so...normal."

He nodded. "I didn't realize they have five different locations. Here, down in Southern California, one each in the Northeast and Southeast. Then what used to be their main headquarters in St. Louis."

"Used to be?"

He was smiling again. "Quinn said everybody seems to be migrating here. He started out in St. Louis, but fell in love with this region, then when he met Hayley decided to stay. His sister started there too—she's the financial genius who funds it all—but she's in love with the guy who keeps all this running." He glanced over to where Grace was looking at the ATV, as if to be sure she was out of earshot before adding, "Who also happens to be an extremely lethal sniper."

That made her blink. "What?"

"Former Marine. Famous for it, apparently."

"Wow."

He glanced over again, clearly keeping track of his girl. Which prompted Ali to say, "Is Hayley here?"

He looked back and nodded in answer. "She's over in the office, pulling strings, I think."

"Good. I want to go say hello." *And leave you two to enjoy this precious time.*

"Okay. Thanks for getting Grace here."

She smiled. "You don't have to thank me every time."

"Yes, I do."

"You don't. Besides, Grace already thanked me in the best way."

She told him about the child's declaration of trust as they'd started their walk, and how she'd been so moved she'd nearly crushed her with a hug. She couldn't quite put a name to his expression then, but it was happy and that was enough.

COLBY WATCHED ALI GO. He found himself more than a little fascinated by the way she moved, that female way. When he caught himself utterly focused on the back pockets of her snug jeans, he tore his gaze away. He shouldn't be looking at her that way, shouldn't be feeling this way. He should be focused on being grateful, not on her backside. After all, the woman had rearranged her entire life to do this, to help them, and she would barely let him thank her for it.

He heard the rapid patter of running steps and spun around to see Grace headed for him at a trot, apparently finding the vehicles other than the ATV just boring everyday cars. Personally, when he'd seen them parked here, he'd realized fairly quickly they could help Foxworth present any image they wanted, from the worn truck Liam had driven to the sleek, expensive import that he had a sneaking suspicion might be put to use impressing people like Liz.

Quinn's sister must be quite the financial genius. Liam had told him she'd used the insurance payout from their parents' deaths in a terrorist attack to build Foxworth, and she'd clearly done an amazing job of it.

"Did Ali leave?" Grace asked.

"She went over to see Hayley in the office."

"Oh. Daddy, we need to do something special."

"Sweetie, every extra minute I get to spend with you is special."

She rolled her eyes, but she was smiling. "I know, but we get to do that 'cuz of Ali, right?"

"Yes. Did you mean you want to do something for her?" He liked the idea, and even more that his girl had had the thought.

"We have to. Tomorrow's her birthday."

He blinked. "It is?"

Grace nodded. "She told me that me trusting her was a great birthday present, but I wanted to give her more, so she said for me to write her a story."

That sounded so like Ali, to encourage his girl in that talent that was already obvious. "Are you going to?"

Grace nodded. "But Daddy, we need to give her something she has to unwrap."

He reminded himself he was talking to his little girl to get rid of the image those words planted in his mind.

"You have something in mind?"

Grace's brow furrowed. "She doesn't like all the stuff the mother likes, jewelry and fancy clothes."

"That doesn't surprise me." No, Ali was too genuine, too real for that. He had the feeling for her it was function over form, not the other way around as it was for Liz. "Have you ever heard her mention something she wants?"

Grace brightened. "Yes!" Her expression turned thoughtful again. He focused on her, thinking he wouldn't trade the challenge of keeping up with his clever girl for anything. "But I don't think we could wrap it up like a present."

"What is it?"

"She wants a...a greenhouse? You know, the glass thing you grow plants in." Well, having seen her garden, that didn't surprise him at all. "Just a little one, but big enough to walk into."

"She have a spot in mind?"

Grace nodded. "Out back, next to the deck. She says it gets the most sun. And she said the reason she didn't already have one was she wasn't sure she could put it together. You can do that, Daddy. You can build anything."

For a moment all he could do was let those words, spoken with such love and conviction, play in a loop in his head. Then practicality rose up.

"It would have to be a late present," he said. "I can't be at Ali's house while your mother's home."

"But she won't be tomorrow." Grace frowned. "Neither will I. She's making me go with her to some fancy thing down near the big mall. She even gave Irene the day off."

"Oh." He tried not to dwell on not seeing her tomorrow and

focused on making this wish of hers come true. "What time is this thing?"

"We have to go at eleven, she said. And if it's like her other stuff it'll take forever."

Colby knew he had to take the exaggeration of time forcibly spent with her mother into account, but even driving time there and back would be over an hour. Liz had never spent less than a couple of hours at these things, doing what she called networking, which to him meant she was cataloging the people there according to their potential to be useful to her someday.

That would give him four hours. More than enough time to put a small greenhouse together. And just the thought of doing something for Ali, something she really wanted, made him feel useful again. Building this shelving for Quinn had kept him from going stir-crazy, but the thought of doing something for Ali…

His mind began to race, with as much energy and enthusiasm as if he were about to build a monument.

ALI HAD BEEN focusing on work this morning, trying not to worry about how Grace was doing at the "grown-ups" party her mother had, in Grace's words, ordered her to. She'd been falling a bit behind lately, because that focus had been faltering. She couldn't seem to stop thinking about Grace.

And her father.

So now here she was, still a little stunned that that father had shown up shortly after Liz and Grace had left. And with a stack of boxes in the back of his truck, with a big, green bow on top.

"Grace wanted me to wrap it all for your birthday, but given the size…"

His voice trailed off, and she realized she was staring at him.

"Look," he began again, "if this isn't a good time or is a lousy idea—"

"No!" She shook off her shock. "I just... I only told her... you did all this since yesterday?"

He shrugged. "I've worked with a guy whose family makes these kits. So when Grace said you really wanted a greenhouse, I got hold of him."

She was still a little rattled by the unexpectedness of it. And the knowledge of how much this had to have cost. "I... wow. This wasn't cheap. Especially now, with people thinking about spring coming."

He shrugged and smiled. "I got a discount."

"Colby, I don't know what to say, except thank you."

"That'll do," he said, and she only realized how tense he'd been by how things changed now. "But I'd better get started if we're going to have it done before they get back. Don't want to blow all our efforts out of the water by having Liz spot me over here."

"Oh, no, we don't," Ali said, but she wasn't happy about it. Because if it wasn't for that, she'd happily have him over here anytime.

Maybe all the time.

He pulled off the big bow and went to toss it, but she stopped him. "No, I want to keep it, to put on it when it's up." She smiled. "A green bow for my new greenhouse."

He paused, then handed it to her. "It made me think of your eyes."

He looked away quickly then, and she was almost glad, because she could feel her cheeks heating up.

The process was fascinating. If she was honest, however, half of her enjoyment came from watching him work. He'd read the rather copious instructions thoroughly, then never looked at them again. He'd laid out the parts and pieces, using a tarp from his truck as a base for the smaller bits, screws and clips. Once it was all organized to his liking, he started the assembly.

He was so thorough it took a while, but in a much shorter

time than if she'd tried to do it herself, she had the exact greenhouse she'd wanted, including shelves, lighting and a fan for air circulation to prevent mold in the rainy season. And mere steps from her back door.

And more importantly at the moment, out of view of her nasty neighbor's cameras.

"I could build you a covered walkway," Colby suggested. "It's only about six feet, so it wouldn't take much. And that way you'd never get wet."

Ali looked at him and smiled. "I'm Pacific Northwest born and raised, walking six feet even in a downpour is nothing." Then she couldn't stop herself from grinning. "Tomatoes! Peppers! Carrots! Maybe even a mini citrus tree! And maybe some dahlias for color, and—"

"And, and, and," Colby said, grinning back at her. "I get it."

The color flooded her cheeks again, and she turned back to look at her birthday present. "You probably think I'm silly."

"I think," Colby said, something deeper, huskier coming into his voice, "you're beautiful. Wonderful. Remarkable. And, and, and."

She couldn't help herself, she turned her head to meet his gaze. And what she saw there in his eyes sent her heart racing. She couldn't look away. It was as if something tangible, something physical, had connected them.

He crossed the space between them in a single step, and when his arms came around her she wanted to cry out at the joy of the contact. She hadn't thought she would ever, could ever feel like this. She thought this kind of heat, this kind of desire, had died with Josh, never to be felt again. Yet for the first time since he'd died, she felt completely alive. Alive and humming.

If anything ever happens to me, Ali, you have to promise me you'll miss me, but that after a while you'll move on. Remember me but don't live like you'd died with me.

Josh's words ran through her head now. And she realized

that until now she'd pretty much been doing that, continuing with the business of life, but setting the emotion of it aside.

Until Colby Kendrick had kidnapped her dog.

And then he was kissing her, and her last sane thought was that promise she'd made, so casually when Josh had asked her all those years ago when they'd been so young and death had been a faraway thing. Now, for the first time since he'd died, she renewed that vow.

And she kissed Colby back, fiercely, feeling as if she had come alive again.

Chapter Twenty-Eight

Colby felt as if the world around him had stopped. As if all the problems, all the tensions, had vanished, as if the evil that was Liz had been boxed up, unable to escape to do her damage. Some part of his mind knew it was temporary, that reality would come roaring back, but right now he didn't care.

Right now, nothing mattered but the feel of Ali in his arms, and her lips against his, returning his kiss, stoking the fire, sending his heart hammering in his chest. It wasn't just that she was the sweetest of heart and taste, or that she was doing so much for him and Grace, it was that she wasn't faking this.

It was real, it was genuine, because he could feel it down to his very soul. She meant it, she wanted this, wanted him, and that quieted the part of him that hadn't believed any woman ever would. The part that had thought maybe Liz was right about how…useless he was.

He felt her hands on his skin, realized his shirt had come—or been—untucked. He wondered if she could feel the pounding of his pulse. She must be able to, the way he could both hear and feel it in his ears. That touch, her fingers stroking across his abdomen nearly made him gasp out loud.

He knew he had to stop her, stop this. If for no other reason than there wasn't time, not now. But he couldn't, he just couldn't, not yet. Not when he wanted to do the same to her, touch and stroke bare skin, more than he wanted his next breath. But if he did, he was afraid what little control he had left would snap.

Finally, somewhere, he found the strength to break the kiss. "Ali," he gasped out.

"You stopped," she murmured.

"I didn't want to. No way did I want to."

"Then why—"

A buzzing sound interrupted her. For a moment Colby couldn't move, even though he knew he had to, because he knew too well what that buzz meant. Then, reluctantly, he pulled the Foxworth phone out of his back pocket. He looked at the screen.

She's on her way back.

He closed his eyes and let out a breath, then showed the screen to Ali. Her brow furrowed. "They were watching her? Foxworth?"

He nodded. "I told them what I was going to do, and they jumped right on it." His teeth clenched for a moment before he could go on. "I have to go. I need to be gone before she gets here. If she sees my truck—"

"I know. I hate it, but I know."

"Do you? Hate it, I mean?"

"That you have to leave…now? Just when we were—" She broke off and looked down, a rather endearingly shy expression on her face. An expression he was certain Liz Hollen had never worn in her life.

"Yes," she went on, still looking down. "Yes, I hate it."

"Good," he said.

He gave her a final, ardent hug, then reluctantly pulled back. And when he started to gather up his tools and the packaging debris, she pitched in and helped him.

"I'll go the back way, just in case," he said, referring to the much more complicated path down some narrow lanes that would eventually land him on the far side of Foxworth headquarters.

She was steadier now, and made a funny face at him. "I feel like a kid trying to hide from my parents."

"I want to hear about them," he said suddenly. "And about when you were a kid. I want to know everything."

"Then we'll trade. Because I want that, too."

He winced inwardly at that. Because Liz had done so much damage there, too. But there was no time now, he had to get out of here, out of sight. For Grace's sake, and right now nothing mattered—nothing could matter—more.

"Call me," he said. "When they're settled in next door. Maybe we can—" He cut himself off. "No, damn, we can't. Because Cutter has to be here, in case Grace needs him."

"I know." He heard her take a long breath. "She has to come first, Colby. I know that. So we have to wait."

"The last thing I want right now," he growled out.

"Me, too. But if it's real, it will keep."

He stared at her for a moment. "It's real," he swore. "More real than anything I've ever felt. But I have to get out of here."

"I know," she said again. "Go. I'll let you know when they've arrived, then try and make contact with her. Say I want to show her the greenhouse I had put up today."

He wanted to grab her, to kiss her again, but he already knew if he did, time would spin out of control and he'd seriously risk being caught.

He got himself turned around a bit taking the unfamiliar back roads, and had to pull over to check a map on his phone and straighten himself out.

That's not the only thing you need to straighten out. Just because she makes you feel things you've never felt, solid, real, glorious things rather than the ridiculous fantasies your mind has spun about what life with Liz would be like, it doesn't change the main priority. Grace. Forever and always, it has to be Grace.

Once he was sure of his route again, he pulled back onto the road. And knew how close they'd cut it when a moment later a text came in from Hayley, saying Liz's car had just gone past Foxworth headquarters. He saw it was cc'd to Ali, so she'd know they were nearly there.

And just as he was pulling into the Foxworth parking area, another text came in.

They're here. Grace looks fine, just cranky. The mother looks more smug than usual, so it must have gone well for her.

He couldn't help it, he smiled at how easily she used Grace's term for Liz. And that she had already realized smugness was Liz's normal expression.

Just as he got inside, using Cutter's door opener, he saw Hayley jump to her feet over at one of the desks.

"Sorry. I should have knocked."

"No," she said, with a smile now, "it's just that when I heard the click of the opener my brain said Cutter. I miss that rascal."

He'd been so glad the dog was at Ali's to help he hadn't really thought about that part. "I'm sorry about that, too."

She shook her head. "Don't be. It's his call. He knows where he needs to be. And I'll tell you, he wouldn't leave even if we told him to, not if he's made up his mind."

"He's...a different sort of dog."

Hayley laughed then. "The tales I could tell you..."

At his request, since he seriously needed the distraction, they settled on the couch and she told him a few of those Cutter tales, until he was shaking his head in amazement.

"Are you sure he's just a dog?"

"Not at all," Hayley said blithely. "The only thing I'm sure of is that my whole life changed for the better the moment he wandered into it."

"You sure he just wandered in?"

That made her laugh. "Actually, no, not at all." Then sounding businesslike now, she gestured him over to the desk she'd been at when he'd come in. "I need you to take a look at some video, see who you might recognize."

When he realized it was security video from the front doors of the hotel Liz had dragged Grace to today, he blinked and stared at Hayley.

"I'm not surprised anymore that you were able to get it, but this fast? Somebody there must owe you big-time."

"A life or two, maybe," she joked. At least, he thought she was joking, but then this was Foxworth, so maybe not.

He settled in to watch, with Hayley pulling over another desk chair to sit and take notes.

"I probably won't be much help," he warned her. "It's been a long time, and I always felt so out of place at the few of these things I went to with her I didn't pay much attention to anything except where to hide, and when I could get out of there."

"Not expecting a roll call," she assured him. "Just a name, first only if that's all you have, a position, what deals they might be involved in, what she's said about any of them, anything at all."

She started the video rolling. He stared at the screen, and actually surprised himself a little, although the memories being stirred up weren't pleasant.

"That's Ben Owen. Runs a local ISP. That guy's named Conway, a local developer, used to be competition, so kind of odd he's there. I think those two are county officials, but I'm not sure. That's Chuck Jeffries, her father's right-hand guy… almost as ruthless. And there's her father."

"Is that Liz's mother?" Hayley asked, indicating the blonde on Hollen's arm.

"Yeah." He left it at that and kept watching. Until he realized Hayley was now watching him, not the video. And then she reached out to hit the pause button.

"Why do I get the feeling she was even worse about you than Mr. Hollen was?" she asked.

He shrugged. "Because you never miss a trick?" He let out a long breath. "If that woman ever said a civil word to me, it was because she didn't realize it was me until after she said it."

"Sweet."

"If it hadn't been for her husband's orders—he wanted the tool of having a grandchild—she would have wiped the marriage off the books, somehow." His mouth twisted. "But I'm actually glad about Liz's father. Otherwise Grace might never have been born."

He watched until Hayley shut off the video when the entrance slowed to empty, but only came up with a couple more IDs, and most of them sketchy.

"No," she assured him, "that's good. You confirmed a couple we weren't sure about."

"Looked like a pretty standard Hollen power meeting," he said. "Full of people they already own, and people they want to."

"So, tell me, what does Grace do during all this?"

"She gets paraded around in some dress she hates that her mother picked out, to show what a loving, family-oriented group they are, then stuffed in a hotel room with a sitter."

"Such fun," Hayley said dryly. Then with an entirely different expression on her face, she leaned back in the chair. "So, how are you and Ali progressing?"

He blinked. Swallowed. "What?"

Hayley laughed. "Did you think we wouldn't notice?"

He shifted his gaze away from her, not knowing what to say and afraid if he kept looking at her she'd read his mind. If she hadn't already.

"Ever notice Cutter getting in your way when you go to sit somewhere, or nudging you when you're standing?"

"Well…yeah, but…"

"Let me tell you about my brilliant dog's other talents," Hayley said, smiling so widely it was hard not to smile back.

He couldn't even guess at what was coming, but after a mere two and a half weeks of dealing with Foxworth, he thought nothing would surprise him.

He was wrong.

Chapter Twenty-Nine

Ali leaned back, stretched, took one final look and closed the file, satisfied. She'd been worried about this one, since it was for one of her most loyal clients, and she hadn't been able to really focus on it—or much of anything—since that day a bloodied, desperate Colby Kendrick had tumbled into her life.

But Grace had given her the inspiration for the project—a redoing of the client's daughter's bedroom. Ali had already redone their living room and kitchen, and that they'd come back a third time made them invaluable in her book. And like Grace, the child, who was a year older, loved to read. So Ali had taken something Grace had said—that she would love a secret place with her books so she could live in that story world—and designed it, raising the bed to give a cave-like spot beneath it, lined with bookshelves and pillows. The parents had been a trifle iffy, but the child had practically shrieked with delight when she'd seen the mockup, and that had decided it.

Unlike poor Grace, who had learned so young not to show enthusiasm for anything she truly wanted, because it would guarantee she would never get it. And if it was for something she already had—like her father—her mother would do her best to take it away. Ali couldn't imagine what it must be like, but to see clever Grace fight back however she could was... well, inspiring.

As for her father…

She sighed. Ran a hand over Ziggy's soft fur. The pup had been snoozing in her lap after a morning spent romping with the big dog who made such an excellent puppy sitter.

She stood up abruptly, feeling the sudden need to move. Ziggy woke, swiped his tongue over her chin, then made the tiny sound that she had a suspicion meant it was time for a trip outside. Cutter was on his feet the moment she was. She looked down into the dark, amber-flecked eyes. In a movement that was almost automatic now, she reached out and stroked the dark head. That same, soothing calm seemed to flow through her fingers to her heart.

"If you can teach him to be one quarter as smart as you, I'll be happy. Not as smart, mind you, because I'd be exhausted just keeping up."

Cutter's mouth opened and his tongue lolled out to one side, and he looked for all the world as if he were laughing.

"Hayley and Quinn must miss you like crazy, but I'm so glad you're here. And so is Grace. We're going to make her life better, aren't we?"

Cutter let out a sharp bark, echoed by Ziggy.

"I'm going to take that as two yeses," she said, laughing herself now.

As she sat watching the two dogs play and admiring her new greenhouse, she instinctively glanced over at the big house now and then, even knowing Grace was still at school. She'd seen Liz leave at about the right time this morning, so assumed she rather than the child minder had dropped her off on her way to the Hollen offices. Irene was here, though. She'd seen the woman arrive just as they were leaving.

Good timing. On purpose?

She wouldn't blame Irene if it was. If she had to work for that woman, she'd avoid direct contact as much as possible. Although from what Grace had said, her minder was almost as strict as her mother. Still, she had little choice. Grace had told her there were nanny cams all over the place, watching every move, every step. She wasn't supposed to know that of course.

I figured it out when she knew I ripped the new dress she bought me. But I did it in my closet, she shouldn't have known. So I did something else—not bad, just something she told me not to do, touch the books on the shelves—and she knew that, too.

In fact, now that Ali thought about it, she wondered if perhaps Liz had some of those outdoor "security" cameras aimed at Ali's house, to watch what happened when Grace was here playing with the dogs.

A chill came over her as a new thought struck her. Would she? Could she?

She pulled out the Foxworth phone. She hesitated, not wanting to hit the red button that indicated everything a red button should, an emergency. Instead she just hit the speed dial for Foxworth headquarters.

Quinn answered on the first ring. "Ali?"

"Yes."

"Everything all right?"

"As far as I know, but... I just had a crazy thought." She told him what Grace had said about the nanny cams. Then asked, "How paranoid is she? Enough to maybe...plant cameras in my house, for when Grace is here?"

Quinn didn't answer her. "Let's go to video," he said, then called out, loudly, "Colby! Question."

It took her a moment to remember how to make the switch to a video call on this phone. As she was doing it, she heard Quinn repeat her question. It was only a moment before she heard Colby's voice saying grimly, "More than paranoid enough."

The video opened just as he said it, soon enough for her to see his worried expression.

"There have been a couple of times when she's been there

and I've had to leave for a client meeting," Ali said. "I haven't seen any sign, but… I wasn't looking, either."

"So she's had opportunity," Quinn said. Then, decisively, "Well, since she's already seen Liam as a coworker, it's a good thing Teague's freed up now. Ali, you just gained a boyfriend."

She'd been focused on Colby, which was the only reason she saw him wince at that last word. And crazily, it gave her a little thrill, that he didn't like even the word let alone the idea that she had a boyfriend. Even a fake one.

"How about a brother," she said. "I get the feeling Liz would react less to that."

"Agreed," came Hayley's voice the moment before her face appeared next to Quinn's. "Good idea, Ali. Here, take a look at your new brother. Think you can sell it?"

Quinn backed away and another face came into view, a guy who looked close to her own age, with sandy-blond hair and blue eyes that were a shade lighter than Colby's darker blue ones.

He was smiling as he said, "Hi, sis." He was cute, but had that same brisk, businesslike air Quinn did, and she'd guess former military. "Teague Johnson, ma'am," he amended.

"I liked 'sis' better." He laughed, and she knew they'd do fine.

"We'll need to work up a story," Hayley said. "Just in case."

"Been thinking about that," Teague said. "Understand Cutter's undercover as your support animal?"

"Yes," Ali said.

"Then how about my wife, Laney, found him for you? She's a groomer, and does a lot of volunteer work for programs like that. That way if she happens to see Cutter being friendly with me, it'll make sense."

"Sounds good," Hayley agreed.

"So I'll come by to visit and see how things are going with the dog, and in the process do a sweep for bugs and cameras. And show you how to do it, so you can check regularly."

"That would be great," Ali said, meaning it.

"All right," Quinn said. "And in the meantime, Liam can get to work on trying to hack into that nanny cam feed, although with some it's tricky because it's completely localized."

Ali had noticed Colby in the background, and that his jaw was beyond tight. She thought she might know what was bothering him, but didn't want to bring it up in a crowd, as it were.

THE SECURITY CHECK was thorough, using some device Teague said their tech guy in St. Louis had developed. She let out a breath of relief when he pronounced the place clean. Then he quickly showed her how to use the handheld scanner, and pointed out likely places for someone to hide any devices. That part made her a little nervous, and she wondered how long it would take her to get that idea out of her head, how easy it would be for someone to spy like that.

He was as nice, and clearly as dedicated as everyone at Foxworth seemed to be. And when he noticed she was a bit antsy about all this, he entertained her with the story of how Cutter had brought him and his wife together. She couldn't help laughing at the tale of the usually fastidious Cutter rolling in every mudhole he could find, requiring a trip to Laney's grooming shop every other day. And how everyone else at Foxworth had magically been too busy to go and pick up the mischievous dog when Laney was done with him.

"If he's got his mind set you belong together, you might as well give in. And by the way," he said over his shoulder as he headed into her office to check her computer gear for any sign of incursion or spyware, "he's never been wrong."

In the time it took him to complete the scans, she worked on convincing herself that all the stuff about Cutter connecting couples who belonged together was just a teasing story they told to put people at ease in stressful situations. She even almost believed it.

The whole time she kept looking next door, warily. But as

it happened, they didn't have to deal with Liz, only Irene, who noticed him getting ready to leave as she was preparing to go pick up Grace from school. Knowing it would be reported to Liz, Ali cheerfully dragged him over as if he truly were a reluctant sibling, introduced him as her brother, neatly dropped in that his wife had gotten her the dog sitting politely between them, and that he was just here for a short visit.

"Nicely done," Teague said with a smile when the woman had gone. "You sure you've never done this before?"

"Never."

He got back into his car, still smiling. "Well, you pulled it off like you've been performing all your life."

"Unless you count a school play once, I've never acted at all."

Except when I told people I was fine, after Josh died. That was the biggest fakery of all time.

As she watched him go, she pondered the memory that had just hit her. She hadn't thought about those days much at all lately. Well, since Grace had come into her life, actually.

And Colby.

That was the biggest shift. She had to admit it. She hadn't denied that from the first she found him attractive. Even when he'd essentially kidnapped her puppy, and they'd found him worried and bloody back in those trees. But when the full story had come out, when she'd realized what he'd risked, how much he'd put up with for the sake of the little girl he so loved, it had moved him way beyond just attractive.

Chapter Thirty

After a day of absolutely no progress, and a night spent more awake than asleep, Colby had finally laced up his running shoes just after dawn and taken off to get rid of some of this tension. He pushed harder than usual, thinking that if nothing else, his legs should be too tired for the seemingly endless pacing he'd done all day yesterday.

When he got out of the shower after the workout, he found that the Foxworths had been and gone, leaving a note saying they were checking out something their tech guy at the St. Louis office had found. They'd also thoughtfully brought breakfast, although the famous cinnamon rolls from the local bakery just reminded him of how Grace had wanted him to take one to Ali. And how much he would have enjoyed doing just that.

But no, he couldn't do that, he couldn't be seen at her place, or with her. And it was driving him crazy, this taking a back seat through all this. Not that he didn't think Foxworth was more than capable of handling this—they'd handled much, much bigger cases, after all—but he felt…useless. Useless and helpless. As he so often had when facing the Hollens and the power they could bring to bear.

But he had no choice. If he pushed, they would somehow take Grace away from him completely, and he didn't think he could bear that. And worse, he was terrified that Grace would do something desperate, something that would blow up everything and endanger her.

When he heard the tires on gravel, he thought maybe the Foxworths had forgotten something and come back. He was startled when the door swung open and he heard dog paw steps. For some reason all he could think of was Quinn explaining to him how with Cutter's toenail length they had to strike a balance between short enough to not cause problems but long enough to use if he needed to, like running over rough ground, or climbing. But that idle memory vanished when the reality of him appearing here hit.

If Cutter was here then so was Ali.

He spun around, nearly colliding with Cutter. The dog dodged him neatly, nudged his hand in greeting, but then started bumping the back if his knees, as if urging him to move toward the door.

"I was going, dog," he muttered, unable not to think about the tales he'd been told about the dog's other capabilities.

"Colby?"

Damn. Just the sound of her voice... Even over the phone it got him revved up. The sound of it here, in person, and saying his name...he had no words for how that made him feel.

And then she was there, a wide smile on her lovely face. Her hair was tied back, and the sight of it just made him want to free it, to see all the colors of autumn tumbling down her back. Those eyes made him think of the spring that was just around the corner, and the trees here in his beloved Northwest that never lost that green.

And when did you start getting...seasonal?

"I was just thinking about you." He hadn't expected his voice to be quite so rough, and he hastily cleared his throat and explained. Or tried to. "Quinn and Hayley brought cinnamon rolls, and I was remembering how the last time we were at the bakery Grace wanted to bring one home to you, in case you'd never had one."

"Are those the famous ones?" she asked, as if she'd noticed nothing odd about either his voice, or what he'd said. She walked over to where he'd gestured at the white bag on the table. And once more he found himself fascinated—a bit too fascinated—with the way she moved, that slight sway, and the way her sweater clung to certain places.

He had to swallow again before he could even say just, "Yeah."

"I haven't had one, yet. Sure have heard about them, though."

"Then you'd better have one of these, or Grace'll never let me hear the end of it."

She chuckled, and he felt his tension ease a bit. Or maybe it was just that he loved the sound of her so much he couldn't stay tense in the face of it. He grabbed the stack of napkins that had come with the rolls, then dug into the bag and got out the delectable treats.

At her first bite, Ali closed her eyes. "Mmm. They are so *not* overrated."

"They really are good."

"Lucky for me they're a bit of a drive, or I'd weigh a ton."

"I was thinking if I ran there and back, it might be a wash."

This time it was a full burst of laughter, and everything, even his situation, seemed lighter. When they'd finished, and he'd gathered up the debris, wondering if licking the last of the frosting off his fingers would be too tacky, he almost reluctantly asked the obvious question.

"Did you need something? The Foxworths already left, but I could call them and see if—"

"I need you," she said. He froze. Stared at her, unable to quite believe he'd heard her right. "Well, that, too," she said, her cheeks pink now. "But I need some plants for my wonderful new greenhouse, and I thought who better to go plant shopping with me than the man who built it?"

He felt as if he were scrambling to keep up, after the shock of that "I need you." He seized on the one thing he thought safe. "You want me to go plant shopping with you?"

"I just thought you might like to get out a bit. We have a few hours while Grace is in school. Unless you think the mother is likely to frequent plant nurseries."

"Uh...no. Not likely."

"Good. Anyway, Irene is at the house, so I thought we should start from here." When he just stared at her, her expression changed. "If you'd rather not, that's fine, I just—"

"No!" *Get it together, Kendrick. Chance of a lifetime here...* "I want to go. I was just...surprised."

"No warning, I know. I'm sorry."

"Don't be. Let's go." He glanced at Cutter, who had settled into what was obviously his bed here, seemingly content to stay in the familiar place while the humans went about their silly business. But then it struck him. "Where's Ziggy?"

She smiled, as if pleased he'd remembered the squiggly pup. "He's with Teague's wife, Laney, getting introduced to actual grooming. She offered, said it's good to start them young. So, everything kind of fell together this morning." Her voice softened. "I thought maybe a couple of hours of not worrying might be nice for you."

He was smiling himself now. "You have—" He stopped himself, then started again. "I was going to say you have no idea, but obviously you do."

It was Ali who thought—of course—to leave a note of explanation for the Foxworths, should they arrive while they were gone. Then they were in her car, since whatever she bought had to go home that way, and on their way to the biggest local nursery. They were out on the main highway—which here meant a full lane and a bike lane each direction—when she spoke again.

"You're really doing all right, not working for this long?"

His gut knotted, and he fought back memories of Liz's denigration of the work he loved. "Yes. I'm not rich enough for Liz, of course, but plenty for me. I've got a nice cushion, so I can do this without going broke."

"Probably just as well it's not enough for her, because I have the feeling she'd go after it," Ali said dryly.

He couldn't explain why that made him smile, but it did. "I see you've got her number."

"Sometimes it's hard to keep it hidden," she admitted. "But I know I have to, for Grace."

She said it as if it were a given. As if she'd do anything for Grace. Just as he would. His throat jammed up again, as it did so often around her.

"Have I mentioned," he said when he could speak again, which wasn't until they were pulling in to park at the nursery, "how glad I am that it was you who moved in next door?"

"You might have, once or twice."

"Not enough. Thank you, Ali."

"Now that, you've done more than enough of. So come on, help me pick out some plants that will live happily in that new greenhouse until they're big enough to move outside."

He'd always liked this place. Surrounded by all kinds of trees and plants, with various habitats built especially for them. They were just getting to one of the more sheltered areas when he heard a shout.

"Hey, Colby! Good to see you. Need help with something?"

He turned to see the son of the owner and founder heading toward them.

"She might," he said, nodding at Ali. "Ali Moran, John Reynolds. His dad opened this place what, fifty years ago now?"

"Almost," John said with a smile. Then he looked at Ali. "And this guy—" he nodded toward Colby as he had to him "—has built about half of it for us. All the new outbuildings, and the shelters so we could carry more indoor plants, and things that need a more protected life than the Northwest usually offers."

"He neglected to mention that," Ali said, giving him a sideways look.

"That's Colby, never brag, just let the work speak for itself," John said. "So, what can I help you find?"

She explained what she was looking for, some of which was familiar, a lot not. But when she described a flowering tree she'd seen and had been wanting ever since, something registered.

"You mean the one outside the library?" he asked.

"Yes, that one. But I don't know what it is."

"I don't either, but I know someone who does. Haven't talked to him since I finished his patio cover last summer, but…"

He pulled out his phone, looked up a number and dialed.

"Jake? Colby Kendrick. Got a question."

"Hey, been meaning to let you know Kim loves being able to sit out in the rain on the patio now."

"Glad to hear it."

"So, what's the question?"

He asked about the tree, and got an immediate answer. He thanked him and was about to hang up when Jake asked, "How's your girl?"

"She's…okay." He flicked a glance at Ali. "Doing better right now, thanks to some help."

"Glad to hear it."

They ended the call and he looked at John. "Japanese snowbell."

"Ah," John said. "Yes, that's a good one. Stays fairly small, not a lot of maintenance unless you want a specific shape, and my wife loves the flowers."

"Sounds like a home run to me," Colby said, smiling now.

Ali was watching him, a rather different expression on her

face. But before he could figure it out she turned to John and smiled. "Lead on," she said.

And I'll follow.

The quip that shot through his mind then seemed to have a lot more weight than it should have.

Chapter Thirty-One

Ali was happy she'd had this idea for more reasons than she'd ever expected. Not only did Colby seem lighter, happier out and thinking about other things, she was seeing a side of him she never had. She was seeing at least glimpses of the man he was when not all consumed with worry. The guy who had a reputation around here, the guy people thought of as a friend, the guy who could make a call to someone he hadn't talked to in months and not only be welcomed, but to have that person ask about his little girl.

And she couldn't help noticing he'd been looking at her when he answered. It told her she was part of that help he'd mentioned, and that warmed her yet again in that way only he seemed able to.

Once they were loaded up, and the back of her little SUV was full of things she was looking forward to filling her new greenhouse with—including a baby version of the library's tree—she headed for the rather winding exit from the parking lot.

"I'm sorry I can't go to help you unload," he said, brow furrowed.

"I'll manage. I've got a dolly in the garage to manage the bigger, heavier stuff."

It wasn't until they were at the one stop light on their route that he asked, "Could we...make another stop?"

"Of course," Ali said to Colby's hesitant question. "We have plenty of time, although I'm not sure we have room for much more."

"I didn't mean more plants... I meant my place. I need a couple of things. It's close," he added, gesturing up the hill.

"Oh, of course," she said quickly. She couldn't deny the spark of interest that flared. She was curious to see where he lived, how he lived, when he wasn't under the kind of stress he was now.

She followed his directions until they ended up on a small cul-de-sac with about a half dozen houses. All were what she'd call tidy-looking, cozy, welcoming. Fairly new, but not starkly so. Each one different, yet they all fit together, with enough in common to suggest the same designer, yet not cookie cutter.

"This is lovely!" she exclaimed.

"Thanks." He sounded pleased, but a little embarrassed.

"I can see why you chose this place. All of the homes here are just perfect. And this one in particular," she added as he directed her into a driveway leading to one of the two houses at the end of the loop.

This one was a bit more secluded than the others, but mainly because of the trees that sheltered it. The house was a single story, with a small yard and a welcoming covered porch. It was painted a light gray with dark gray trim, which could have made it a bit stark, but not next to all the greenery.

Once she'd parked the car, she glanced over at him. He was looking pleased again, which pleased her in turn. Funny how just seeing him react in any kind of positive way warmed her heart. But there was something even more in his smile this time. And after a moment she had it.

"You helped build these, didn't you?" she exclaimed.

He looked startled then. "How did you know that?"

"Because you looked proud. And the only other time I've seen that look on your face is around Grace."

That seemed to startle him, but his smile widened. "Do you

want to come in?" His mouth quirked. "I don't remember how big a mess it is, I kind of left in a hurry."

"I'd love to."

It didn't look messy to her, but then she'd been living half-unpacked for three weeks. Sure, there was a coffee mug in the sink, a pair of boots on the floor inside the back door and a jacket and shirt tossed over the back of a chair, but to her that just meant lived-in.

As was instinct with her, she noticed some things—very few—she would do, give him a drying rack for those work boots, maybe a bit of tile on the floor for wet and muddy days, and add a splash of color here and there, but all in all this felt like a place she'd finished with, not one she needed to work on. And down at the end of a hallway she saw a door open, to a brightly colored purple-and-pink room with toys and books strewn about, and stuffed animals and more books on every shelf.

Grace. There was no question. She thought about the cold, sterile room the child was relegated to in her mother's house, and felt another jab of sorrow and sympathy.

Then they walked through to the main room, which had more of the neat, functional feel. And the stack of books on an end table were a positive, even if they weren't exactly neat. But all of it barely registered when she saw the view out the large back windows. Not just the expansive deck but, in the distance and between more of the trees she loved, as if they were a frame, the water of Puget Sound. It was a lovely blue today under the clear winter sky.

"Colby, this is beyond wonderful," she said when she heard him come up behind her.

"Kind of plain, I know—"

"It's not plain, it's functional. And who needs fancy inside when you have that—" she gestured toward the sparkling water through the trees "—outside? This spot up on this hill is the perfect place, and I love that you didn't mow down all the trees to take advantage of the view."

"They talked about it, but I told them I was buying this one and to leave them. To me, they frame the view, not distract from it."

She turned around quickly as he used exactly the word she'd thought of a moment ago. She hadn't realized he was quite that close, and before she knew it she was up against him. She wobbled a little, and his hands instantly came out to steady her.

And then she was in his arms, looking up at him. She thought she saw something flash in those blue eyes, something hot followed by an effort to look away that was underlined by the tension in his arms, as if he were trying to let go but his arms wouldn't cooperate.

"Colby," she whispered, her voice coming out husky because of the tightness in her throat. And then he was kissing her.

It began almost harshly and definitely hungrily. Fierce, even. She let out a low moan without even thinking about it, because she couldn't have stopped it anyway. He broke the kiss, and she felt him start to back off.

"No!" she protested, and reached up to pull him back to her.

"Ali, I…can't do this."

"Oh." She felt a chill go through her. "I thought…you wanted to."

He let out a low, harsh laugh. "I do. God, do I. But I'm afraid you'll regret it."

"What is there to regret that I don't already know about?" she demanded.

He just looked at her for a moment, his expression softening. He let out a low, wry and short chuckle. "Point taken. You pretty much know it all."

"I want you," she said firmly. "*You*, Colby Kendrick. Who you are, now and from now on."

She saw the change come over him then, and before she could even put a name to it heat rippled through her in response. Then she realized it was fierceness, the same kind she was feeling. Heat, want, need all billowing through her in waves so potent she even imagined she could see the reflection of it in his eyes. Or maybe it was his own need, finally cut loose.

She hoped so.

And then he removed all doubt by sweeping her up into his strong arms as if she were as light as a leaf from one of those plants waiting outside. His mouth came down on hers again, heat spiked again and she barely noticed they were moving. She didn't even register the room as he pushed open the door. All she saw, all she wanted to see was him, all she wanted to feel was his mouth on hers, and anywhere else he wanted to put it. Which had her thinking of all the places on him she'd like to kiss, to taste.

She wasn't sure who removed what clothing, thought she might have tugged at his jeans while he was pulling off her sweater, but it didn't matter. What mattered was within moments they were skin to skin.

He was as beautiful as she'd expected, strong, leanly muscled, powerful. They hit the bed, and the only thing she noticed about it was that it just might be big enough.

He reached over and pulled open a drawer in the nightstand and pulled out a small, clearly unopened box of condoms.

"Sometimes," he muttered, "I'm thankful for my smart-ass friends."

"If they provided those, so am I."

He laughed, and she felt it down deep where his abdomen was pressed against her. She also felt the prod of another powerful part of him, clearly ready and able. He fumbled for a moment, sheathing that part, telling her it truly had been a while for him. As it had for her.

He rolled back, half over her, cupping her face in his hands. "You're really sure?"

"So very sure," she answered. "Just…it's been a long time, so I'm not…used to this. Just don't stop."

"I won't." He almost growled. "But I'm going to go slow and easy until you tell me not to. And then, look out Ali Moran, because under all the chaos, I've been wanting this since the first time I saw you."

"Ditto, Colby Kendrick."

Then his mouth was all over her, finding places she'd forgotten existed, feeling sensations she'd forgotten she could. And when he finally slid into her, long and slow and deep, it was only a moment before she did exactly as he'd said, and told him not to be so careful.

And even in this it seemed they were in tune, because the moment she felt an incredible wave of sensation making her convulse around him, he groaned out her name and pulsed inside her. And there were no words she knew that could describe the wonder of it, of him.

Of them.

Chapter Thirty-Two

Colby turned his head away from the clock on the nightstand, but it didn't change anything. It was still time.

"I know," Ali said quietly as she sat up in his bed. "We need to go."

The memories of the hour and a half they'd just spent exploring, discovering and, in his case, learning his body was capable of things he'd never realized, flooded him. The last thing he wanted to do was leave this unexpected bit of heaven.

To leave her.

He didn't dare watch her get up and start to dress. Just looking at her, at those curves, the soft, sleek skin, that glorious fall of red hair that he now knew was completely natural, made him ache all over again.

"I wish…" It was all he could say.

"Me, too. But Grace will be home from school soon, and Cutter and I need to be there."

"I know."

With an obvious effort at cheer, Ali said, "I think I'll ask Liz if she can go with me to pick up Ziggy at Laney's shop."

"Grace would like that."

He tried to put some enthusiasm in his voice but failed. Right now he wanted nothing more than to spend the rest of the day and all of tonight right here in his bed with her. And a whole lot of the nights after that.

But instead he was facing a yawning, empty hole.

"You sound…" Her words trailed off, but he knew what she meant.

"Yeah. Can't wait to get back to where you have to do everything, or Foxworth does. While I sit around and do nothing."

"Nothing but stay out of the mother's way, for Grace's sake."

He let out an exasperated breath. "I know."

"And I know it's totally unlike you to be a bystander when something critical is happening, and probably close to impossible when Grace is involved. But you've got one of the biggest forces around backing you up now, precisely so that you don't have to fight this battle alone."

He stared at her for a long, silent moment. Then, softly, as softly as he had whispered her name when he had been buried to the hilt inside her, he said, "With you on my side, I can fight anything. Even her."

She gave him a smile that made him want to pull her right back down on these sheets and start over. But he knew she was right, they had to get moving. His girl would be home soon.

They hastened through a process that went surprisingly well, as if they'd already learned how to coordinate. He gathered up what he'd actually wanted to stop here for—he'd never expected it to end up like this, never even hoped—and looked over at her. She glanced at the book in his hand, the one he'd been in the middle of when all this started, and the copies of legal papers Quinn had advised him to bring so they could turn them over to Gavin.

"Do me a favor?" she asked, her gaze locking on his now.

He wanted to say "Anything," and would have meant it, but he couldn't seem to get even the single word out. So he just waited.

"Grab that box of condoms, too."

She was out the door and headed back to her car, leaving him standing there barely able to breathe.

He was still processing as they headed back to Foxworth.

His brain seemed to be careening in a dozen directions at once. Trying to analyze the implications of her wanting those condoms available. That there would be hours while Grace was in school when they could be together. That she would have to come to him, which made him nervous and oddly revved up at the same time. And which would also require explaining to the Foxworths, should they happen to walk in on them in his generously loaned living quarters.

He was still working on that last one when they arrived. The Foxworths' SUV was parked in its usual spot, making Colby remember the note Ali had left for them. Somebody's brain was working, at least. Cutter raced out the door to meet them—he still boggled a bit at the trust they gave that dog—before they were even fully parked.

Oddly, the dog skidded to a halt about a yard away from them instead of romping up demanding the usual pets and scratching behind his right ear. He stood looking at them, with his head tilted as if questioningly. As if he somehow knew or sensed something had…changed.

Okay, now you're buying into that alien-in-a-dog-suit thing Liam talked about, Kendrick.

And then Cutter covered those last few feet at a trot, head and ears up, tail wagging. As if whatever had made him stop in the first place had now met with his approval.

"That dog," Colby muttered.

Hayley wasn't far behind her dog. When she reached them Cutter had turned to face her, but sat down between him and Ali. His tail was wagging again, vigorously, and he had what Colby had to call a grin on his face.

Hayley stopped almost where Cutter had, and studied them for a moment almost as the clever animal had.

"Well, well," she said quietly. She shifted her gaze to her dog. "Another win, huh?"

Cutter let out a soft woof that sounded almost self-satisfied. And Colby was thrown back to that day when Hayley had explained about Cutter's most unexpected gift, that of simply knowing when two people belonged together. And when his gaze met Hayley's steady one, he knew she'd had the same thought. He rarely blushed, but he could feel his ears getting warm, and was very glad he'd stuffed that box of condoms deep inside his jacket pocket.

"Told ya," she said with a grin. Thankfully, before he had to try and explain that to Ali, Hayley went on. "Nice selection," she said, looking at the plants and the small tree in the back of Ali's car. "I gather the greenhouse install went well?"

"Perfectly," Ali answered before he could shrug and say his usual "Okay."

"Excellent," Hayley said, then glanced at her watch. Before she could speak, Ali responded to the action.

"I know. I need to get moving if we're going to be there by the time Grace gets home."

Colby felt a jab of disquiet. He knew she had to go, but he didn't want to let her leave without kissing her one more time. It felt awkward, here in front of Hayley. But then Cutter's mom laughed.

"Would it help if I said it would be no surprise to any of us that you want to kiss her goodbye?"

"Goodbye...for now," he amended, his voice more than a little rough.

Then he did kiss her, and thought that if the Foxworths hadn't been here, he would have wanted to carry her inside to resume their earlier joyous activity. And as he watched her drive away, with Cutter now secured into the front passenger seat, the only one not full of plant life, he marveled at how things had changed.

He'd assumed he would forever have to fight alone for Grace. He'd assumed someday he might lose that fight, and thus lose his precious girl. He'd assumed he would never again risk getting close to a woman, certainly never let her in to batter his heart.

But now he had the thought that life seemed determined to turn everything he'd always assumed on its head.

ALI HAD JUST slid the tree off the dolly in its selected spot when Cutter, who had been sitting and watching all the plant arranging with apparent interest—more than she would have expected from a dog, anyway—suddenly leaped to his feet, spun and headed for the door.

That she had almost expected. Because when Grace and the mother had arrived home about twenty minutes ago, she'd heard the girl's wailing "I hate you!" even from inside the greenhouse. It made her stomach knot, because her first instinct was to run to the girl and comfort her, but she knew she couldn't. She had to play this as if she didn't know a thing.

And she had to let Cutter do his job. Which included responding to the whistle she couldn't hear.

But that didn't mean she couldn't watch. And she did as the dog ran over to the back of the big house next door. Normally Grace would appear on the back porch, ready with a note to place in the tiny canister on the dog's collar. But this time there was no trace of the girl.

Cutter sat, waiting, for a minute or two. His head tilted, as if he were trying to figure out why she wasn't there. Then he moved back along the side of the house, stopping, to her surprise, at the window to Grace's bedroom. The same window Colby had broken that day, which seemed so much longer ago than just three weeks. The window where Grace now appeared, although she was looking back over her shoulder.

They'd warned her that the new cameras would show if she tried to open or climb out that window, warned her that everything on that side of the house was being watched, yet she seemed to be trying to slide the sash-style window up. But she stopped, turned and vanished back into the room, and Ali let out a breath of relief.

Then Ali saw something else. Something small and white

falling to the ground. Something Grace had slid through the tiny gap she'd made at the window sill. Cutter was on it immediately, picking it up with his teeth. Then he spun on his hindquarters and raced back toward her. She stepped outside the greenhouse and shut the door behind her, thinking rapidly.

She tried to picture what that would look like on those cameras. She hoped it would seem the dog had come over to play, but when he got no response had given up and left. Would the thing the dog had seized be recognizable? Would it even occur to Liz or anyone else who saw the video that the dog could be this clever?

She had no more time to dwell on those questions because Cutter was there, offering the carefully folded note delicately.

She won't let me be with Daddy on Saturday and I can't come see you anymore at all. She thinks you're telling me bad things. I can't even play with Cutter or Ziggy. Tell Daddy I'm going to run away, I can't be with her anymore.

The knot in Ali's stomach tightened even more, making her faintly nauseous. Did the woman really think Colby would just take this lying down? Did she know so little of how much he loved his daughter? Of how far he would go for her?

Well, you're about to learn, mommy dearest.

She made herself walk back into her house at a normal pace although she badly wanted to run. Once inside and out of sight from next door she did run, to the counter where the Foxworth phone was. And this time she hit the red button.

Chapter Thirty-Three

"You don't seem surprised," Quinn said.

Colby grimaced as he stopped pacing the Foxworth headquarters. "I'm not. I've been expecting this."

Hayley tilted her head slightly as she looked at him with that intensity he'd come to expect from the woman. The intensity that meant she was hearing much more than his actual words. Then she looked at Ali, who was sitting almost huddled in on herself, hugging Ziggy close as if the pup could ease the pain. As if she were hurting as much as he was.

"You answered her?" Hayley asked.

Ali nodded. Managed a small smile and a nod toward Cutter. "That dog of yours... I wrote that I was calling right away—I figured she would know who—folded it up and gave it to him. Not in the note holder, since Grace couldn't get to it without getting into more trouble. And darned if he didn't run over there, plop it on the window sill and nudge it with his nose until it caught in that tiny sliver of an opening she left, right where he picked up her note."

Colby had no words for the amount of amazement and gratitude he felt for this animal, so settled for a stoke of the dark fur on his head. And felt yet again that odd, calming sensation, as if somehow things would work out.

Ali let out a long breath before going on. "I thought I'd best stay out of sight, so I just watched on our monitors. It was maybe five minutes before she came back to the window and found it. Once I knew she had it, I headed here."

Hayley nodded, then she and Quinn walked over into the office area, and started to make calls. That was one thing he'd learned about the Foxworths, they didn't waste any time when the ball needed to roll.

Ali shifted her gaze from Hayley back to him. "You've been expecting this? That she'd clamp down like this?"

He nodded. "Ever since the day you hugged her outside, in the clear."

She drew back, her eyes widening. "You think she saw me do that?" He nodded. "And that...that's all it took?"

"For her to be wary of you, and of the influence you have with Grace, yes." He grimaced again. "No one, but no one, owns her child except her."

"'Owns'?"

"That's how she thinks of her. A helpful possession. Something to make her seem more human to the people she wants to manipulate. Same reason she allowed the dogs." For a moment Ali just stared up at him, her expression pained, as if she were feeling queasy. He shrugged one shoulder as he shook his head. "I can't explain her. Any more than I can explain how I was so stupid for so long."

"I should have thought," Ali said, her voice even more troubled now. "We always wait until we're past the trees to pick up Ziggy and start to head here fast. I should have thought first, shouldn't have hugged her out where she could see."

Colby sat down on the edge of the big coffee table directly opposite Ali. He took her hands in his, squeezed them. "You couldn't have known. You're sane, normal, your mind could never work like hers does. Thank goodness."

She managed a slight smile. She looked at their clasped hands. Then, with a tiny gasp, her gaze shot back to his face. "You don't think she knows, do you? About...us?"

Now, that hadn't occurred to him. He thought about it,

trying to see from all angles, then said with some certainty, "I don't see how she could. Not already." She looked nervously over at the Foxworths, and his mouth quirked. "Oh, they know."

Ali drew back slightly. "What?"

"They've been expecting...what happened." She blushed. And he kind of liked it. "Remember what they said about Cutter's matchmaking?"

She blinked. "That was a joke, wasn't it? Or anthropomorphism?"

He shrugged. "I don't know. But Hayley insists he knows when people...should be together. And does what he has to do to make it happen."

"I know they say he brought them together, but..."

"And Liam and his wife. Teague and Laney. Even Gavin de Marco and his wife. Who is, by the way, your local librarian."

Her eyes widened. "Katie? I met her when I went in there right after I moved in, when I needed an internet connection and mine wasn't hooked up at home yet. She's married to Gavin de Marco?"

He nodded. "Hayley said his most extreme case was that sniper I told you about. He tried to walk away and Cutter literally put him on the floor. Now he's about to marry Quinn's sister. And that's just the Foxworth part of the list, apparently. All of it thanks to this guy," he said, reaching out to give Cutter a scratch behind the ears.

When he looked back up at her, she was staring at him, still wide-eyed. More than this amusing but silly idea warranted. Then her eyes darted away quickly, as if she felt...caught? Embarrassed? Simply upset?

The Foxworths came back to join them in front of the fire, interrupting his rather crazed string of questions.

"Let's get the dogs outside for a bit," Hayley said. "We have some planning to do. Cutter, outside?"

Ali set Ziggy down on the floor, and the moment the bigger dog headed for the back door, the black-and-white puppy scrambled after him, as if he remembered it led out into that expansive meadow.

"We need to know," Quinn said to Colby in a businesslike tone as the door closed behind the dogs, "that you're still up for going full bore on this."

"I won't let her steal Grace out of my life, if that's what you mean. No matter what it takes."

"You trust us to get it done?" Hayley asked. "Even if it means you may have to pretend a bit?"

He flicked a glance to the woman in front of him. "I trust you and Ali, yes."

Ali's head came up, and she was smiling now. And he had the thought that he would give a great deal to see that smile often, and for a very long time. But then he made himself focus.

Quinn nodded. "All right. We're going back to our old friend Sun Tzu, then. When in conflict, don't rely mainly on physical and material power, but on mental power."

Colby drew back, his brow furrowing. "Mental power?"

"They're not used to having people stand up to them, especially people they feel beneath them. So you convince her you won't…before you do."

"So…she'll be surprised. Off-balance maybe."

"Yes. You'll have to judge carefully, you can't roll over too easily or she'll be suspicious. But at the same time let her think she's won, that there's nothing you can do."

Colby dug back into the memories of those days when his father had read the philosopher strategist to him. "When we are able to attack, we must seem unable…"

"Exactly."

He nodded slowly, but with a wince. As if she'd read his mind, Ali said softly, "What about Grace? She'll think he's giving up, too."

His jaw tightened at hearing it put into words. Just the idea of his girl thinking he wasn't going to fight for her, that she wasn't worth everything to him, up to and including dying for her, made him even more determined.

"You still have your three hours tomorrow, right?" Hayley asked.

"Unless she tries to yank that, too," Colby said grimly.

"Then we need to decide if we're going to tell her anything about the plan," Quinn said.

"I think we have to tell her something," Ali said. "We can't just let her think Colby's given up on her. She already said she'd run away, and I think that might tip her over the edge."

She already knew his girl so well. Much better than the mother did. "Ali's right."

"That's putting a lot of weight on a seven-year-old," Quinn said, sounding wary.

"But a very smart, very special seven-year-old," Ali said firmly.

"All right," Hayley said, briskly now. "But we have to keep it to a minimum. The less she knows, the less she can give away under pressure."

"I'd say we should meet up here," Quinn said, "but if she's followed you on these visitation days before, she might be triggered enough to do it again now. We've been lucky so far, but…"

Colby nodded. "You're right. If she's edgy enough about Ali to tell Grace she can't even play with a couple of dogs next door, she's on guard and will be watching closely."

"So you'll need to take her someplace open, public, where people go," Quinn said. "She still hasn't seen Teague, or me, so we can be in the area without raising suspicion."

"I'm glad you didn't say without attracting attention," Hayley said to her husband, with a glance full of a very pointed kind of heat.

Colby might not be the most tuned in to nuances, but even he didn't miss the twitch at the corner of the imposing former

Army Ranger's mouth or the heat that flared in his gaze. Colby risked a glance at Ali, who had one of the sweetest smiles he'd ever seen on her face as she watched the couple. He couldn't blame her, they fairly reeked of "this is forever."

And suddenly, like a misguided hammer blow, it hit him. Why she'd looked so odd when he'd told her about Cutter's track record in the matchmaking department.

Every couple he'd mentioned had gotten married or was about to. Did she think he was implying that the same thing would happen with them? Was that what had had her so rattled?

The images that thought paraded through his mind were breath-stealing. And unexpected. He'd never really thought about getting married again, had thought himself a charter member of the "once burned, forever shy" group.

But this was Ali. And Ali was different. Special. Real. True.

He could have gone on for ages with all the things she was. And somewhere down deep he knew that he was as right about her as he'd been wrong about Liz.

And what better to build a life on?

Chapter Thirty-Four

Ali thought she'd never seen a couple so in tune, so well matched. She and Josh had been great together, but they'd never had this sort of communication-without-words thing.

"—decide where you're going to take her," Hayley was saying, making Ali tune back in. "Someplace public, but not crowded, so you can talk without being overheard."

"And you'll have to convince her how crucial it is that this is kept secret," Quinn added. "She's been good so far, but this is the crunch. You'll have to tell her in a way she won't forget."

"The lighthouse," Ali said suddenly. They all looked at her. "She's talked about it, that it's so close but she's never seen it."

"I... She never said she wanted to," Colby said.

"I think when she's with you, she doesn't care about anything else," she said, trying to explain the idea that had hit her. "But if you take her there, she'll remember because it's the first time for her, and you can tie it to what you're telling her. That it's...it's the light in the darkness, and like it, you'll always be there for her."

They were all staring at her now. Surprisingly, it was Quinn who shifted his gaze from her to Colby, gave him a smile and said, "You're a lucky man, Colby Kendrick. Finally."

Colby looked at her, then answered simply, "Yes."

Ali felt a kick in her pulse. Maybe he had meant it, when he'd linked them to all of Cutter's apparent successes. Heaven knew she'd seen enough of the dog's uncanny cleverness to at least consider the possibility that it was true. All of it. The idea made her very hesitant to leave now, but she knew she needed to be home for Grace's sake.

When she got back home, Cutter immediately looked over to the big house, as if he knew it was out of the ordinary for them to have left while Grace was at home. There was no sign of the child now, through the window or anywhere else. And the dog didn't indicate he'd been called.

After a moment he made what she'd come to think of as his rounds, checking every bit of her house. He didn't react to anything, so she felt fairly safe, although she did the camera check that had become routine. Then she turned on her flat-screen to her own monitors, so she could watch Grace's room without getting caught staring out her window. Cutter went over to nose Ziggy, who had plopped on his bed, clearly tuckered out from the romp in the Foxworth meadow.

They'd discussed her possibly putting that red square of paper in the window, to indicate Grace needed to come over and play, but decided it was too risky until Colby had talked to her. They didn't want Liz to crack down even more, and maybe try and stop Colby from having his paltry three hours with her tomorrow. It would be his last chance before they started to move. Grace had to be clear on what was happening, on what to do, and more importantly what not to do. Ali had a lot of faith in the child, but she was still a child.

But the worst part of it was that she couldn't even be around. It made sense, if Liz or someone she'd assigned was spying on them, it could blow up everything if she was seen with them. But that didn't mean she liked it. She already felt so much a part of this, and had even before that afternoon when she'd discovered that hot, female part of her wasn't nearly as dead as she'd thought it was.

That afternoon when Colby Kendrick had shown her she could still fly.

But now she was relegated to pacing the floor, feeling worse than helpless, feeling useless.

She stopped mid-step when a memory hit her. Colby's words rang in her mind, and she knew she was truly understanding them for the first time.

Can't wait to get back to where you have to do everything, or Foxworth does. While I sit around and do nothing.

No wonder he was so on edge. It was driving her mad, she could only imagine how it made him feel to just stand by.

It also led to a sleepless night for her. Which in a way turned out to be a good thing, because she was awake when her phone chimed an incoming text. She knew who it was, who it had to be.

Going crazy. I wish you were here or I was there.

She thought of all the possible platitudes she could send back, that it would be all right, that he just had to hang on, they were on the edge of making their move.

In the end she went with the simple truth.

Ditto.

There was a long pause, as if he were thinking as hard as she had been. And in the end he, as she had, went the simple route.

This weekend?

She'd wondered about that. If Liz and Grace were both going to be gone, to whatever event Liz was using as an excuse to take Colby's full day with her away from him, then maybe they could…revisit. Discover if it really was as explosive as she remembered.

Please.

She'd typed and sent it before she thought much about it. It was time, she decided, to go with the truth. She felt a qualm after the "message sent" notification appeared, but then Cutter was there, nudging her hand. She automatically reached out to pet him, and at that first stroke of his head it was there again, that sense of calm, that reassurance.

Yes, it was time for the truth. She was where she never thought she'd be again. Looking at a future suddenly very different from the one she'd had just a few weeks ago.

She walked over and picked up Ziggy, needing to cuddle the little ball of fluff. He squirmed a little, but once she sat back down and he realized he was safe in her arms, he settled and went happily back to snoozing. And with her puppy on her lap and Cutter at her feet, she felt comforted.

But this weekend, with Colby, she would feel whole again. And that, she had never expected. That if he meant what he'd said, that wholeness would include the sweetest, smartest child she'd ever met, who would be the frosting on the cinnamon roll her life seemed like it could become.

Chapter Thirty-Five

"Can we come back here, and bring Ali and Ziggy and Cutter?"

Just hearing her link them all reached a place in Colby's heart he'd only recently discovered existed.

The day Ali welcomed you, made you feel whole again.

He rested a hand on his girl's shoulder, trying not to think of how not so long ago he could only have reached the top of her head without bending over. She was growing up so fast, and these short interludes with her were just not enough. Which steeled his resolve to fight.

Helps that you have the best cavalry around at your back now.

He smiled at the thought, and at the certainty that Ali was included in that force to be reckoned with.

No sooner did the thought form than he heard Quinn's voice through the earbud in his left ear.

"Looks all clear. The two subjects out on the point are from the US Lighthouse Society, and the family that are out on the beach arrived in a car with Idaho plates."

He knew the man had them in sight, so he just gave a thumbs-up to indicate he'd heard.

"Can we, Daddy?" Grace drew him back to her initial question.

"I hope so," he answered. "And soon."

That made her smile. Then her brows rose sharply. "Oh! I almost forgot!"

She reached into her jacket pocket and pulled out what looked like a couple of folded pages torn from a notebook. It looked rather like that story he'd found, about the little girl and the monster.

"This is for Ali. I promised it to her, for her birthday. She said she didn't care if it was late, since her birthday was last Sunday." Grace expression shifted to a sad frown. "You have to give it to her, since I'm not allowed to see her anymore. And we're leaving in the morning anyway, to go over there. Again."

She waved her hand in the general direction of the city. He took the folded sheets, tamping down his anger at Liz's latest tactic. "I guess I shouldn't look at it, if it's hers, huh?"

"You can," Grace said, "if it's okay with her. But she should see it first, 'cuz it's her present."

He tucked the pages carefully into his own jacket pocket. "I'll see she gets it. But right now, Gracie-girl, we need to talk. Very seriously."

His girl's blue eyes, so like his own, looked up at him. "Is this about...fighting her?"

"Yeah. Yeah, it is."

"We better sit down," she said wisely, and looked around. One of the north-facing benches was empty, and she scampered that way. Colby ran to keep up, loath to have her anywhere outside of arm's reach, as if Liz could somehow swoop down and grab her.

Like the vulture she is.

Sending up a silent apology to the birds that were a necessary part of the system, he sat down beside his daughter. He'd thought a lot about how he was going to approach this, what he was going to say. He knew his girl, knew how she thought, even if she sometimes almost scared him with how smart she was.

"How would you feel if I gave up fighting for you?"

Grace stared at him for a long moment. He could almost

hear her brain racing, processing. Then, finally she shook her head. "You wouldn't. You just wouldn't."

He couldn't help the sudden stinging of his eyes, and the tight, grateful smile that tugged at his lips. He blinked rapidly a few times, put his arm around his precious child and pulled her close.

"No. No, I wouldn't. And I won't. Ever." Remembering Ali's words, he pointed to the tall light behind them. "I will always be there for you, just like that lighthouse is there for the ships going by."

His girl looked at the solid, steady fixture, and smiled. "I know you will."

"But honey, I'm going to have to pretend that I'm giving up. Give up fighting at all over her taking tomorrow away from us. And more, I'm going to have to tell her that I'm not going to fight her anymore at all. No more arguing with her when I pick you up or bring you back."

Grace looked up at him, her brow furrowed. "Why?"

"So she'll think she's won."

"Why?" she repeated.

Although it wouldn't surprise him if she could totally grasp Sun Tzu, he went for a more modern explanation.

"Because if she thinks she's won, maybe she won't be so... careful. Maybe she'll get careless, overconfident." His daughter's brow furrowed again as she processed the words. He shifted to something he knew she'd understand. "I know she'll get smug, think she's better than anybody else, that nobody would dare challenge her."

Grace made a sour face. "She already thinks that."

God, he loved his girl. "I know. But now we're going to use it against her. Lull her, then come up from behind and shock her. But part of that is I have to act like she's won. Like I gave up."

Again he could almost hear that clever brain churning away. "How should I act?"

"How do you think you'd react...if it were true?"

She shook her head. "I wouldn't believe it."

"Then act that way. Like you don't believe it."

Grace went very still for a long, silent moment. Then she looked up at him, with an expression he could only describe as mischievous on her face. "Can I call her a liar?"

Despite his tension, Colby nearly laughed at her glee. "I don't think so, honey. That might tip her over the edge, and she might really lose it. Lose her temper, I mean. She might even try to hit you or something."

Grace shrugged. "She's done it before. It wasn't so bad."

Colby went rigidly still, all humor vanished. In his ear he thought he heard someone swear. "She what?"

"Well, she slapped me once, when I told her I wanted to go live with you. It hurt, but only for a little while."

"You never told me that."

"It was while you were gone, working up on that island."

His jaw tightened. Last year he'd been on a crew repairing storm damage on an emergency clinic on one of the San Juan islands north of here. He'd hesitated about being gone that long; it had been a monthlong job. But it was the only medical clinic on the island, so it had needed doing, and the money had been good and steady.

"You should have told me," he said, a little tightly.

Grace looked up at him, and for one of the few times in her stubborn life he saw actual fear there. "I was afraid you'd get really mad at her, maybe do something... She always talks about that, that someday you'll do something stupid and she can keep you away from me forever."

He pulled her into his arms, hugging his beloved girl tight. "You might have been right, if I'd known she dared to hurt you." Then he pulled back enough to look into her eyes again. "Why did you tell me now?"

"Because now you're going to fight her anyway," she said simply.

He gave a wondering shake of his head. "What am I going to do when you're the genius out there saving the world and I'm just your dumb ol' dad?"

"I don't wanna save the world," she said, hugging him back rather fiercely. "I just want us."

"So do I, Gracie."

"Then so be it," came Quinn's determined voice in his ear.

"Amen," Colby muttered.

But hope was burgeoning, because he had the feeling that if it could be done, Foxworth could do it.

Chapter Thirty-Six

Ali blinked rapidly, but it wasn't enough to stop the tears. One trickled down her cheek, then another, until she had to swipe at them before they fell onto the paper she was holding.

It was a simple story, in a child's simple hand.

It was also simply beautiful.

"Have you read it?" she asked Colby, not even caring that the powerful emotion she was feeling had tightened her throat and made her words a little shaky.

He put the mug of coffee he'd poured for her down on the counter in his kitchen, then sat on the stool next to her. She'd watched Liz and Grace leave early this morning, and confirmed that Irene was still in the house. That had started Foxworth moving. Quinn and Teague would be tracking them on the other side, keeping in touch, while Colby prepared for the engineered meeting on Monday. He had an appointment with Gavin de Marco tomorrow morning to go over the plan, but had asked her if she would come here today so he could give her Grace's gift.

"No," he answered now. "She said you had to read it first, since it's your present." He seemed to hesitate before adding, "After that, it's up to you."

"You should read it. I know how hard that was on you yesterday—this will make you feel better."

He grimaced. "You mean telling her I give up, I can't fight her alone anymore?"

"Yes. Even if it isn't true, it had to sting."

"Slash, more like," he muttered. But then he gave her a sideways look and an almost smile. "But it really isn't true, is it?"

She put everything she had into the smile she gave him then. "No, it's not. And boy, is she going to be surprised."

She got a much better smile back then, and it warmed her to the bones. She held out the story his little girl had written, a fairy tale of sorts, about a family who had come together in a different sort of way. A handsome prince who had fought bravely, a princess who had had sad times, and a little girl who wished more than anything for them to be a family. And a very smart dog who seemed to think they already were.

And they needed a dog of their own so a little black-and-white puppy came to live with them, and they were all happy forever after, and the evil queen went away because she didn't like being around people who were happy.

She remembered that ending word for word. She thought she always would. The assessment of the mother was razor-sharp, and Ali thought anyone who ever underestimated Grace Kendrick would soon learn the size of their mistake. But more important to her was the clear, simple certainty that the prince and princess and little girl would be happy, because they'd be together.

Forever after.

She watched him read it, saw his expressions change as he did, from a smile simply because it was from his precious girl, to his eyes widening as he realized who she had cast in the parts of her little story, to quickened breathing as he neared the end. And she saw his eyes were glistening in a reaction just like her own.

For a minute, maybe two, he just sat there staring at the end of the story. Then he spoke, without looking at her, but sounding as if his throat was as tight as hers had been.

"You ever read a fairy tale and wish more than anything that it was true?"

Ali's heart leaped with joy at his reaction. "Yes," she said softly. "Just now."

He looked at her then. "You mean it?"

"I mean it."

Colby looked like a man who had opened a door and found paradise. And also as if he couldn't quite believe it. And it made her love him all the more.

Her heart took another little leap as she acknowledged the truth. If you'd asked her a month ago she would have said she didn't think she'd ever love again, not the way she had loved Josh. Now...now she knew better. And somewhere deep down she knew that Josh would approve of her choice. They would have been friends, these two, had they ever had the chance.

Colby swallowed hard. "I mean it, too. I know this is...a crazy way to have met, and a crazy mess we're in, but...when things calm down..."

"After you win, you mean?"

A flicker of his old fear flashed in his eyes. "What if I don't?"

She let out an intentionally snorting bit of laughter. "Foxworth took down an evil governor and a crooked senator. Do you really think they're going to let the likes of *the mother* beat them?"

It worked. The fear vanished, and it was the Colby who knew he had a small but very effective army at his back who was smiling at her now.

"Then...can we try and make this—" he held up Grace's story "—come true."

"We'll do more than try. We'll plan out life after you've won," she said. "But for now...could we take advantage of being actually alone together?"

His smile became the one that she remembered, from the afternoon spent in his bed. An afternoon she wished to repeat. And even as she thought it, he swept her up in his arms and proceeded to make the wish come true.

Colby settled the earpiece in his ear, more for something to do than because it needed it. It was in his right ear, facing away from the rest of the big dining area that was rapidly filling up, probably with a lot of government types given the county seat was just a couple of blocks away.

He was a little peeved at himself, because just the thought of being in the same room with Liz was bugging him more than sitting across a small table from a world-famous attorney. As if he'd read his mind—and given his courtroom abilities, Colby wouldn't be at all surprised if he could—Gavin de Marco reminded him of their rehearsal.

"You're happy. You know you're going to win. And when you spot her across the room—after she spots you—you're going to…?"

"Laugh," he said.

"Believably," de Marco suggested rather wryly. "Think of Grace, and being where you should be in her life." The man lifted a dark brow. "Or think of Ali. I gather that should put a smile on your face."

Not for the first time since Ali had come into his life, Colby was glad he wasn't a blusher. "Who told you that?"

"Hayley told me early on that Cutter had decided."

He hesitated, then asked, "He really got you and your wife together?"

"He did. And believe me, it wasn't easy. I was stubborn. My logical, fact-based brain did not want to even play that game with him, but he made it impossible not to. Thank goodness. Katie's the best thing that ever has or ever will happen to me." He tilted his head slightly, assessingly, before adding, "Just as Ali will be for you, I think."

He remembered last night, and the long, sweet hours they'd spent together. And smiled. "I love her."

De Marco smiled. "That's obvious."

"If you two are done, the play is about to begin."

Quinn's voice in his ear startled Colby, and considering

what they had just been saying, he could only hope they hadn't been listening all along on the Foxworth end. Especially when he knew since Grace was in school Ali was there with them, no doubt hearing everything. But then, he'd already told her those words last night as he'd held her close, finally letting himself believe.

Good, because I love you, too. I think I have ever since I realized everything Grace says about you is true.

The joy ran deep, and he couldn't help smiling.

"Now, that's the happy Liz needs to see," de Marco said. Then, for the sake of the earpiece that was in his left ear so neither of them would be visible from what would be Liz's table, he said, "Ready when you are, Quinn."

"No changes," Quinn said. "She's with the Community Development guy we researched."

Colby remembered how they'd been happy to discover this was the first public engagement of the two, because it implied she was just beginning to try and reel the guy in. She probably needed some rules bent, and would offer to make it worth his while to bend them.

"We're on," came Teague's voice a moment later, from where he was stationed outside the door, wearing something Liz would be sure to overlook, a waiter's outfit. "They're on their way in."

"Rick is ready, too," Hayley said.

She was back in the restaurant's office with Rick Giles, the manager who was readying to step on stage. Colby had met him briefly, when they'd first arrived. The man was middle-aged, a bit round, and looked slightly nervous as he fiddled with the mic Foxworth had rigged him with, attached invisibly to the back of his name tag. They would be able to hear the entire exchange at the table, for as long as the man could manage to be there.

Oddly, his nerves had calmed Colby a little. This man, who didn't know him at all, was going to play a crucial role in his fight for Grace. And when that man turned to him and said, "Foxworth saved my life, and my son's. I'm honored to help them do the same for you," Colby had never felt more humbled.

Except when he'd first held baby Grace.

And last night, when Ali had said she loved him.

He'd spent so long afraid to hope. But now here it was, bubbling up inside him like the untouched glass of champagne on the table before him.

"We're celebrating, remember?" de Marco had said when he ordered it. "We've found what we need to take her down, and we're delighted."

Colby had stared at the face he'd seen in the news so many times. "How much of what you do is acting?"

De Marco had burst out laughing. "Oh, so much," he'd said.

And then they were there. Liz strode in as usual, dressed to the nines, head high, phone at her ear.

"You said she always does that, the phone thing?" de Marco asked.

Colby nodded. "Half the time, probably more, it's not even real, she's not talking to anyone."

"But she wants it to seem like she's so in demand that her guest should be grateful that she's allotted him some of her precious time."

He smothered a laugh. "You sure you haven't dealt with her before?"

"Yes. But I've dealt with her sort dozens of times. They're half the reason I went to work for Foxworth."

They stayed quiet after that, according to the plan. The food on his plate would have been appealing at any other time, under any other circumstances, but right now his gut was churning enough that putting anything in it seemed like a bad idea. But he tried not to let it show, tried to present the demeanor of a man who had found a solution to the biggest problem in his life, thanks to the man sitting across from him.

That it was possibly true was what got him through the

next few minutes. And then it began, when he saw Mr. Giles stride across the dining area to greet his guests, doing an excellent job of appearing overjoyed that someone on the level of Elizabeth Hollen would grace his humble establishment.

And then he heard that painfully familiar voice in his ear. "Mr. Harkness here recommended it for our meeting. I'm glad to see he was right about the management appreciating the level of clientele."

Colby happened to be looking at de Marco at that moment, and seeing him roll his eyes as if she'd fulfilled his every negative expectation almost made him laugh. But it wasn't time yet, so he stifled it.

"I'm having quite a day here in my little restaurant," Mr. Giles said, sounding delighted. "First a world-famous attorney, and now you."

"World-famous?" Liz didn't snort, but her voice had taken on that tone Colby knew meant she would be the one to decide who was well known enough to rate that description.

"Absolutely," the manager gushed. "I mean, Gavin de Marco? Here, in my little place?"

Colby couldn't stop himself from risking a glance, figuring she'd be fixated on the man who'd just done that huge name drop. For no doubt one of the few times ever in her life, Liz looked taken aback. "Gavin de Marco? *The* Gavin de Marco? Here?"

"Yes," Giles said with just the right amount of pride. "He brought a client in to celebrate, something about having found exactly what they needed for their upcoming court action."

"I don't envy whoever they're suing," said the county official. "I mean, the guy took down our sitting governor."

Colby heard Quinn's chuckle through the earpiece. "Couldn't have written a better line for him than that."

"And rightfully so," Giles said enthusiastically. "But I agree, I don't envy his opponent, no matter who it is. He's lost what, one case in his entire career? And then won it in the end on appeal."

"Wonder what this one's about?" the official said.

Colby blinked as the man asked for the info Giles had been about to drop. It was hard not to look over there, but that wasn't the plan. "You sure you didn't arrange this guy, too?" he whispered. De Marco laughed.

The manager handled the shift perfectly, sliding in what he'd been going to say anyway, just in a different form. "I heard him mention a child custody case that was turning into a criminal one. Sounds exciting, doesn't it? I bet it will be all over the news soon. I mean, Gavin de Marco, in the headlines again!"

"Great job, Rick," came Quinn's voice. "Seeds planted, feel free to fire the last shot and then disengage."

"Please, enjoy your meal," he said with all the charm of a host. "I need to go make sure Mr. de Marco and his client enjoyed theirs."

Then, as planned, he walked over toward their table, staying in Liz's line of sight, blocking her from seeing Colby, who was intentionally turned mostly away from their table anyway.

"Great job, Rick," de Marco echoed Quinn's words to the man. "And by the way, the crab melt was great, too. I have a feeling you'll be seeing some Foxworth folks here more often."

"I would be honored," Giles said with a bow.

Then, at de Marco's nod, he turned and walked away. And Colby, as planned, shifted in his chair to where he could be spotted from that table across the room. In the same moment, de Marco lifted his glass of champagne. Colby did the same.

"A toast to victory," the lawyer said.

"I'll drink to that," Colby answered fervently, tipping his own glass to clink lightly on de Marco's.

"Now," Hayley's voice said in his ear, "would be the time for that laugh."

Think about how it will feel when she's beaten, and you did it. Think about the look on Grace's face when you tell her.

Ali's words echoed in his mind now. The pure delight on her face when she'd said it had made him laugh joyously then, and Hayley had immediately seized upon the sound of it as a weapon.

The memory of Ali saying it did it again now. And he let it out, not even trying to muffle it.

"That did it," de Marco said with satisfaction. "She looked, and I only wish you could have seen her face when she recognized you. Now drink that last bit down—happily—and let's decamp before she has a chance to get her bearings."

Smiling purposefully, he gave the famous face across from him a wondering look. "You're really enjoying this."

De Marco laughed. "I am."

He downed the last swallow and they both stood up. "I know it's tempting, but don't look," Hayley warned in his ear. "You'll get to see it shortly. Teague got some great video of her reaction. Ali is still dancing gleefully over it."

And that mental image alone was enough to enable Colby to stride out of the dining room, the famous lawyer at his side, looking as if he owned the world.

Chapter Thirty-Seven

"So," Quinn said as they leaned back on the couch after watching the video Teague had shot, "do you think we got to her?"

Ali watched Colby as he sat there, slowly shaking his head in wonder, staring at the now-blank screen. She had a feeling she knew just what had him so gobsmacked.

"Could we watch that moment when she spots Colby again?" she asked. "It just does my heart good."

Hayley laughed and rewound the video. The moment when Liz's eyes widened was wonderful, and the next instant when her jaw dropped, heedless of the fact that she was out in public, was even better.

But the best of all was the moment when fear flashed in her normally cold, gray eyes. That was absolutely priceless.

"As well you should be afraid," she murmured.

Colby heard her, because his head snapped around to look at her. "So... I'm not imagining that?"

She reached out and took his hand, squeezed it. "That scared look in her eyes? No, you are not. Isn't it wonderful?"

He laughed, then looked up toward the ceiling, biting his lower lip. He closed his eyes, and she wished she knew what was racing through his mind at that moment. When his eyes abruptly snapped open and he looked down, she saw that Ziggy was pawing at his leg, trying to climb up. But before the pup could do it, and even before Colby could reach down for him, Cutter was there.

He picked Ziggy up just like Quinn and Hayley had told them he had when he'd brought Ziggy to them, and plopped the wiggly bit of black-and-white fur in Colby's lap. Colby simultaneously patted Cutter and picked Ziggy up. He held the squirmy pup against his chest, and Ziggy reached up to swipe his chin with a pink tongue.

Even my puppy loves him.

For a moment she allowed herself to think beyond this crisis, to a time when things would settle and they could just be together. When this horrendous strain was behind him and Grace, and they could actually be happy. But then Quinn spoke, yanking her back to reality.

"We'll be watching her carefully. Teague's on her now. I suggest you remain here, Colby, so she can't corner you at your house. I have a feeling she's going to react rather strongly once she gets over the shock."

Colby nodded. Ali reluctantly glanced at her watch. Hayley noticed, and nodded.

"Yes," she said, "you need to be close by when Grace gets home from school, to make sure she doesn't take any heat from this."

She felt Colby stiffen, and reached over to grab his hand. "I won't let her hurt Grace. If I have to go kick down the door or make up a story and call the sheriff."

"We'll call them, if necessary," Quinn said. "We've already alerted Carly that things may be starting to move."

"Good," Colby said flatly. "Grace's safety comes before anything else."

"I'll come with you," Hayley said. "I think we can get away with another visit from your old friend."

"Thank you," Ali said, meaning it rather fiercely. She had the feeling things might start happening fast, and if she couldn't have Colby at hand, Foxworth was the next best thing.

They only had a few minutes, so her goodbye with Colby was much shorter than she would have liked. But he blew all other thoughts out of her mind when, hugging her close, he whispered, "I can't wait until this is over and we can just be us together."

"All three of us," she whispered back. She felt a ripple go through him, and knew she'd found the right response. And she meant it with all her heart.

They made it to her place ten minutes before Grace usually got home. Irene was still at the house next door, which usually meant Liz herself was picking her up from school.

"I hope that's not a bad sign," she muttered.

"We won't assume," Hayley said. "She does pick her up frequently, and she was already out. But we won't assume it's nothing, either." She gave Ali a reassuring smile. "Now, show me this new greenhouse of yours. I've been thinking about one myself."

"I still can't quite believe he did it," Ali said with an almost embarrassed smile as she led Hayley to the newly installed—and filled—structure, Cutter at their heels.

"I can. Because I can see how he feels about you."

"Sometimes I can't believe it's even real," she admitted, not even bothered by the fact that Hayley clearly knew how close she and Colby had become.

"Then trust Cutter. He knows it is."

They walked around inside the small greenhouse, much warmer than the February chill outside, where her plants were already showing how much they liked it. It might be crystal clear and the sun might be bright enough to make you squint, but that didn't mean it was warm here in the Northwest. Sometimes February was one of the harshest months of all.

They'd gone back inside for some hot chocolate when Cutter alerted. He trotted over to the window and stood still, watching.

"Must be her car," Ali said. "I swear, he can tell even cars apart."

Hayley laughed as she went and turned on what Ali had taken to calling the spy cams, the ones that showed the house next door, including the driveway, at the edge of their broad visual field.

"I don't even question anymore," she said as the images popped to life on Ali's flat-screen.

And sure enough, a moment later when a car pulled into view, it was Liz's top-end luxury sedan. The garage door began to rise, and the car pulled straight into the garage. But not before Ali spotted the passenger. Definitely Grace, she could tell even though the child was slouched almost below the level of the windows of the vehicle.

"She didn't look happy," Hayley said.

Ali sighed. "She never does when the mother picks her up."

They watched until a light came on in Grace's room at the back of the house. Cutter finished making his rounds, interrupted by the arrival next door, then settled into the bed Ali had made for him from a soft throw. Ziggy, adorably, had begun to imitate his big companion, following him around the house as he checked every door and window, then plopped down beside him on the floor.

"You know, you could rent him out as a puppy trainer, along with all the zillion other things he's good at," Ali said.

"Now, there's a thought," Hayley said with a smile.

Ali watched the screen. "I wish she wasn't so careful about having the house checked for bugs or cams. I'd love to know what's going on in there right now."

"Agreed. We even thought about giving Grace something to record with, but the risk was too high that if her mother found it, she might hurt her."

Ali grimaced. "Even higher, now that we know she's hit her at least once," she said, remembering that moment when they'd been talking on the lighthouse bench. She'd felt a little uncomfortable, as if she was eavesdropping on something very personal, but it was all part of knowing what they had to know to rescue Grace.

And that particular bit of knowledge was well beyond infuriating, it was enraging.

Time passed and it was starting to seem like just another day next door when Cutter's head came up. He got to his feet and walked over to the window. Ali looked at the screen and waited, trusting the dog's incredible hearing. And about a minute later a car pulled into the driveway. It wasn't on a par with Liz's favored luxury model, but was the same make.

"A rideshare, maybe?" she suggested to Hayley. "We don't have much in the way of taxis over here."

"I'd agree, if the driver wasn't acting like that," Hayley said dryly, nodding at the screen.

Ali looked back at the man who'd gotten out from behind the wheel. Tall and burly, he looked around. Not at the house number as she would have expected if he wanted to be sure he was at the right address, but all around him, lingering long enough on her house to make her uncomfortable. Then he turned to look back the way he'd come, as if he were checking to see if anyone followed him.

"Security?" Ali asked.

"That would be my guess."

Ali grimaced. A Foxworth operative would likely know one when she saw one.

They couldn't tell who had come to the door, since they didn't step outside, but watched as the man went into the house. Quiet reigned again. Cutter was more restless, as if he'd somehow sensed the new arrival was…different. Or maybe she was just starting to believe the dog was as amazing as the Foxworths said he was. He'd certainly done nothing to disprove that. But finally he settled back into his old spot, and she went back to snuggling with Ziggy, who didn't have quite the calming effect petting Cutter did, but there was something about that soft fur and tiny body, and most of all the utter trust, that soothed her all the same.

Cutter suddenly scrambled to his feet. He raced to the back door and looked back at them, letting out an almost urgent bark. Hayley headed toward him while Ali grabbed up Ziggy to keep him from trying to follow. Playing together was one thing, but Cutter was obviously working now.

Hayley opened the door, but stayed inside. Cutter raced into the yard, leaped over the short fence in one scrambling bound, and headed for Grace. Hayley stayed at the door while Ali ran back to the screen, where she could see Cutter had already reached the window of Grace's room.

The window that was open.

She watched, with her heart pounding, as the child leaned out as Cutter reared up on his hind legs to reach her. Grace's hands went to his collar, and Ali guessed she was putting a message in the little canister.

The pounding in her chest became a wrench as Grace looked back over her shoulder every few seconds, as if she knew she was being pursued. Still the child took a moment to stroke Cutter's dark head, and even in the small image on the screen Ali could see her smile. So even at times like this—or maybe especially—the clever, protective dog could provide comfort.

And then Grace pulled back inside, slid the window closed and darted back into her room and out of sight of the camera's field. Cutter wheeled around and started back toward them at a dead run, head down and tail out straight as if he understood speed was of the essence. Which made Ali feel that painful twist in her chest again.

She spun around as fast as the dog had and hurried over to where Hayley was waiting, arriving in time to see him clear the fence again. Hayley murmured something soft and loving to the amazing animal as she opened the tiny container and pulled a tightly rolled piece of paper, larger than the previous ones had been.

Ali you have to help me!!! She pulled me out of class. Some stranger is here. She's packing stuff. She told me we're going away and not coming back. I asked her where and she said I didn't need to know. I asked her why and she wouldn't answer. I said what about Daddy, and she got really mad and said it's all his fault. Help!

"So she's going to run," Ali said.

"Or try to," Hayley said, with a hint of steel in her voice that calmed Ali a bit. She reached for the Foxworth phone. But before she even picked it up, the red light lit up and the urgent-sounding notification went off. Hayley hit the red button. Quinn's voice came through immediately.

"We think she's making a move."

"We know she is," Hayley countered, and relayed the contents of Grace's note. "What happened on your end?"

"Liam's been monitoring, and in touch with our contact over in Everett at the airport. He heard the pilot of the charter jet they use just filed a flight plan. Two passengers. And one of them is a child."

Chapter Thirty-Eight

"It was filed IFR," Quinn said.

Before he could ask, Colby heard Hayley explain it in her response.

"Instrument Flight Rules?" she asked. "But it's severe clear out."

Colby recognized the local term for this kind of day, when you could see from Mount Rainier to Canada. His brow furrowed as he studied the video feed from the cameras at Ali's house.

"Exactly," Quinn said. "Why not just Visual Flight Rules? So Liam kept digging. Turns out the only real weather anywhere close is some heavy clouds with potential snow later tonight hitting the Rockies, west of Denver."

Colby tensed and his gaze snapped back to Quinn. "Her family has an office in Denver, and a house in Beaver Creek. Near Vail."

Quinn looked at him. "Address of the house?"

Colby gave a disgusted shake of his head. "I don't know. I've never been there. Grace either. I only know about it because I overheard her father bragging about it to someone. About how big the house is, and what big wheels they are around there."

"Liam!" Quinn yelled toward the stairway.

"On it!" came a return yell from the second floor, reminding Colby all of this was going on live via those rather heavy-duty Foxworth phones.

Quinn looked back at Colby. "Her father bragged about it, but she never told you about it?"

"No."

He didn't even try to explain how typical that was, that once he'd refused to become part of their world, they shared nothing with him.

"So she has every reason to think you don't know anything about it?"

"Yeah, I—" Belatedly it hit him. "So it's the perfect place to hide Grace."

Quinn nodded. "Liam," he called out again, "you copy that part about her pulling Grace out of class?"

"Already called Ria," came the answer.

Quinn turned back to Colby. "Ria is his wife. She's also a local teacher, who knows several others who work at Grace's school. She's already reached out and they're checking for us."

Colby wondered if the Foxworth network had no end. Then Hayley's voice came over the speaker.

"Ali and I could go over there, see if we can find out anything."

"Put that on hold," Quinn said. "We don't know who that guy who arrived is yet."

Hayley sounded tense. "We need to be sure before we commit. If we guess wrong…"

"Maybe Grace could help." It was Ali, and Colby couldn't help the little jump of his pulse when he heard her voice.

"How?" Quinn asked.

"Maybe she could get a look at what her mother is packing. If she's taking heavy, winter-type clothes, or if she's overheard anything…"

"Excellent idea. If she and Cutter can pull it off."

They decided it was worth a try. Hayley had Ali write a quick note, then sent Cutter off to deliver it. They watched on screen as the dog raced over to Grace's window. The child was there almost immediately, pushing the window open. Then she vanished, but was back in under three minutes, wrestling with Cutter's collar. So they had an answer much more quickly than they'd expected. And with more than they'd asked for.

Ali read it out loud for them all.

She got out her big pink puffer coat. She called somebody and said to get the house ready. And I heard that nasty guy say something about mountains. We're going now.

"It ends in a kind of scribble, like maybe she heard her mother coming and had to rush," Ali said.

"That's it, then," Quinn said. He looked at Colby. "I really would like to hire that girl of yours when she's a bit older."

Colby let out a sharp laugh. "I have a feeling we may all be working for her."

"Truer words," Quinn agreed.

"Quinn! They're leaving," Hayley said urgently. "Shall we try and stop them?"

Colby held his breath, hoping Quinn would say yes, but when he said no, he sadly understood.

"We need a plan in place first. And I think getting away will lull her, put her off guard."

Colby didn't like it, but he knew Quinn was right. They both turned as Liam came running down the stairs. He rattled off information at a rapid clip.

"Ria says she pulled Grace out indefinitely. Got the address, and pulled some info. Big place—figures—overlooking the golf course at the resort. My guy over at the airport says they're scheduled to take off in an hour. In this."

He handed Quinn a scrap of paper with something scribbled on it. Colby could just make out the word *Citation*.

"Fast. So we can't beat them in the air. Any idea if they're flying into Denver and then driving?" Quinn asked. "There's a county regional airport a lot closer, I think. With a nice long runway, because of the weather they have to deal with sometimes."

"He's checking," Liam said.

Quinn looked at Colby, who had to shake his head. "Depends. They've got a fancy limo there in Denver, but if she's in a hurry she might risk the short drive in a possibly grubby ride."

"But if you had to guess?"

Colby knew the "had to" part was true. This was Grace. "I'd say the luxury limo. She avoids us peons whenever possible."

"All right. Hayley, you get all that?"

"Copied. All of us?"

"I think so. We want max shock value."

"Good idea," Liam said. "I could—" He broke off as his phone chimed. He looked, sent a quick answer to a text, then looked at Quinn. "Denver."

Quinn gave Colby a nod for his accurate guess. "Excellent. That's at least a two-hour drive, maybe more this time of year."

"Cutter, I assume?" Hayley asked.

"Of course."

"Prepping now," she said, and Colby could almost hear her smiling as she ended the call on her end.

Quinn went to the office in the corner of the building, which Colby now knew was his. He was on the computer there in seconds, and was quickly reading the screen and tapping a thumb on the desk.

When he saw Colby in the doorway, he glanced up and said, "Figuring timing."

He went back to the screen.

"This model jet has a cruising speed of about three hundred twenty knots an hour." He glanced again at Colby. "Say three hundred seventy-five miles per hour. So an estimated three hours plus a bit flight time. It's got just enough range without refueling, but only if they don't have to dodge anything or wait in the air very long. Pretty risky."

"I think they'll stop," Colby said hesitantly. "She'll feel safe once they're on their way. That jet makes her feel…"

"Privileged? Special?"

"Yes."

"Then she has a surprise coming." Quinn said it with such cool Colby felt that hope battering down his qualms. "They're not leaving for an hour. With driving time from Denver, that gives us roughly six hours, probably more when you add in delays and ground transit. And a lot more if they do stop to refuel."

Colby stared at the man. "Why do I get the feeling I'm about to meet Wilbur?"

Quinn grinned, widely. "Won't be as fast—it'll take us two hours or so more flight time—but ol' Wilbur's steady. With a range of five hundred miles more than we need, and that's with a nice fuel reserve left over."

"And you can top the Rockies?"

"Max altitude is twenty-five thousand feet. Cabin's pressurized, rare for a small turbo prop. We're good."

"What about that weather?"

"Always the X factor, but like I said, we've got the range to go around a bit if we need to. Especially since we're not heading into Denver International's traffic pattern."

"So you think we can beat them there?"

"No, but we'll be close on their tail. If Mother Nature cooperates and holds off until tonight."

"You mean Foxworth doesn't have any pull there?" Colby asked in mock shock.

Quinn laughed. "Good to see you're able to joke."

"Hope," Colby said, solemnly now, "is a powerful thing."

"Yes, it—" He broke off as another call came in. Quinn looked at the screen and then put it on speaker. "Gavin. Go."

"Just saw the case update Liam sent. Thinking I should go along."

"We've got room," Quinn said. "You have a reason?"

"Two. I've got a former client in the area who happens to have some legal pull."

Colby didn't doubt that. Back in his headline days, Gavin de Marco handled nothing but people who had some pull. Or a lot of it.

"And reason two?" Quinn asked.

"If I was enough to scare her into running from here, imagine what me showing up there might do."

Quinn laughed. "Our own personal boogeyman."

"I've been called worse," de Marco said with a chuckle. Colby was sure he probably had been, in those years when if there was a lawyer all over the news, chances were good it was him.

Liam appeared in the doorway. "ETA on Wilbur ready for takeoff is forty-five minutes."

"Excellent. You copy that, Gavin?"

"I did. I'll be there just about then. And I'll have to play it by ear, but I may have something worth using."

Quinn ended the call and turned to face Colby. "What did that mean, something worth using?" Colby asked.

"Knowing Gavin, it means something that could turn the tables completely. Just like he used to do at court. We'll have to leave that to him," Quinn said briskly. "It'll probably be pushing an hour by the time everybody gets there and we get loaded up."

"How many people can Wilbur carry?" Colby asked, trying not to leap on that bit about de Marco having something and chewing it to death.

"Five, plus the pilot."

"Who I assume is you?"

"Yep," Quinn said, looking nothing less than delighted at the fact. "So Hayley, Teague, Liam, Gavin, and you."

"And Cutter?"

Quinn grinned at that. "Yeah, him too, but since he's only about seventy pounds, we don't worry about it."

"That'd be one of Liz's suitcases," Colby said dryly.

Quinn laughed. "Hope you pack lighter."

He did, grabbing up whatever clothes were clean, including some of his heavier work socks he was glad he'd grabbed, given the weather they were heading toward. Quinn apparently had a go bag ready at all times, because the only thing he grabbed was his laptop with all the details he'd just researched and a couple of heavy jackets off the rack by the door.

Thanks to the fact that his stay here was temporary, he didn't have a ton of things to include, so was able to be ready only a couple of minutes after Quinn.

"What about Hayley?"

"She's got her go bag in the car. Along with Cutter's."

"The dog has a go bag?"

"He does. Food, water, collapsible bowls and some of Liam's gear we sometimes use with him." Quinn grinned again. He was obviously looking forward to flying. "He's even got a coat and some traction boots, so if that snow hits, he'll be ready."

Colby was still marveling at it all as they drove south to the small local airport Wilbur was hangared at. And his first look at the sleek little airplane had him, oddly, thinking better this to tackle the Rockies than the helicopter, although he suspected Quinn wouldn't cringe at that, either.

All those thoughts vanished when Hayley's SUV pulled up and two women got out. And only one of them had a backpack slung over her shoulder, looking ready to get on that plane and fly.

Ali.

Chapter Thirty-Nine

Ali let Hayley do the selling, since her opinion would carry more weight with Quinn. And hopefully Colby, who had seemed a bit stunned that she was there at all, let alone ready to roll.

"I'll hate not being there, but Ali has some very good points," Hayley was saying. "Seeing Gavin will worry her, especially now that she knows he's working with Colby. And if she sees Liam she'll connect him to Colby."

"If she even remembers me at all," Liam drawled. "Me being one of those peons, and worse, a country boy."

"If she saw me," Hayley went on, "she might wonder, but I doubt she even remembers me from our brief interaction. But seeing Ali appear out of the blue will shock and startle her, because she'll have no idea what she's doing there." Hayley paused, then added quietly, "Maybe you won't need that moment when she's too stunned to react…but maybe you will."

Quinn looked from his wife to Ali consideringly before saying slowly, "And Grace trusts you."

"Yes, she does," Ali said, thinking she was prouder of that truth in this moment than she'd been of almost anything in her life.

"You're sure?" Quinn asked. "It could get messy."

"I'm sure I don't want Grace in her hands a moment longer than she has to be."

"All right, then."

The head of Foxworth turned to the business of loading up. While Ali turned to look at Colby. He was still staring at her, but his expression was different now, looking not stunned but more...awestruck. Like a man who couldn't believe his luck.

His lips moved. "I love you," he mouthed.

She smiled at him. "And I love you."

She said it aloud, not caring who heard. And judging by his quick glance around, that she was willing to say it aloud in front of witnesses made a difference. Because she thought she saw him blink rapidly a few times as he turned to help Teague load some gear into the small cargo area of the plane. What on earth she didn't know, but knowing Foxworth, it could be anything.

And she laughed when she heard Teague say there was almost twice as much baggage space inside, but when they had a full complement of passengers a chunk of that was reserved for the comfort and convenience of their most important operative, the furry one.

After all these days spent with Cutter, she believed it.

And then Colby straightened abruptly and turned back to look at her with a worried expression. "What about Ziggy?"

That he'd even thought of her pup under these circumstances told her just how right she was about this man.

"Hayley's seeing to him until we get back. Until all three of us get back," she added with emphasis, which got her a flashing smile that somehow filled her with faith that this would somehow work out right in the end.

Teague, who apparently was in the process of getting his pilot's license as well, sat up front with Quinn. Liam and Gavin were in the two seats behind them, facing the tail of the plane, leaving the other two forward-facing ones farther back for her and Colby. She would have thought the arrangement coincidence had she not noticed the way Cutter had nudged people around as they boarded...and the way he settled down into his spot behind their seats with an expression she could only describe as smug.

As they prepped for takeoff, she also noticed Liam talking animatedly with the famous lawyer, who was grinning a lot. Funny, in all the video and photos she'd seen of him from back when him merely being involved in a case put the case in the headlines, she'd never seen him even smile much, let alone grin like that. From what she heard, apparently his wife, the librarian, and Liam's wife, the dog groomer, had become great friends.

She sighed inwardly, happily, envisioning a future like that for them, where happiness was the order of the day, even under stress. Or maybe they weren't stressed, maybe they just had so much faith in Foxworth they didn't worry. And why not? So did she.

Ali had always loved mountains. She admitted the waters of Puget Sound were gorgeous, and she loved the evergreens, but when it came down to it, no matter where she was, as long as she could at least see mountains she was happy. She put it down to being born in the flat heartland. Now she was headed for some of the most magnificent mountains in the country, although Mount Rainier could give even the tallest Rocky a run for its money.

She should be nervous, she supposed. They were, after all, headed for a confrontation with one of the few people she'd ever met whom she would actually call evil. But she had faith in Foxworth, and the need to stand up for both Colby and Grace was more than enough to keep everything else at bay.

Once they passed the rolling hills of the Palouse in eastern Washington there wasn't much that couldn't be called mountainous. But they reached the Rockies—the true mountains among mountains—much sooner than she expected. She'd known they ran from Canada all the way to New Mexico, but she hadn't quite realized how wide they were west to east in spots.

She heard Teague saying something about Class A airspace, which apparently meant over 18,000 feet. Somehow that made it more real to her. It got a little bouncy in a couple of places, and she couldn't deny it made her a bit nervous, never having flown in a small plane before. But as if he somehow knew, Colby reached out and took her hand, squeezing it gently. Then he leaned over, his mouth teasingly close to her ear.

"Quinn's still letting Teague take the controls, so it can't be that bad or he'd take over," he whispered.

What he said made perfect sense, but she was a little slow in processing it because of the shiver of sensation that having his breath tickle her ear caused. And then Cutter lifted his head and poked it between the seats, resting his chin atop their clasped hands.

"Yep," Liam said from his seat about four feet across from them, "just like I expected. You've got the Cutter seal of approval."

They both looked, and the young Texan was grinning widely.

"To be greatly valued," added Gavin, very solemnly. And Ali looked up at Colby, whose gaze was lowered to the dog, but who also wore the sweetest smile she'd ever seen.

She wasn't sure how the four and a half hours of flight time slipped by so quickly, but it seemed the next thing she knew they were prepping for landing. She had the feeling she should be thankful she knew little of flying in smaller aircraft, because this place, in this narrow valley with lot of snow still on the ground, seemed a bit hair-raising.

Quinn was back at the controls, his headset now over both ears as he talked back and forth with what she assumed was the controller in the tower she could see in the distance, and maybe other planes in the area.

Teague looked back at them. "They're hanging onto ski season, so there's a bit of traffic, but we're cleared for landing next."

They dropped rather quickly, or so it seemed to her. Then they were passing over a fence and went from buildings and small roads to empty space, with the runway ahead. It went smooth and quick, and only moments after they touched down they were taxiing off the runway and over toward the hangars on the side opposite the tower.

Liam had told them all angles were covered. There would be a car waiting, a crew to see to the plane and prep it for the return flight, the local authorities—particularly someone Gavin had made contact with, because he'd helped him out of a mess once—were apprised, and Liam had the video equipment ready to go. And once Cutter had the "protect" command, nothing would stop him from keeping Grace safe.

But now Liam was grinning at them as he said, "Is now a good time to mention this place is on the list of the ten most extreme airports?"

"Considering we have to turn around and take off again, perhaps not," Gavin said dryly.

"Why?" Ali asked. "There's no snow or ice on the runway. And that landing seemed really smooth."

"That's because you've got a pro at the controls," Liam said, nodding toward Quinn. "Unless it's actively snowing, the main weather you have to worry about is wind. And the simple fact that we're at six thousand feet and the thinner air makes approach and landing speeds 'a bit interesting,' as Quinn would say."

"Less drag," Colby said. "Never would have thought of that, but it makes sense. I helped build a place over in Steamboat Springs once, and I remember having to catch my breath a lot."

The were offloading before Ali got the chance to say, "I didn't know you'd worked nonlocal."

He shrugged. "It was one of the things that made Liz think I'd go along with her plan. Because I was known enough to get called in on jobs in various places, so obviously I must be ready to go higher."

"And here I'm thinking it's way more than enough that your reputation precedes you that much."

At that he leaned over and kissed her.

Chapter Forty

The place was even more pretentious than Colby would have guessed. It was nestled on a hill above the golf course—at least as much as a house that size could nestle. Three stories tall, the bottom level of custom-hewn rock, and the upper two of wood pretending to be cabin-like, with views to forever, he was sure. Ironic, for a family who looked only inward.

If he had to guess—and given his occupation he was pretty good at it—Colby would put it at 10,000 square feet or better. He didn't know what prices were running around here these days, but he'd bet this one was into the eight-digit range. Liz would have seen to it. After all, a Hollen couldn't have an address less distinguished than that.

They drove around and parked out of sight from the driveway at the back of the house. It was situated so nothing faced the neighbors or the street. All the views were out toward the open side, so it probably seemed as if they owned the mountains around them. Liam had already had an aerial view ready, and from that Colby could see that it wasn't quite as isolated as it seemed. Good planning on somebody's part. He doubted very much it had been a Hollen.

But most importantly, the garage door was open. Colby didn't know if that meant they were already here, or if the house was just being prepared for their arrival.

"You three stay here," Quinn said, "until we get this scoped out."

The three Foxworth operatives—because that's what they were at the moment, geared up and ready to skulk through the woods—headed out and split up to circle the house. Liam, because he'd been seen by Liz before, took the most hidden path, through a thick stand of evergreens. Ali watched them go, looking a little anxious.

"They're really good at this," de Marco assured her.

Colby didn't doubt it. With both Quinn and Teague being ex-military, and Liam having learned from them both, he was sure they'd get this initial recon done without being noticed. And they did it much more quickly than he expected.

"Movement, lights on, but we can't see who," Teague reported when they got back to the car.

"I'm going to take Cutter for a little walk," Quinn said.

Colby blinked, but wasn't about to question the man. So he just watched as he and the eager dog took off, looking for all the world like just a guy and his dog out for a stroll.

Until they got to the driveway and Cutter alerted. Quinn edged a bit closer to the house, as if letting the dog pick the path. Then Colby saw that dark head go down to the concrete, nose twitching. He couldn't see from here, but he recognized the motion. The dog had started toward the front door of the house when Quinn pulled him back and walked quickly back to the road. Colby frowned, not sure why he hadn't let the dog continue. But then he saw someone jogging down the roadway, a woman who paused when Quinn said something to her. She answered him. He smiled, she laughed, and then continued on her way.

The pair were back to the car in moments.

"They're here."

Colby blinked. "How do you know?"

"First, the way Cutter alerted up near the door. He scented

Grace, and you said she'd never been here before. And second, that lady saw the limo arrive about twenty minutes ago."

It still amazed Colby how the dog could apparently focus, ignoring what had to be a lot of other new and interesting scents, to home in on the one he was here to protect.

"Liam, you have the comms set up?"

"Will have in less than a minute." Colby didn't doubt it. He'd started messing with the gear the moment Quinn had said Cutter had scented Grace.

"You gonna take the bodyguard, or should I?" Teague asked Quinn, as casually as if he were asking about the weather.

Quinn looked at Colby, as if asking his opinion. He had no idea why, until it hit him that whoever didn't take the bodyguard would probably be the one to confront Liz. And Teague was slightly less intimidating at first sight. Was that what they wanted? He had to assess, quickly. But it wasn't that hard. Dressed in his rugged gear, Quinn looked like what he was, a man able to take on anything. He had no doubt Teague was also, but he didn't look the part in the towering, fierce way Quinn did.

"We want her off guard until we move, right? Then it should be Teague."

Quinn smiled. "Points for figuring out what I was really asking."

Teague didn't take offense at all. In fact, he ran to the back of the rented SUV, pulled his duffel open and yanked something out. Then he shed his tactical jacket and pulled on the item of clothing that, to Colby's surprise, was nothing less than a well-tailored, expensive-looking suit jacket. He'd apparently had it rolled rather than folded, so it looked no worse than if he'd worn it on the plane. And when he put it on over the sweater he was wearing, he looked downright a successful businessman.

"Damn," Colby muttered. "Perfect. She'll think you've come to connect with the family on business."

They'd discussed at length on the flight the aspects of the Hollen businesses, including some things Colby hadn't known about but Liam had discovered in his seemingly endless research. And then they'd gone over one last time the plan for the encounter. With more what-ifs than Colby could have ever thought of himself. But then, Foxworth had quite a history of cases to provide possibilities.

"Liam, you have those business cards?" Teague asked.

"Side pocket," the young Texan answered without looking up from his laptop.

Teague reached into another duffel bag and pulled out an envelope that held a small stack of business cards. He marveled even at that, because no one the Hollens would deal with would walk around with just one to jam in someone's face. Every meeting was a business meeting, and had to be put to some use.

"These folks are out of Denver, too. But the best part," Teague said when he saw Colby watching him, "is that the Hollens have reached out to this company and been brushed off. I've got the details on that, so I can drop some on her."

"So she'll think they've caved and now want to deal," he said, knowing that was exactly how they'd react.

"But what if she calls the company, to verify you're who you say you are?" It was the first thing Ali had said since they'd arrived.

"They'll say yes, I'm one of their main front men, the one who makes the deals."

Colby blinked, but Ali only smiled. "You helped them out before, too."

Teague grinned briefly. "We did."

Liam was fussing with what were apparently body cams now, one for each of them, so small he was amazed. He'd have to remember that, that it was all going to be recorded live. He knew what buttons to push that would get to Liz the most, if necessary.

"She'll be totally distracted while I take the bodyguard out of the equation," Quinn was saying. "Then Colby, you and Gavin make your grand entrance and we take advantage of the shock. She won't know if or how Teague fits in. But his and Gavin's presence should make her think twice about doing anything stupid."

"She's many things, but she's not stupid," Colby said. "But she's also never been cornered like this."

"Point taken," Quinn said with a nod. He looked at Ali. "And you search the house with Liam, out of the target's sight, until we have control. And have Grace safe."

"Unless…" she said quietly, and Colby felt a gut wrench at her willingness to walk into this mess.

"Yes," Quinn agreed. "Unless." He turned to the lawyer, who was looking at his phone. "What you said you had…" he began.

"First," De Marco said, holding up the device, "as of right now I have an agreement to reopen the custody case, which is enough for us to rescue Grace. And we got that because of what I had before, now confirmed. The Hollens' attorney, Colby, is now under official investigation for accepted bribes, and various other offenses. And that judge is looking at even worse, as in immediate arrest." He glanced at his watch. "In fact, should have happened while we were in the air."

"I'll find some news video," Liam said instantly, and went back to his keyboard. An amazingly short time later he had it, the district attorney, the county sheriff and the mayor of the jurisdiction all there as the DA read the charges to the gathered media.

"They all look like they're at a funeral," Ali said.

"In a way, they are," de Marco said. "That judge has been around a long time. And unless I miss my guess, some of the dirty threads they've found will lead right back to the Hollens."

And Colby thought the odds of Gavin de Marco missing a guess were probably pretty darn slim.

He'd never expected to actually do damage to the Hollens. All he'd ever wanted was Grace, and he would have left them alone completely if they just would have been decent about it. But the name Hollen and the word *decent* were the biggest oxymorons he'd ever encountered.

And now, finally, they were going to pay the price.

Chapter Forty-One

It was like listening to an old-time story podcast, and it required some focus. Colby couldn't tell exactly what the quietly speaking—and probably timid, knowing Liz—woman who'd answered the door said, other than something about Liz having just arrived and wasn't ready for visitors.

But Teague very politely, and with the same assumption of joyous welcome Liz always had, explained that she would be delighted to see and talk to him. And managed to provide them valuable information in the process.

"I'm more than happy to go to the third floor to see her, just tell her on that intercom that I'm here and who I represent. She'll want to see me."

Third floor and there's an intercom. Just like that we know where she is and something to be wary of.

The woman gave in, clearly unsettled. After a moment when Colby could only hear the woman's voice as a muted sort of sound in the background, Teague whispered into his hidden mic that the front door was now unlocked, and he would make sure she didn't think to go back to secure it.

"I imagine you should take me to her," Teague said normally, his tone firm but genial. "I wouldn't want you to get in trouble for letting a stranger roam the house."

"I... Thank you," the woman said, sounding surprised. "There's an elevator over here."

"Of course there is," Teague said in that same amiable tone. "Perfect."

"Indeed," Quinn muttered. He gave them all a quick glance, and Liam and Gavin both nodded.

"Who's that outside, over by the hot tub?" came Teague's voice. "I was given to understand Mr. Hollen wasn't here?"

"Oh, he's not, no one else is. That's just the security man."

Colby barely had time to register how good Teague was at this when he made a comment on the brand of elevator, indicating they were there and stepping inside.

Then Quinn left at a swift but silent pace toward the other side of the house, clearly knowing exactly where the target was. Colby listened tensely, half expected the sounds of some nasty fight. But all he heard was a low grunt and the sound of something—or someone—large hitting the ground.

"Guard down," came Quinn's voice. "We'll have half an hour before he wakes up. Liam and Ali, set Cutter on the search."

Colby hated seeing Ali leave, but trusted Liam as he trusted all of Foxworth now. Particularly that black-and-brown furry critter. It was going to take time to search the massive residence, and the dog would make it so much quicker.

"He'll ignore anywhere there's no sign of Grace," Quinn had explained, "unless he comes across something dangerous, like weapons or explosives."

Colby remembered his startled reaction at the idea of the Hollens hoarding such things, with all their public declarations about them, but they were hypocrites about everything else, so why not this, too? Besides, the laws never applied to them, and even if they did, they would, as they had, hire someone else to do the dirty work.

"This is it? Second door on the left?" Teague asked, as if merely curious.

"Yes," the woman answered. "It's the family gathering

room." She said that last as if she was surprised he was being allowed in.

Colby had sat in on a few business encounters with Liz early on, before he realized she wanted him there not in support as her husband, but to see his future path. Now he listened to Teague, talking as if he were exactly what that business card said he was.

But he listened more closely to Liz.

He pressed the button to activate his own mic, and said quietly, "She's fired up to pull this deal off. She wants to be the one to do it. To be able to tell her father he has her to thank for it."

He heard Teague work the word *copy* into his next sentence, and knew he'd heard. The wait resumed. He knew Quinn was circling the outside of the house, looking for signs of other people, security or otherwise. Meanwhile Liam and Ali, led by Cutter, searched for his precious girl, although she hadn't been here long enough to leave much of a trail. But at least they were looking.

While you sit here doing nothing.

He fought down the long-instinctive guilt. He had his role to play today, and it was crucial. He just wasn't used to having help, that was all.

"Clear outside," came Quinn's voice. "Coming around."

So there were no other guards outside. Inside, they couldn't be sure. The thought of what else Quinn had mentioned, that she might have brought a guard along solely to keep Grace in line, made his jaw tighten, and he clung to the fact that she'd done this in such a rush there likely wasn't time. But that didn't mean more armed help wasn't coming, especially since he was sure there were security people at the office in Denver.

They listened to Teague work the situation, so perfectly Colby would have sworn the guy was exactly who Liz thought he was. And then Quinn was there, looking exactly as he had when he'd left.

"That guy have any clue at all what happened to him?" Colby asked.

That brief grin flashed, and Colby had a sudden image of how deadly this guy must have been in a war zone. "I left him snoozing peacefully in one of the patio chaises. Hoping he'll wake up thinking he just dozed off."

"I wouldn't be surprised if—"

Colby cut himself off sharply as something changed in the feed coming in through his earpiece. It wasn't much, just a shift in Liz's voice, an undertone he recognized. He keyed his mic again.

"She's ready to close this. She thinks she's going to pull off what her father couldn't, and she's euphoric about it."

"I think that's your cue, gentlemen," Quinn said. "I'll follow and be right outside. Liam?"

"Still nothing. Second floor now."

"Then let's proceed."

Colby couldn't help it, he was looking forward to this. Looking forward to seeing the look on Liz's face, not just when someone dared to interrupt this crucial victory, but when it turned out to be him…

De Marco didn't even knock. He simply shoved the door open. Colby heard a click and whoosh as the automatic closer kicked into action. De Marco ignored that, too, just strode into the room as if it were his. And Colby realized he was now looking not at the caring, empathetic Foxworth man, but the firebrand lawyer who had made headlines around the world.

Liz stared in shock. But then she saw Colby, and the shock turned to fury. "What the hell are *you* doing here?"

Colby couldn't help himself; he grinned. Her expression was even better than he'd hoped. She seemed to have forgotten her business meeting altogether. Teague was on his feet now and, Colby suspected, ready to move in any direction in the large room. It was a nice room, Colby noted out of habit, with a fireplace over by another entry door, and French doors leading out onto a deck that probably had a fantastic view up here on the third floor.

Nicer than the Hollens, anyway.

"He's here," de Marco answered silkily, "for his daughter. The child you have smuggled out of state without notifying her father, after breaking the custody-sharing agreement two days before."

"She's my daughter," Liz retorted loudly. "And I have every right to bring her with me."

De Marco smiled, as if he knew that would only set Liz off more. "Not without notifying her father."

Liz gave Colby a look of utter disdain. "Avoiding any time with the likes of him is good for her."

"You might want to rethink your attitude, Ms. Hollen," de Marco said, his voice still smooth and unruffled.

Liz swore, loudly. Considering whom de Marco had come up against in the past—and beaten—Colby thought she ought to be a bit more careful. But he was very glad she didn't see it that way.

"So you lied," she spat out. "When you said you wouldn't fight me anymore."

Colby smiled. "I leave the lying to you, since you're an expert. I only said *I* wouldn't fight you anymore. Not that the fight was over."

"But it is now," de Marco said.

"I don't care how unbeatable you think you are, de Marco, you picked the wrong side here. Judge Boras will slap you down with fines and maybe more if you interfere with me."

Colby tried to stifle a laugh, then realized nothing would push her over the edge faster, so he let it out. De Marco's smile widened. "If you mean your bought-and-paid-for judge, you'll want to rethink that, too. He was charged with multiple rather salacious crimes just an hour ago, and his time as a judge is over, for good. And he's going to take you and your family down with him."

Liz's eyes widened. "I don't believe you."

De Marco shrugged. "Check. It's all over the news. We'll wait."

She did just that, picking up the phone that lay on the arm of the chair she'd been sitting in when they strode in. A few taps and a half scroll and she stopped. She paled as she read, and Colby knew she'd found the story.

She looked up at them again, and this time in addition to the fury, there was a touch of fear. Just the idea of being held to account clearly frightened her.

"Well," Teague said as if he were still that businessman, "obviously you're not the kind of person my company wants to be associated with. You can consider this discussion over, and the deal officially dead. And I'll make sure everyone we do business with is warned off."

She let out a little sound as she spun around to look at the man she'd clearly almost forgotten was here. She wasn't used to being afraid, and she did not handle it well. She let loose a tirade so loud it made Colby's ears ring.

A noise came from another entry door he'd noticed by the fireplace. Colby saw Teague spin around, then take a long stride to put himself in front of both him and de Marco. The assistant coming to check because of the noise? Or worse, more security they'd missed? Or—

His mind went blank and his every muscle went taut as the door swung open and the person on the other side rushed in.

Grace.

Chapter Forty-Two

Cutter was practically dancing, but Quinn held him back.

"Daddy! I heard her and I knew it was you. You're the only one who makes her so mad."

The joy in the little girl's voice made Ali's heart skip a beat.

"Shut up, idiot child."

The fury in the mother's voice made a chill go down her spine.

"You shut up," Grace retorted.

And then she heard a yelp from Grace, a shout from Colby, the sound of a door opening and a "Don't even think about it," from Teague.

Her first instinct was to charge into the room, but Quinn held her back. "Not yet. Timing is crucial. And evidence, to win in the end."

That reminded her this was all being recorded. It was an effort, but she stayed put.

"You take one more step toward us, you bastard, and she goes over!" Liz was shrieking now. And beneath that horrid sound, she thought she heard a tiny scream of fear.

"Boss?" Liam's voice sounded like she felt, and Ali didn't like that. The young tech wizard held out his phone for them to see.

Liz was out on the deck, had Grace in her grasp, and even as they watched, pulled the child up onto the railing.

"Take another step," Liz screeched, "and I'll drop her!"

Three stories up, nothing but rocks and a stone patio below. A fall would kill her.

Quinn looked at Ali. "I think we need that moment."

She nodded. Steeled herself. She knew what her goal was. Grace, and Grace alone. She pasted the biggest smile she could manage on her face. With Cutter at her heels she grabbed the knobs and pushed the double entry doors open and strode into the room.

"Liz? Oh, there you are," she said cheerfully. "They said I'd find you here."

The woman gasped and spun around, gaping at her. And in that moment Grace pulled free of her mother's grip. Ali saw her start to grin victoriously, but then she wobbled and started to fall backward. That fatal drop. She screamed in fear.

Cutter ran. The dog arrived just in time to catch the sleeve of Grace's jacket in his strong jaws, using the vertical bars to hold himself back from the drop. And in the next split second Colby was there.

Without hesitation he went over the rail himself. He hung on to the decking with one hand as he reached down with the other. He caught Grace's wrist just as her jacket began to rip. Ali wasn't sure how he did it, but knew she was seeing just how strong he really was as he pulled his precious girl to safety.

Only when she was safely back on the deck did he start to pull himself up and over the railing. There was an instant when he nearly slipped and Ali gasped. But then his strength overcame gravity, and he was safely back. Grace clung to him like the lifeline he was and he hugged her fiercely.

Liz had turned as if to run toward the doors, but the moment she realized the woman was going to run, Ali stepped in front of her.

"I don't think so," she said, letting all the contempt she was feeling show in her voice.

Liz tried to shove her aside, but froze as Quinn stepped

between them. Liz gaped up at the man she'd never seen, but whose steady stare had likely made worse people than her back down.

Gavin spoke, and sounded just amused enough to put the icing on Liz's humiliation. "Lovely." He plucked the disguised mini camera from his shirt collar, and let her see it. "And now, in addition to the recordings the sheriff will obtain from your nanny cams, we have you on video for child abuse, assault and attempted murder. And investigations will be opened in the next few days into many of the Hollen financial dealings. Say goodbye to your luxurious life, Elizabeth Hollen. Oh, and you might call your father, when they let you near a phone, and tell him you've managed to destroy his life, too."

"Are we going to go home soon?" Grace asked hopefully.

"Very soon," Colby promised.

Quinn had had them all decamp to a meeting room at a resort lodge Foxworth had rented down the hill, based on the accurate assumption that none of them wanted to stay in that house any longer than they had to. Then he had told them he would be flying them, including Grace, home as soon as the weather made it possible. Liam was busy gathering all their gear, then he would fly back with Gavin, who would stay as long as it took to deal with the locals. Then the attorney would head back himself to deal with the fallout at home, including any government agency that might want to get their hands on Grace.

"Where were you in the house?" Ali asked the girl. "We searched the bottom and second floor, and Cutter didn't find any sign of you."

"I was hiding in the library. Down the hall from where she was in that room. She never goes in the one at home. I was figuring out a way to sneak out."

Colby was still holding her tight against his chest with one arm. Ali was next to them, and his other arm was around her.

He felt a bit drained, but that didn't matter, not when the three of them were together. And having Cutter at their feet, Cutter who had essentially saved her life by delaying that fall that precious second so he could get to her, was beyond comforting.

"Then what were you going to do?" Ali asked.

"I saw out the window there were some kids playing in the snow down the hill, with a dog." She paused to stroke Cutter's dark head. "I thought I'd go to them, and ask for help." She looked up at Colby. "I know not all parents are like her."

"Thanks to your father," Ali said softly, "you know that some of them are wonderful."

Colby swallowed hard, his throat tight. He was still feeling a bit dazed. But Grace smiled widely and nodded at Ali. Then she shifted her gaze back to him.

"I yelled at her, when she put me on that airplane, that you'd come for me. She said you wouldn't. That you didn't love me, I was just how you got back at her. She's a liar."

"A big one," Colby agreed. Grace snuggled against him, clearly never having believed a word of Liz's propaganda.

"I'm glad you're too smart to believe that," Ali said.

Grace looked up at her. "I'm glad you're here," she said simply.

"As am I," Colby said, looking at Ali now. "More than glad. Delirious with happiness."

Ali didn't answer, but looked at Grace. "And there's something I've been waiting to tell you. How much I loved my birthday present."

The child smiled. "You did?"

"I did. So much."

"I wish it were real."

Only then did Ali look back to Colby. She saw him swallow, hard, then he looked at his precious child and said huskily, "Maybe we can work on that when we get home. Making it real."

"That would be good," Grace said, and lowered her head to rest against him.

For a while they just sat there. Together, holding on to each other. Ali thought she'd never been more tired, but also never more exhilarated. It was all over but the cleanup, and Foxworth would see to that.

Ali's phone chimed and she pulled it out. It was a text from Hayley, with a video attached.

I think he misses you!

She laughed and held it out for Grace and Colby to see. Ziggy, curled up sleeping on Ali's couch, burrowed into the very sweater they had used to give Cutter Grace's scent.

Grace laughed, and Ali saw Colby close his eyes as if to savor the sound of it.

"Will you miss Cutter, now?" the child asked.

"I'll miss him," Ali admitted. "But I won't miss trying to keep up with him."

"Story of my life." Quinn's amused response came as he arrived beside them, a smile on his face. "And speaking of life, would you like to get back home and start rebuilding yours?"

They all looked up at him. "Now?" Colby asked, sounding hopeful.

"Now," Quinn confirmed. "Just checked the weather and it's all north of here. Clear sailing, and if we head out now, we can be airborne before it gets dark."

One day. One day and Foxworth had undone Grace's short lifetime of damage.

"I'm for that," Colby said, almost reverently. But then he looked at Ali. "Unless you want to—"

"I'll beat you to Wilbur," she said fervently.

"Who's Wilbur?" Grace asked.

"You'll find out soon," Colby promised.

"Good," Quinn said, then added with a smile. "Not a bad day's work."

"Quinn," Colby began, but the man shook his head.

"Time enough for all that later. Cutter, on me. I think your work here is done."

Cutter scrambled up, gave one last look at her, Grace and Colby, and she'd swear the dog was grinning.

"Yeah, yeah," Quinn said with a chuckle. "You did it again. Now let's go home."

Ali liked the sound of that. Tried not to dwell on the clever Foxworth dog's apparent matchmaking abilities. But it did suddenly occur to her to wonder where exactly that home was going to be.

Grace yawned widely. Ali didn't blame her—the post adrenaline crash had to be close. She snuggled up even closer to her father, but she didn't let go of Ali's hand.

"Ali's going to stay with us, isn't she?" she asked her father as he got up, still holding her. "So she doesn't have to look at that house next door?"

Ali felt Colby go still. But as if now that he had Grace back and safe, nothing could daunt him anymore, he looked over and met her gaze.

"That's her decision, honey. But it sounds good to me. Really, really good," he said.

Ali thought her heart would burst, her chest felt so tight. "I'd like to be with you. We have a lot of things to work through, Gracie."

"But it's over now, right?" the child asked, a trace of the old worry back in her eyes. "I don't have to be with the mother anymore?"

"All over except the details," her father said.

"Details?" She shifted her gaze from Colby back to Ali, still looking worried.

Ali smiled at her. "It's like a big firecracker exploded," she said. "Now the big bang is over, but there's some junk to clean up."

"Oh." As if that made it all make sense to her, she settled back down.

"You know the rest of that unpacking you mentioned?" Colby asked.

"Yes?"

"Put that on hold," Colby said.

And that, Ali thought, answered her big question. They were going to clean up the junk, and then…well, Colby was an amazing carpenter, a man who built. And now, with the weight that had been dragging him down gone, Ali had no doubt he could build an amazing life for them. Because this time he wouldn't have an anchor weighing him down, but a partner. Her. So together they would build that most precious of structures.

A family.

A short time later they had indeed introduced Grace to Wilbur, and Colby made her laugh when he explained the name, which the child thought was exceptionally cool. And it apparently made her ask if she could please, please not ever be Brianna anymore, but be Grace forever.

"We'll work on that, too," her father promised.

At takeoff, the child's sleepiness seemed to vanish at the excitement of flying in this smaller plane, or perhaps it was just because of her companions. In the end it didn't seem to matter, as long as they were together.

Home. They were going home.

Ali looked away from the small window to find Colby watching her, with a smile that held so much promise it sent a thrill through her. With Grace beside them, they flew into the sunset, to prepare for the dawn of three new lives.

And behind them, Cutter yawned and settled in for a nap, his work done.

For now.

* * * * *

COMING SOON!

We really hope you enjoyed reading this book. If you're looking for more romance be sure to head to the shops when new books are available on

Thursday 21st May

To see which titles are coming soon, please visit
millsandboon.co.uk/nextmonth

MILLS & BOON

FOUR BRAND NEW BOOKS FROM
MILLS & BOON MODERN

Indulge in desire, drama, and breathtaking romance – where passion knows no bounds!

OUT NOW

Eight Modern stories published every month, find them all at:

millsandboon.co.uk

LET'S TALK
Romance

For exclusive extracts, competitions and special offers, find us online:

- **f** MillsandBoon
- **X** @MillsandBoon
- **◉** @MillsandBoonUK
- **♪** @MillsandBoonUK

Get in touch on 01413 063 232

For all the latest titles coming soon, visit
millsandboon.co.uk/nextmonth